DEVIL'S KEY

Also by Elisabeth Graves
BLACK RIVER

For Kayleigh –

DEVIL'S KEY

Hot – very hot – off the press!

ELISABETH GRAVES

Elisabeth Graves

Northampton House Press

This is a work of fiction. All the characters and events portrayed in this novel are either products of the author's imagination or used fictitiously.

Cover design by Naia Poyer. Cover photos: mangrove tree in Everglades © lightkey/iStock; ram horns © PhilipCacka/iStock; red sunset © zaozaa09/iStock.
First Norwegian edition: 1999 by Egmont Boker, Oslo
First English edition: 2016 by Northampton House Press
ISBN 978-1-937997-69-4
Library of Congress Control Number: 2016939461

And the souls mounting up to God
Went by her like thin flames.

– Dante Gabriel Rossetti

He did not see any reason why
the devil should have all the good tunes.

– Rowland Hill

PROLOGUE

The silent man drew back into the shadows behind the stairs of the Wenger Social Sciences building. He was watching a young woman climbing the concrete and steel steps above him in the echoing concrete stairwell. She was going to class, though not one he took with her. One night last semester, when their study group had gone for pizza and beer, he'd tried to ask her out. Tried, but somehow never got a chance in the loud, greasy, off campus pizzeria. Never got close, much less private enough to shout a question into her ear: *Would you like to . . . Maybe sometime we could—*

Yeah, right.

What I really want, Timothy Carling thought, still looking up the stairwell, catching a glimpse of pale bare inner thigh, is to—

To kill her.

He flinched and pressed back against the wall, muffling a gasp in the sleeve of his sweatshirt. Where the hell had that come from? Like a strange voice in his head.

OK, he *was* lurking—looking up her short black skirt. But he couldn't think of any other way to get close to her. She never noticed him, though he'd spent half the last hour of anthro staring at her instead of taking notes. He wanted to ask her to a movie, maybe kiss her. Then take her to his room. . . .

He blushed, trying to imagine that scene unfolding,

though it was hard to see her in his stuffy, closet sized dorm, with the crumpled Doritos bags under the bed, his roommate's lacrosse gear, mounds of dirty boxer shorts kicked into the corners.

You mean you want to fuck her. Then kill her.

The voice, which came simultaneously from the dark around him, and from inside his head, was deep, rough—not his own.

"No," he said aloud, startled and getting a bit frightened, too. The denial echoed in the stairwell. Had she heard? Was *she* looking down, could she see him now? Oh God. . . .

No, the pneumatic door on the upper landing was just hissing shut. He was safe. Probably. But that *voice*—

Something touched his shoulder.

"God!"

He whirled to see a wispy old man in a wrinkled tie and gray cardigan standing behind him. He was short, thin, even less substantial than Tim. He didn't seem threatening. Except . . . except he was dressed like a suit from the registrar's office, so probably he'd seen him staring up like a perv, and now was about to bust him. The college had a real bitch of a sexual harassment policy. They could get you for anything, even a random smirk.

"Hey, I . . . I wasn't . . ."

The man in gray smiled and shook his head. "Of course not. I just wanted to advise you not to bother with that one."

"What? W-which one?"

"Miss Fowler. She's not for you. She told me so. In fact, she's told everyone, by now, I'm sure."

"But I—" He swallowed. "I never, I mean—"

"*Tsk.* Women know how you feel, young man. Surely you're aware of what they call you here."

His face flamed. "Y-yeah." His nickname on campus was The Moth. His mannerisms, his gestures, had always been sweeping, fluttery. He got nervous in public. Then he stuttered.

People assumed things. They were real bastards. He'd been hoping she hadn't heard that.

"The only way to impress a girl like that is with a show of strength."

He frowned. "You mean, like, in football, or—"

The gray man laughed. "Not team sports, no." Then smiled, as if at some juicy private joke, and slung a bony arm around his shoulders. "I believe I can help you out, Tim. Get you what you—what we both—want."

How did this old dude know his name? Was this some kind of Student Services personal counseling program, like, an intervention? The skinny suit was really creeping him out. "No thanks. I really gotta go, I—"

The pale, gray face was suddenly thrust right into Tim's, barely an inch away. As it neared, it changed—no longer mild and bland, soft and wrinkled; instead it darkened, swelled, the eyes bulged and the teeth, *oh Christ, those long yellow . . .*

Tim felt heat run down both legs, heard a trickle, smelled piss. He didn't care. He wanted only to get away from this horrible, staring, elongated thing that was holding him hostage with slitted sulfur-colored eyes and breath like the whiff of dead skunk he'd gotten once from under his grandmother's rotten porch, back home.

He blinked, and suddenly the twisted visage snapped back to normal. Pressing one clammy hand to the back of Tim's neck, the man slipped the other into a pocket of his sweater and pulled out a small feathered bundle. Before Tim could ask what it was, the man raised the object to his own lips. A small bird, not any species Tim recognized. It struggled feebly. Black, with some bright scarlet in the breast and wings.

Without another word the man bit the bird's head off. Worse, next he shoved the tiny corpse's spurting, severed neck against Tim's clenched lips.

"Drink me," the man said, his voice higher now, hollowly mimicking a little girl's. As if they were in Wonderland and Tim had agreed to play Alice.

"*No*," he said. But to do that Tim had to part his lips. Big mistake. The old man jammed the flopping bird in, past teeth and tongue. It filled his throat with blood and fluffy down and then he could not breathe and oh God he was choking, drowning. How could a stupid little bird have so fucking much blood in it?

What else could he do but chew, gag, and swallow?

"That's my boy," crooned the colorless voice, as if Tim were three and had just cleaned his plate. "Now, there's only one way to take care of this problem. You know the answer. Isn't that right?"

Tim—somehow down on hands and knees on the cold concrete behind the stairs now, with the man bending over him—swallowed again, sucking the last of the blood from his tongue. It hadn't tasted as bad as he'd feared. He wiped his sticky mouth on the shoulder of his blue sweatshirt, leaving a dark smear.

"Yeah," he mumbled, glancing up at the empty stairwell. "I know."

"Good boy," said the old guy. "Good *man*."

Which was weird, because by the time he heard those words and looked up, the guy was gone. No door had opened or closed, no footsteps had clomped up to the second floor. But all the same, Tim was alone.

ONE

Lucy Fowler ducked behind her laptop screen to hide a yawn, then started keying in notes as the professor read to the thirty-five students in his cultures and belief-systems class:

"Then an Araibande tribesman said, 'The dead have power. They watch all that we do, and never rest. They dream angry dreams while their bodies dry up in the earth. We are what they dream about. Our lives, our breath, the warm blood flowing through us. While we live in dread of the cold doorway they have already passed through.'"

Lucy glanced up. Around her people were scratching or typing notes. She counted two snorers—one drooling on an open textbook—and a girl listlessly playing Sudoku on an iPad. They looked zombified themselves. Like mannequins in a Macy's window display, only without the nice outfits. But the end of a semester always seemed to have that effect.

She squelched a desire to check the time on her iPhone. Instead, her fingers found the silver medallion that hung from a heavy chain around her neck, thumb caressing the bottom edge where the cool metal felt rough, as though a piece had broken off.

"This subject," Dr. Grove droned on, "was a long-time resident of Port-au-Prince, Haiti. He claimed during the interview that the dead have this so-called power because the living allow and believe in it. Due to fear, or guilt they've done the deceased a wrong and now can't make it right." He looked around. "So. How does this outlook compare with last week's material on the African Dahomean folklore of death? See any parallels . . . conflicts?" One hand rose tentatively. He nodded.

"Is it true, what you read?"

Lucy knew the sophomore, an honors student with cropped blonde hair and a waiver to attend this graduate-level course. Her name was . . . Summer?

"I mean . . . do you believe what you wrote there, Dr. Grove?" the girl added. "That spirits exist beyond death?" Someone in back snorted, and she blushed.

The professor did not smile patronizingly—as Lucy had expected, because Grove was not known for his patience. "Well, Summer," he said, removing rectangular black-framed glasses to polish the lenses on his tie. "We're speaking here of a developing country. That they go about the production of knowledge—yes, knowledge, not 'superstition'—differently than we do, does *not* make their perception of reality any less valid than ours."

Summer frowned. "What do you mean? I guess it's not their fault, but aren't they just ignorant of science, of—"

"Are they?" Grove shrugged. "Say a South African man dies after being gravely ill for a long time. His family might say his death was *isidliso*. Does anyone know what that means?"

Lucy raised her hand. "I think . . . the work of witchcraft."

Grove nodded. "Exactly. A biomedical doctor—one of ours—would say he died of AIDS. Still another person, elsewhere, might say, Yes, he died of AIDS, but a witch exposed him to the virus."

A few sniggers rose from the back. Grove frowned and they subsided.

"Whatever etiology model you attribute to his disease, some *force* has acted to kill that man. However you explain it, he's still dead. Does our culture's explanation deserve precedence over his?"

"Well, sure." A lanky student in the front row leaned back, stretching his legs into the aisle. "I mean, we got scientific proof, right?"

Grove inclined his head. "Perhaps. But then again, how would biomedical science even attempt to prove that the AIDS was *not* sent by someone with a grudge against the man?"

Lucy frowned. Somehow the professor's tone did not match the bantering words.

In any case, this was obviously not the answer Summer had been looking for, either. "But Dr. Grove, you've been to places like that. Couldn't it be true the dead might . . . well, like, make contact, or continue to, um, like . . . "

Lucy looked down at her keyboard to hide a smile.

Grove smiled too, but not kindly. Summer was probably a Harry Potter fan. "The culture of western science says no, Summer. But feel free to join the Araibande, if witchcraft seems more appealing to you than reason."

Lucy grimaced. Did he have to be so mean? She'd been Grove's graduate assistant the year before. He was smart about everything except how to treat people.

More muted sniggers. Another hand shot up—the girl who'd been playing Sudoku. Grove's wiry gray eyebrows rose. "Yes?"

"Will that be on the final?"

He sighed and closed his book. "Ten minutes left. Let's call it a night."

Students filed past, vanishing like ghosts returning to another dimension, as if afraid he might change his mind and call them back. Lucy stuffed her laptop into her backpack. Thank God only two weeks were left in the term. Then her internship, Florida in December, and no classes until the third week of January. She'd looked forward to this for months.

She slung the pack over one shoulder—ugh, so heavy—and staggered down the hall.

In Reicher Library she kicked open the door to the

study carrel she shared with another grad student and dumped everything on the desk. Loose papers and notebooks cascaded onto the floor.

"Well, if it ain't Loki-Lani, goddess of earthquakes."

Lucy jumped. "Jesus, Prince. Don't you ever make any noise—like breathe, for instance? Stop lurking in the dark like a fucking vampire!"

The slender, androgynous-looking man lounging in the open doorway behind her laughed. "The Gender and Sexuality tests I'm grading for McKean look better in dim light."

He watched her retrieve papers, re-stack the pile, and drop into her chair. She tilted it back to smile at him.

He raised his eyebrows. "Now you look festive."

"I'm going to do some real work. On my own, for a change."

"Right. The lurid bestseller." He pulled on his long blond ponytail, the one familiar to all the university's students. Hal was very popular with both sexes.

Lucy threw a pencil at him. "It's called a dissertation, you dork. Don't be such a snob. Maybe I won't turn Sir James Frazier green, or outsell Steve Berry. But by next summer, it'll be on its way to a publisher. So stick that in your stinky pipe."

"You wound me and my beloved meerschaum deeply, Bird Girl." He clutched his chest and slid down the doorframe.

She ignored his mock death-rattle and began re-stuffing her backpack, thinking about what she needed to do before she left for Ibo Key. Proctor Grove's final exams. Take Hercules to the kennel.

But tonight, all she really had to do was pick up a quart of milk and some kibble at the Co-op. Which closed—she looked at her cell—in a half hour. She slung the bag over her shoulder again and stepped over Prince. He looked up beguilingly, one eye half-open. Lucy was not charmed. She'd already had her little fling with the Prince of Hearts, back when she'd first arrived at Pottsburg. He was good, yes—but she'd been inoculated.

Outside the wind gusted refrigerator-cold, carrying a few icy flakes. She wrinkled her nose at a whiff of something truly foul—methane? sulfur?—like someone forgot and left the door to Hell open. Probably the paper mill on the industrial Northside. Five years at Pottsburg University and she still hated the sporadic lye-soap-and-spoiled-eggs stink. When the wind shifted you could scent the chocolate factory to the west. Much better. To the locals, it probably all smelled more like money. Understandable.

For a wistful moment she thought of chilled, clean air, crisp as a winter apple, scented with pine smoke and evergreen sap. What she'd be breathing now if she'd stayed in Vermont. But graduates seeking fellowships couldn't take seasons or sentiment into account.

A gust rattled the sickly maples flanking the cement-block arts and humanities building. Wind lifted curling strands of springy dark hair and tickled her face. She tucked them behind her ears impatiently, shrugged her jacket together, and started across the B section to her car.

The lot's crime lights ought to have highlighted it with their overlapping circles of urine yellow glare. But tonight the two over it were burned out. Her shadow-gray Toyota was nearly invisible in the drifting fog from the Johnson River. She shivered and zipped her jacket higher.

"Stupid," she muttered, glancing around for reassurance in the shape of a three-wheeled security patrol, but there was none. She shook her head, gripped her keys tighter, and made her stride long and confident.

Leaning against the car at last, she fumbled at the lock, dropped the keys and then squatted on the dark asphalt, the heavy pack dragging her sideways as she groped for them, cursing. As she straightened, a shadow detached from the minivan next to her. "Ah!" she gasped, flinching away.

"S-sorry. I didn't mean to s-startle you."

She peered up into a shadowed face. Pale and thin, awkward posture. Paper-bag-colored hair. A stutter. Timothy Carling, the quiet, earnest guy who'd been in a Grove seminar with her last semester. Some of the students in their study group had referred to him as "The Moth." She didn't know why, and hadn't cared to ask. She sighed and relaxed. "Oh, hi. What's up, Tim?"

"It's, uh, my car. You know, the red Volvo wagon? Won't start and my roommate's not home, and I d-don't have change, and wondered, uh, that is if it's not too much trouble, I mean if you could, that is . . ."

God, this could take all night. She could almost see the CLOSED sign on the co-op. She reached into her pocket, found her cell, and held it out. "Oh sure. Here."

As he looked down, she suddenly withdrew the phone. "You know, I'm going right past the Mobil station. They have a tow truck, if it turns out you need one."

Even in the unlighted lot, Carling's blush was visible. He seemed to be struggling more than usual to get the words out. "Don't," he rasped suddenly, face contorted. "D-don't."

She blinked. "Excuse me?"

He coughed, then shuddered as if suddenly chilled. He looked up again and smiled. "I only meant, don't go to any trouble just for me. But if it's not, well . . . that sure would help out."

Funny, his stutter was suddenly gone, his voice even seemed deeper. Kind of . . . hollow. Was he trying to impress her, putting on this husky, raspy persona like an actor? She shrugged. "It's no problem. Just throw your stuff in back. Jiggle that door handle too, it sticks like a bitch."

"So, plans for the holidays?" Lucy asked as she turned onto the main road. He was so quiet now it made her feel awkward.

Carling shifted in the seat to face her, high, narrow forehead creased with a frown. "What? No. No plans," he snapped, as if angry she'd asked. His face was shadowed, so she couldn't make out his expression. She felt uneasy again. How stupid, spooked by The Moth. Besides, the Mobil station was only a few miles up—

Just as she thought this he lunged for the steering wheel, spinning it hard, right out of her hands.

"Hey!" She fought to grab it again and turn the car back onto the road as it swerved over the double yellow line and bounced into the rutted entrance of a deserted service road, narrowly missing a ditch. She stood hard on the brake and the Toyota slewed to a stop in a storm of pale red dust fifty yards down a patchy, half-paved lane, headlights illuminating wind thrashed bushes. "What the hell, Tim!"

His face looked phosphorescent in the green glow of the dash lights. He smiled. "I want to stop here."

Here? But—

Time slowed to a crawl. She noticed the top button of his oxford cloth shirt was loose. It hung from a single thread, swaying like a hypnotist's crystal. She raised one hand to touch it, to say, *You'd better fix that.*

The button came off in her hand. After that, things happened quickly, yet still slowly enough to sear the tiniest details into her brain.

Tim reached out, too. For her. She grabbed the driver's door handle. They both spilled onto the road, him on top, the impact and his weight crushing the breath from her so thoroughly she wheezed like an asthmatic. At last she sucked in a blessed lungful, seeing a meteor shower of black dots and jagged white lines.

By then Carling was crouched above her. He grabbed both arms at the wrist, dragged her farther down the road, and shoved her flat to the pebbly dirt again. The rock studded clay flayed her skin like a cheese grater, but she felt no pain. She scrambled up and faced him, panting, ears ringing with a shrill, constant whine.

What should she do? Where could she run?

He dragged a hand down his sweating face, then stood staring over her left shoulder, as if listening to something or someone she couldn't hear. It seemed like a good time to bolt, but she'd taken only two steps when he jerked her hair from behind so hard a whiplash pain shot down her spine. One arm tightened around her neck like a steel choke collar. He flung her down again. "Stop screaming!"

The words grated in her ear like a wood rasp; not like Tim's voice at all. There was that other sound, too: the high-pitched keening she'd assumed came from their nightmarish surroundings. A siren, a factory whistle. Until he spoke, she hadn't been aware the noise was coming from her own bruised throat.

"Shut up," he added, "or I'll kill you, slut!"

Her mind struggled for reason, for a plan. For some sense of why he was doing this. Why now?

No. Forget about why. What does he want, and how can I use that to get away?

His hand slid down over her hip and squeezed. "Nice ass," he said, in the growl she could hardly believe was Carling's voice. "I think we're ready to play."

She went rigid with the realization he didn't want her car, or money, or just to knock her around.

Her skirt was already hiked halfway up her thighs. He jerked it roughly to her waist, then pressed a ropy arm across her throat again. She gagged. Spots and jagged flashes fractured her vision, as if she were watching cable with a bad connection. The whine in her ears became a waterfall roar. Cloth ripped, flecks of spit spattered hot against her cheek.

She could move only her head and shoulders. One arm was still trapped under her back, the other imprisoned in his painful grip.

"Stop it. You don't—Let me—Tim, *let me go!*" The weakness, the high-pitched hysteria in her voice frightened her too.

The only answer was a snarl in her ear and his nails tearing her underwear, snagging on the thin cotton. The elastic snapped like a worn rubber band. Cloth tore like paper. It was appalling, this sudden strength from the frail Moth. Drugs? It must be. The shy, gentle guy she knew from class surely wouldn't do this.

He clawed at her breasts until warm blood trickled down her sides. Then he was pushing roughly, brutally into her. She screamed as inner membranes burned, abraded, and tore. He cuffed her as a lion would a misbehaving cub. The casual blow bounced her head off the ground. He shoved harder, bruising her stiff, resisting muscles.

No, she thought. *This isn't happening. Not to me.* Or if it was . . . then nothing else was real, either. She sobbed and cursed him, revolted by the hot, coppery smell of his body, the greasy sweat dripping from his face onto hers. Grunting each time his body slammed against her. This snarling thing which pinned her to earth like a specimen butterfly was the same scrawny, stuttering guy she'd given half her mocha latte to during an all night study group. The one who, taking the venti cup from her hands, had blushed.

Then something happened that was stranger still.

The essence of herself lightened until it weighed less than the frigid air. It pulled away from her body like mist rising from a pond in winter. Higher and higher it rose, like an Olympic diver called to heaven in mid-flight. She hovered, then looked down. Two struggling figures outlined in a faint greenish light were sprawled on the cracked dirty pavement. She gazed with detached wonder as they writhed and fought like ants under a magnifying glass. What was happening? What did it mean?

Was she dying?

How strange it felt. Not terrifying. Not painful. Just strange.

An animal howl burst from the one on top, and she was dragged down in a whirlwind grip, flailing at the insubstantial night, the sickening rush of wind. No—she wouldn't go!

Yet she fell and fell, until there was a slight impact, as if she'd been bumped from behind by someone hurrying past on a crowded sidewalk. And she was back inside herself.

Don't look at him. Don't look.

Inside her clenched eyelids, light burst like a second sunset, and dimmed away into featureless darkness.

The asphalt was hard and cold under her bare back. A sharp stone stabbed the soft flesh between her shoulder blades. She tried to rise, but fell back, gasping at the pain that shot through every inch of her cold, bruised body. When she opened her eyes again, someone was standing over her. *Thank God.* She reached out a hand for help, then froze as, through slitted eyes and swollen lids, she recognized the stained jeans, the grimy black sneakers.

He was still here. Breathing hard, looking down on her.

Her keys dangled from his hand. He'd taken everything there was to take. Maybe now he'd leave. Or maybe he'd kill her.

She made herself inhale slow and deep, until she felt alert again. Then coldly reviewed all the advice she'd ever read and heard about what to do in a situation like this.

Scream and run. No—only in a public area, like a mall parking lot.

Don't fight, especially if your attacker is armed. Was the Moth armed? She didn't know. He hardly needed a weapon, he was so much stronger than she would've ever believed possible.

Talk him out of it. Show sympathy. Shame him. A bit late now.

Throw up on him. Somehow she doubted he'd care.

An icy droplet of fear trickled from her mind and ran down her spine, its crystalline rivulets chilling her heart as it passed: *He's not finished with me yet.*

The toe of one Converse crashed into her ribs, and something snapped. She rolled into a fetal crouch, cradling her head. Tim dropped to his knees, yanked her onto her back again, and began punching her face. She sensed rather than saw his hair, lank and dark, swinging over a pale, sweating forehead. The thin mouth a brutal knife-gash. But his eyes . . . as he grunted and flailed, they seemed different. Didn't go with the rest of him, with what was happening. Why was that?

"Why?" she screamed.

He stopped, panting. Jumped up and stood with head tilted as if listening. Then, just like that, he was gone. The muffled thud of running feet floated back to her over the empty pavement.

When she heard the hesitant gassy cough her car always made starting up, she had just enough strength left to crawl to the shoulder, drag herself within the gnarled, protective roots of an old oak, and collapse.

Her Toyota roared past, swerving wildly. It skidded to a stop with an agonized squeal of worn radials. Gone? No. She heard it idling there and moaned. Then he was backing up.

Instead of stopping and getting out, Carling proceeded to drive back and forth wildly over the spot she'd just left. To run over, she saw now, her wadded-up winter coat—as if he'd mistaken it for her, and now was crushing and grinding even the *idea* of Lucy Fowler into a smashed, bloody pulp. Back and forth, back and forth. Then he peeled out again, taillights blinking back redly like the malevolent eyes of a demon flying away in the dark.

Then they, too, were gone.

She huddled against rough bark, sobbing. At a new sound she tensed, lifting her head.

There it was, the thing that must've chased Carling away. Distant voices, faint laughter. She tried to push herself up too quickly and toppled back. Her head was pounding, her sight blurred. She gripped the rough knobs and whorls of the ancient tree as she clung fiercely to consciousness. After a few moments, though, her fingers loosened, slipped over the rough bark, went limp.

After that she heard nothing. Nothing at all.

TWO

The frightened middle-aged couple stopped their LeBaron under the awning at the ER entrance. The woman gently helped Lucy out of the back seat.

"We aren't married to each other," the man explained apologetically, glancing back but not meeting her eyes. "So we can't come in. They'd ask for our names. You understand."

Then they sped away across the hospital lot, tires squealing at the turn back to the highway.

Ten other people were already huddled under the bluish fluorescent lights when she limped in through the sliding glass doors. Only one besides her seemed to be bleeding. The others gave her dull glances, then turned back to their own personal miseries.

A half hour dragged past on the digital clock over the receptionist's desk before they were finished with questions about insurance. Things were complicated by the fact that her wallet was in her backpack, still in the stolen car. She suspected only her silk shirt and expensive boots made them believe she wasn't homeless and indigent.

Another thirty minutes passed before she was summoned by a nurse.

The massive swinging door hissed as she limped through, ears assaulted by electronic beeps, the clatter of stainless steel instruments into enameled trays. Beneath the racket ran a liquid murmur of voices, some calm and detached, others choked with sobs. Somewhere, far off, an infant howled. Her nostrils flared at sharp disinfectant and stinging alcohol. And copper, perhaps the blood that crusted her face and splattered her torn shirt. She pulled the ripped material closed, wishing it had even one button left.

The nurse led her to a curtained alcove packed with chirping monitors, gleaming trolleys, pregnant canvas laundry bags on the very verge of birthing piles of rumpled, stained green and white linen. Lucy limped to the examining table, hugging herself hard, teeth clenched to pin down the scream that had been building since two giggling, overaged lovers had stumbled upon her in the woods back of the campus. Now, at the sight of the twin metal stirrups, she almost bolted.

"Doctor'll be here in a minute." The nurse patted her arm. "Here's a gown. Take off everything, honey. You okay till he gets here? Who do you want us to call?"

She took the paper smock, assuming, from waiting at her gynecologist's office, that 'a minute' probably meant the doctor could be there in five—or forty-five. She nodded to the first question, shook her head at the second. "No one. Thank you."

The nurse retreated to the other side of the curtain. Lucy stripped off her clammy, dirty clothes, wrapped herself in rustling green paper like a soiled, secondhand gift, and curled up on the table. Something in her rib cage shifted and she stifled a moan, turning her face away as the nurse returned. After a few seconds crepe soles squeaked away across tile.

She wanted to go home. No, scratch that. She wanted to be somewhere clean and distant and cold, preferably uninhabited. Like North Dakota. Or Saskatchewan. Better yet, Antarctica. Then maybe she could wake up tomorrow and believe she had not really just been raped by a classmate. A quiet guy who bit his nails (the ragged ones that had shredded her underwear, scored her inner thighs).

Who stuttered when he spoke in class, and had thanked her in a dazed, happy-puppy way when she'd complimented a paper he'd posted online last spring.

Yes. That sounded right. A place cold and clean, quiet and empty.

The curtain rattled back on the track. A tired male voice murmured, "Miss? Or is it Mrs.?"

She opened her eyes. The white-coated man who stood there looked kind enough, but very tired. "No. I mean . . . yes. It's Miss" she whispered.

He nodded. "I understand you've been through a terrible ordeal, Miss, uh,"—he glanced back at the chart—"Fowler. We'll try not to keep you here any longer than necessary."

She raised her head, winced. "Where's the police. The investigator? The triage nurse said there'd be someone to take a statement."

He shrugged. "They usually show up promptly, unless it's a busy night. Not that your case isn't important." He was tall, thin, with very pale skin. His brown hair was graying, so he was obviously a lot older than the Moth. Still, the tousled hair, the pale blue eyes, reminded her of—

She clutched the sheet to her chest and narrowed her eyes. "What's your name?"

"Dr. Jacoby." He tapped a plastic card on a lanyard, then extended the stethoscope.

She flinched away. "Where's the nurse?"

"Right here." The one who'd escorted her in earlier stepped into the examining cubicle and twitched the curtains closed. She carried a white tray, something folded within it.

Eyes fixed on the blank desert of ceiling tiles, Lucy struggled not to cry as cool, rubber-sheathed fingertips probed her body.

"Hmm," the doctor murmured.

She sucked air as the chilly jaws of the speculum slid

into her. Tim Carling loomed in her mind, and her hands jerked up to cover her eyes. But the twisted face hung stubbornly in her self-imposed dark. And at last she realized what it was that had puzzled her, even through the beating, and the rape.

The eyes. His eyes.

While the rest of his face had been contorted to a snarl, alien with rage or savage joy, his eyes had looked wide and full of tears. Like the imploring gaze of a frightened child.

She limped back into the waiting room, breathing shallowly to minimize the pain of the cracked ribs. Though she wasn't the only person there wearing green scrub pants and shirt, the loose garments made her feel out of place, dreamlike, as if she were walking through the Johnson Valley Mall in her pajamas.

The reception nurse pointed out a stocky, middle-aged man in a blue windbreaker and khaki pants. "The officer wants to talk to you."

The man rose and removed a battered Yankees baseball cap. "Mrs. Fowler?"

"Yes, but it's not Mrs. Are you—?"

"Bob Reshenko. Investigator, Pottsburg Police Department." He unfolded a leather ID case. "I know you been through a lot, but we get better information while it's still fresh in the victim's mind." He held up both hands. "But only if you can handle it. You decide, ma'am."

The victim. That was her. She stifled an impulse to laugh at the 'been through a lot' part. What could he possibly know about it? She didn't feel like deciding anything right now. Still, his matter-of-fact tone had a calming effect. He looked her in the eye, and didn't act as if she was totally damaged, or—

Her rigid shoulders and clenched fists loosened. But that made her want to let go and cry. And she didn't want to. Not here.

"I . . . yeah. I guess I can handle it now. But not here."

"We can go down to the station. Or is there somewhere else you'd feel more comfortable?"

"I want"—she pressed her lips firmly together, then tried again—"to go home," she managed to say.

But Carling was still out there. Oh God. Did he know where she lived?

Reshenko reached out as if to touch her arm, but his fingers stopped a few inches away. "Well, my car's out front. But if you don't want to ride with me, I understand. Wanna call someone—friend, relative?"

"No," she said. The only name she could think of was Hal Prince, and she didn't want to see him, or anyone from class. To have to explain what had happened . . . forget that.

"Miss Fowler? Lucy."

She shook her head and look up at him again. "What?"

"This same thing—it happened to my wife a few years ago. A teenage kid who mowed our lawn. He knocked one night I was on patrol. She thought it was okay to let him in. She knew his mother. I don't mean to say I know how you feel. But I know what it's like to want to do something about it. And I *will* do something about this."

He sounded angry, though not at her.

She took a deep breath. "Well, I guess we should go to your office, Mr. Reshenko." Then she remembered: *Hercules.* "Wait—my dog. I have to let him out."

"Yeah." He nodded. "Sure."

"Take me home. I'll let him out, shower, and put on my clothes. Then I'll talk to you."

The station was a noisy one-story box of tan cubicles. A few cops in dark blue uniforms were shouting back and forth, laughing, answering phones. She felt less self-conscious in her own jeans and sweater. She'd stuffed the wrinkled scrubs in the kitchen trash. And the shredded, bloody skirt, the ruined shirt? "These will be evidence," the nurse with the rape kit had said firmly, as if Lucy might insist on keeping the stained scraps as a souvenir. Reshenko carried them now in a sealed plastic bag.

He led her down a narrow pine-paneled hall to a door on the end.

"Wow. I thought my carrel was small," she murmured.

A dented steel desk almost filled the office. Most of the remaining space was taken by a half-dozen metal filing cabinets and a battered wooden armchair. She had to sidle between them and the desk, then swivel carefully to sit, or else bang her knees. That there were no windows somehow made her feel better.

Over the next hour she told her story three times, first to Reshenko, then to a female investigator, and finally to an older, heavy-set man she guessed was their boss.

"We'll get a photo from the DMV or the registrar's office," Reshenko said finally. "Email it out to the papers, TV stations. In case he's fled."

She didn't know where Carling lived. The detective made some inquiries, then dispatched two officers to an apartment a half-mile from campus. They called back ten minutes later to report they'd woken his roommate, who told them Tim hadn't been home since that morning. There was no sign of Lucy's car on the street or in the apartment lot. They did find Carling's rusted old Volvo, a spare key secreted underneath the chassis in a magnetic holder. It started on the first try.

At one a.m. Reshenko took her home. He'd waited outside the first time he'd brought her back to change. Without being asked now he came inside, looked around, casually opened closet doors, peered into the bathroom, under the bed. "Nice place," he said.

"I like it better than a dorm," she conceded. "But—" She glanced around at all the windows.

"Worried about staying here tonight?"

"No. I don't think . . . he won't be coming here." She felt certain, somehow, that this was true. "Besides, I have Hercules."

Reshenko frowned and looked around, until he spotted a German shepherd lying quietly beside the couch. The dog gazed back silently with mild brown eyes, gray-flecked muzzle resting on paws.

"Uh—that's Hercules?"

She smiled. "Well, he is strong. He's obedience-trained as a companion. Makes a good sentry, too."

Reshenko raised an eyebrow. "He didn't have much to say about me walking in."

"Because you were with me. But don't take my word for it." Without glancing in the dog's direction, she snapped, "Herc—guard!"

The shepherd suddenly loomed before Reshenko, legs braced, ninety-five pounds of bristling, wolfish dogflesh, showing well-polished canines down to the gum line.

Reshenko froze. He cleared his throat. "Huh. Impressive, considering all the silver hairs." He smiled uneasily. "Can I move now, or what?"

The dog, on point, still had not uttered a sound.

"Out" she said with calm authority. The shepherd return-ed to the worn spot on the carpet and lay down again and stared up straight at him.

"You know," said the detective, edging toward the door, "My pop was a mail carrier for thirty years. He always told me those were the ones to watch out for. The quiet, sneaky dogs."

For the first time that night, she smiled. "We'll take that as a compliment, Detective."

After the cop left she went to her room and lay down, though she didn't expect to sleep. Anyhow, it was already four a.m. Hercules padded in, sniffed at her outflung arm, and sank beside the bed with a satisfied groan.

She woke up once, around four A.M. Terrified, crying. But she hadn't been dreaming of the attack. Instead, she'd been in class—the seminar from last semester. Tim had been sitting across from her, smiling—but in the old, shy, kind way. She looked away, then back, and he was gone.

After a few minutes, her heart slowed to normal, and she fell asleep again.

Next thing she knew a large insect—a bee?—was buzzing in her ear. She bolted upright, brushing at her face and hair. God, she hated flying bugs.

It was only the alarm, set as usual for six-thirty. She moaned and fell back onto the pillows. But there would be no more sleep, she could tell.

Stay here? No. Better to keep busy at the university. She got up and stumbled into the bathroom. Looked in the mirror over the sink. Her eyes and jaw popped open.

The furrows Carling had clawed into her breasts were inflamed, swollen, highlighted with iodine. She closed her eyes and leaned on the sink. Then reached blindly for the ratty terrycloth robe hanging on the back of the door. Once covered, she peeled off the taped gauze on her face and inspected the stitches holding together the split flesh over her cheekbone.

"That'll be ugly." She'd always figured she was kind of vain, but the thought of a scar didn't move her in the least now.

She carefully washed her face and walked out, then remembered she hadn't done her teeth. She went back. Stared at the brush and tube blankly for a moment, then picked them up and brushed like a robot set on slow.

After that she kept moving from bedroom to bathroom, forgetting things. Hercules got up and began to pace behind her, whining. She stood for almost fifteen minutes staring into the closet, unable to decide what to wear. Or no—it wasn't exactly that. She couldn't seem to remember what she was *supposed* to put on. What item, which colors, what patterns? Did this match that? She forgot which drawer bras and underwear were in. After an hour of wandering, she took the dog out, then went back to bed. She'd go in late, do some reading. Work on her dissertation. Yeah, that was a good plan.

The phone woke her.

"Hey, Bird Brain. You planning to show up? We were supposed to have lunch at The Alley, remember?"

"Prince . . . Hal," she mumbled. "Uh . . . yeah. I just—what time is it?" The iPhone screen seemed out of focus, an indecipherable glow.

"Past two. You okay? Sound weird, man. Should I bring over a case of Red Bull? A pack of Tums?"

Her sweating palm made the phone slippery. Possible stories flew in and out of her head like gray moths.

"Hey—Fowler. You still there?"

Everyone would see her face and notice how she winced each time she had to bend or turn. Know she'd been singled out, attacked. She thought of Hal's bantering voice, his slim, androgynous figure in the various retro outfits he loved. The brilliant paper he'd once written on queer rape survivors. If not Hal, who could she tell—ever?

She took a deep breath and let it go. "Hey—Hal? Can I say something?"

"Sure," he said without a pause. "Anything, Fowler. You know that."

She smiled. "Yeah. I know. But you won't believe what happened to me last night."

The rest stop bathroom was a stinking concrete box of gore. Reshenko wrinkled his nose. He'd seen worse, just not lately. But man, he hated murder scenes.

The sheriff's deputy nudged him. "This's the guy you were lookin' for, right? The rapist. Some mess, huh. Maybe a revenge hit by the vic?" He chuckled.

Reshenko looked up from the body to stare at the uniformed deputy. The other man shuffled his feet and looked away. "Anyways. Janitor found him 'bout five this morning. Poor slob. Still dry-heaving."

Reshenko frowned. *No wonder*. He was swallowing back some bile himself. "So where is he?"

"In the cleaning staff office, round the corner. But we already took his statement . . . sir."

"I want to see him."

"Um, yessir." The deputy faded away.

Reshenko looked at the corpse sprawled on the concrete a few feet away. Thank Jesus the county guys hadn't mucked up the scene, stomping around in all that blood. He'd gotten the call twenty minutes ago. A deputy had said, "Think we found the perp you put an APB out on two nights ago. Rape suspect? Driver's license says Timothy Wayne Carling."

Reshenko had perked up immediately. "Yeah—where?"

"Rest stop outside Bear Creek on 309."

"Don't take any statements till I get there," he ordered, hoping rush hour traffic had peaked. "Just Mirandize him and—"

"Uh, won't nobody be taking any statements. Suspect's deceased."

"Ah shit," Reshenko had muttered, and slammed down the receiver.

He should take some evidence before the sheriff arrived, since this was a homicide on the county's turf. He snapped a few photos. Then, glancing at the body but not touching it, he took out a pad and began to make notes.

Carling had pulled up at the rest area around three A.M., driving a gray four-door Camry registered to Lucy Emilia Fowler, reported as stolen night before last. He was the only one there, or maybe had just waited until he was. They could check the security camera footage on that. Apparently he'd dragged a yellow sawhorse-shaped CLOSED FOR CLEANING sign in front of the women's rest room and shut the door.

Footsteps echoed on tile. Lourdes Martinez, the county medical examiner, was coming in with a black canvas bag and a Big Gulp Styrofoam cup. "Hey Marty," he said glumly. "How's the coffee?" He hadn't wanted to take the time to stop for any.

She shrugged. "Maybe lethal. But what the hell."

She knelt by the body and took a rectal temp, bagged the hands, the usual stuff. At last she stood, peeled off her gloves, and drank some coffee.

"So?" he prodded.

She yawned. "Sometime between three and five A.M. the deceased took a boxcutter—I'm guessing that one in the corner, the cheap kind sold at any Walmart—and cut his wrists." She shrugged. "Just a guess, mind you."

"Ha. Ha."

"After that . . ." She paused to toss back more coffee. "Things got weird."

"Yeah." Reshenko rolled his eyes. "I noticed."

Carling had apparently used those sliced, freely-bleeding wrists to smear two-foot-high letters on the cream-painted wall of the restroom. The concrete block was finished in rough-textured stucco. The words had come out ragged, blurred at the edges. Yet readable. Ouch, Reshenko thought. But where in hell had the guy been since Wednesday night?

"Not an ideal writing surface," said Martinez.

"It had to hurt like a bitch." Reshenko winced, able for a moment to feel the pain of dragging open flaps of severed flesh over a surface with the consistency of extra-coarse sandpaper. "So then what? He got impatient or pissed off that he was still alive, and turned the knife on his throat?"

She sighed. "I'm trying to concentrate, Bob." After a few

moments she muttered, "Yes. He inflicted such a nasty slash that—look here—the head's nearly severed from the neck. See?"

Reshenko swallowed at the sight of stringy tendons, the truncated hose of windpipe. "What about that?" He pointed with the toe of one shoe to a gleaming object in the opposite corner.

"What about it?" she asked, tucking the empty coffee cup into her bag. The restroom's trash bin was stranded like a tall metal island in a pool of coagulated blood.

"Too far away. Wrong angle. I say this boy didn't shuffle off on his own; he had some help. 'Cause look, Marty. See what we're standing on?"

She nodded. "Uh huh. Concrete."

"Wrong-o. A small patch of clean concrete. And yet the blood is, like, everywhere. The walls, the stalls . . . so how'd Carling keep this spot clean?"

"Well, do you see any prints leading out, hand or foot, that don't belong to us? I'm skeptical he had any guests at this going-away party. For now I call it suicide."

Reshenko snorted. "You're saying he whacked himself, then pitched the knife all the way across the room, with a thirty-degree curve. Or dropped it, then raced over here, spewing like a fountain, wiping surfaces clean as he went." He eyed the basins and stalls again. "Does he look like some kind of neat-freak to you?"

"He just looks deceased to me." She shook her head. "But it's freaky, I admit. Maybe the bloodwork will show traces of something—dust, crack, crank. Something. Just committed a violent rape, didn't he, with no priors?"

"Yeah . . . yeah," Reshenko conceded. "But I think—"

She patted his shoulder. "If it's not self-inflicted we'll find out at the autopsy. But . . . face it, Bob. No indication anyone else entered or left before or after the decapitation. Nothing on the camera, the deputy tells me. Not till Joe the Janitor showed up."

He grimaced. "So we'll be calling it suicide."

She nodded. "I think so. Probably."

Reshenko ran a hand wearily down his face. "OK. Say you're right—for now. What about the words? On the wall."

She turned to look. "Yes, I wondered about them too."

He nodded eagerly. "Right. 'NOT ME.' Like that stupid comic strip, been around a hundred years—*Family Carnival*? *Family Circus*, yeah. Every time one of the fat little kids breaks a vase or tracks up the floor they all say, "Not me!" And there's a short, pudgy see-through guy—a ghost—always running away from the mess. The parents can't see him. On his chest is printed NOT ME. You know how kids are, never want to take the blame."

Martinez sighed, glanced at her empty coffee cup. "Your point?"

"So Carling, he's a suspect in a nasty rape case. Guilty and ashamed, but not wanting to admit it, even to himself." He paused, sneaked a look at Martinez's face.

The deputy Reshenko had first spoken to reappeared. "Hey, that janitor dude wants to talk to you. Wants to know who's gonna clean up this mess. I told him, 'Most likely you are, bro.' Just messin' with his head, you know? A little humor. And he busts out cryin'."

"Why didn't you tell him there's a service that—oh hell, I'll be there in a minute." He waved the guy off. "Hey, Marty. Got a spare buck?"

"Jesus, Reshenko. Every case you bum cash." She dug into the black bag. "Don't they ever pay you? Wait, let me guess—it's volunteer work."

"Yeah, I'm a regular, fucking Mother Teresa," he muttered.

He went outside and got a tiny flimsy cup of anemic coffee from the rest stop vending machine, took a sip and scalded his tongue.

"Shit," he muttered. Setting the cup on a low wall, he slipped a scrap of paper from his wallet and laid it flat on top of the wall. Squinting, cradling the collapsing paper cup in the other hand, he thumb-punched Lucy Fowler's number into his cell phone.

THREE

Lucy stood in the parking lot of her apartment complex, dangling a rawhide bone. "Come on, Herc! Get in back."

The big shepherd put his head down and walked toward the Camry's open door, so slowly he might've been an outlaw ascending the gallows.

"Come on, come on, boy."

The dog's ears drooped. He slowed to a tail-dragging crawl.

"Oh, for—here, Hal. Hold this." She passed the dog treat to him. Then, with a few encouraging boosts, got Hercules to climb into the backseat where he hunched, head hung over the front passenger seat.

"Poor guy," said Hal, scowling at the rawhide. "He needs some chocolate. Not this shit."

She took the beef chew back. "He'll be happy once we get out of town and he realizes we've passed the vet's office. So, any last questions?"

"Let's see." Hal ticked off slender, nicotine-stained fingers. "Feed the guppies, but just a pinch. You decided not to stop the mail, right? So I'll check the box every other day. Oh yeah, and call you at this number in, uh"—he dug into the pocket of his WWI jodhpurs, and produced a folded scrap—"in . . . Eye-bo Key, if that's how you say it. But only for something that's, like, really urgent. About your dad—or from the Reshenko guy."

She nodded. "It's EE-bo. And I don't expect anything, but just in case. So, like, eat anything in the fridge you want. Be sure to shut the windows on the porch if there's a storm. And when you water, be careful with that big staghorn fern."

"Yeah, sure. Is it—valuable?"

"Only to me." It had been her mother's coddled favorite. "Oh, and Hal? Stay out of my hair products, OK? And don't go rummaging through my private drawers. You know what I mean."

He shrugged. "Right. Absolutely. Not."

Her cell played "Don't You Care About Me Anymore?" When she pulled it out of her bag, the screen said DET RESHENKO.

"Oh." The breath went out of her all of a sudden. "Hold on. I better take this."

When she passed the first rest area off I-10 at Starke, the iPod was channeling the Decemberists; "The Abduction of Margaret." She clicked it off, palms slippery on the wheel.

Reshenko had called to tell her they'd found Tim Carling. Or rather, his body. "Thought that might make you feel, you know, safer."

She'd thanked him.

"Yeah, well, so—not to pry or anything but there's a Rape Crisis Center at"—she'd felt her face heat then, with anger, though that made no sense—"No. I mean, I'll think about it," she'd said, glancing at Hal, who was staring at her with raised eyebrows. "But really," she'd said slowly, exhaling, turning her back to him, "keeping busy is best for me."

The detective didn't pursue it.

What this cop doesn't understand, she thought, was that after the first night she hadn't feared Carling would come after her again. Maybe she should have. But she knew, somehow, it wouldn't happen. What seemed worse was that she'd been a total fool, had misjudged and been betrayed by somebody she'd assumed she knew. If it happened once, it could happen again. How could some crisis center prevent that? She didn't want to talk about it, just to put it behind her. And not trust anybody in that naive way ever again.

But gradually she'd grown afraid to *leave* the house. Especially at night. Inside she felt safe. Outside, as if she had a sign on her back: HELPLESS. TARGET. HURT ME. Finally, she decided the answer was to never go anywhere without Hercules.

At the university she moved in a cottony cocoon. She'd told a few other students she knew, because it would be in the papers anyhow. They'd guess. There was the bruised face, the stitches. Better to get it over with—the sympathy, the curiosity. Instead of trying to act all cheerful and *fine*.

Hal had offered to come over, or for her to come stay with him. That wasn't going to happen. She didn't need a sympathy relationship, a disaster-movie romance. Still, when she'd turned up in the library, he was waiting in their carrel.

"Look, Fowler," he said before she could blink. "I'm not good at cooing and patting shoulders. And let me be the first to say that I don't have *any* idea how you feel. But guessing you don't want me to snivel and pule all over you."

She sank into her chair, saying nothing.

"So OK," he went on, looking nervous. "Let's just put it all up front. I hate like hell what happened. I'd murder the shitty little perv if he hadn't beat me to it. In fact, I'd like to dig him up and kill him again, but that probably wouldn't make you feel better. Or would it? So should I go away, stay in here? Write you a paper, carry your backpack, buy you a chai latte? Offer my face as a punching bag?" He paused for breath. "Damn. Why don't you say something?" He actually had tears in his eyes. Who'd have thought?

"Hal." She reached up and touched his arm. "I don't need you to do any of that stuff. Though every nutty thing you said was just right."

He patted her shoulder. "Well, okay then," he mumbled. "Now, got to run to British Mystic Poets." He pushed out. Was that muffled sniffling she heard as he stamped off down the hall?

Word traveled fast in a university, which was like a small, gossipy town. The biggest surprise was the offer from Summer, the earnest blonde sophomore, who pulled her aside after Dr. Grove's anthro class.

"Hey, so would you like to, um, come along and maybe join my community?"

Did she mean a gaming club, a Harry Potter fan thing?

"The BDSM community," Summer explained.

Lucy frowned. The term was tantalizingly familiar but—Oh, right. Bondage Dominance and . . . .

"OK, yeah, it's like, bondage and dominance," Summer confirmed patiently. "But everybody's got it all wrong. We are the gentlest, most respectful people in the universe."

"Oh." Lucy nodded. "Well, uh, thanks. But I . . . I don't know what I want to do right now. Not yet."

Summer had smiled and rubbed her nose. "Sure, that's cool. Just let me know." Then she'd shouldered her bag and walked off—and yes, carrying a copy of *The Deathly Hallows.*

Lucy received offers of pepper spray and stun guns. Some mute, embarrassed glances. Sometimes conversations halted when she came into a classroom or the student center coffee bar. Once, as she was walking down the dimly lit hallway of the social sciences building, her neck stiffened as if wrenched violently from behind. And, for a moment, in her mind, she was thrust back into the woods with a lunatic. She woke most nights and couldn't go back to sleep until she reached down and laid a hand on Herc's broad, furry back.

Hercules went everywhere with her now. To class, where he sat outside the door. She sneaked him into the library carrel. Hal complained that the dog farted, but otherwise seemed not to mind sharing the space. At a store or gas station, Herc sat patiently in the back seat until she came out again. On walks he trotted beside her. As long as he was there, she was OK.

But now, as she drove over the South Carolina-Georgia border, he climbed through the gap between the seats, then pressed his nose to few open inches of passenger window, snorting in exciting scents. It'd been tough getting the hotel in Ibo Key to agree to a large dog. But the clerk had relented after she'd promised to pay a big damage deposit up front.

"What the hey," he'd sighed. "We've had worse guests. And there's no carpet here anyway."

On I-95 she stopped outside Brunswick, Georgia, to walk Herc in a roadside park. He frisked in circles, panting.

"You're a great tourist, buddy," she said. "One more lap around the park, then back in the car. We're not searching for a hotel in backwoods Florida after dark."

The Island House Inn was a historic hotel in downtown Ibo City. She'd seen it mentioned on a photocopied article from the Crane County Public Library. A box labeled *Per your request* had been checked off. She'd frowned. She hadn't requested anything from this place . . . had she? But she'd been working on the dissertation sporadically all the last year. It was hard to remember sometimes where she'd left off.

Anyhow, a reporter for the *Big Bend-Sun*, a Panhandle paper, had done a feature on Esther Day, the oldest living midwife in the South. She'd never lost a baby, she claimed, or a mother either. In the grainy photo, a heavy, square-jawed woman with permed white hair squinted at the camera, standing behind a kitchen table spread with stainless implements and jars. The caption read: "Tools of the Trade: Midwife Esther Day in the kitchen of her Ibo Key home."

Lucy needed an interview subject for a chapter on plant lore and evolution of medicine in rural America. She'd read the diary of Martha Ballard, an eighteenth-century New England midwife, and been amazed by the birth records for that time in history. Granted, these were informal documents, but it seemed the infant mortality rate had been fairly low as long as midwives practiced alone. A sharp rise occurred in reported deaths as doctors, previously only summoned by status-conscious, wealthier families, began to take over more deliveries later in the century. The educated male physicians saw a chance to profit from the lucrative new practice called obstetrics.

Lucy had emailed the reporter, who gave her an address for Day. "She doesn't go online," the woman added. "Check 4-1-1.com."

So Lucy had gotten the address, and written an actual letter. Only a few days later she received a packet of articles on Day, some dating from the 1950s. What a quick response! A letter arrived the next week. Day would be available for a meeting in early December. *I will pull out all my old scrapbooks and dust them off. I suggest you stay at the Island House. There is a snowbird motel on the island,* the midwife wrote. *But they charge an arm and a leg.*

Lucy was elated. She'd showed the letter to Hal, who'd grunted. "Just don't get in trouble with the natives on Mysterious Island. Beware the giant chicken."

She'd snatched the page back. "You're the only giant chicken left on earth. So I'll be safe there."

Her doctoral dissertation was on folklore and naturalistic medicine and the role they played in structural violence in the biomedical system. She was going to finish it by the end of next year. Nothing and no one—not even a fellow student gone insane—would stop her from doing that.

Three hours later, they were in northeast Florida, heading west. Outside Gainesville she passed a green highway sign that read ABATON 5. At the next county road, a left pointing arrow announced IBO KEY BRIDGE 7 MI. By then Hercules was snoring, head hanging over the seat, nose touching the floormat.

"Thank God, we're almost there," she groaned. She was stiff, sore, and bored. And for the last twenty miles of empty two-lane she'd kept remembering what was waiting to be done when she returned to Pennsylvania in mid-January.

She'd seen a gynecologist two days after the rape. The doctor had checked her over, listened to a recounting of the attack, and never once glanced at the wall clock. Then she'd blown a big hole in the day. "I'm sorry to tell you this. But, in addition to checking for the usual STDs—syphilis, gonorrhea, chlamydia, Hepatitis B and C, and HIV—we ought to do a pregnancy test."

Lucy had nodded numbly. The doctor leaned forward and laid a hand on her arm. "Not one of those home kits. You want to be sure in a case like this, so there's plenty of time to decide . . . whatever you decide. We could send you to the lab right now. Just to be sure."

God, God, God. She'd slid off the examining table then, paper wrapper crackling. "Thanks, but—the ER already gave me a morning-after pill. And I've had all the bad news I can stand in one day." She turned away and began dressing, so the doctor wouldn't see she was crying. The possibility that she *might* actually be . . .

"Um . . . OK. Where's the lab?"

After they'd stuck her arm and drawn a vial of blood, the lab tech came back with a hypodermic. "Roll up your sleeve again, please."

Lucy frowned. "What's that?"

The dark-haired woman shrugged. "Vitamins, honey. Dr. French ordered this."

"Wait—in a shot? But she didn't mention it to me."

As if Lucy hadn't spoken, the lab tech grabbed her wrist, shoved up her sleeve over the crook of her elbow, and pinned it to the padded arm rest attached to the chair. The syringe was filled with something luminous, red, a thick substance that glinted weirdly under the flickering fluorescent of the lab.

Lucy frowned. "What kind of vitamins?"

Silently the tech slapped her arm for a good vein.

The stuff looked pearlescent . . . but also kind of like blood.

"I don't want it," Lucy had said, and knocked the hypodermic out of the tech's hand. It bounced on the linoleum. She bolted up. "Sorry, sorry."

The tech didn't answer. She was leaning on the counter next to the blood-drawing chair, face pale, a hand on her forehead as if she didn't feel well, either. "Could you . . . tell the nurse to come in?" the woman said weakly.

Lucy nodded. She rushed out, down the short hall toward the reception area. A nurse was standing near the exit door, weighing an elderly lady. "The lab person needs help," Lucy told the nurse. "She's . . . I don't know. Sick."

Without waiting for a response she'd pushed through the door. Paused at the check-out window and smiled and nodded automatically at the receptionist. Made a date for a follow-up appointment, which she immediately forgot. Then she'd left, climbed into her car. As she sat there, sweating, staring through the windshield it occurred to her for the first time that she was sitting in the same seat, on the same fake leather Tim Carling's body had pressed after . . . after he'd—

She wrenched the doorhandle, jumped out, and stood beside the car. She took in a huge breath. Her body went rigid, then shook, then stiffened, over and over again. She stood frozen for so long a yard-service guy trimming grass set his edger down and came over. He leaned to peer into her face. *You all right?* His lips had seemed to be saying.

She couldn't hear any sound, though. When he touched her sleeve she'd flinched. "I'm fine!" she'd snapped, then got back in the car and pulled away, thinking, *Fuck, fuck, what the hell was that, a seizure, a blackout, am I going crazy?*

The blood test had come back negative. The morning-after pill had made her nauseated, and for a few days she'd bled. At least that much of the nightmare was over—she wouldn't have to carry and give birth to the child of her crazed rapist. But as for the rest . . . that would all have to be dealt with later.

Now wind through the driver's window whipped hair across her face. She pushed it back. "So *am* I going crazy, Herc?"

The dog, startled from sleep, looked up. His tail thumped.

"Damn right. You and I are the sanest people we know." She tapped the dash. "Knock on plastic."

A second later came a muffled, answering *thump*.

"What was that?" She snapped around to look. Her bag hadn't fallen off the back seat. The rearview mirror showed nothing in the road. But Hercules had his ears laid back, his nose sniffing overtime on the shelf beneath the rear windshield where a small feathered bundle jerked and flopped. "Herc, leave it!" He pulled away from the shelf and sat, whining in concern, his ears perked. Yellow and red smeared the glass. She whipped her head left and saw a trail of gore along the back side window, all the way across the seat upholstery. An unlucky bird had collided with her side mirror and cracked open like an egg.

Wincing, she pulled onto the shoulder. By then the creature had concluded its death throes. When she got out a small, brown, gelatinous object tumbled off her lap and lay quivering on the cracked asphalt. The bird's . . . liver?

Trying not to retch, she searched for a rag, even some leftover fast food napkins. Nothing but an empty hand sanitizer bottle and a crumpled Hershey wrapper beneath the seat. Cleanup would have to wait.

Miles later a rusted steel bridge loomed like an abandoned

erector set, spanning a wide stretch of water. On the far side lay a smudged green-black tree line. Ibo Key, she guessed. No town visible yet, but then the three-story Island House, the owner had proudly informed her, was the tallest structure there.

She'd read about the area online. Until 1933 there had been no bridge. Passengers and freight were all carted overland from Panama City or Tallahassee, then ferried on barges or skiffs across this Gulf inlet. Lumber was sent back to the mainland on the same vessels. On the north end lay treacherous currents and frequent thick fogs where the murky, always-cold Black River met the warm Gulf of Mexico waters. Still, in the late nineteenth and early twentieth century, the island had thrived.

In 1889, a New Jersey lumber baron decided to extend his narrow gauge railroad to Ibo, where trees and cheap manpower were plentiful. But he went broke in the panic of 1891, his bridge only half built. She'd seen this same view on Google Earth: creosoted pilings like a stumpy fence across the Gulf, vanishing suddenly into a sepia-toned sea a mile short of Ibo Key.

Roosevelt's WPA, forty years later, had built a real highway bridge of concrete and metal gridwork beside the old railroad project. According to www.VisitOldFlorida.com this narrow span was the only way, other than by boat, to reach Ibo Key.

As she drove on, the bridge rattled and hummed. The surging green Gulf was visible through the rusted steel gridwork. On the left, the time-eroded pilings of the railroad bridge crouched, half-submerged, like the charred backbone of a dead dragon. Hercules hung his head out the open window, whining and barking at seagulls, at mist, at God knew what.

"Good grief, sit down. It's just a bridge."

But the dog trembled and whined and would not be quiet. She gritted her teeth and ignored the din.

A rising breeze whipped hazy ghosts off the water;

vapor-spirits that twisted and curled, then spun up out of sight. Mist drifted over, blotting out the Key. A moment later they were wrapped like a child in a mother's shawl. The enveloping echo-chamber bounced back the hum of car and splash of waves. Visibility dropped to a few feet. She'd noticed no one approaching in the opposite lane, but slowed to twenty anyhow.

A glance in the mirror showed the same mass of white vapor through the smeared back window, blotting out the mainland behind them. She fought the urge to make a U-turn in the middle of the bridge and floor it a thousand miles, all the way back to Pottsburg.

"Get a grip," she muttered.

Then the fog thinned and vanished, raising a curtain on a green tropical Eden of water oaks, pines, and palmettos. Spanish moss draped the trees like gray tinsel. Her Toyota rumbled off the bridge, still echoing with Hercules' sound and fury, smeared with vile avian fluids. Seagulls wheeled away, white-feathered bullies shrieking insults. Pelicans lurched off pilings and into flight, like fat-bottomed dowagers.

She exhaled. OK, solid land again. Beautiful, too. Herc sank back, quiet. The bridge had deposited them on a two-lane that must lead to town.

Gradually, though, the place began to look less like Eden. The road was lined with rundown seafood shacks and vine-strangled gas stations turned junk stores, still with rusted pumps. A boarded up oyster packing plant, and plywood covered storefronts. A few charming cottages were interspersed with peeling clapboard shacks hoisted on bricks or pilings, mute testimony to a storm tide's potential reach.

She overtook a figure on a wobbling bicycle pedaling as if pursued by demons. Pelicans and seagulls flapped behind him like miniature Furies. Bringing up the rear was a lone egret. As her car drew closer the big white bird veered off, honking like a bicycle horn. The bike had boxes, bags, and pails strapped to every fender, crosspiece, and handlebar.

As she drew alongside, the rider turned to grin at her. A stringy weather-darkened man of indeterminate age in baggy khaki shorts and a warp-brimmed Jacksonville Jaguars baseball hat. He threw a salute, then leaned into pedaling again. The buckets swinging from the handlebars were full of fish. So the waterfowl were in hot pursuit of nothing more ominous than dinner.

When she reached the main drag, things looked more upscale. But Ibo *City*? Village, more like. The shabby brick, stucco, and clapboard business district had a quaint if rundown early nineteen-hundreds look. Northern money had not yet remodeled this place into the pink-and-aqua cuteness of Key West. No Conch Trains full of parboiled vacationers, no ghosts of dead writers to boost tourism. Just a hardware store, a post office, a few shops, a small farmers' market, a fishing charter, and at least one restaurant.

Beyond these last two, on the right, rose a towering white Vic-torian hatbox: The Island House Inn.

The lobby looked even more retro—like a nineteenth century parlor equipped with a front desk. Huge mahogany-paddled ceiling fans revolved like balky windmills. Thrift-shop sofas and worn armchairs were grouped next to a shelf stuffed with battered books and old *National Geographics.*

She slung her bag down to scarred heartpine. "Herc, sit. Stay." He snapped to attention next to the dufflebag, her own fur-coated guard.

Behind the desk a man in crow black stood. "Miss Fowler?"

"Um—yes. How did you know?"

"We've been expecting you and your, uh . . . the animal. So I put two and two together." His gaze lowered. "Big fella."

"Yes." She decided not to call Hercules by name and give

the wrong impression. "But obedience trained. Impeccably housebroken."

"Hmm." The clerk rummaged in a drawer, pulled out a registration card, and slid it in front of her. "If you'd just fill that out. You said Visa, right? May I have it? Thanks. Your room's 202. A nice rice planter's bed and of course a Gulf view. Breakfast in the dining room between seven and nine. No AC, but this time of year not needed. I'm Gary. Anything I can do to make your stay more pleasant?"

"Oh—yes," she said, still filling out the card, "I'll need a hose."

His smile wavered. "You mean the garden type?"

"Um-hm. And some rags. Or a big sponge. With some liquid soap."

He leaned forward. "I can assure you the room's been scrubbed spic and span. The bath, too. If you see it's not to your liking"—

She'd been hoping not to have to explain. Laying the pen aside, she sighed. "OK. Picture this. It hit my car. Something like a—a bird bomb."

He stared in horror. "A *bomb*?"

"No! Let me back up," she said quickly. "See, I was driving along, minding my own business, when . . . "

She pushed the last clean rag around her Toyota's back window. All the grisly feathered gunk was gone. The mangled corpse she'd buried under a thorny rugosa rose next to the inn. It would've felt heartless to pitch a once living creature into the dented green Dumpster, as the clerk had suggested. The finch sized black bird—not a crow or a cowbird or anything else she'd seen before—had red markings on head, wings, and breast, as if it'd been flicked with a loaded paintbrush.

She backed out of the cramped seat, wincing at a jab from her broken rib, despite the elastic wrap. All right, so this didn't seem like a good beginning, but things would get better. She'd interview the midwife tomorrow. Maybe the woman liked dogs. If not, Hercules could wait outside.

Once he realized all the washing paraphernalia was not for a bath, the shepherd had slipped out of hiding, yawned, and stretched out in a shaft of sunlight. Lucy was about to flick him with a rolled up rag when she saw a furtive movement up on the porch.

The damp cloth slowly unfurled in her hands as a shadowy figure stepped from between two wicker rockers. A dark skinned boy of seven or eight, barefoot, in worn, faded jeans and a white T-shirt with an amateurish tie-dyed pattern. Just a child, yet something about him creeped her out. But that was silly. "Hi there," she said, smiling. "What's your name?"

He didn't answer. Then she noticed his head. The left side was dished in, concave at the temple. A severe birth defect, a terrible old injury? She felt sorry for him.

"Oh, I see. You're not supposed to talk to strangers. Well, that's smar—"

He raised a thin arm and pointed solemnly at someone, or something, behind her.

She turned and saw only the boat rental office. Beyond that, the marina, where two motorboats, a small fishing trawler, and a catamaran were tied up, gently bobbing. No one on the pier. Beyond them only empty water, cupped by the curve of the comma-shaped island's southern shore. When she turned back to ask what he wanted her to look at, the boy was gone.

"Oh well." She gathered up bucket and hose, and started up the steps. "Come on, Herc."

She stopped halfway up, thinking of the strange child, the misshapen head, hollowed as if depressed by a giant's thumb. Her chest tightened. Anyone who'd survived such an injury would surely be brain damaged. So, as for the pointing finger—it probably hadn't meant anything.

By five P.M. it was dark and cool, the sun a mere glowing line on the Gulf horizon. Water Street was crowded with people, many wearing green scrubs or white medical coats. The sight made her recall a billboard on the mainland, a few miles before the bridge, advertising a resort-type retirement home:

GULF REST IN BEAUTIFUL IBO KEY

STAY A NIGHT, A WEEKEND . . . FOREVER!

It must be the main employer here; a roost for elderly snowbirds who preferred not to fly back home.

Jimmy Buffett was buzzing out "Margaritaville" from a dented speaker on the Merry Cat Café's patio. A weathered sign hung over the door, just like an English pub, with a painted boat sailing azure waves. The captain, a gray tabby, wore an eyepatch, red neckerchief, and jaunty grin. But above the jaunty, grinning feline hung a dark cloud pierced with a gilded thunderbolt.

A chalkboard next to the door advertised grilled tuna, blackened catfish, cheese grits, jalapeño cornbread, fried okra. And Caribbean dishes: Mandazi bread, conch chowder, black beans, fried plantains, and yucca. Her stomach growled loudly. She found a vacant table on the patio and Hercules lay down beneath it.

The waitress was a teenage girl with spiky red hair and a gold nose ring, wearing a faded *Linkin Park* T-shirt and a quiet demeanor. "Your dog's so cute," she whispered.

Lucy smiled. Hercules wagged at her hopefully.

"Aww! Look at that face. Wait right there, puppy!" The girl returned a few moments later with a fresh knuckle bone. "OK if I give it to her?"

"Him." Lucy nodded. "Sure."

Soon he was gnawing happily. "My spicy grilled tuna will be just as good," Lucy told him. "Don't look so smug."

The other diners appeared to be fishermen, Gulf Rest employees, or seriously tanned retirees. Some glanced at her; a few stared. Oh well, she thought. A stranger in a small town. She could ignore a little curiosity, but wished she'd brought a book or her iPad.

While chewing the last sweet bite of plantain, she noticed a middle-aged woman, tall and lean, arms folded over a stained chef's apron, standing in the doorway. Her eyelids drooped; an unlit cigarette dangled as she scanned the patio. Her what-the-hell look gradually softened to a satisfied smile. She glanced once at Lucy, then slipped back inside.

The chicory coffee was good, not bitter like Starbucks'. Hal Prince, who always complained about the university sludge, would love it. For a moment she wished he were sitting across from her. Back when she'd arrived at PU study carrels were in short supply. She'd been annoyed to have to share one. Though Hal had turned out to be attractive, funny—and much less messy than she was.

She'd just ended a three year romance at her former college and didn't feel like jumping back into the shark pool. She'd felt homesick for Vermont, and hadn't been out with anyone for months. Late one night they were at the library, passing back and forth a bottle of wine he'd smuggled in, and she'd confided this. Next thing she knew he was kissing her neck, then her lips, and then—almost like a jump cut in a badly edited film—they were at her apartment, in bed.

But the next week he was hanging out with a beautiful criminal justice major. Then a creative writing undergrad. Not that they'd made any commitment, but—this was more than she'd bargained for: Polyamory *and* a tiny shared space? No thanks. They'd agreed to go back to platonic. At least, that had been her impression. Sometimes Hal seemed to be hinting otherwise. But he was a friend, and she was glad they'd finally made the time last week to go out.

Now the mere thought of being physically close to anyone had less appeal than a nude swim in a leech infested lake. She sucked a breath as her brain once more projected the same horrible jumbled slideshow: deserted road, pleading eyes in a crazed, cruel face, the racing engine of her own car. Then green scrub suits, needles drawing blood. *Her* blood, splashed all over. She twisted the napkin in her lap, taking slow deep breaths, until the images receded.

She paid the check and whistled softly. Hercules rose, tail wagging, and followed her back through the mild winter night, the well-chewed knuckle bone clamped in his jaws.

"Message for you, *Dottore* Fowler," said a short, dark-haired woman in a pink sweater set, knitting as she sat behind the hotel desk.

"Thanks, but I'm not a—never mind." Lucy took the note from the night clerk. Was that an Italian accent? This place wasn't just a melting pot, but a spicy, mixed-up gumbo.

The crabbed, old fashioned Palmer script was from midwife Esther Day. Ten o'clock in the morning was the time she agreed to be interviewed. The house was just off Water Street, the main drag, so it ought to be easy to find.

She began the climb to her room, prodding her left side tentatively. The broken rib seemed to be healing. The scratches on her chest were fading red lines.

Three steps behind, Hercules's tail brushed *whisk-thump, whisk-thump* like a straw broom. He hadn't liked these stairs at first; she'd had to coax him to climb.

At the bend that made a small landing, darker shapes seemed to scurry ahead of those cast by the dim electric lights. The foreshortened figures startled her until she realized they were just her own silhouette and Herc's, cast against white-painted wainscoting. The hushed whispering, like drifts of blowing sand thrown against window glass, was only Herc's tail brushing the banister rails.

Still, a trickle of sweat ran down her side beneath the elastic Ace corset. A tingle numbed her arms and legs. Her mouth was so dry her throat clicked. The pounding in her temples echoed the erratic lurching of her heart. Suddenly her stomach took a sickening drop, as if she were coming down on a Ferris wheel.

"Only a panic attack," she whispered. "Be gone in a minute." She stopped on the landing, counting slowly to twenty, trying to stop the floating-up feeling, the urge to leave her own body every time this happened. To repress the message both body and mind were sending: Go. Run. *Now.*

After a couple very long minutes she opened her eyes. Hercules was staring up, whining. "God," she whispered, blotting her face on a sleeve. "Well, come on. Don't let's just stand here!"

She closed and locked the door, shaking her head. Strange how something as harmless as the flicker of her own shadow on a wall could trigger such paralyzing terror.

FOUR

The Day house was a two story clapboard Greek Revival cottage. A short square tower rose from the flat middle of its tin roof. The marker attached to the weathered picket fence out front read:

OLD PUBLIC SCHOOL
This structure, erected prior to 1874, was used
as the city school until replaced by a new brick
building on East Bayou Street in 1949. It has
since been a private residence occupied by the
Turner and Day families.

So that tower had held a brass bell that once called generations of children to giggle and squirm in rooms full of wooden desks and dusty chalk boards. *Turner and Day*, she mused. Such a big house. Did Esther have a husband, family? Maybe scads of grandchildren. Or a social position to keep up. Or maybe just too many closet skeletons to fit in a U-haul.

Lucy straightened. "Ok, boy. Sit; stay." She left the dog in a shady spot just inside the gate. The place was silent. Even the bird song from the trees next door seemed muffled. As she closed the wooden gate, its rusty hinges screeched. A startled crow took flight in an explosion of leaves from the live oak in the front yard.

She carefully climbed the wooden steps, which looked

warped and felt loose. No doorbell. She was about to knock but then spotted a ship's bell mounted on a column. One hard pull and it pealed like a brass banshee.

"Comin'! I'm comin'," called a rough querulous voice. After a few moments the door began to creak open in short jerks. "Shoot! Daggone humidity," muttered the disembodied voice. "I mean to tell ya!"

At last it swung wide to reveal an elderly black woman—thin, bent, head topped with white hair fine as a bouquet of baby's breath. She regarded Lucy with an osprey sharp squint.

Well, clearly this wasn't her interview subject. Mrs. Day, in the newspaper photo, had been large, heavy-set, and white. Perhaps this woman was a companion or housekeeper, though with that frail body—

"Well?" The voice, all smoke and rusty steel, didn't fit the rest of the package. "Kitty-cat steal your tongue?"

"No. Sorry." Lucy blushed, realizing her scrutiny had been noticed. "I'm here to talk to Mrs. Day. My name is—"

"I know who you are, Miz Doctor Fowler." The woman doubled over suddenly and coughed. Lucy put out a hand, but she waved it away. "Never mind, it's the cancer, had it bad last year. But *that* ain't beat me yet, uh-uh. Well, step in. Been expecting you."

"I'm not a doctor. I mean, maybe later, but—anyhow." She slung her backpack beside a sprung Victorian sofa, hoping her lack of a terminal degree wouldn't be an issue. "This is going to be for my doctoral dissertation."

"You a doctor, then." The old woman nodded. One thin brown arm waved imperiously for her to sit. "Well that's just fine."

"No, I'm not a—not yet." She tried to sit on the middle cushion, but it was like trying to mount a bad-tempered horse, so at last she perched on the springy outer edge. "I'm sorry, I didn't catch your name."

"Didn't throw it." The woman limped to an overstuffed armchair, lowered herself, and groped across a wobbly side table. She picked up a pack of Marlboros, lit one, and drew deeply. Held in the smoke, eyes shut, then through cracked lips exhaled a chain of ghostly wisps that obscured her face. She coughed again, but less violently. "I'm Eugenie Lee, Mrs. Esther's assistant. And she isn't home."

"Oh. But I thought . . . I mean, she sent me a message last night, at the hotel, to come this morning."

"No, *she* didn't. That was from me, child. Mrs. Esther's gone. Two weeks now."

"Gone?" Lucy exhaled. Surely she didn't mean dead?

Lee shrugged. "May not be comin' home for a long while. At least"—she smiled wryly and regarded the glowing tip of the cigarette—"that's what the doctor say."

"But if she's in the hospital, why send a note telling me to come today?" She frowned, mystification sliding toward anger. "You said she's been there two weeks? Look, I'm sorry to hear she's sick. But I made a long drive from Pennsylvania, rented a room for two weeks, all just to interview her. I wish somebody'd told me before—"

Eugenie Lee went on mildly, as if she hadn't spoken. "Yes'm, they took her off to the Manor two weeks ago this Friday. Poor thing just out of her head. I'd of let you know, honey, but it seemed a shame, you wanting to get here for an interview, and her not able to talk. Well, I known Esther Wadley Day for nigh-on fifty year. I can tell anything you need to know, for that book you're writin'."

Lucy felt her face heat again. "Well, it's not exactly a—sorry, I'm still confused. Who are you again, please?"

"I first come here to be her assistant as a girl, barely fifteen year old. She twice my age then. Though not no more!" She chuckled. "We about caught up now."

"Oh. So you helped her in midwifery?"

"Been her right hand all along. God bless and forgive

me." Lee gave a rasping cough and stubbed out the cigarette on a china saucer. "Damn. Let's go out on the porch and sit where it's cooler."

Leave, or stay? Eugenie Lee wasn't who she'd come to interview. But being Dr. Grove's graduate assistant had taught her to never overlook found material. He'd gotten some of his best interviews in Haiti that way. She could talk to this gravel voiced companion now and follow up on Day. Then the trip wouldn't be a total waste.

As they stepped out the front door, a shadow at the far corner of the porch flowed like spilled mercury around the side of the house. Her heart lurched and skipped. Then the sun brightened, casting more moving shapes across the same stretch of planks. Just wind tossing the gnarled wisteria vine twining the columns, throwing long wavering arms of shadow.

Taking two splintery rockers, they faced each other. Lucy set her cell phone on a three-legged stool near Eugenie Lee. As she leaned forward to press the record icon, the heavy silver medallion slid from the front of her shirt, swinging like a pendulum on its serpentine link chain.

The woman glanced at it. Her mouth fell open. Lucy braced for another storm of coughing. Instead, Lee said softly, "O Moses. Ain't that a piece of work, that old African silver. Look soft enough to mash with bare fingers."

"It is." Lucy was surprised. Most people guessed it was old, though not how very old. But only twice before had anyone commented on its origin. Dr. Grove, of course. The other had been an artist who made jewelry. Quite taken with the piece, he'd begged to buy it. Lucy had refused, despite her pathetic bank account. This was the only tangible thing that had accompanied her mother, as an infant, when she'd arrived at her adoptive parents' home.

"It mean a lot to you," said Lee.

"Yes. I try to be careful not to damage it. How'd you know it was African?"

"My daddy worked in silver. Had designs handed down from *his* grandaddy, who'd been a slave. Blacksmith on a sea island plantation in Georgia." She smiled without humor. "He said, the way my grandaddy talked, it weren't no Tara."

Lucy nodded. "I'm sure." What a pity she wasn't looking for oral histories on slavery. "Now, let's see. . . . Do you mind if I record us on this? I can't get everything down fast enough, just taking notes."

The old woman squinted at the silver iPhone. "After all the things I seen and heard, a little box don't scare me."

Lucy opened a new file, recorded date, place, Eugenie's name, then turned to her again. "Now, Mrs. Lee—"

"Child, please. I never married. Don't call me that, or I'll think you want my dead mama. Call me Miss Eugenie. Like Esther always done."

Lucy smiled. "All right. Now, Miss Eugenie, you said you've known Esther Day for fifty years. That you became her assistant at age fifteen. Tell me about growing up here on Ibo Key."

Eugenie Lee leaned back with a sigh. "Back then everyone thought the Key a good place to live. There was work then—the cedar mill and pencil factories was still running. Teppentine mill, too. And one where they made brooms out of palmetto fiber."

"Um . . . teppentine?" Lucy looked up from notetaking. "Oh, *turpentine*."

The old woman scowled. "That's what I said. Anyways, my folks was among the first cullud homesteaders here. Daddy worked tappin' trees for pine oil. On his one day off, and evenings, he built us a home of cedar logs so snug and tight an ant couldn't get in to look for sugar crumbs. Company railroad tracks run behind the place. I grew up with an engine whistle for a lullaby." She paused, gazing straight ahead, looking sad. Then, with a shake of the head, said, "But you want to hear about Esther, too."

"Yes, please."

"Well, we lived on opposite ends of the island. Guess you know why."

Lucy nodded. "It must've been segregated then. And you lived on which side?" She made a note. "So you're saying there's another town besides this one. What's it called, and how do I get there?"

Eugenie Lee's knotted hands began twisting the fabric of her skirt. "Oh well, it was one. Just a small place called Revelation. Black folk all lived over that way." She jerked her head vaguely south. "Ain't there now. They all picked up and gone north to the cities. On account of needing work."

"Right," said Lucy. "The Great Migration."

Lee shrugged. "Call it what you like."

"So how'd you meet Esther Day?"

"Her daddy was my daddy's boss over at the lumber mill. She'd come to the office every afternoon bringing him—Mr. Bay Wadley—a dinner pail. About the same time my mama always sent me over with my daddy's dinner. Biscuits and ham, cracklings, fried oysters or Nile perch. We girls didn't exactly speak—but I knew she was going off to college in Tallahassee, to study on being a nurse. Kinda late, but she still single. And Esther, she *look* like a nurse!" Eugenie laughed, then wheezed. "All prim and starchy."

Lucy smiled, imagining the woman she'd seen in the paper—younger but already serious, with a determined presence.

"She go off and come home two years later, a real nurse. First one the Key ever had. Open a little office downtown, call it a clinic. Publish a notice in the paper, saying she gonna bring modern medicine and . . . hygiene. Then she wait. And wait some more. But nobody come to get treated modern."

"People don't like change." Then, envisioning a scowling

Dr. Grove, Lucy added, "Um, not that their ways are necessarily wrong, of course."

Eugenie shrugged. "You got the degree. Well, some Wadly cousins come in, naturally. A few friends. Nobody know better than Esther that don't count. Still she don't act worried. Instead, she hire me to clean, do laundry, answer the phone, like she in way over her head. 'You be my assistant now, and I teach you how to work in professional medicine,' she tell me." Lee snorted. "Fifteen and a half, and for the first time I got my own money. She coulda hired me to midwife possums, for all I cared."

Lucy laughed. "Please, keep going. It's interesting."

"I don't know where your people's from. But small town folks stubborn as ten dollar mules. Bound to keep goin' round in the same circles. Rich ones went to see a fancy doctor on the mainland. There was an old root doctor name of Pop Taylor, too. Poor folks went to him for warts, colds, and whatnot. That where part of the business Esther want was going. Pop already older than Moses, not bound to last. But then there was Solange Koumari."

"Wait. I'm sorry . . . can you spell that?" Lucy typed the name. "And who was she?"

"A light skinned Negress from New Orleans. Tall, green eyed, the longest, shiniest black hair that fell in waves. Voice like music playing on the radio. *She* got a lot of the other business, and all the birthings.

"When Esther come back, she also marry her high school sweetheart, Turner Day. He was right handsome, thick arms strong enough to lift a pine log at the mill all alone. He hadn't been happy about her going away. But she a stubborn daddy's girl. By the time she back home he become a millwright. So she didn't *have* to work. But she want to, just *got* to.

"Pop Taylor not only old but so sick most days he just stay in the bed. Esther figure somebody got to inherit his practice, why not her? But then he pass, and most switch over to Solange. So Esther decide to go after the liver and lights of her rival's work: the midwifin'."

Esther did not start out as a midwife, Lucy typed on her laptop. *A business decision, to expand her practice.*

Eugenie broke off in a coughing fit so violent it vibrated the floorboards. "Maybe we should quit," Lucy said. "I don't want to tire you out."

The older woman dabbed at her lips with a faded handkerchief, looking disappointed but also relieved. "If a body lives long enough to get in my condition—and I ain't so sure they should—you got to take everything in small doses."

She left the old woman sitting on the porch fanning herself. The heat was definitely rising. It was already after twelve. How fast the morning had gone! Hercules sat panting by the gate. She cupped a hand and poured bottled water for him to lap. Then, boosting the dog into the back, she decided to drive around town. In between interviewing Eugenie Lee, and checking out Ibo Key, she could start editing her dissertation. Last month a university press had answered her query, saying they'd take a look at the manuscript when it was completed.

As she reached for her keys, she heard the thump of footsteps. Her head snapped up. A tall, brown-haired man was running down the street. Fast. She tensed, then noticed he wore running shorts and wasn't looking her way. Still, she flattened herself against the car as he drew nearer, hurrying to get the key in the lock.

He gave her a nod and a tight, pained grin. His clothes were sodden, face scarlet, legs and arms slick with sweat. As he puffed past she got a whiff of male sweat, faintly metallic, filtered through laundry soap and damp cotton. Enough to thrust her back into the dark woods, the bruising grip of a madman.

"God," she whispered, passing a shaking hand over her

face, feeling a laugh or maybe a scream beating its fists against her diaphragm. Sweat prickled her face. She yanked open the door and slid inside the Toyota, a soundproof, upholstered womb. The automatic lock clicked. For a moment she sat gripping the wheel, listening to the comforting rasp of Hercules panting in the back. Then, slowly, put the car in gear and drove on.

FIVE

Lucy set her phone next to her laptop and pressed PLAY on the smooth touch screen. The hoarse, smoky voice of Eugenie Lee filled the hotel room. *". . . so she decide to go after the liver and lights of her rival's work: the midwifin'."*

She frowned. For some reason the old woman's words sounded lifeless, faint, tinny. After a few moments a machine gun burst of static wiped them out altogether.

She tapped the SKIP icon, then PLAY again. The static returned, at times breaking up the conversation like a bad Skype call. It rose, blocking out the voice, or distorting it into gibberish. Luckily she'd taken notes, which made it easier to figure out the bad portions.

Weird. Sometimes the noise was just garbage, a howl of electronic wind. Then, off-and-on, it twisted the words so it seemed like the old woman was saying things Lucy knew she hadn't heard while sitting on that porch.

In the early part, according to her notes, fifty years back people thought Ibo Key was a good place to live. Eugenie Lee had said so. Now an electronic shriek, just after "Ibo Key was" made the next words sound like *a dead place*. She frowned. Maybe the local economy had a foot in the grave, but it was hardly a ghost town yet.

During Lee's recounting of the rivalry between Day and Koumari, other voices muttered like cross-talk on a

61

phone line. Nothing clear. Except once, craziest of all, when playing that part back at the loudest section of interference, Lucy thought she heard a woman's voice whisper, "Murder . . . it was murder." Popping and crackling overwhelmed everything else.

Too weird. She'd never had this happen before. She pressed END. Obviously she'd done *something* wrong. Forget transcribing for now—she'd call Key Manor and find out whether Esther Day was up to seeing people today.

"Thanks," she said, making a face as she hung up. Visiting hours were any time you liked. That is, unless the person was assigned to the 'special unit' where Day was hospitalized. Then it was early to mid morning, a time slot she'd just missed, and from two to four P.M. But Day was scheduled for tests and couldn't see anyone this afternoon.

Her own fault. She'd slept late then lingered over poppy seed toast, mangoes, and strong coffee with cream. "I'm getting on island time," she muttered. So, get going earlier tomorrow. This afternoon she'd explore the place from the water.

Out on the hotel steps she adjusted her sunglasses against the glare of noon. It was really hot. She slapped on sun block, though her olive skin rarely burned. The hotel clerk and waitress had both commented on it. A December heat wave had settled in. Rumor was even hotter weather was on the way.

She'd noticed a sign for boat rentals and fishing charters across the street. Anhinga Tours. That seemed a good place to start.

The marina office was narrow as a cigar box, its thick air stirred by an ancient cast-iron pedestal fan that nodded from left to center, and then flopped left again. She slapped the bell on the counter, and stood where she could hog the fan's breeze. The shelves on one wall held baseball caps with a dust-fuzzed logo. It looked like a buzzard, a snaky-necked bird perched on a piling. Also small plastic spray bottles of insect repellent—what the heck was 'ozone' scent?—and some fishing paraphernalia she mostly didn't recognize. On the end sat a stack of badly-photocopied guidebooks with a crude illustration of some unidentifiable shore bird, perhaps commissioned from an artistic ten-year-old.

No one answered her ring. She slammed the bell a second time. "Hello! Anyone here?"

A muffled crash from the back, where a blue curtain hung across a doorway. Someone muttered, "*Shit.*" The curtain, wrenched aside, ripped from its track and fell to the floor.

"Shit," the tall dark-haired man repeated. He wore a T-shirt and ragged denim shorts, and was rubbing bleary eyes. He peered at her like a bear roused too early from hibernation. From the aura of beer, stale smoke, and sweat, he was in serious need of a shower. She took a step back.

"Sorry," he mumbled. "Where's Jesus?"

So it was true, what she'd heard about the Southern obsession with evangelical religion. "I'm not here to be saved," she said firmly. "Just to rent a boat."

He combed his hair awkwardly with one hand. "Sorry. I mean, look, I have a new assistant, and he—I meant to say *Hay*-suess. He's supposed to be here working, but . . . ah, forget it." He smiled, looking less sleepy, and suddenly she recognized him. The runner who'd passed her yesterday in front of the Day house.

"Nick Yulee. I do the charters. I'll get you a boat. And, um, excuse the way I look. We played a gig at Weird Sister's, up near Gainesville. Didn't get in till . . . well, never mind. What kinda boat?" He leaned on the counter and raised an eyebrow.

That explained it. He did smell just like a scruffy off-campus bar. "I'd like . . . um . . . a skiff, I guess. A ten or twelve-footer? And a map, I mean chart, of the area."

"Don't need one to putt around those islands. Hard to get lost. If you capsize, just stand up. Usually no more'n four foot, even at high tide." Then he frowned. "Going out by yourself?"

She felt first annoyed, then angry. Summers, growing up, she'd handled a small sailboat—first with her father, then on her own. "Would you like a note from my mother? Wait, let me guess. A permission slip from my boyfriend."

He raised a hand. "I don't care if you're male, female, or none of the above. Long as you can run an outboard and sign your name to this-here waiver." He slapped a sheet down on the counter and sighed. "Sometimes we get tourists who'd sink a boat in a bathtub. Sounds like you can take care of yourself."

Too late, she thought, not returning the smile. She dashed off a signature, slapped down a credit card, and drummed her fingers while he slid it through the machine. Good-looking, maybe, but this guy was annoying.

On the dock the warm breeze was heavy with salt. Boats bucked and rolled like tethered aluminum horses. "Your pick. Except for that'un. Might need her later today." He pointed to a sleek cabin cruiser. The name HOT TUNA scrolled in red across the starboard side.

Just what she needed—a beach-babe taxi. "This one looks fine." She pointed at the biggest, least battered skiff, one she hoped was sizeable enough to take the Gulf chop.

"Good choice."

Like she'd asked his opinion. She raised two fingers to her mouth and gave a shrill whistle.

Yulee took a big step back when Hercules galloped around the corner and launched into the rocking skiff. "So you do have an escort." He handed over a pair of oars from a battered wooden gear locker.

She tossed them on the thwarts, then turned her back and coiled the stern line. "I'll be back by five."

"Sure. Now, that's Rattlesnake, the bird sanctuary, way over there. Uktena Key to your left. Off limits. It's a federal bird sanctuary." He pointed at various smudges on the horizon. "None of those other islands are inhabited. Might want to check out Teach's, on the far side of Pelican Key. Behind the two I pointed out."

She glanced over one shoulder. "Why's that?"

"You know Blackbeard, the pirate? Teach's is a nice place for sunbathing."

She raised an eyebrow. "He used it for that?"

Yulee looked flustered. "N-no. They say he really landed on Pelican, and buried his loot along with some of the crew, to stand a skeleton guard over—"

Oh, right. *They* say. The Urban Legend Factory. "Save the corny spiel for the tourists. I'm here doing research." She swung down into the skiff, then turned and looked up, shading her eyes. His back was to the sun, face in shadow. "By the way, you've got some of that fable wrong," she said. "It's the Devil who guards ill-gotten treasure."

She started the outboard on the first pull. He tossed the bow line down and she threw the Yamaha into reverse, aiming the little skiff between two pilings beneath the fishing pier and then, toward open water.

She cruised by Rattlesnake—uninhabited, as he'd said, except for hundreds of brown pelicans nesting in every scrubby bush and palmetto—then pointed the bow toward Pelican Key. But not, she reassured herself, because of some hokey tour-guide monologue.

As she rounded the far side of Rattlesnake, she spotted Uktena—larger, its shore walled by stunted, salt-gnarled pines. 'Uktena' meant 'monster' in many Southwestern Indian dialects. There'd been Creek and other tribes in Florida as early as the seventeenth century. And then Cherokee, who'd later joined with runaway slaves to form the Seminole tribes.

"Monster Key" didn't sound inviting. Had those early dwellers believed an Uktena—a terrifying winged serpent, huge and scaly, with deer horns on its fearsome sharp-fanged head—inhabited this small, benign-looking hump of sand? More likely they'd wanted outsiders to think so, and stay away.

Pelican Key was just ahead. The boat-guy's four-star tourist beach. It did *look* great—sugar-white sand, tall swaying palms—in a vacation-postcard way. Its narrow white ribbon of beach was scattered with sun-bleached shells. A great blue heron stalked, stiff as a hieroglyph, in the shallows. White crest whipped by the breeze, he nodded like a judge at each slow-motion step. When a covey of herring gulls swooped past, shrieking, he ignored them. Beyond the gleaming sand, live oaks and mangroves sprouted up between cabbage palmetto and prickly pear.

Lucy sat for a moment, the outboard humming in neutral, gazing at the island. The right kind of place to go—safe, predictable. It would've bored her. Before.

Something splashed nearby. Startled, she dropped the throttle. Fear like an electric current shot a numbing tingle down to her fingers and toes. Beside the skiff a glistening sickle of fin broke the surface, a broad back of dove gray. One sleek porpoise rolled in the calm water to eye her. Two more surfaced beside him. Hercules barked, paws braced on the gunwale. Lucy shook her head and laughed, passing a shaky hand over her sweating face. Terrified by Flipper? Lame.

She glanced over her shoulder, back at Uktena. The forbidden place. The bird sanctuary. *Place of monsters.* Monsters were not usually so helpfully labeled, though. She felt a chill, even with the sun beating down on her back.

So, on to the approved tourist sunning spot on Pelican—to Teach's Cove?

No.

Suddenly resolute, she pushed the outboard in gear, twisted the throttle, and turned the skiff back toward Uktena.

After a half-hour in the sun she moved beneath sheltering trees. Lying on a towel on the warm white sand she felt lazy, content. A breeze gusted in, cooling her, drying the sweat from sun-warmed skin. She rolled over to look out at the lapis Gulf, sighed, and closed her eyes. No monsters here. Just blessed escape from people, from questions, from the assessing glances of men. That she wasn't supposed to be here at all made it feel even sweeter.

Sometime later she opened her eyes again. How long had she slept? The nap had been deep and dreamless. Her cell phone screen said it was already pushing four. Hercules lay a few feet away, sprawled on his side, snoring.

She was starving, but there was food in the blue canvas bag. Valencia oranges bought on Water Street from a man selling fruit and vegetables from the bed of an old pick-up. She peeled and sectioned one, then bit into a plump crescent. Cool juice ran down her chin.

The dog raised his head and gazed at her. "Are you drooling? OK, OK." She dug in again, and tossed him a Milkbone.

She popped another section of orange, glanced up, and noticed the sky. To the west thunderheads were massing like a flock of dingy sheep. The breeze was cooling, picking up strength. A bolt of lightning like a warped silver knife split the darkening sky. "Uh-oh," she said to the dog, the next slice halted halfway to her mouth, juice curling a sticky bracelet down wrist and forearm. "Looks like more than a little squall there."

The dirty clouds were scudding this way. But if she left now, surely they'd beat the storm back to Ibo. She brushed sand off her legs. "Come on, Herc. Into the boat!"

He scrambled up, shaking head, then hips, ears

flapping. Flying sand stung her cheeks. She bundled things up while the dog paced in circles like an impatient boyfriend. All he needed was a wristwatch to glance at. But down at the boat she stopped short, staring in dismay. She hadn't considered the tide. Apparently it'd been past the high mark when they'd set out. She had run the skiff right up to the sand and beached it. Now, it lay high on an exposed sandbar made mostly of jagged gray oyster beds. Their rough shells were stacked like the towers of sand castles, but with edges so sharp they'd shred the rubber soles of her flip-flops. She'd have to drag sixteen feet of heavy aluminum plus an outboard over an obstacle course of razor-edged shells and slick mud.

What had she been thinking? She *knew* about tides. "Shit!" She grabbed the stern. With a hefty tug it rocked slightly, like a giant's cradle. Not going anywhere.

"Well, great," she muttered. Scooping her belongings from the damp sand, she dumped them into the bottom, grabbed the stern again, braced her feet and pulled hard. The skiff moved a couple inches.

She glanced back at the approaching storm. Sweat and salt mist stung her eyes. They could wait it out here, but the thought of huddling under dwarf trees lashed by howling wind, driving rain, and random lightning strikes wasn't attractive. Anyhow, in a flat landscape you didn't shelter under trees in a storm, unless you aspired to become a broiled shish-kabob. Even if the squall blew over quickly, she'd still be stranded till the tide rose. Maybe even after dark, and there were no running lights on the boat. Could she find her way back at night? The town lights might guide her in, but sand bars and other obstacles would be invisible.

She gripped the bow line, debating how she might use Hercules as a draft horse without lacerating his paws, when she heard the rumble of a large motor. Shading her eyes she saw, out beyond the lagoon, a white boat. As it drew nearer, a man climbed on the bow and heaved out an anchor, then waved. She groaned. *Hot Tuna*, Yulee's charter. How had he known she'd be here, trespassing? OK, maybe she shouldn't quibble, but what price rescue? . . . Why couldn't it have just been a passing fisherman?

Annoying too was the graceful way he splashed through the mucky shoals of the treacherous oyster bed in bright-green watermens' boots. "Dr. Fowler, I presume?" He grinned and held up a coil of nylon line.

"I'm not a—oh, never mind." If only her stupid dog would stop grinning back, and wagging like a fool.

He squinted. "Say what?"

"Nothing. Um, so what brings you out here?"

He jerked a thumb over one shoulder. "Weather took a turn. Like to make sure my boats don't get lost. And my customers don't get wet."

"Well, I—" She avoided his eyes, feeling torn between gratitude and annoyance. At last she shrugged and forced a quick smile. Suck it up, Lucy.

She nodded. "Yeah. I guess we could use a little help."

They skimmed over the whitecaps past Uktena Key. He'd said nothing about her trespassing on a posted sanctuary. Then again, who would he tell, out here?

She was about to open her mouth, to ask why he'd decided to look for her there, when the squall caught up to them.

"My God," she said. Had all the toilets in heaven flushed at the same time? She was drenched in seconds, shivering, teeth chattering.

Yulee flapped a hand, and shouted, "Duck inside the cabin!"

She shook her head and clung stubbornly to the lifeline, already feeling too much like Helpless City Woman. As long as she was still standing, she couldn't possibly be drowning, right?

The icy rain finally did drive her inside. Before descending the ladder she took a last look at the empty skiff trailing behind, bouncing less wildly now because it was half full of water. She and Herc could've been out there in that—but afloat for how long? Imagine the headlines in the PU *Cauldron*: "Doctoral Student Drowns While Island Hopping with Dog."

Her knees buckled and she sank onto one of the cushioned passenger benches.

Hercules, however, stood right beside the wheel, all four legs braced, wagging and nosing Yulee's free hand, as if their savior were an old buddy.

Finally the downpour eased, blowing off east toward the mainland.

Yulee dug into a locker and tossed her a towel.

She rubbed her snarled, dripping hair. "All the excitement . . . guess I, uh, haven't actually thanked you."

"No need. I'd do it for anyone. Coastal weather's unpredictable. Out here, sort of like a . . . a vortex, maybe you'd call it. Storms come up fast. Used to be a pile of shipwrecks out there in the Gulf, way back, just like around Cape Hatteras. Even locals get caught short. The marina's right up here."

She leaned out to dump her things on the dock, then tried to coax Hercules to jump. Yulee scooped the big dog up and set him on the sun-bleached planks. She scrambled out before he decided she needed a lift too.

"Say," he said. "I've been thinkin' on the best way to ask. How about some time you and I—"

A loud hoarse honk made them both jump. A familiar bicycle was parked at the end of the pier. The same wiry dark rider was leaning on it, feeding a fish to a snowy egret perched on the handlebars. The bird gulped, then loosed a stream of green guano.

The man smiled at her, revealing snaggly brown teeth. He looked her up and down as if she were the fish and he the hungry egret.

She looked away and wrinkled her nose. "Who in the world *is* that guy?"

Nick shrugged. "Boy Jackson. They call him the Egret Man. He's harmless, lives nearby. Pedals that rolling fish store around. Takes care of hurt birds. That old egret is his pet. Now, what I was gonna ask, was—"

No. She couldn't do it. It wasn't so much him . . . he was kind of attractive, in a rough, salty way, but—no. She grabbed her phone. "Oh my god, it's after five! Got to go. But, um, maybe some other time?"

He looked disappointed. "Oh. Well, I—"

"Sorry." She waved and turned to walk away. Hercules's toenails clicked on the planks as he scrambled to keep up.

"Hey, hold on a minute!" Yulee shouted. "This week my band plays the Cat, at nine. You could drop by and catch a set."

She called over one shoulder, "Sure! Might do that." Then walked faster, around the building, toward the street. He wasn't ugly, or creepy, or pushy, but—she wasn't ready to go out with any guy. Anywhere. Not yet.

It occurred to her only later, while she was pulling on a dry set of clothes back in her room at the Island House, that no matter how close Nick Yulee had stood—whatever he did or said—she hadn't felt the least bit nervous. No sweating, no shakes, no panic to numb her arms and legs. Even out alone on a deserted island. Even on a boat in the Gulf of Mexico. Now, why was that? The only other man she might be able to say that about anymore would be Hal Prince.

And so what? Because her impressions of people meant absolutely nothing. Not anymore. She wasn't going to make that mistake again.

SIX

The next morning, on the Day house's shady porch, Lucy set her phone on the mildewed wicker table as close as possible to Eugenie Lee. It was fully charged, ready to go. This time she swore she'd get a static-free recording.

"Yesterday you said Solange Koumari was Esther's biggest rival for a medical practice. Was Koumari born here?"

The older woman rocked slowly, frowning. A warped board beneath her chair creaked rhythmically as a cricket's song. "No. She wan't local."

"Do you know where she was from? And how she became the local midwife—or practitioner? I'm not sure what it was called then."

Lee laughed, hunched shoulderblades protruding like sprouting wings. "You full of questions about *where* and *how*. Like a three-year-old. Next I s'pose you'll start askin' why this, Miss Eugenie, why that, Miss Eugenie."

Lucy felt her face heat up. "Sorry. I just—"

"Child, hold onto your panties. I'm getting there! Most of the black folks here descended from slaves. But Solange Koumari was born in New Orleans. Though her mama came there from the islands—the West Indies.

"She taught Solange the herbs for bringing on sleep, for healing wounds, for stopping fits, for calming anger, to cut birthing pains, stop bleeding, and make a baby come faster.

She could look at the sky, listen to the wind, then tell you a storm was fixin' to hit—long before it come."

I sure could've used her yesterday, Lucy thought. "So she was brought here as a child?"

Eugenie frowned. "No. Grew up in Louisiana after they lynch her mama. She roam around a little; finally settle here."

Lucy was incredulous. "They—they hanged her mother? But . . . why?"

"For being too smart. Too pretty. For knowing how to do things men couldn't. Now, Solange was sure something. But they said her mama was even more beautiful. Anyhow, one day this man see her in Jackson Square—"

Lucy made a note. "You mean New Orleans. In the French Quarter."

"Yeah, that old part. Anyway, he follow her home to Burgundy Street. When she won't open the door, he knock it down. Just one of them flimsy shotgun houses they used to build. He rape her right in front of the little girl."

Lucy's pen hit the porch floor with a clatter. She reached a shaking hand down and groped blindly, but it was gone. Then she sat up too fast, and black spots dipped and spun like a swarm of gnats before her eyes.

Lee said, "Never mind, sugar. It roll between the cracks, fell clean through. Want me to fetch you a—"

She took a deep breath. "No. No problem. I have another." Eugenie's gaze was sharp, but Lucy pretended not to notice. "So . . . so she was, um, attacked by a man. But why was *she* hanged if he—"

"I'm gettin' to that part. Afterward, he throw a few coins down and say, 'Now you cain't say you wan't paid for your services, nigger.' Then he laugh. Maybe that's what done it. Or maybe the little bit of money scattered over her own clean floor. But when he turn and walk out, she grab up a machete from behind the door, follow, and kill him right out in the street."

Lucy shivered, feeling a perverse joy. Then she shook her head. "But that—wouldn't it be self-defense?"

"Those days, not so long ago, a black man didn't dare strike no white man. Never mind a black woman lifting a hand. For *any* reason."

Lucy felt sick to her stomach. What the hell—was she coming down with something? She swallowed back a bitter taste. "Yes. I've read about . . . about that." Accounts of lynchings, of Klan cross burnings. On the Internet she'd seen old photos of swollen black bodies washed up on riverbanks, or noosed and hanging from lampposts. "I . . . know what you mean."

Eugenie Lee's raised brow seemed skeptical. Just then three chickens—black, scruffy creatures—ambled around the corner of the house and began scratching and pecking in the grass and walkway. Hercules raised his head, then heaved up and scattered them in a hurricane of feathers.

"Herc. No!" shouted Lucy. She scrambled down the steps and grabbed his collar.

That hoarse laugh rose again from the porch. "Never you mind, honey. Them no-account critters a nuisance. Little exercise do 'em good."

Lucy was mortified. When the dog lunged again she gave his collar a sharp little jerk and snapped her fingers. "*Stay.*" His ears dropped, but only a bit, as he tracked the chickens' zig-zagging progress across the yard. They disappeared under a hedge.

Eugenie snorted. "I got to come feed the sorry things ever day while *she* in the hospital. Worthless old biddies. Don't lay no eggs. Been making inroads on 'em, though." Her eyes gleamed with mischief. "You like fried chicken?"

Was she serious? "Uh, I—well, thanks but no thanks."

"Shame. Neighbors been complaining 'bout the rooster."

"Herc, heel," Lucy said, and led him back to his shady spot. Then she returned to the porch and resumed recording where they'd left off. "So young Solange came here . . . how long after that?"

"Some kin raise her up to nearly grown in Louisiana. But all the people there look at her funny, you know? As if it be a child's fault bad things happened. "'Course this was a girl born of a woman who used herbs to make love charms and heal, and also hacked a grown man to death in the street."

Lucy nodded. "In other words . . . a witch?"

"That do tend to make people nervous." Eugenie grinned. "So when little Solange get older, she understand from the whispers, the dead chickens left on her doorstep, the signs to ward off the evil eye, that she was no more welcome around there than the prohis."

Lucy held up a hand. "Prohis? What's that?"

"The gov'ment men, sugar. Prohibition back then, and moonshiners. Crazy times, but the daughter of a so-called crazy woman wan't welcome. A whore and a ju-ju witch they call her mama. Maybe think she studying on following her footsteps.

"So she leave that place, come to Florida, only sixteen years old, and settle down to practice what she know. First in Key West, then Ybor City, the old Spanish quarter in Tampa. Finally she wash up here. Why she choose Ibo Key no one ever know. Some say, to get away from a man. Some, to escape the law. She have a reputation, even before she arrive—but mainly for healing. She was working root cures long before Miss Esther ever go off to learn fancy city medicine."

"Was Solange married?"

"Never mention a husband. But she bring two li'l children, a boy and a girl. Heard their daddy was a white man. Or maybe a rich Frenchman. Even heard tell it was the Devil hisself. But folks like to talk about anyone they jealous of, you know.

"She teach them to respect everything they see: land, sea,

air, fire. That everything that live and breathe have a *soul*. And no man, never mind color or fine clothes or fat wallet, is master." Eugenie smiled. "Now that way of thinking not too practical back then, way before anybody hear about civil rights. But Solange knew how to get along with white folks, mostly. And those Koumari children was sweet. Strong, handsome. They shined like a bright light, a hope of what could be, what might lead all of us—all of us—"

Lucy heard a sniffle and looked up from her notes. The old woman was brushing tears away with one palm. "Oh! You need to take a break?"

"No, ma'am. It's just—back then, like most of the girls, I had a weakness for Julian Koumari. Not that he ever looked at me! And what would I do—ask his own mama for a love mojo?" She laughed. "He liked growing things. Was set to go to that agriculture college up in Tallahassee. But of course after they . . . he never . . . well." She trailed off, cleared her throat, and spat over the porch railing, then scowled over at Lucy. "Child, if you ever gonna visit Mrs. Esther, best collect your things and get on over."

"Oh." Lucy glanced at the iPhone and blinked. "You're right."

The interview was over. Some sort of invisible but tough shell, a calcified mask built up against old pains, had closed the lined, weathered face against further questions.

She gathered notebook and phone and stood. "Thanks for your time. What we talk about might bring back painful memories, but . . . if we get it down, that history won't be lost. People forget, even the most terrible things. Your story could help make sure this kind of stuff never happens again."

Perhaps she'd gone too far, somehow insulted or condescended. The other woman turned that sharp, penetrating look on her again. Not anger or disdain, exactly, but something else. Almost like . . . pity? As if she knew something about Lucy that she herself didn't.

Eugenie Lee lit another cigarette. She squinted, exhaling smoke in two serpentine streams. "You a nice young lady," she said. "Come back tomorrow if you want."

Tall stands of longleaf pine cast deep shadows, nearly obscuring the pristine crushed-shell drive that led to Gulf Rest Manor. As she passed orderly lines of royal palms, Lucy caught her first glimpse of the well-advertised "rest home." A long white stucco plantation house stood surrounded by several one-story brick outbuildings, sort of like vacation cabins. They studded a wide lawn of clipped emerald grass. The landscaping imitated the lush tropics of wealthy South Florida: Sabal palms, Schefflera, pothos, azaleas, weeping fig, mossy live oaks, bromeliads, and leather fern defined the borders.

"Look, Herc. A place where no dog has gone before," she pointed out, smirking.

She parked in the visitors lot. Clusters of well-dressed older folks strolled broad brick walks lined with mondo grass and mounds of Gerbera daisies. A few old men played at shuffleboard and *bocce* on the sunny lawn, while frailer individuals were wheeled along by staff wearing the green scrubs Lucy had noticed her first night, at the Merry Cat Café.

Only at the portico did she see a small, carved cypress sign with gilded lettering:

GULF REST A CONTINUING CARE COMMUNITY

A stylized blue heron flanked the words. So discreet, you could easily miss it. Maybe that was the idea.

A mirror would've envied the finish on the oak parquet foyer. The Persian rug she crossed looked muted, old and threadbare, a sure sign it was extremely valuable. From behind a curved antique desk, a slim woman in a white silk suit, honey-gold hair sleeked into a french twist, gave her a Mona

Lisa smile. Camellia blossoms floated in a crystal bowl on the desk; the woman's hands rested on the felt blotter, slender fingers entwined like a bisque figurine's.

"I'm here to see Esther Day."

The receptionist tapped at a concealed keyboard. "You'll need to go out and walk all the way to the back of the complex. Last building. The Magnolia. For Special Care guests. Look for the carved white flower over the door."

"Thanks."

The stylized painted bloom on the last brick unit told Lucy she'd arrived. Past its heavy oak door she was enveloped in the faint lemony scent of magnolia blossoms, mixed with pine cleanser and a faint under-layer of mothballs.

This floor was shiny too, but it was practical, polished green linoleum. The visitor area was furnished in polyester tweed. A stocky woman sat alone on a couch as if waiting for someone. Her hands, puffy and swollen, laced with veins and mottled with age spots, lay entwined in her ample lap, as if parodying the porcelain receptionist.

From down a long corridor came murmurs, the carbon-iferous scent of burnt microwave popcorn, and brief bursts of staccato noise: loud music, a television spewing canned laughter. An aide squeaked past on thick crepe soles with a steaming popcorn bag and vanished through an office doorway.

Lucy cleared her throat and turned to the seated woman. "Excuse me. Are you by any chance Esther Day?"

The woman flinched and looked up, slightly bulging blue eyes watery behind plain black bifocals, but she didn't reply.

"Sorry, didn't mean to startle you. I'm Lucy Fowler. Mrs. Day? You wrote to me last month."

She nodded slowly, peering over the bifocals. Lucy smiled, enduring a few moments of unabashed scrutiny, then said, "Mind if I sit down? I'd like to use my cell phone to record the interview. But if that bothers you, I can just take notes."

The woman muttered, "Makes no never-mind to me how you do it."

"Great." Lucy dug into her shoulder bag, then set the iPhone on the coffee table between them. "I'm gathering material for my dissertation on local medicine and systems of herbal healing. I'd like to talk about your midwifing experiences. I've taken oral histories before, but I'm really excited about yours. One chapter in the book is incomplete. It's on the call to healing, and you—"

Esther Day's eyes widened. "Missing? You mean to say there's a chapter gone. But where did it go? No one could have—" She broke off and began nibbling a well-chewed thumbnail. Her lower lip trembled.

Perhaps this wasn't a good day for an interview after all. "I don't mean missing, as in *lost*. I just haven't written it yet. That's why I'm here. All you need to do, if it's OK, is answer a few questions."

Day's lower lip crept out. "Like a test, you mean? I already had plenty this week."

Lucy shook her head. "No, no." This woman was not at all what she'd expected. More like a survivor of some terrible trauma. She suddenly felt she was doing well in comparison, even if she did still flinch sometimes at shadows or overt shows of masculinity. "No grades, no medical procedures, and you certainly can't fail. More like a . . . a memory game. I ask a question about the past, and you say what comes to mind. If you don't remember, no big deal. People are usually amazed at how much comes back, one they begin. Pretty simple, right?"

Esther Day nodded, looking somewhat convinced.

As Lucy leaned over the coffee table to touch RECORD, a red blur flashed by the window behind the couch. Perhaps a cardinal leaving a feeder in the side yard.

Day flinched and clamped both hands over her face. "Is it gone?" she whispered, glancing through her fingers, gaze darting to the window then quickly away.

"You mean the bird? Yeah, it flew off." Wow, this poor woman was a wreck. There were bird phobias, of course, but . . . "Are you still OK to do this?"

A slight, fearful nod. She looked away, out the window again.

"Great. Let's start with your childhood. The town of Ibo City the way it was sixty years ago. What events stand out most in your mind from back then?"

The old midwife turned back to her with such a blank, abstracted expression Lucy's heart sank. Then, just as she thought she might as well stop recording, Esther Day began to speak.

". . . and that's when I knew I was born to work in medicine. Never dreamed of being a doctor, of course, women didn't think that way then. But more than a nurse— a practitioner. If I went off to Jacksonville or Atlanta, I'd just be one more white hat in the hospital. Call it vanity; a wicked sin. But to go off and come back a better person, why, I'd be something, then.

"So I applied to the women's college in Tallahassee, not tellin' Daddy and Mother. When the college wrote back accepting me, then it was a train too late to stop." She smiled, remembering. "So I went, though I'd never been off this island before except to shop with my folks in Gainesville. Never alone, if you can believe that! Three years later I had a diploma and a true calling."

Lucy nodded. "So many people hope for that. It's great you got to follow yours." She stopped recording, and scrawled a note for later: *recruitment to healing role: self-selection.*

After twenty minutes of reminiscing, Esther's face had regained color and animation. She even looked younger. Well, that's what therapy's made of, Lucy reasoned. A narrative, and a person to listen to it. "Shall we stop now? I don't want to tire you out."

Day smiled warmly. "I'm so glad you came, honey. When you wrote, I wasn't sure it was for the best. You travel a lot? Young girl like you, roving on her own. No telling what might happen." Her tone was a motherly scold, but the eyes seemed pleading, hungry for something else. Lucy couldn't fathom what.

Day drew closer, leaning across the low table. "Know why you were chosen, out of all the world? Have you got a plan? Because, if not, what earthly good can you do us now?"

Lucy frowned. What the hell? "Well, I, uh . . . I don't know exactly what you mean by 'chosen'. No one told me to study folklore or anthropology. I decided that myself. And came here on my own, to interview you." To lighten things up, she added, "It's a degree, not a religious calling. Or maybe I'm just nosy. People's stories—I like to collect and preserve them. One day, when I publish the book, I'll—"

Day flapped a hand, face screwed up in agitation. "Shhh! Don't speak of . . . of *it* . . . so loud."

Lucy bit her lip. "Mrs. Day, are you feeling all right? You understand I'm only here to interview you for my dissertation, right? Remember, we corresponded and agreed I'd take down the information you could give on midwifery."

The old woman's face had faded from scarlet back to pale. Beads of sweat glistened on her forehead. She shook her head. "Never mind all that. You don't have to say a thing outright. I know we got to be careful. But I declare, why'd they send *you*, of all people? Indeed He moves in mysterious ways. 'Course you're here for the Book. *Her* Book." She glanced around the room. "But it's too dangerous. Paid for with blood, by that evil—"

She broke off, lips clamped, neck out-thrust like a snapping turtle's. Her eyes cut sharply right, once, as if to warn of the approach of someone unfriendly, even dangerous. Mystified, Lucy turned to look.

They were no longer alone. A man she assumed must be another patient, judging by his attire—pajamas, gray flannel robe and slippers—was shuffling toward the front door. He didn't glance over, but whispered something under his breath as he passed by. It sounded like, "Hello, Miz Fowler."

Lucy's turn to flinch. Before she could answer, the man stopped. He was pale, slight, with brown, thinning hair. He gave off a strange smell, vague but unpleasant, a bit like rotten eggs. She held her breath.

Still not looking at her, he said in a low voice, "You like riddles?"

She tried to push away her unease. Esther Day had probably been talking about her impending visit, had mentioned her name during a group meal or something. "Well, sure. Sometimes. And you are . . ."

He turned then to smile at her with bloodless lips that stretched thinner until they were nearly invisible. He looked unhealthy. No, more: he looked somehow . . . wrong. She couldn't pin it down more precisely than that.

"Here's one I like," he murmured.

> When I went up to Sandy Grove
> I met a Sandy Boy-o
> I cut his throat, I drank his blood,
> And left his skin a hanging-o.

"Ugh," Lucy said involuntarily. She noticed a bowl of oranges sitting on a counter by the nurses' station. "Wait. That's not so hard. An orange, right? Probably an old English nursery rhyme; maybe eighteenth century? You know, those are the basis for most Appalachian rhymes. Did you know that one, Mrs. Day?"

Esther was silent, staring at the man as if transfixed.

"How did you know my name?" Lucy asked, turning back to him.

He was no longer standing there.

Weird. No, totally creepy. "Do you know that man?" she asked Esther. "He seemed to recognize me. Did you mention I'd be visiting?"

Day shook herself, and turned to Lucy again, looking at her with a strange blend of horror, knowledge, and—pity? If she'd been asked to describe the emotion on the old woman's face, Lucy would have had to say, *entirely hopeless.*

SEVEN

The next morning she went out to the café for breakfast. A few minutes later, a hand slammed down the apple-walnut muffin she'd ordered with such casual violence the plate nearly skated off the table. A harsh contralto growled, "Hear you're studyin' us. Which fancy college got a belly-ache and shit *you* out?"

Lucy lowered her book, blinking. The heckler was spotlighted in a shaft of sunlight, butt perched on the rickety café table across from hers. The woman's short red hair was spiky, her arms were crossed. One leg swung idly. An unlit cigarette dangled from her lower lip. The same woman who'd stepped out of the kitchen and scanned the dining room with such satisfaction, Lucy's first night on the island.

She raised her eyebrows. "You seem to know me better than my own mother. Have we met?"

"Nah. Just a lucky guess." The woman rose and swatted at the tabletop with a worn dishtowel. "Ah, don't mind me. I like to show off my two talents."

Lucy smiled. "Which are?"

"I can cook like God's own chef, and I got a tongue like the devil's switchblade."

This might actually be fun. "You're being too modest," Lucy shot back. "There's that talent for analogies, too. Maybe you should write my paper, and I should tie on that apron."

85

"Analogies?" The woman burst out laughing, then dragged a chair across the floor and sat. "Cora Cisneros. I own this mess. Pleased to meet you. Maybe."

She shook the proffered hand—its palm warm, slightly greasy, with a light dusting of flour—which felt as though steel wires lay just beneath the skin. "Lucy Fowler. I'm here doing pretty much what you said. And something's got me stumped."

Cora raised an eyebrow. "No shit?"

"A phrase I heard at the fruit market. You're a cook, so I figure you'd know. What's a saltwater grit?"

"Any damned soul born on this floating fish factory. In the beginning, the Lord took some fire, and a little seawater, and ground corn, and He created—"

"The Southern breakfast of champions?"

Cora scowled. "I hate it when people step on my punch-line. Hey, Starr Lynn!" She mimed pouring motions at a girl across the dining room. The teenager's spiky hair, sharp features, and lanky body made her a younger version of Cora. She silently brought over another cup and pot, pouring Lucy fresh coffee, too.

"My baby," said Cora proudly, stroking one of the colorful tattoo-sleeves that decorated the girl's slender arms. Starr rolled her eyes and drifted away.

"She's waited on me before," said Lucy. "Very efficient."

"Bet your ass." Cora slid a battered box of kitchen matches from an apron pocket, flicked fire with a thumbnail, and lit the still-dangling cigarette. "So, what kinda books you write, exactly? If I walked over to the public library back of the courthouse, could I check one out?"

Lucy fiddled with the handle of her coffee cup. "Well, no. I'm still writing it. For my dissertation. I'm just . . . a graduate student. But I plan to publish someday." She explained the project briefly.

"Midwives and root doctors and *childbirth*, oh my." Cora snorted and gulped coffee. "Give me a nice flounder and a filet knife, any day. Glad to be done with all that mess. So you been talking to old Miz Day and Eugenie Lee? I tell you what, though—" She broke off, frowning.

Lucy waited, but Cora was looking away, toward the front of the café. Two men, one in a dark suit and flamingo-patterned tie, the other in khakis and golf shirt, were just entering.

"Something wrong?"

"No, honey," growled the café owner. "Just checking out the new arrivals. I prefer not to let certain creatures dirty up my nice clean tables." She cast a disgusted look over at the corner where the two were seating themselves. "But business is business," she sighed. "I guess."

The suit picked up a menu by one edge, as if he feared germs. "Look, Randy," he said in a loud, wondering tone. "Gator tail. People actually eat that shit?"

Cora called over sweetly, "Cooked specially, boys. The skunk bile marinade makes it extra tender."

They exchanged worried glances.

Lucy whispered, "Why don't you want them here?"

Cora flicked ashes into a saucer. "Land developers, honey. Midget crooks stuffed with hot air and bullshit. When Walt Disney, rest his technicolor soul, sent a bunch to buy up all the land cheap and turn Central Florida into a big plastic dimestore, I moved here to Ibo. Thought we was so far off the path, I'd never see such as them again. But looks like it's only a matter of time till they pump bilges here and float some cardboard condos on bottom slime and dead oysters."

"What part would developers be interested in buying?" Lucy asked doubtfully, thinking of the tumbled fish shacks, abandoned storefronts, and rank-smelling salt flats.

Cora snorted. "Just the biggest, cheapest ocean-side

parcel they could lay tentacles on. That waterfront at the south end with nothing but a falling-down house on it." She lowered her voice. "I'm gonna try not to accidentally spray roach killer on their food." She threw a sweet smile their way. Starr was slouching beside the table, ready to take the order.

"Really? Who owns the part you're talking about?"

"Hurley Yulee. Or rather, his boy does. Old Hurl was a half-cocked pistol, a mean son of a buzzard. But now, Nick, all he inherited besides the land was that nice tight Yulee ass."

Oh. The marina guy. Her storm-tossed savior. Lucy nodded, then shook her head, lest Cora think she was seconding the ass compliment. "Oh, I see—right. His land."

"Some mainland realtors been out here already. A shiftless bastard would sell it off like a shot. But he's a born island man, no come-here. He sent 'em packing."

Lucy looked again at the two men talking loudly as if to impress Starr, who looked only bored. To her eye, they could be bankers or lawyers or doctors on holiday. How could Cora size them up just on appearance?

She turned back to ask, and saw the café owner's back disappearing through the swinging kitchen doors. Conversation over.

She sighed, stood, and left five dollars on the battered tabletop. Resisting the urge to stare with pity as she passed strangers so obviously unaware they'd been found wanting, if not damned. Lucy wouldn't want to feel the terrible wrath of Cora Cisneros directed at her—or worse, at her food.

She walked Hercules, then left him in the room while she set out again for Gulf Rest. It was too hot to leave a dog in the car, and there was a strict no-pets policy posted at Gulf Rest. She'd expected to feel anxious without him at her side, but today she didn't. Maybe because the place was so small, so far removed from the recent past. The panic attack on the stairs several nights back had been a one-time deal.

She ducked into the farmer's market for a bunch of flowers to take to Esther Day. There wasn't a single bloom to be found, only some drooping potted plants. She settled for tangerines, and handed the cashier an incredible sum for the skimpy net bag of wrinkled, abused citrus. There were some financial drawbacks to living on a secluded island, it seemed.

On her way back to the car she nearly walked right into Nick Yulee.

"Hey, it's the history buff." He eyed the tangerines. "Ten pounds of pure vitamin C? Hope you didn't catch cold out on the water."

She forced a smile. "It's a gift for somebody. And I'm not in history, exactly. It's anthropology—folklore."

He looked puzzled. "Oh, sorry. Hey, listen. Maybe I came on too strong the other day at the marina." Uncertainty softened his face. He fidgeted like a nervous teenager angling for a first date. It was appealing somehow, at odds with the rough exterior.

"Well, I don't know."

"I just thought . . . I mean, you're not from here, so . . . it seemed like if I didn't say something, we'd never, uh . . ." He stopped. Good grief, was that a blush?

"Don't worry about it. No offense taken. After all, you did save me from a dunking. And maybe a bad cold."

He brightened. "Then you'll consider what I said, about coming to hear us one night?"

Her turn to fidget. "Well . . . "

He grinned. "If I'm on a roll here, maybe I should move up a square. How about dinner tomorrow night? Nothing fancy, just local food." He quickly added, "If that's not how things work in your culture, we could go Dutch. Oh, damn it all. You win. OK, you can pay for mine too."

She couldn't help laughing. Maybe a night out would be nice. Even healthy. Half the world was male, after all— well, ok, not strictly male. She knew Hal would insistently correct her in his oh-so-proper Gender Studies way—but in any case, she'd have to work alongside plenty of men, for the rest of her life.

"Mr. Yulee," she said sternly, and he looked crushed. "I don't usually fall for this sort of line, but—all right. Dinner. What time, and where do we meet?"

"Meet? Oh . . . well." He thought a moment. "You want to see what it was like way back, right? There's the Cat, but you want more local color. So, Oatey's. Good seafood, nary a tourist in sight."

He gave complex directions involving a burned-out chimney, a fish house that used to be on a particular corner but was now a gas station, and an unpaved, unnamed road.

She almost backed out then. No wonder the place was patronized only by locals. But it sounded like island color, for sure. Finally he insisted on sketching a rough map on the back of a paper bag.

"I'm sure I can find it." She squinted up at him, now outlined in the white glare of noon. "See you at eight."

He walked off whistling. She headed for Gulf Rest.

EIGHT

"My sweetheart, Turner Day, waited for me to finish school in Tallahassee, though he didn't give a hoot for the idea," Esther Day told Lucy. "We wed at the First Baptist, then he went back to the sawmill. I set up my clinic downtown, where the barbershop sits now. Not many patients at first. Takes a while for word to get out."

Lucy nodded, noting the testiness that crept into Day's voice as she spoke of this. "So competition also affected the practice, at first?"

Day frowned. "Meaning what?"

"Well, uh—were people used to going somewhere else? Like, to doctors on the mainland?"

She nodded, frowning. "Some did."

"Or maybe a local, traditional source, if they had less money." She flipped back to her notes on the talk with Eugenie Lee. "The names I have are Pop Taylor and Solange Koumari."

The old woman had seemed almost lively, before. Now her skin took on a pale, sickly hue, as it had the previous day. She raised a trembling hand to her face.

"Turner said it was revenge for a wrong to his lawful wife. Wronged or not, he beat me senseless after he and the other men come back. I couldn't show my face out of doors for a week. He said no white woman can be . . . attacked . . .

unless she didn't fight. She should die first. He hollered ugly things while I dragged myself to the kitchen pump to wash the blood off my face."

Lucy stopped writing and stared. "Attacked?"

She sighed. "God forgive, it was *me* told the boy to steal it and bring it to me. My fault, don't you see? He wouldn't thieve from his own mama. A good boy, no matter what folks and the newspapers said later." Her voice rose to almost a shout. "Now I'll be punished! We all will. The dead will rise and take vengeance on the living. The guilty be thrown from the grave!"

Lucy rose, reaching out. "Mrs. Day? I'm sorry, I didn't mean to upset you."

"No!" She gripped the arm of the couch as if the feel of its rough tweed would help in the tremendous effort to compose herself. "No. I'm all right." She waved off the proffered hand. "But listen to me, girl." She grabbed both Lucy's hands in a grip so tight she could not free herself. "It was my doing. I paid many times over. Lord knows, sweet Jesus, all the babies. Not even one left to me! Every other woman on this island carried home the children I pulled from them with my two empty hands."

Lucy frowned. "But—you never lost a baby. Isn't that right?"

Esther Day turned a drowning look on her. "Oh, I paid a thousand times. So will those others, one day soon. The innocent don't deserve to suffer with the guilty—but they will. I know what's coming, haven't I seen it in my dreams?" Her eyes widened, staring at some unnamed horror. "You put a stop to it. Take the damned thing. Use it if you must."

"I'm sorry, I don't understand. What thing do you—"

"The Book, *the Book!*" she cried, pounding a fist on one knee. "Use *his* cursed instrument to put a stop to this, or we'll all die. Just like, like . . ." She paused, panting. "God help me, I can't say it. Not out loud. Come closer."

She pulled Lucy, whose aching hands were still trapped, even nearer.

God, the woman was raving. Time to call for help. She's strong enough to break my hands, Lucy thought, looking around for some staff person.

Day whispered in her ear something tiredly indistinct wafted on a faint gust of peppermint and denture powder. Then suddenly released her and stood abruptly. Face calm, composed. "Can't talk no more today," she said. "You come back later. After I rest." She shuffled off like a lifer, down the hallway to her room.

Lucy rose, staring after her, rubbing red, sore wrists. She called after the slowly retreating back, "Mrs. Day! Are you sure you're OK?"

No reply.

She hesitated, then started down the hall, looking for someone who worked there. Someone who would see how disturbed the woman had been. She must have serious physical and mental health issues. It could even be dangerous.

Lucy passed a lounge or day room where a few people sat watching a talk show on a flat screen TV. None looked up, but she heard a soft female voice say, "Go careful, daughter."

She turned back to look into the room. All five patients, elderly men, looked up slowly, vacantly. Had it just been the TV sound track? She glanced down the corridor and saw a lone male orderly pushing a cleaning cart. Day was no longer in sight. The whole place was creeping her out now.

She turned on one heel, swept up her things from the lobby, and left Magnolia House a good deal more quickly than she'd come in.

For most of her life, Lucy had kept a journal. Not every day, though that was always high on her list of New Year's resolutions. At three A.M. she sat at the wicker desk in her hotel room, the red leather-bound volume staring up like a silent accusation. She hadn't written a thing for over a month.

This late, it would be no good to get back in bed under the mosquito netting and try to sleep. So why not catch up? Keeping track of daily events obviously included recording strange dreams. So why was she still just sitting there, not writing?

"Move, fingers," she whispered. At last she opened the journal and picked up a pen.

> Tonight went to bed @ midnight. Woke 3 hours later, crying. In a dream I'd been walking down a street where all around wooden buildings were on fire. The heat singed my hair, scorched my skin. No one was trying to put it out. No one else there. Only me.
>
> I ran out of the burning town to a field where men were working, though it was night. A full moon made it bright enough to see. So I thought maybe they were farmers behind on planting, trying to catch up. But why ignore a terrible fire close by? A plow with a huge blade was guided by 2 men. A tired mule pulling it. Other men stood around talking. When I came up they got quiet, nudging each other.
>
> "There's a fire!" I shouted.
>
> They burst out laughing.
>
> "Can't you go help? What're you doing

here that's more important?"

They ignored me.

I picked my way back across the field—tripping, determined to catch up with the plow and see what they were planting. But the faster I went, the farther away it got. I was barefoot and my long nightgown kept tripping me. Tired, sweating, even (how stupid) worrying a damp nightgown might be see-through.

As I reached the first row, I lost my footing and stumbled into the nearest furrow, deep as my waist. I looked down, and saw I was standing not on fresh-turned dirt or seed corn but dead bodies. All ages, all sizes. Men and women. Newborn babies whose froggy limbs were tangled with those of older children. All wounded—shot, stabbed, burned. Some tied with ropes that had turned red in places. Some were mutilated. The ground was dark and sticky, watered with their blood.

I noticed a faint, feeble stirring. As if some were not dead—not yet. So I ran, screaming and stumbling, not daring to look where I stepped, or on what. The whispering men were gone. But a huge gray snake barred my way, coiling and uncoiling, raising its head to strike. I picked up a hoe lying in the dirt and chopped it into a hundred pieces. Then scattered them to the wind. And then

I woke up, crying.

She shut the book, shoved it away, then realized something else: the dog. She pulled the journal back, turned to the last passage, and beneath it wrote:

Hercules is always with me. But he was nowhere in this dream.

She lowered her forehead to her arms. She hadn't even written everything down yet. After she'd awakened, sweating and terrified, there were shadows in her room. Retreating dark shapes that dragged themselves away slowly, painfully, to the dimmest corners. Vaguely human figures that stirred and groaned and sighed as if wounded. Beside the bed Hercules paced, growling, putting his bristling body between them and her.

She'd bolted up, tangled in the cobwebby netting, and grabbed one tall, carved bedpost just before she fell. Then stumbled to the door, clawing for the switch. She'd darted around the room breathlessly flipping the lights on, then stood in a glowing pool cast by the overhead fixture, rubbing her bare arms as if the infinitesimal heat of a forty watt bulb would take away the chill. Gradually she'd stopped hyperventilating and sat down at the desk. Whining, Hercules came over to lick her hand, then propped his head on her thigh, gazing up.

Now, still wide-eyed, she watched till the first rays of sun turned the dark corners gray with rosy yellow light. Only then could she bring herself to get up, cross the floor to the bed, and try to go back to sleep.

NINE

A muffled thud roused her. She squinted at her iPhone. It seemed to say eleven-thirty. Ridiculous. She dragged up from damp, tangled sheets. The room was stifling hot, steamy. She crossed to the window and with a lot of cursing and shoving was able to heave the warped sash a few inches higher.

She closed her eyes and let a faint warm breeze dry the sweat on her face. When she opened them again she shrieked, stumbling backwards over the rug.

On the outer sill lay mounds of bloody feathers. Several dull onyx eyes stared back sightlessly as tiny black buttons. She scrambled up onto the bed, heart pounding. Hercules whined.

She whispered, "Birds, Herc. Just some dead birds." Back at the campus, songbirds often bashed headfirst into the broad glass sections of the tall buildings, which deceptively reflected trees and sky. Tiny souls shattered, fallen, and forgotten. Her pulse slowed, her breath eased. She got up and went back to the open window.

She looked up at dozens of red smears in different spots on the panes. As if each bird hit not just once, accidentally, but had slammed into the glass again and again. But that was crazy. No animal would behave that way. She shook her head. Her over-reaction was probably because of the nightmare she'd had last night.

Simply sweep the bodies off the ledge.

No, she couldn't. She picked them up one at time, by limp wings or curled claws. She carried each corpse to the bathroom, where it received a toilet paper shroud and silent interment in the wastebasket.

Then she sat at her laptop and typed in the browser: "black bird random red markings Gulf coast Florida" and got back from her computer: "Sorry, cannot access the page you requested."

"Shit," she muttered. "Typical."

While getting dressed she felt a morbid urge to unwrap one of the tiny white bundles to look more closely at the strange bird again. Beneath the smears of blood, those black-and-red-feathered bodies had resembled the one that had hit her car a few days earlier. Some local variety, plentiful as lemmings—and, it seemed, just as suicidal.

That evening, at five after eight, she opened the battered door of Oatey's Place and was met by a wave of hot oil and breaded seafood. Nick Yulee was sitting in the back at one of the newspaper covered picnic tables. He met her gaze and waved her over.

A harassed-looking waitress swung past bearing a huge tray of iced-down oysters on one arm and a monstrous platter of fried shrimp on the other. "Any trouble finding the place?" he asked.

"None. Unless you count the five-mile detour I took because weeds have overtaken your so-called burned brick foundation. No worries, though. My phone has GPS."

He made a rueful face. "Damn, never thought of that. I'm so used to the scenery I probably still see it there. Sorry. But you're here. How'd work go today?"

She looked away. "Oh, well . . . I got a late start. Spent the afternoon in the library, at the courthouse. Looking for some historical stuff. Not much there."

"No kidding. That closet can barely hold some used best-sellers and a set of twenty-year-old encyclopedias. What you oughta do is pay a call on Mrs. Waters."

"Who?"

"My seventh-grade English teacher. Retired, but she keeps this, like, free lending library in her house. A big local history buff. Was talk at one time of forming a historical society. She'd have been the, uh, curator, I guess you'd call it? Never happened. In hard times folks're more worried about buying groceries and making payments on their trailers and fishin' boats. Not much interest in the past when the present looks shaky."

She nodded. "Well, sure. I get that."

"But she kept all the stuff in boxes. Lends books. Got more volumes than the library, even delivers them to old folks, shut-ins, like that."

"Thanks for the tip." She picked up a laminated menu. "So what's good here?"

He caught the same waitress's arm as she rushed past, and ordered plates of oysters, blue crabs, and fried mangrove snapper. The red-faced woman scribbled the order on the back of one hand, and stamped off muttering.

Nick shrugged. "Posey Teabo. She's always like that, even if you're the only table in the place. Grumbling's her hobby. Can't blame her, she's been married to Bird Dog Teabo for thirty-five years."

"Who's this Bird Dog guy you keep mentioning?"

He grinned. "Prime specimen of Ibo Key manhood. Getting on, but still tells a mean story. Never forgets a thing. Fisherman, millhand, medicinal moonshiner. Always smells like fish, booze, and pine resin. By now it must be ground into his pores." He nudged her arm. "You'd like him." At her doubtful look he smiled. "I mean from a professional interest standpoint."

"Think he'd talk to me while I'm here?"

Yulee looked crestfallen. "Sorry. Bird Dog's been around all my life, I keep forgettin'. He's been over at Gulf Rest since late November. Had a stroke. He's a lot older than Posey. All he says now is cuss words and 'shine recipes. Still grabs all the nurses, though. Even the men."

Lucy rolled her eyes. "Sounds charming. Too bad I missed him." She reached for one of the beers that had appeared in front of them as Posey swept past, scowling like a thunderhead. "Yesterday, you said your band had a, um, a *gig* at the Merry Cat."

"Through next Friday. That's Christmas Eve. You like bluegrass, Americana?"

"It's all right." Actually she liked both, so why didn't she want to admit it? "What do you play? How have you got time for that and a charter business?"

"Still in interview gear." He laughed. "Well, I play fiddle, mostly, and mandolin. Both just eight strings on a box. Finding time's no problem. Maybe you overestimate the tourist traffic here."

She smiled. "Maybe. So, are you good on that fiddle?"

He colored a little. "Well, tolerable, sure."

She thought of something else. "American folklore claims the Devil invented the fiddle. And that nobody can outplay him. Is that why you named the band Scratch?"

"No." He laughed again, this time without humor. She waited, but he didn't elaborate, just fingered a faint white scar on one cheek.

Dinner turned out to be a kind of food orgy. When the gargantuan platters of fresh seafood arrived—steamed, raw, blackened, fried—it looked like enough for a family of four.

Nick talked and joked. Kept urging her to dig in. She was soon putting away huge quantities, not caring she was sitting with a near-stranger, stuffing herself greedily, fingers slimed with melted butter, a pile of shattered crab claws and empty oyster shells mounded between them like an Indian midden.

At last she sat back. "OK, I give up. I understand the newspaper tablecloths, now. What a mess!"

They ordered coffee. After it arrived Nick said, "A shame Bird Dog's in no shape to talk. He's full of stories. But he was sick even before the stroke. Emphysema. Three packs a day. Unfiltered Camels."

"God. That nickname, Bird Dog. Did he hunt a lot?"

Nick laughed. "That's his Christian name. His daddy gave it, on account of how *he* loved to hunt. But yeah, Bird did his share. Poaching too. His daddy claimed to have invented the bird-dog boat. So who knows which was named after the other?"

She put down her fork. "The what?"

"At the marina, did you notice some small boats had an outboard mounted through the center of the hull, not on the back? So they won't tilt back at high speed. Then nets tossed off the stern don't get snarled in the prop. I know you noticed the water here's awful shallow."

"Hmm. Fishing." She ignored the reference to her boat grounding, his convenient rescue. "Haven't been since I was twelve, when a nasty neighbor kid in Vermont slung his cane pole and hooked my hand." She showed him a small raised scar on one thumb joint. "They had to cut it out. After that, I identified too much with the fish to want to catch them."

"Huh. Hasn't hurt your appetite for seafood." He lightly touched his own scar again. She wondered how he'd gotten it.

"True." She slid both hands away, under the table, and clasped them in her lap. "What do you do when you're not playing or having dinner with tourists?"

His face lit up. "This time of night, between tides, I take a bird-dog out."

She laughed. "The guy or the boat? Oh wait, there's the canine, too."

"Ha! Good one. No, with weather this warm, I'd go to my secret spot, catch some mullet. At high tide, they hide in the sea grass. At low, you can't float a toy boat out there. Ever cast a net in the moonlight and drag it in full of silver fish like a live pirate treasure?"

She laughed uncertainly. "Well, uh . . . no."

He stood, waving at the waitress again. "Posey! Bring that check."

Outside the restaurant, Nick looked from Lucy to the grinning, panting shepherd. "You're kidding. The dog goes along?"

She felt her face growing warm. Then thought—fuck him. It's none of his business. She nodded. "Yeah."

"Well, a good dog . . . s'pose it's not outside the bounds of Southern hospitality."

All three climbed down into the bird-dog, which was indeed an odd-looking contraption. But, as Nick had said, it ran quiet as ripping silk.

It was almost dark. She raised her eyebrows. "No running lights?"

"Worried I'm a pirate? Well, the water's too spotty here for the Coast Guard. I know this part of the Gulf like my own back yard. Who needs lights?"

After that she concentrated on not flinching while he sped around oyster beds and mud banks—all but invisible until they were nearly on them. Hercules seemed to enjoy the harrowing ride, though, front paws braced against the starboard side, tongue trailing like a pink pennant. She finally had to move toward the bow, away from the shower of dog spit.

Nick stood in the bow, which had no guard rail, one hand on a long pole equipped with throttle and gear controls. In the other he held a Q-beam, shining it along the sand bars and oyster beds, spotlighting gleaming mullet as they leapt and pirouetted away.

"How about here?" she called when a large school broke the surface.

"Not my spot," he shouted back. "Be like poaching."

"What, you even have to pay rent on the ocean in Florida?" she muttered. A loud splash sounded, very close. "Hey! What was that?"

He slowed hard and swung the light in an arc, illuminating two glowing orange orbs. Then moved the beam more slowly to reveal the scaly length of a twelve or fourteen foot alligator on a mud bank, a writhing mullet clamped in its jaws. Hercules leapt and barked. The gator's hiss was muffled by his catch. He slid into the water.

Yulee laughed. "There goes the competition we got to beat."

She shook her head. "I wouldn't compete. He might decide to change the menu."

"Oh, he's not interested in us. I know what you mean, though. I stepped in a gator nest once. If there was one in it at the time, he never showed his face. But tell you what, I did a double-dance gettin' out." He pointed at Hercules. "Better get a grip on your buddy, though. Gators love a nice juicy dog."

"Good God," she whispered, and grabbed Hercules's collar.

They beached next to an unoccupied mud bank. Two bottlenose dolphins popped up a few feet away, then swam for open sea. "Scared the hell outta them," Nick observed.

After a few awkward tries she was able to cast the net from the stern. Yulee walked along the bank, slapping a paddle on the water like a giant flyswatter.

"What in the world are you doing?" she asked. "What if another alligator comes along?"

"Pshaw. I'm too tough for them. Just wait."

The water around their sandbar slowly began to perc, like the inside of a boiling teakettle. Suddenly mullet were leaping everywhere, charging headlong into her out-flung net. She flinched as several sailed into the boat, flopping at her bare feet. Now *she* did a dance to avoid the slick, flailing fish. Hercules bounced with her, panting and grinning. The boat rocked so alarmingly she finally ordered him to lie down in the midst of the writhing silvery horde.

Nick donned heavy gloves to sort out undersized fish. "Stone shame to have to loose these," he muttered, throwing a large squirming redfish back over the side. "But so sayeth the law." Mullet and sheepshead he slapped into a plastic beer cooler.

Also trapped in the net were a few stingrays and catfish. "Worthless," he grunted, wrestling with a barbed grandaddy cat. "Foul the net, sting like goddamned mothers. Ouch, shit!" He called each one he took out a "son of a sea-bitch," bashed it headfirst against the side, then threw it up on the bank to die.

She opened her mouth to object, then recalled the livid map of criss-crossed scars on his wrists and shins she'd seen in the light of the waterproof flash, when he'd rolled up his jeans. This was his culture, his world—not hers.

They headed back toward Ibo then. Rounding the south end of the island, through the shoreline's tangled scrub and sea grape she spotted a patch of peeling white clapboard glowing ghostly under the full moon. High against the moonlit wall rose a crumbling, vine-choked brick chimney.

"Hey, what's that place—that building there?"

He didn't answer.

"Nick!" she shouted, pointing at the ruins. "What's over there—an old farm?"

He shook his head and shrugged. He seemed evasive, even sullen. What was his problem? She wasn't a cop or the IRS. "Hey, let's stop," she announced. "Pull up on shore and look around."

"No!" Then, meeting her startled gaze, he said more gently, "I mean, we can't land there. It's—too swampy. And there's snakes. Lots of snakes. Anyhow, I need to get back, or I'll miss the first set."

"Oh." She nodded, feeling rebuffed. "Well, sure."

"You know," he continued in a rush, almost over her own words, "Your hair's pretty. So thick and wavy, but natural. You don't curl it or use that sticky spray stuff, do you? Looks nice, all loose here in the breeze."

It seemed an odd moment for the island boy come-on. But he'd hit on her one real vanity—her hair. And the compliment didn't make her feel uneasy. Why should it? She'd just spent the last hour on a remote sandbar with a man whose only real hostility seemed to be toward ugly stinging sea creatures.

"Thanks," she said. "From the texture and curl, I used to think there must be African blood in my ancestry. Or Jewish, or Arab? Something. I asked my mother once, but she was adopted. So she didn't know."

His expression changed. He frowned and looked tense. Almost horrified.

"What's wrong? You feeling sick?"

"No. I'm fine." But he passed a hand over his face, staring at her with an odd expression. He'd seemed all right until she'd started talking about possibly being part black. Oh, shit, she thought. So he really is a Good Old Boy—*Boneo Antiquus Puer*, as she'd once figured out in high school Latin class. A backwater racist.

Annoying, yet she felt something else, too. Disappointment, or pity. Imagine Nick Yulee on the university campus, or at a party surrounded by the people she knew. All colors, cultures, and viewpoints. That picture simply didn't develop. He'd never fit in, not where she felt at home. No more than she'd want to live out here, assaulting sea life and dodging alligators.

Anyhow, what difference did it make? It wasn't like she'd be packing him in her suitcase along with her books and notes.

When they reached the pier, he lifted Hercules up onto the dock. As he turned back to securing lines and tarps, she climbed the ladder.

"Look," she said. "I'm, uh, going on to my car, if you don't need help. All right? I know you've got to get to work."

"Yeah, I guess—"

"So thanks for the cruise," she added in a rush. "Interesting. Really. Well, I've got to be up early tomorrow, so I won't be going to hear you at the Merry Cat. Sorry, and thanks again. Well—later."

He looked up with open-mouthed surprise. She turned away without waiting for a reply and walked off toward the street, the dog trotting to keep up. Her car and Nick's Jeep were parked side by side in front of Anhinga Tours. As she walked, she tried to brush off her last glimpse: his face slack with disappointment, the tanned, broad shoulders slumped. So what? It wasn't her job to boost his ego. "Bigoted asshole," she muttered, fishing for her keys. "Who cares?"

But she wondered at her growing anger.

Forget it, she decided, sliding into the driver's seat. We have nothing in common. I don't owe him a thing.

She was going to move the car from in front of the store. But it felt foolish to start it up and drive one block to the hotel. She sighed. Got out, locked the doors again and started walking back toward the Inn.

An emaciated old black woman was sitting on a bench beneath the huge gnarled oak in front of the unlit courthouse. Dimly illuminated by a shaft of moonlight through its branches, the woman's clothes seemed oddly dated, of another era. The cloth tattered, even brittle, somehow blackened at the edges. Lucy was surprised. It hadn't occurred to her they might have bag ladies here, just like in a big city.

"Hi," she said as she passed, expecting an answering nod, maybe a request for a handout. She had a few singles in her pocket.

No response. Not even a glance. No indication the slight, bent figure even noticed her.

She shrugged. At the curb, about to cross the street, she looked back toward the big tree. The moonlit bench was empty.

TEN

She was pulling a cotton nightshirt on when it occurred to her that the ruins spotted from Nick's boat might be part of the vanished black community Eugenie Lee had mentioned. She froze, the cloth bunched around her neck. The indecipherable word Esther Day had whispered in her ear at Gulf Rest—could that be the name of the place? What did an old woman's babbling about an abusive husband and a bunch of angry men have to do with it? Perhaps in between research and revising she could explore a ghost town. Maybe interview some older Ibo residents, discover who'd lived there besides Lee. Check out the ruins, get a photo or two, and—now here was an idea: write a short article for the university's literary journal.

Hal Prince was the editor, and he kept asking her for a contribution to *The JB Harmonium*. The biggest weakness on her CV was its scant publications. Here was a perfect opportunity to add something. And it would fill the time until she knew whether Esther Day was reliable or not. At least her trip would not be wasted. What was it the woman had whispered? It'd sounded like "Weird one" or maybe "Where wool?" Neither interpretation had made sense back in the nursing home. Calling Day at Gulf Rest to ask again didn't seem a great idea either. But she could check maps in the morning at the library, see if anything remotely similar was a place name. She was pretty sure there'd been nothing like it on her Google map, coming down, but lost bits of the past were always waiting to be discovered.

She'd also phone Hal to ask a favor. The Internet connection here was slow as frozen maple syrup. She was beginning to think the whole town shared a single DSL connection. And it went out a lot—too unreliable for research purposes. But maybe he could cajole one of the university's library staff into a quick newspaper archive search for articles on the area. Their electronic files would date past the forties and fifties. A side task to keep her occupied. It was important to stay busy. When she was working, she hardly ever thought about Tim Carling or the marks he'd left on her. Except for the one nightmare of the burning town, she rarely even dreamed now . . . thank God.

Hal called back at noon, while she was out walking the dog. "The library found two articles in the Tallahassee *Democrat*. Emailed the files. You get 'em?"

She shifted the phone to her left hand as Hercules tugged at the leash. "Nope. Connectivity sucks here. I'll check when I get back."

"OK. Well, anyhow—the town is spelled I-B-O K-E-Y. But there's only a one-sentence reference in the sources I checked," he said. "Weird, since it was, like, the main labor pool for the lumber mills. Pine, turpentine, and cedar wood for good old number two pencils. By the forties trees were sparse, though. They didn't bother with little details like replanting back then."

"Great. Thanks, Hal."

"The articles were both on the same week in December 1952. Apparently there was some kind of, uh, disturbance. Hard to say what. You know . . . papers reported shit . . . McCarthy era. Lots of editorial . . . short on . . . no hard data."

"You're breaking up, Hal." She frowned at her iPhone. "Can you—"

He didn't seem to hear. "Anyhow, Jan . . . periodicals . . . fax stuff . . . headline: 'Woman . . . Suspects Hanged. Negroes Flee.'"

Good grief. All written up as if it'd been a Neighborhood Watch patrol to foil mailbox bashers. "That sounds like a . . . a lynch mob."

"Yeah." Hal's voice was clear again. "Not so unusual back then, right?"

"Well, no. But—what was the supposed crime?"

Silence. She thought maybe the call had dropped. "Hey! You still there?"

"Uh-huh. It was, um, supposedly a, um . . . a sexual assault. Of a white woman, by a black man."

"Oh." She took a deep breath. "Well, from what I've seen, there may not have been any 'authorities' then. The county sheriff is on the mainland. I've read the weekly paper—all two pages. Not much crime now. Some domestic violence, public drunkenness, check kiting. Oyster poaching. What's the other article?"

"Even vaguer, believe it or not. Something about the white sheets stepping up to help get everything under control." He read the brief account, which made the Ku Klux Klan sound like first responders on a natural disaster.

"That's it? Nothing else about the town or what became of it?"

"Well, something ten years later. Probably not related. A stringer for the Tallahassee *Democrat* told his editor he was going to Ibo Key to write an article for a Sunday feature on Florida ghost towns. Maybe he had some personal problems, or the story was going really shitty—"

"Hal!" she interrupted. The dog was straining at the leash, dragging her down the sidewalk. "What happened?"

"Sorry. Hang on." She heard paper rustling. "He was found in his car, on the mainland, at the foot of some three mile long bridge. With a bullet in his head. A gun with his prints lying on the passenger seat. No sign of foul play. The county coroner ruled it suicide. Nothing after that."

"Damn," she said, wincing as the dog nearly jerked her arm out of socket. Hercules was usually much better behaved. Now he was snuffling and rooting in a nearby bush. "Herc, sit!"

"Maybe back in the fifties the KKK could clean up a town so well it turned invisible. Even now some guys—girls too—would probably like to slip into white designer sheets and do something radical about the evils of social equality. And not just down South."

Lucy sighed. "No doubt. The Klan was everywhere. Reborn in Indiana in the twenties, remember? But thanks for all the help. Maybe I can put together an article for your lit-crit rag now."

"I'll anticipate it eagerly." Then his tone dropped, turned more serious. "But how are you doing?"

She chose to misunderstand the question. "Not bad. It's hot as hell in the daytime. No AC in the hotel. Oh—and my main interviewee is flipping out. Never mind, long story. Maybe I won't find what I really came for, but I'll get something worth the long drive."

"*Fowler.*" His voice was clipped with exasperation. "I'm not talking about a damned dissertation, you twit. How are you—are *you* doing all right?"

She laughed. "Great. Really. It's just what I needed. I'm dealing in my own way, Hal. Which doesn't include spilling my guts in front of a bunch of people. Thanks for the concern, but—"

"Butt out, I know. Just remember your friends who worry. About you. Oh shit, I just got sentimental in a non-ironic way. You won't repeat that, will you?"

She smiled. "Your secret's safe. Bye, Hal."

As she pressed END Hercules backed out of the bush with something clenched in his jaws. Long, ivory colored, dirty. "Hey! What did you dig up, fella?"

She squatted and pried the thing from his mouth.

"Ugh," she said, wrinkling her nose, about to drop it. "Prehistoric beef bone? Honestly, dogs are so—"

An odd mark on it caught her eye. From the long thick shape it almost certainly was a cow's femur. Carved with some markings that looked not so much tribal as crudely obscene. Short, thick curves meant to represent vaginal lips, maybe. Or rounded breasts. Faces with gashed eyes and pouting lips. It felt less like folk art than an obscene, secret souvenir. A stinking trophy of some unspeakable act. Though where these thoughts came from she had no idea.

Whatever. She wanted nothing to do with this foul artifact. She started to pitch it back into the oleander shrub, but hesitated. The thing was a relic reflecting some sort of local weirdness. The ritual markings made it a religious artifact, of sorts. Suppressing her disgust, she tucked it in a side pocket of her backpack and dragged Hercules whining in the opposite direction, back to the hotel.

The Merry Cat was half empty after the lunch rush. She tied Hercules in a shady spot and took a table near the back. Starr slid a basket of jalepeña corn muffins in front of her. She decided on conch chowder and hearts of palm salad. The pale girl nodded, scribbling. Just as she turned to go put in the order a muffled crash sounded from the kitchen. Diners flinched as Cora burst through the swinging doors like a gunslinger looking for trouble. Starr paled as her mother glowered around the room. Cora stalked over and slid into the chair across from Lucy.

"Believe this heat?" she growled. "I mean, yeah, we're in the sub-frigging-tropics, but it's almost Christmas. Should be sweater weather, at least, this late."

"I know," Lucy sympathized, though it seemed better to her than shoveling a couple feet of snow back in Pennsylvania. "That's what I packed for—cool weather. Now I'm washing out the same three things in the bathroom sink." She looked around. "Heat hasn't chased your customers off, though."

At the next table retirees juggled fried grouper sandwiches that dripped tartar sauce at each bite. Most of the tables were full, watermen and local merchants, a few sunburned tourists. "Food this good—a little hot weather won't keep people away," she added.

Cora curled her lip. "Yeah, 'cause they got so many other choices for fine dining downtown." She lowered her head and scratched at a spot on the tablecloth.

"Had any more run-ins with developers?"

"Nah." Cora flicked her dishtowel morosely at a fly. "Next it'll be talent scouts for Chick-Fil-A coming in, to hire away Starr Lynn."

Lucy suppressed a laugh, ignoring Cora's melodramatic tone. "Nothing stays the same. That's one reason I decided on folklore. Old customs, stories, superstitions—they'll just be forgotten. History, too. Unless we can preserve the past somehow—"

Cora's eyes were glazing over.

Whoa there, Lucy, she thought, hearing the evangelical tone creeping in. You'll bore the sources into a coma. She cleared her throat. "Speaking of the past, I've got a few questions about Ibo Key."

Cora frowned. "Such as?"

She leaned forward. "About fifty years ago, there was a black community down at the south end. Seems it just disappeared, like, overnight. I was wondering about it."

The other woman's gaze looked flat now, even unfriendly. "Why?"

"To write an article. Like I said, I like to preserve stories, practices, legends, folkways. Things that, whether we realize it or not, construct the way we live now."

Cora smiled again, but not warmly. "Only 'preserving' I ever done was in mason jars. You know, a newspaper reporter did come around about that once. Only we weren't fooled. He wanted to lie and stir up trouble, make headlines. Slap a label on this place, then piss all over it. What did he know about us—or anything here? Scaring up victims to make himself look good. Well, we're all victims, right? Some just ain't in fashion no more."

Lucy bit her lip. "I didn't mean to—"

"What in hell did he know about us?" Cora repeated, as if she hadn't spoken. "Just wanted his fifteen minutes, like that creepy old white-haired artist said . . . yeah, I know about Andy Warhol. We're not all stupid rednecks, like they claim back where you come from. Quaint, colorful, ignorant rubes. That way the bastards can make it sound like a public service when everything you love gets torn down and cemented over, while they rake in cash."

"Cora, I didn't—"

"Well, that news hack couldn't hold his own life together, much less write up ours. How's *your* goddamn mental health?" She stood abruptly, chair scraping back on the tiles with a screech that made Lucy's ears throb. "I was right about you. A fucking scribbler come to gawk at the grits, make notes about our savage customs, snigger later with the other fucking scribblers. You turkey buzzards all make me sick." She slammed back through the kitchen doors, which flapped again for several seconds.

Lucy felt her cheeks burning. Curious diners turned her way, like the glaring old man two tables away dressed in the faded coveralls and white rubber boots of a waterman. Or was she just paranoid? She took a sip of tea, then a slow deep breath. You should expect rough treatment from time to time, she reminded herself. Some people don't understand what research is all about. They don't get that asking questions, reexamining the past, is important. In the line of duty, for her.

And a newspaperman ventilating his head in the front seat of his car, was that in the line of duty?

She gulped more tea. That was a different situation. The guy's problems had nothing to do with her. Maybe he was ill. In debt. Feeling like a middle-aged loser. She had problems too—who didn't? But she could handle them. Hadn't she been doing just that?

Yet Cora's words stung. Of course she hoped to get something out of her work. Why not? That prickly café owner didn't peel and chop and mix and cook all day in a hot kitchen, then go out on the street and give meals away for free. Why should Lucy Fowler spend all her time researching, planning, organizing, filing, writing, and not expect to be rewarded? Somehow, in some way.

Of course, her job was different from running a store or a restaurant for a profit. More like a public service that at its best yielded a lasting gift to the world. To preserve how people had seen things, done things, to reveal the part the past still played today. It wasn't as if she'd make millions, like some hack turning out crappy spy thrillers. Or some freaking land developer. A little money, maybe a good teaching job. She stopped in confusion, still hearing Cora's mocking words: *They want to cash in on us . . . like a public service. . . .*

But that had been different people, prying into Ibo Key's past for other reasons. No, she was onto something historically important. And she'd keep working on it—with or without the help of Cora Cisneros.

Starr reappeared suddenly at her elbow and slid a plate gingerly onto the table, as if serving raw meat to a Bengal tiger. Lucy didn't feel hungry anymore. She thought of Cora's earlier joke about lacing land developers' meals with insecticide.

God, I am getting paranoid.

"Thanks, Starr," she murmured. By then it seemed important to casually spread the bandana napkin over her lap, then slowly and deliberately eat every bite, and act as if she really, really enjoyed it.

After forcing down the last tasteless mouthful, she paid the check, untied Hercules from the patio post, and set out for the Day house.

This time the old woman seemed a mere shadow, out on the porch rocking and smoking. A sweating pitcher of tea sat on the table by one elbow. Lucy climbed the steps, itching to tell her about Cora's insults in the café. Why, though? A minor unpleasantness. Still, she couldn't resist a comment.

"You've been so nice and helpful. So has Mrs. Day, as best she can, I think. But I get the feeling Southern hospitality might be a bigger myth than the yeti."

Lee frowned. "Miffed? Thought you looked out-done about something."

"No, sorry. I'm muttering. A myth, like a made-up story, an old legend."

"Oh me, you just now figure that out?" Eugenie laughed at her. "Do me good to hear a college-educated doctor don't know everything."

"I'm not a—oh, never mind. It's just, I had a run-in with a person who seemed friendly at first, and then . . . well, it's not only that. Last night I said hello to a woman sitting on a bench, to be polite, and she refused to even look at me."

Eugenie Lee gazed at her, waiting. Lucy was wringing her hands, getting wound up, and couldn't seem to stop. "And you know what else? I've seen a handful of African Americans in town, but they always seem to be walking off, or just rounding a corner, like they can't wait to get away from me. Aside from one little boy, that is." She recalled the child with the misshapen head. "It's like they're, I don't know—shunning me. Take that woman last night. She deliberately ignored me, then left in a big hurry." She flung her hands up. "Why would they all act like that?"

Eugenie was looking at her so strangely. With

astonishment, or fear—almost horror.

"I mean, I—what's wrong?"

The old woman sucked her lips in, till they made a line as thin as a scaling knife. "Except for me, missy, they ain't no black folks on Ibo Key. Haven't been for years and years."

"What? But I've seen them."

Well, a few anyway. A warning chill crept into her mind. Was Eugenie Lee getting demented like Esther Day? And if so, what good was any of the material she'd recorded? Surely the old woman wasn't lying. What would be the point? The contradiction just made her more determined to find out why it was taboo to even mention a vanished town to anyone in Ibo City.

She sat down, tapped the screen and selected the RECORD option. "I'm sorry, complaining like this when you've been so helpful. Well, let's do it. Miss Eugenie Lee, Ibo Key, Session Three, December 21. . . . Please, tell me what went down in Revelation back in 1960."

No answer.

"Was a crime committed?" she prodded gently, without looking up. "Did a mob attack residents?"

The phone sat there, recording silence. Lucy looked up from her notepad.

The old woman was slumped in the chair, nodding. Apparently she'd just dozed off. Lucy sighed and reached out, her finger headed for the STOP key.

Before she could touch the screen, Eugenie Lee's lips moved. "Mama, Mama! I see some men. Coming up the road!"

Goose-bumps rose on Lucy's forearms. This voice was high-pitched, not Eugenie's whiskey-rough alto but the tones of a small, frightened child. A little boy. No falsetto imitation, Lucy would swear. The dry, withered lips moved in sync with the childish words as if Eugenie were merely an amplifier for an unearthly recording. A living ventriloquist's dummy. But who was working the dummy's mouth?

"They got dogs. And guns, lots of guns! Look like they comin' here! Mama—"

The voice broke off abruptly, as if a harassed mother had snatched the child and pulled him inside, cutting off his shrill commentary.

Lucy froze, staring, expecting Eugenie Lee to open her eyes. To laugh at the confusion she'd just caused.

Instead, the child's voice was replaced by the calm but firm tones of a woman. "Son, go out the back. Hide yourself somewhere. They will search here first. No, no! Listen to me. I know you've done nothing wrong. What does that matter? It has never mattered. Whether you are innocent or in the wrong, it is only sport for them. And you the game they hunt!"

Perplexed, enthralled, Lucy edged the phone closer to not miss a word. Was this a prank? Dementia? Weirdly it brought to mind black and white movies in which a medium draped in scarves and big hoop earrings rolled her eyes up into her head and claimed to be in contact with departed souls. And, just like one of those badly acted old films, it was perversely enthralling.

But this was no late night rerun. She was on a warped wooden rocker on a front porch flanked by peeling white columns facing a steaming asphalt street. Sweat soaked her cotton shirt. She was sitting bathed in sunlight, across from a shrunken old woman who chain-smoked Camels and—up to now—had seemed about as mysterious as a supermarket checker.

"Miss Eugenie?" Lucy whispered, and reached out to touch a wrinkled hand. She paused halfway across the space that separated them. Was it dangerous to startle someone in a trance, to bring them out too quickly? Or was that only for sleepwalkers? No, no, old movies again, she decided. How agonized and distressed those actress-mediums had always appeared, as if the "spirit voices" were being wrung from their livers by invisible hands.

But Eugenie Lee didn't seem to be in pain. Now her lips were producing the voice of the same woman as before, alternating with that of a girl with a Creole accent. Yet all the while her expression remained tranquil, her features motionless.

"Silence! I must finish talking with your brother. . . . Go to the woods. Later, to Mr. Flowers' store if you can," the low, soothing female voice was saying. "A good man. Perhaps he will help. If you cannot, stay in the marshes until they leave. Go now, before the hell-hounds catch your scent. Remain hidden until dark. Then there will surely be a way off the island." A pause, a sigh. "My son, I knew about you and that woman. But I never thought this—" The voice broke off suddenly, as if the speaker were listening for something. Then, a fierce whisper: *"Go now!"*

The same voice murmured, as if reflecting to herself, "Food, of course. And my medicine bag. And the Book. It must go with us, protected from them, or be hidden. Of course—the key. Julian, wait! Take this with you."

Suddenly, the desperately placating voice of an older man broke in. "I tol' you, Boss Jimmy. Don't know where he at. Ain't seen him since yesterday. But Julian, he always been a good boy—oh!"

A moment of taut silence, then the male voice was back, slightly slurred, with a note of tired resignation. "No suh. I tell what I know. You don't believe no how. I never done you no harm. Worked for your daddy nigh on thirty year. And you treat me like this, when—"

The plaintive words were replaced by a blood-chilling scream. The fine hairs on the back of Lucy's neck rose. She jumped up and her chair keeled into the porch wall and toppled. Should she call 911? Was there an emergency service on the island? As she reached for her phone the screams faded, resolving into the old man's voice again. High as the little boy's now, shrill with unbearable pain.

"Lord Jesus! *My hands.* What you done, you killed me!" A weak moan, then, "Sweet Lord God."

Lucy froze, staring at Eugenie Lee. Unbelievably, the old woman's face was still tranquil. It hadn't altered even while the old man keened in mortal agony. The high-pitched wail went on and on. Lucy covered her ears, but could not escape it. She couldn't stand any more. I'll go crazy too, she thought. Call somebody, anybody.

She snatched up the phone but then merely held it, staring, paralyzed, as the old woman rose from her chair, lips working as if to shape that horrible scream again.

Instead, an impossible jumble of sounds and voices poured from her open mouth as if from a loudspeaker. The hoarse shouts of angry men, the famished crackle of flame, the snarling of enraged dogs. Screaming women and howling babies, mocking laughter and curses and cries and prayers. All of it sounded from the frail body which stood impassively, eyes closed, expression detached, blank as a radio babbling to an empty room.

And the high whine beneath it all was not coming from Eugenie Lee at all. Hercules stood at the foot of the steps, gazing up, hackles raised, ears folded back, trembling all over.

"Please." Lucy crumpled, a hand outstretched, until one knee struck the porch floor. She scarcely felt the numbing pain that shot up her thigh. "I don't know what to do. For God's sake, please stop!"

A blessed silence fell. The older woman sat back on her rocking chair, silent. After a moment her eyes fluttered open, as if she were waking from a nap. She took a deep, shuddering breath. And then—then, she smiled.

Now Lucy was losing her mind. She felt sure of it.

Eugenie took a second breath, slow and deep, as if for the first time she actually savored the air she breathed. "O Moses," she sighed. "Never could tell it before, even among ourselves. Bottled up and kept in the dark like old preserves, till it explode and bust the jar. Feels good to let the words pour out, bitter as they be."

She looked over at Lucy, too, as if for the first time. "Well, girl. Wanting to know it all, are you? Sure you can take that—what comes after the knowing? Then walk on back here and set yourself down. And I'll tell how pure Evil itself came one night to Revelation."

ELEVEN

That evening back in her hotel, as she worked in the yellow circle of light from the overhead fixture, Lucy recalled her own dream of a burning town and a mass grave. Right now it felt as if a bat were trapped beneath her breastbone, trying to escape that cage of ribs. What she'd heard on Esther Day's front porch was part of her own nightmare, like the missing soundtrack to an old film. Sweat prickled on her skin as the grotesque dream images came rushing back. She forced herself to slowly count to ten, twenty, then a hundred—waiting to be left in peace. There'd been no more such dreams to record in her journal. But she didn't think she could stand even the sight of the Book now, knowing that the horrors recorded between its innocuous red covers were apparently no dream.

She'd tucked it away in the night stand, next to a dusty Gideon Bible and the horrible carved bone. She went over and opened the drawer as cautiously as if a small fierce animal lived inside. Snatched the diary out, carried it to the desk, and began to write.

Today I again interviewed subject named Eugenie Lee. The result was a very unusual—

She stopped, frowning, and struck through that sentence.

123

Then in a rush, began again.

I've never experienced anything stranger than what happened today. Never in my life. If somebody ever told me a story like that at the college, in a classroom, even at a bar—I would've listened politely, then gotten the hell away, thinking Nutcase Alert! Or No more alcohol for you!

Well, now I have to decide. Either I'm the nutcase (because I haven't had a drink all day) or else the sounds on this tape are the audio-record of a horrible massacre committed sixty years ago. And maybe—just maybe—proof of some existence after death. At the very least, evidence the dead leave a lingering impression on our world.

As Dr. Grove had said in his lecture. Though that seemed like a lifetime ago, now. She paused, then scribbled one last line.

Could my recent dream be tied into this, somehow?

She stared at the shakily-scrawled words. What to believe, and what to do about it? Easy enough to claim with a sort of proud academic objectivity that realities other than our own might be equally viable. But this was not a theory essay. She was starting to feel the vastness of the leap from abstract theorizing to actual . . . belief.

The iPhone sat on the desk. She'd already played back parts of Lee's interview. What she'd heard on that sunlit porch a few hours ago was trapped inside that flat white

Pandora's box. The fine hairs on her arms and neck had risen when she'd listened to voices, shrieks, cries, other chilling sounds impossible to reproduce with human vocal cords. They might sound a bit more remote, threaded with intermittent static—but were undeniably there.

What wasn't, of course, was what she'd seen: a frail flesh and blood being become a remote transmitter for some unearthly, invisible force.

The implications were frightening . . . and exhilarating. Yes, that was what she felt beneath the animal fear: pure energy, intoxicating excitement. Jolt enough to keep her awake for days. She felt charged with life, determined to *prove* it was real—not just acknowledge it with detachment on some anonymous page or screen. Never in her studies had she felt so focused, so riveted. A seductive high, a driving force to act, to move. She could not let this opportunity slip away.

What was less clear was how to begin.

Before she left the Day house she'd quizzed the old woman about a book mentioned by one of the voices. *The Book.* She had almost heard the capital letters, spoken huskily by a female Eugenie had later claimed was Solange Koumari. That ghostly voice, clear yet frightened, struggling for control, had spoken of hiding this book. Of keeping it safe. Almost as if it were more important than the human lives around her.

"Solange Koumari's Book," Miss Eugenie had explained, "Said it hold all the knowledge and power for Doctor-Woman's mother. She bring it to New Orleans from her island. The daughter inherit it, you see?"

Rumor had held that its antique leather binding was made of tanned human skin—the white hides of sugar-plantation owners murdered by their black slaves. That it was so old it had aged to the reddish-brown of Haitian mahogany. Cradled between these gruesome antique covers lay fantastic histories, impossible cures, deadly spells, knowledge beyond what any human mind should know.

The old woman leaned closer to whisper, "A mighty fearsome tool in the hands of an evil person. I never seen it myself. But Esther Day knew about it. Fact is"—Eugenie Lee's tone dropped lower, until Lucy had to concentrate hard to hear—"she want it for *herself*."

"For what?"

She'd sat back, nodding. "Oh, not to use. Mrs. Esther didn't believe in such as that. I expect just to *know*. To keep it out of Solange's hands, so people would come to her instead. Her modern medicine. To her it just be like . . . business."

Lucy had felt the prodding of excitement then. It still made her ears ring and her hands tremble now, as she wrote. The voice had spoken of hiding this Book. Could it still exist? The people had been dispersed, the town burned. But—if someone had protected it, hidden it somewhere? Amazing artifacts had been recovered before. From dusty attics, garbage heaps, cave systems, burial grounds. Even the virtual ashes of a community. A discovery like that would make her reputation even before she held a Ph.D. diploma in her hand.

Beyond that, who knew? A great job. Instant respect. And who needed that kind of security more than Lucy Fowler, with no one but herself to rely on. Her mother dead, her father, who'd been fifty when she was born, in a nursing home in Vermont. A frail, vacant old man who blinked and gazed at her blankly when she visited. The money left in his account would cover long term care for him. But who would care for her if she had no job? If she got sick? *The HIV test,* a whisper in her mind added. *When you go back. What if—?*

No. She refused to contemplate that. But yes, she was on her own. And so, more vulnerable.

But who wouldn't want real achievement? Not that

recognition should be most important in a situation like this. But damn it, she wanted to feel she was doing more than just following some preordained grind. Was it wrong to want that, just a little? Sometimes late at night in her study carrel, she'd looked around at the cheap fabric covered partitions, thinking, *What am I doing here?* Sometimes, she stared at the professors, the students around her, and saw a dreary monastic order which had ordained it unseemly, even sacrilegious, to aspire to anything else. To make money, to own anything too luxurious, to even drive a car nicer than, say, a three-year-old Subaru.

Well, they could sneer all they liked. Now she understood why she'd been working nonstop. From earliest memory, she'd never been able to satisfy the expectations of her parents. It seemed to have something to do with her mother's origins, an unwanted baby adopted from some unspecified birthplace. Her grandparents had all but given up hope of ever having a child. So many years of dreams and hopes hoarded and cherished, saved up and then poured out, must've nearly drowned one small child. Her mother, Philomena, had been nervous, slight, thin hands always moving, as if searching for something lost so long ago she'd forgotten what it was. And dissatisfied with everything, it seemed.

How could Lucy ever measure up? Not with grades. Each six weeks she'd dragged home with report card clutched in damp palms. Always high marks, but rarely perfect. The fleeting glimpse of disappointment tamped down, the carefully blank expression, the limp hug, all conveyed how her mother really felt. She'd gotten her bachelor's degree, though not with highest honors. Which had only whetted the maternal appetite for a Master's to brag about at the Thursday bridge game. She'd sweated that out. Then, with the scroll barely safe in Lucy's sweating hand, Philomena had observed, "It would be a shame not to go on for a doctorate, sweetie."

Even now, with her mother dead of breast cancer and her father past knowing or caring, the drive to satisfy them haunted her.

Throughout college her single-minded pursuit had left little time for attachment to anyone. Roommates, acquaintances. A few men. Actually she'd slept with lots, mostly other students. To be brutally honest, she'd have a hard time recalling all the names. But each time a relationship seemed about to develop, she'd pick a fight. Or, failing to provoke one, flee in panic.

At least, thank god, she'd never gotten pregnant. In some cultures, that would be yet another failure, a black mark. Oh, who was she kidding—in her society, too. Maybe she didn't truly belong anywhere. If she didn't put all her talent and energy into finding this wonderful so-called Book, she'd feel that sense of utter failure again.

Perhaps such obsession wasn't normal. What was wrong with her?

Once, huddled at night under the covers with a book and flashlight, after her parents were long asleep, it had hit her: She was not one of them. Her mother had been adopted. Who knew what strange features her genetics might hold? If she couldn't feel she belonged in her own incurious family, how could she expect to be part of some other world? Unlike other adopted children she'd read about, who yearned even as adults to find their roots, her mother had never seemed to hunger to discover her beginnings.

Two years ago, she'd had to check her father into the private nursing home. Alzheimer's had crept in like a slow-moving thief, taking a memory here, a name there. His brain shrank, dwindling like fruit left too long on a drying rack. Until finally he no longer recognized his daughter. A small kindness, she supposed, that he didn't seem to miss being able to read, write, talk, or dress himself. Indeed, he seemed to have no recollection of the vigorous life he'd once led, the dreams he'd pushed Lucy toward. Now she could become the first female president, or a homeless drug addict with a police record—he wouldn't know the difference.

She frowned, plucking at the silver talisman around her neck. But she could still prove something to herself. She wouldn't leave Ibo Key without two things: the concluding section to her dissertation, and this mysterious old book—if it still existed. And if that meant she had to spend hundreds of hours listening to the ramblings of crazy old women, sifting through jumbled words like a miner panning for gold dust, then so be it.

She glanced at the time on her cell phone, and smiled. Visiting hours at Gulf Rest's special care unit began in an hour.

At ten minutes to one the Gulf Rest lobby was occupied by a lone man in a gray suit and dark tie, gazing at a crinkled copy of *People*. Cora would probably classify him as an underfed lawyer. Or was that an oxymoron? Just another soul, waiting as she was, to visit a friend or relative.

She took the armchair opposite. A low wood-grained coffee table held vintage issues of *Field and Stream*, *Good Housekeeping* and *US*. She found a lone *Marie Claire* and flipped idly through, skimming advice on orgasms, photo-spreads of overpriced lingerie, an article on celebrity mistresses. She dropped it back on the table.

"Funny," said a male voice.

When she looked up, the man across was smiling at her. She tilted her head. "Sorry. Did you just—"

"I said, 'Funny.'"

"What is?"

"You don't seem the fashion magazine type. Then I remembered I read such rags, too, when I'm waiting. Like at the dentist." He held up his magazine. "Funny. We both do that."

"Oh." Oh brother. Was this some lame pick-up line?

She decided to grab a new magazine fast, before the guy felt encouraged. Then she noticed someone coming down the hallway.

Not Esther Day. Instead, four elderly men shuffled in and sat at a corner table. One broke out a pack of cards from a pocket in his robe, and dealt. They bowed heads over their hands and began arguing in low voices. Suddenly a tall, cadaverous oldster with wispy white hair stood so violently his chair toppled backwards.

"The hell you will!" He pointed at a fat man, who rose and snarled back. The two still seated reached out and jerked them back into their chairs. The game resumed.

"Now, that bunch," the man in gray remarked to Lucy. "They play cards same time every day. Always have the same argument. Can't get along for five minutes. So much in common, yet they hate each another. That's funny, too."

"Seems sad to me," she said, then regretted it. She didn't want to carry on a conversation with this vaguely creepy guy.

He shook his head. "But sad is subjective. Each of those fellows was once involved in state-sanctioned killing, and it eventually drove them all mad. Yet do they feel any group loyalty, any *esprit de corps?*" He flapped a hand. "Might as well be strangers. Now, I find *that* sad."

She glanced at the card players again. "They're all war veterans?"

The stranger grinned, exposing small, bright teeth, almost too white. They looked unreal. "Something like that. Though they knew many of those they disposed of, which would make any sort of war more . . . challenging . . . don't you think?"

Wow. First, she really didn't like his word choices. "Challenging," for God's sake! Second, she didn't like him at all. She thought about moving away, across the room.

Again his thin lips stretched in a knowing smile. As if he'd read her mind. "Oh, you may not like it, but it's true.

That sort of challenge is enhanced by familiarity. Why, I myself—though I was, in a manner of speaking, not myself at all—once killed and ate my entire family. Beginning with my dear wife. We had a large, frost-free freezer in the garage, so I could enjoy them for quite some time. Waste not, want not. I saved the baby for last. Delicious, tender as a lamb chop."

Lucy stopped breathing. She rose unsteadily, afraid to take her eyes off the man, who was still droning on in a pleasant, conversational tone. This was no visitor. He must be a patient. This part of the facility was supposedly reserved for "special needs." Just how special hadn't been made clear. But surely madmen like this should not be wandering freely, when Gulf Rest was courting applicants for the luxurious retirement section.

Of course, perfectly harmless individuals, due to age or infirmity, could suffer from confusion, memory loss, dementia. But he wasn't elderly, nor did he seem the least bit infirm. He spoke calmly and lucidly, and like a natural storyteller was making every detail very vivid.

"Every day I wiped down the white enameled freezer lid. I hate a messy kitchen, don't you? That is, after I took out one of the rigid blue limbs, so nicely coated with frost, to thaw," he was murmuring.

The images unreeled in her head like a slasher movie. A perverse thrill of horror held her in place, face averted, arms crossed against the revulsion his images conjured. "Look, I—"

"Then I took a cast-iron pan, and—"

Enough. She turned and walked away, past the card game, toward the hall, where she'd noticed a sign for a nursing office. She tapped on its frosted-glass door.

A woman in a green aide's smock, chart in hand, poked her head out. "Help you, honey?"

Lucy took a deep breath. "Yes. There's this man—one

of your patients—sitting out there." She cleared her throat and made her tone flat, so she didn't sound hysterical. "Who's becoming sort of . . . well, he's scaring me. I'm sure he's not actually dangerous—I mean, you wouldn't let him roam around then, right? But could I possibly wait in here?"

The woman was peering over her shoulder. Looking perplexed. "One man? Just by hisself, not our regular card players? I don't see anyone else out there."

Lucy turned to look. Except for the four players, the lobby was empty.

"Oh well," the woman went on cheerfully, "some of our visitors is stranger than the inmates, honey. Old rascal probably slipped on out the door. Sometimes the older gentlemen try their hand flirting with young ladies. Come get me directly if he gives you any more trouble, honey."

Old rascal? Flirting? She shook her head. "Um—all right. Thanks. I will."

She returned, giving the card table a wide berth, and sat down on the lumpy couch again. Picked up a battered travel magazine, and tried to be interested in diving in Aruba, dog-sledding in Saskatchewan. She glanced up at the wall clock. Twenty minutes had passed. Where was Esther Day?

In fact, why was she even in here, housed with what seemed to be the criminally insane, or close to it. Though the strange man in gray was the only one who'd actually claimed to be a killer. Perhaps a deluded street person, making up stories?

But his suit had been clean and pressed. His shirt and tie neat. And with such intensity and a calm lucidity. She'd swear he'd known exactly what he was saying. And worst of all, had meant every word.

The press of cool fingers on one bare arm almost made her shriek. It was the woman from the office again. "Honey, you by chance Miss Fowler? OK, well, I just come out to tell you Mrs. Day won't be seeing visitors today. Feeling poorly."

Lucy felt a stab of anxiety. "She's ill?"

"Lord, no. She enjoys her food, probably had a bit too much at lunch. Tuesday is Italian day. All that heavy cheese and sauce lays on the stomach like a stone, in some."

"Oh. I see." She felt no great disappointment at getting away from a place that fed Italian lunches to people who claimed to prefer a much more sinister diet. "That's fine. Please tell her I'll be back tomorrow."

Gathering her bag she rushed out, feeling liberated. Poor Hercules was waiting patiently, head out the window of his backseat prison. She returned the favor, pulling off just outside the gates to let him take a well-earned pee.

When she got back to the Inn, the older woman with the accent—Stellina, her name tag read—called out as she crossed to the stairs. "Another message for you, *Dottore.*" She smiled. "A nice gentleman this time."

"I'm not a—never mind. Thanks." Lucy took the slip of paper she held out across the counter and read the scrawled message.

Please call B. Reshenko. 547-551-2112.

The police detective back in Pottsburg. She sighed.

"Good news, I hope," Stellina murmured. "Such a nice voice he had."

Right. "It's nothing much really. But thanks again." She climbed the stairs to her room, Hercules following, panting in the rising heat.

Reshenko. Yes, he'd been nice. But she dreaded his solicitous calls, so evenly spaced, as if he were tracking her state of mind the way he'd run surveillance on an elusive suspect. As if he expected her to just . . . snap. To crack one day like the over-tightened lid on a too-full jar. Of course he was probably trying to help, but she didn't want to follow his kindly, well-meant advice. It was *her* mind, her body. Who knew better than she what to do for it?

Anyhow, she was too busy right now to return calls. She'd catch up with him later. She'd finished talking to Eugenie, and Esther Day wasn't available. So she would go exploring—to track down the ruins of Revelation herself.

In the end, to find the lost town, all she had to do was follow Water Street south. This main road bisected the entire crescent-moon of island, turning from asphalt to shell-paved road, then at the far end to rutted, weedy, hardpan clay. Terminating in the town of Revelation.

Or more precisely, its remains.

She stopped as the road dead-ended into a tangle of wild grapevine pierced by the pale limbs of fallen dead trees. A fine drizzle was thinning out to clammy mist. Could this be all that remained of a thriving community dead only fifty years—a weed-choked plot of charred, broken brick foundations, scrawny second-growth pines thrusting through rubble?

A few fireplaces strangled by kudzu creepers stabbed jagged accusing fingers at the sky. The lone recognizable building was a hollowed, hulking clapboard house, what was left of its painted skin leprously peeling. The porch roof had caved in, giving it a curiously blind face. Painted on one side in tall black letters was FLO   RS' GROC RY D Y GO D. So that must've been the community's general store.

"Herc!" He was snuffling in some bushes again. He trotted over and she snapped on the leash, to keep him from wandering where he might step on rusty nails or broken glass. Now, belatedly, she also thought of snakes. She wore leather hiking boots and heavy cotton socks, but khaki shorts wouldn't protect her shins from a startled rattlesnake or water moccasin. She slapped her left leg for him to heel. Slowly, cautiously, she crunched through dry leaves and pine needles, kicking at fallen logs, making plenty of noise to give any hostile wildlife a chance to retreat.

The crackling she'd heard on the tape, so much like flames, made more sense now. The remaining wood was charred at the edges, the fallen bricks blackened with soot. This place had been thoroughly torched. Termites and rot and creeping vegetation had finished the job. She couldn't tell whether the foundations she saw had been homes or shops or schools or churches. What hope was there of finding a single lost book in this jungle?

Well, it wasn't going to hop out of the trumpet vines and poison ivy and greet her by name. "All right then," she muttered, pulling denim sleeves down over her wrists and buttoning them. She carefully eased into the nearest tumbled thicket.

One by one she walked the remains of almost a dozen buildings, looking for trap doors or inset bricks that might mean a hiding spot. Or depressions in the earth that might indicate a buried object. A curious scrub jay hopped from tree branch to broken chimney and back, offering terse comments on her progress. A sleepy armadillo peered from beneath a collapsed shed before lumbering off like a toy tank into the bushes.

After an hour or so she was sweaty and scratched, smarting from the wounds of a thousand blackberry thorns. But by then she felt secure enough to let Hercules off the lead. Then she was freer to move around. To crawl inside blackened fireplaces with bricks loose as rotten teeth, so she could shine a flashlight up, then cautiously stand and feel around inside for niches or secret cubby holes that might conceal the lost Book mentioned by both her interview subjects.

She discovered several pieces of bent flatware, a broken picture frame, and some rusted tin cans. Reaching up inside a chimney she heard some animal scuttle farther back inside. Before she could jerk her hand out something latched onto her sleeve, and she jerked the arm out in a panic. A gray squirrel tumbled onto her head, bounced off her chest, and hit the ground. They regarded each other for a stunned moment, then fled in opposite directions.

It could've been a poisonous snake, or a rabid raccoon. She decided to retreat from the ruins and take a look inside the abandoned general store. No question of entering by the front door—the collapsed porch had sealed that off. Around back, on the loading platform, one corner of a heavy sliding door listed from the top track, but it was secured with a massive rusted padlock. She rattled and jerked, but the hasp held tight to the doorframe.

She looked around and espied an old shipping crate with slats intact. Trickling sweat burned her eyes and stung her cuts, scratches, and scrapes as she dragged this around to one side of the building, then heaved it under a window with a broken pane.

When she scrambled up on the box it sagged only a little. The interior of the store was dim, thanks to thick dirt on the window glass. She wrapped one fist in her shirt-tail, knocked out the rest of the broken pane, then poked her head through the knife edged hole.

The long aisles held empty wooden shelves with drifts of litter in between. A thick tablecloth of cobwebs and dust draped a huge butcher block. Something—a grayed, lumpy rag rug?—lay on the floor near it. She shoved at the rotted sash and two more panes fell inward and shattered.

If she could just reach in and undo the lock. But as she slid one arm in to the elbow, the bulky gray rug shifted. She froze. A low buzzing rose from the writhing rug, which seemed to be unfolding itself slowly. Then several individual strands unwound and slithered away, disappearing beneath a dusty shelf.

"Oh my God," she whispered. The low buzzing intensified. A dozen wedge-shaped heads rose from the remaining mass, bobbing and swaying in the gloom.

The grocery store had become a sanctuary for rattlesnakes. So many she couldn't count them. Slowly, carefully, she withdrew her arm and jumped down from the crate, whistling softly for Hercules. Besides an elderly German shepherd, the most lethal weapon she'd brought along was mosquito repellant. That would hardly disperse the Gordian knot of reptiles inside the decaying building.

She tugged at Herc's floppy left ear and whispered, "Let's go. That's all the excitement I can stand in one afternoon."

She kept her eyes fixed on the ground as they walked slowly, carefully, back to the car.

Her room cooled to the temperature of a sauna by evening. Strands of hair stuck to her neck like limp seaweed. At last she pinned it all up, then squinted into the clouded glass of the mirror atop the pine dresser. Sort of retro-washer-woman, but definitely cooler.

Just then a blur flashed past her cheek, whirring like a bumblebee. She crouched, covering her head. It whizzed by again. When she risked a glance between her fingers she saw it was not a giant insect on the rampage, but another of those damned black and red birds. She felt a sinking dread out of proportion to the size of the thing.

"It's just a bird," she muttered. "Small. Harmless." Unlike a nest of rattlers.

All right. But why the *same kind* again, as if she were cursed with a personal albatross? She glanced around for something to shoo it with.

It darted and flapped, caroming off walls and ceiling like a feathered handball. Lucy felt like crawling under the bed or locking herself in the bathroom. But that wouldn't make it go away. She waved both arms, trying to urge it toward the window.

Hercules jumped, barking, as if they were playing a new game.

"Down!" She tripped over dog and furniture following the wheeling, diving bird. Her best hope was that open window.

Where had its screen gone, anyhow? She'd demand a replacement from the front desk soon as she got rid of the flying visitor. Considering the racket they were making, if anyone was staying in the room below she'd soon be hearing about it.

The bird swooped low and her fingers brushed its tail feathers. It feinted away. Then, inches from the open window and freedom, it wheeled away and crashed headlong into the mirror. She heard a faint crack, as if clumsy fingers had just snapped the stem of a crystal goblet. The limp feathered bundle fell to the dresser top and rolled off onto the carpet.

She stood by the bed, panting. Feeling not just shaken but persecuted. Drafted again to play avian undertaker. She sighed and lifted the still, small body by the tail. As she did its breast feathers rose as if alive with breath. She shrieked and dropped it before realizing a breeze had merely ruffled the feathers of the still, dead bird.

She got it into the bathroom and began the now familiar ceremony of the tissue paper shroud. The corpse had the same odd red-on-black coloring, the markings almost like demotics. At least I've discovered *something* here, she thought. Maybe a new species: the flying lemming. Her giggle, a little too high-pitched, echoed in the small tiled room. She flung the body into the wastebasket with relief and shame.

But really, what *was* her strange allure for these even stranger birds? She wasn't wearing flowery perfume, or stepping out with pockets full of sunflower seeds. They must cover the landscape like flies, though so far she'd never noticed a single one outdoors doing any normal bird-like things—hunting for worms, singing, perching in trees. The doomed ones chose to favor her with their agonized final moments. Her hand hovered over the phone, as she debated calling the front desk.

Look, I'm being followed by some crazy red birds. I want it stopped right now! Why can't you control your local fauna?

Cora's harsh spiel on tourists came back to her. She

shook her head and left the handset on the base, then crossed the room to pull down the sash. Tomorrow she'd look the bird up online. If the Internet was up, surely some ornithology site could tell her whether this was a rare species genetically programmed for suicide. Or at least incredibly stupid, even for a bird-brain.

Through the open window, from down the street, she heard music. Fast-paced, happy. The room was sweltering with the window closed. But what if another bird happened by? She reached up to raise the sash again, to cool off the stifling airless box of room.

The music picked up in tempo. Must be Yulee's band playing at the Merry Cat. Suddenly she wanted more than anything to be out, with people, lost in a crowd. Not by herself. Not alone.

She went back to the bathroom and splashed cold water on her face. The small beveled circle over the sink said "disheveled, frazzled girl" was the only phrase to describe her now. Whatever. She glanced at the make-up bag she'd set on the counter above the sink, the one she had yet to use.

"Screw that," she said, rubbing her face dry. Foundation and powder in this humid heat? No way.

"Come on, Herc. Let's go have a drink and hear some tribal music."

The Cat was packed, but she spotted a small empty table near the back. Only one chair, which suited her. She slipped into it and Starr materialized at her elbow. "Oh, hi . . . uh, a Corona, please."

The girl nodded and vanished into the smoky crowd. Lucy turned back to the stage, a rough wooden platform rolled out for the occasion. There, under a dangling light, was the band: three men and a slight woman with long blonde hair who cradled an acoustic bass, the huge rotund instrument dwarfing her. One of the men was hunched

over, changing a broken string on a fiddle. He straightened
and nestled it under his chin. It was Yulee. He raised the
bow with a flourish and a grin, and the audience broke into
applause. The local favorite.

She propped her chin on one hand and waited.

When he drew the bow slowly over the strings there
came a moan, a low prolonged note of mourning. A pause,
then in a flurry he sawed at the instrument; slowly at first,
then faster, as if he meant to cut it in two. She recognized
"Dog House Blues." Not due to great expertise on her part—
only because she'd heard it at a campus party last term.

He made the wooden box wheeze and wail. Made it imitate
the many tongues of a mockingbird, the vibrating croak of
frogs at night, the ringing brass of church bells. Other sounds
too, maddeningly familiar yet not quite identifiable. All of this
seemed unlikely to be produced by a mere wooden box with
strings, and yet—it was.

So entranced was she that she almost overturned a wineglass at her elbow. So Starr had come and gone without her
noticing. Yulee finished in a lightning-fast burst, elbow a
flying blur, and the room erupted in whoops and applause.
She found herself clapping too, until her palms prickled.
What had kept such skill and talent here in this island
purgatory, running sunburned tourists around in old boats?

She sat through a half-dozen more tunes, spellbound.
Then, the craving for noise and people sated, she reached
for her wallet. Starr was across the room, threading the
needle around tightly packed tables. Lucy raised a hand to
catch her eye. On stage, the musicians were setting
instruments down, stretching. Yulee yawned and cracked
his knuckles. Before she could look away, he spotted her.

Damn. Now he'd assume she came to see him. "Crap,"
she muttered. Where was Starr? She pulled out a five and
set the empty wineglass on top of it. She was scraping back
her chair when suddenly there was music again. She

glanced up. Alone on the platform, Yulee had traded the fiddle for a mandolin. He began to sing in a velvety tenor.

> The Devil rode in off the ocean
> Chained lightning to his wheel
> Stepped foot on this damned island
> And the wicked hearts did yield.
> The mothers grabbed their children
> And they all began to cry
> Oh, Lord God please have mercy
> If we all are bound to die . . .

The smoky room, packed with chattering humanity, suddenly fell silent. So abruptly her arms and back prickled. Suddenly she didn't want to hear any more of this strange, folkloric ballad.

She sidled quickly through that dark smoky cave and out into the humid night. Hustling Hercules down the street, not looking back. Because if she did, she might want to return. To sit, and listen, and that could lead to things she didn't want to contemplate. Not now. It wasn't what she'd come for, what she wanted. No, not at all.

TWELVE

The next morning the hotel coffee somehow managed to taste both weak and burnt, but she wasn't ready to risk another scene with Cora. Not even for decent caffeine. At nine she'd call on Miss Eugenie again, go over notes of the last recording to decipher the indistinct passages. She felt anticipation and dread at seeing the old woman again. What next, ectoplasm and floating trumpets? Well, it could all be material.

In the afternoon she'd be free to poke around the library. Maybe inquire about the best way to get rid of rattlesnakes. Ask about those creepy red birds. Hadn't Yulee said something about a woman with boxes of historical records in her home? But the name . . . maybe the librarian would know.

She recalled Yulee as he'd looked on stage the night before. The smoke of a hundred cigarettes, the glow of the dimmed lights forming a hellish orange halo over his head. Sweat gleaming on the sharp-chiseled face under the lone unshaded lightbulb. His shirt soaked, shaggy black hair plastered to his forehead in commas and question marks. The persistence of the image disturbed her. She pushed it away, out of mind.

She marched right back to the front desk. "I'm having trouble with my Internet connection again," she told the pale, gloomy clerk, the black-clad man who'd checked her in on arrival.

He nodded. "Yes, I know. Our connection is out."

She waited expectantly for some good news: like, a projected repair date. He said nothing, only blinked dolefully as if *she* might have the answer.

"Well, when will it be fixed?"

He looked surprised. "It's an island." He spread his hands on the marble-topped counter in apology or surrender. "We have to wait until someone comes over from Gainesville."

Well, at least they were working on it. Sort of. "Uh, right. OK . . . thanks."

Her cell never got good reception in the hotel—horsehair and plaster walls might as well be castle stone. So she slipped into the antique oak-sided phone booth around the corner and pulled out the number for the Day house.

As it rang, she racked her brain for that other woman's name—the one Yulee had tossed out casually as a dog biscuit. Nothing came. She tugged at a springy lock of hair and grimaced. Six rings, seven. Ten. No answer. So it was the library, then. She'd rather not confront the fiddler in his morning-after lair.

Just as she set the receiver back on its hook, a faint tinny hiss escaped the earpiece. She clapped it back to her head. "Hello, Miss Eugenie?"

Silence on the other end.

"Are you there? It's Lucy Fowler."

A harsh puff of breath, then silence.

"Hello . . . hello?"

A low male voice said, "Mrs. Day is not at home."

Lucy paused. The voice sounded familiar. But she'd never seen anyone, aside from Eugenie Lee and the scruffy black chickens at the Day house. Eugenie hadn't mentioned any relatives or guests. Of course someone could have just shown up to visit.

"Yes, I know," she said. "May I please speak to Miz Lee?"

A definitive click. The hum of an empty line.

Charming. Who was this guy? She reached out to dial again. Maybe they'd been cut off. But no—why bother if some soft-spoken joker was just going to hang up on her again? The old woman was expecting her. If today was a bad time, she could always come back later.

But no one answered her second knock, or third. Lucy shifted from foot to foot at the front door, thinking of the elderly woman's hacking cough, her chain smoking. Though it went against all she'd been taught, growing up, at last she tried the doorknob. It turned easily, the door swinging in with the same screech of rust on elderly metal. She stood peering into a dim cool foyer, a staircase rising to her left. Dust motes spun and whirled.

"Miss Eugenie, it's Lucy Fowler. You all right?"

Silence. Only the creaks of an old wooden house settling back on arthritic haunches. She crossed her arms and called out, "Hello?"

No reply.

She couldn't bring herself to step all the way into that gray interior. What if the anonymous voice had been an intruder? Perhaps she'd better call—who? A neighbor, the police? At what number? She wasn't even sure anything was wrong. What idiot burglar would answer the phone, anyhow? Probably Eugenie was just out on a quick errand, the rude jerk a mis-dialed number.

Or maybe, jabbed a nasty whisper in her mind, *the old lady's lying in there, bleeding and helpless. Like you were, remember? While you cool your Sketchers in the foyer. Wouldn't that be just like you, to miss the boat by a few seconds—to misjudge, to leave someone when you could save her? To let the big prize slip out of your butterfingers.*

She gnawed on a knuckle until the pain made her wince. A snail-track of sweat crawled down the map of her back, into the waistband of her shorts.

I can't just go in. Not without being sure something's wrong.

Say what you really mean, the voice prodded.

Someone might be in there.

And who might that be? You mean *him*? The dead one? The—

"Don't say it," she whispered to the empty hallway. Hercules whined and nosed her hand.

Moth! Her relentless mind mocked. *MothMothMoth!*

She spun away from the staircase and fled down the steps. Hercules reached the gate first and stepped in front, leaning his furred bulk against her legs as if to herd her in a different direction. Looking down at his broad brown back, the long black stripe of fur, she stopped, reassured.

His ears were pitched forward, still monitoring the house. They stood regarding it, waiting. And as they hovered in the gateway, like the Gemini twins, she began to feel foolish. Less frightened.

A harsh, guttural growl roared through one open window suddenly, and she flinched.

Oh good grief. Someone was vacuuming.

She laughed and rubbed Herc's ears. No wonder Eugenie hadn't heard her, if she was upstairs cleaning, shoving a rackety old Hoover around that funhouse maze.

And the man's voice on the phone? Wrong number, obviously. True, he'd mentioned the Day name. But it was an old local family, probably stuffed with second and third cousins. She pushed her doubt into a locked room and slammed the door. She was never worth much in the morning. Not before coffee. OK, she'd had coffee. But it was easy to dial one digit wrong, and—

But the voice was familiar. Wasn't it? The whisper insisted through the keyhole of its mental prison. Frankly, she was getting sick of the damned little inner voice. She wished it would fuck off and leave her the hell alone.

"Come on, Herc. You sit on the porch. I won't be long."

The door was still ajar. She pushed it with two fingers and it swung in a few inches. "Hi! It's—"

The vacuum motor roared and coughed.

God, she's deaf. I'll have to go find her, try not to sneak up and give the poor thing a heart attack.

The old house exhaled stale cigarette smoke and black mold. She went left from the foyer, past the stairs, toward the whining roar. Halfway down the hall, she heard a tortured wheeze. Senile gears chewed spasmodically, then fell silent.

As she passed an empty parlor, someone called her name. Eugenie's raspy, faded voice. She turned back. "Sorry, didn't see you." She turned back and stepped into the room. "Could we—"

The old woman was there, sitting upright in a tattered green wing chair. Her eyes rolled up so far the whites glowed in the dim room like the blind chiseled sockets of a statue. Her mouth was open, but from it came not a greeting but a sudden garbled shrieking and howling. As if she were picking up static like an old fashioned radio.

As Lucy stood gaping, paralyzed, the old woman's face took on a dark, purplish hue. Oh my God, Lucy thought, she's choking! Choking on her own tongue and what the hell do I do? I knew it, knew I should've taken that goddamned CPR course last fall. Oh hell, why didn't I—

"Daughter. You are one of us."

The voice jolted Lucy like an electric prod. The same disembodied tones—the same words—she'd heard in the television room at Magnolia House that first day as she'd walked past. It had not been a rerun of *Oprah*, nor her overtaxed imagination. Eugenie Lee had her dial set on a different station, one that had ceased broadcasting a half-century ago. Lucy had the evidence in her bag, in the tiny digital prison of her cell phone, like an insect mired in amber. Ghostly voices, crackling flames, a horrible murderous soundtrack. And this one voice, that of a Creole woman named Solange Koumari, long dead, yet it spoke. To her, Lucy Fowler.

Eugenie Lee's eyes and mouth slowly closed, a grotesque parody of a child's baby doll. The congested blood, the eggplant hue was slowly draining from the wrinkled cheeks. In fact, the old woman seemed to be turning lighter: face, hair, even the shapeless flowered housedress she wore. Her weathered skin took on an ashy hue. And then, as Lucy stood trembling, cold even in the humid musty house shuttered against the unseasonable winter heat, patches of the old woman's skin began to peel. To flake off and blow away like the blown petals of a dying rose.

Lucy's knees buckled as the body of Eugenie Lee slowly faded, disintegrated, down to a heap of bone shards and ash on the faded brocade upholstery. Only when the same spirit broom whisked this last remnant away, too, did Lucy become aware, and distantly ashamed, that a hot trickle of urine was running down one of her quivering legs.

She bolted. Ran blindly through the house, arms thrust before her to ward off anything else that might be concealed in it. She wrestled open the front door, whimpering, and dashed out. Hercules scrambled after, claws clicking and scrabbling on the porch floor. He caught up at the sidewalk, where she'd paused, panting and shaking. She dove at him, hugging his neck, gripping the studded leather of his heavy collar, inhaling the sweet woodsy fur, welcoming the usually forbidden pink tongue on her face.

She had to get out of there, leave that place. For good. And Ibo Key, too? Yes. No. Maybe.

She rose and pulled at Herc's collar to herd him to the car. But now a dark figure blocked her path.

An old black man in worn work greens and heavy, laced work boots knelt on the sidewalk, right in their path. His lips were moving as if in prayer or supplication. Agony etched every line of his ravaged face. Six feet of knotted hemp dangled from his neck. His lips worked on and on, but no sound reached her. She stumbled back and rubbed her face, but when she looked again he was still there.

Her stomach lurched. So it was true—she was losing her mind. She could feel sanity leaving her, fleeing like a refugee from a hurricane-tossed island. She swayed, clutching the gatepost, grateful for its rough splinters, the chipped, chalky paint that flaked and stuck to her palms. Wondering if she should fight off this coming faint to unconsciousness or welcome it. She'd never swooned before, and up till this moment had thought the whole antiquated idea silly.

But she did not pass out. Two horrible details still held her fast to this world.

The first was that the old man's hands were gone. Cut off. Dark blood oozed and dripped from the ragged stumps of wrists, pooling on the cracked concrete walk.

The second was that she could see the sidewalk, the street, and her own car, right *through* him.

"Oh my God," she moaned.

She shoved off from the gatepost and ran, because there seemed no other choice, right *through him* to her car. A momentary coolness as she passed through the spot where he knelt, like the clammy kiss of sea fog on bare skin. As she scrabbled in her bag for keys, she glanced back. He was gone. Then she heard a new sound. A high mewling cry, coming from the empty weed-choked lot next to the Day house. By now she doubted it was anything as prosaic as a stray kitten.

Don't look, she thought grimly. Just *don't*. Get in the fucking car and drive away. But these thoughts weren't being received by her faithful dog, apparently, because he was now slow-motion crawling toward the lot on his belly, ears forward, whining softly.

"Herc, stay!" She lunged for his collar and missed, but

snagged his tail. Got him in a bear hug to drag him back to the Toyota. Out of the corner of one eye she saw, nestled in onion grass and thistles, a ghostly infant clad in a bloody scrap of diaper. Skull smashed, brains leaking a pitiful gray porridge onto dirt and broken, bleached shells. It lay still, eyes closed, yet the high thin keening persisted.

"Uh," she said, all breath punched from her. She didn't wait to see if this tiny specter would vanish like the mutilated old man. Sobbing, cursing, she manhandled Hercules into the passenger seat, wrenched open the driver's door, and slammed all the locks down. She tried, with shaking fingers, to start the car. The key seemed too large for the ignition; it skittered and scraped off the metal circle. She kept jamming it to no avail, her breath rasping in the closed space.

"Calm down," she whispered. Her chest was tight, her arms and legs tingled. "One . . . two . . . three . . . get a grip," she whispered. "Four . . . five . . . six . . . seven . . . can't drive like this. I'll kill somebody . . . eight . . . nine . . ."

No use. She lowered her sweating forehead to the steering wheel. All right then. I may be going crazy. These things can't actually be there. But what kind of emotional aftershock or delayed stress syndrome would make me see the mutilated bodies of people I've never even met? I'm not a soldier, or a war refugee.

Her hands tightened on the steering wheel. "Be brave now," she whispered, the way her mother used to when she had skinned her knee or been stung by a wasp. But she was getting tired of being brave, of always having to get a damned grip.

What to do, then. Treat it as . . . some natural phenomenon, a thing to be observed and studied. If she could find the guts not to run screaming away. Because if it were a hallucination—or even actually a whole pack of chain-rattling ghosts—then what she saw couldn't hurt her, right?

Ghosts were not really there. They were more like . . . pictures in the air. An old DVD someone had forgotten to turn off.

She took a deep breath. Calm down, think. Then decide what's real, and what's not. And what, if anything, could be done about it.

Otherwise, I will go crazy. For real.

She took a few more slow, deep breaths, making sure to exhale just as deeply to avoid hyperventilating. The overwhelming suffocation eased. Hercules whined and licked her arm over the seat. After a minute or two she was able to start the car and drive slowly, carefully back to the hotel. All the way she kept her eyes firmly fixed on the road, expecting some new, horrific tableau to pop up on the faded center line.

By the time she finally parked in front of the Island House Inn, her hands were cramped, aching claws, still rigidly, painfully locked on the steering wheel.

THIRTEEN

In the end, she did not go to the library. Nor try to tell anyone about her experience at the Day house. Who would listen? Anyhow, she couldn't seem to get up off the bed in her hotel room. Staring at the ceiling, at a lopsided oval water stain like a Venetian mask, she narrowed her eyes. Yes, a grimacing carnival mask. Leering, twisted, evil. Obviously male. It seemed familiar, one she'd seen before. Somewhere.

She rolled her head to one side on the pillow and closed her eyes. Jesus. Seeing portents on old plaster in need of a coat of latex. I *am* losing it. All her self-reassurance about calm observation, detached study, of harmless phenomena in the air. What good did that do if her shattered, traitorous mind wouldn't get with the program? Maybe she didn't have the guts to face her problems. The courage, the control.

Ever since the night Tim Carling had metamorphosed from a shy fellow student into a psychotic rapist, dragged her from the car and thrown her down on a deserted stretch of cracked asphalt, she'd lost all control: of emotions, actions, thoughts. Of her whole fucking life. Now she was afraid to be alone, afraid to go out, afraid of the dark, afraid to close her eyes and go to sleep. Soon she'd be afraid to wake up and face the sunrise.

Maybe Detective Reshenko was right, maybe I do need help. More than a project on this haunted, hopeless island can offer. Therapy. Drugs. The whole deal. Maybe it *is* PTSD. She laughed bitterly. Too bad I couldn't delay it a little longer!

Her laugh sounded more like a sob. Hercules rose and licked her out-flung hand. She did feel, in a way, as if she'd been through a war. But no one got awarded a medal just for going on living.

So she maybe should do what Reshenko suggested. Leave here, go home. Join a support group. But the recollection of that expectant circle of other stricken faces nodding, listening gravely, when she'd gone just that one time had made her shiver. The other victims, saving her a seat in the circle.

Maybe group wasn't for her. Okay, then. See somebody alone. Before her final, winter term started. Or else how would she make it through the next semester, much less the rest of her life?

Yes. Yes, but. If she left, she'd still lack the last piece of history needed to finish her dissertation. And she knew, somehow, with a sinking certainty, that if she didn't get her shit together now, her unfinished dissertation would sit on a shelf. Until finally it became a dust-coated paper brick, an embarrassment to be stuffed in a drawer or a box. Whisked out of sight like the mad wife in the attic in *Jane Eyre*. Good only for a time capsule.

"Shit," she whispered. That terrible sense of a sudden fun-ride drop, the trajectory of a comet of fear traversing her guts, shooting sickeningly from her heart down her legs, to her feet and back. She drew her knees up. Oh good, Lucy—already assuming the fetal position. She hugged her legs more tightly, breathed faster. Back home, in this kind of shape? That would look great to Hal, other students, to Dr. Grove and the faculty, even strangers on the street. *Her? Oh yeah, that's Lucy Fowler. Sad case. Can't go out to buy milk without a big dog to protect her. Too bad, she seemed competent at first, but now . . .*

She'd be handicapped, groping in the dark, suddenly gone blind . . . though she was pretty sure the most timid blind person on earth had lots more gumption. She'd be a slow-witted turtle stranded in the middle of a busy highway, waiting for the fatal tire with her name on it, as the rest of the world whizzed by.

A blind turtle. A conversion disorder. What the fuck?

She started to laugh again. What a ridiculously mixed metaphor, that self-pitying image. Was she really slow-witted, dull, overwhelmed—stupid? Bullshit. That wasn't her at all. Anger jerked her upright so quickly her head reeled.

OK then, a tortoise. Like in the fable her mother used to read to her. It'd seemed a little silly even then. And boring: *Slow and steady wins the race.* Plenty of time to lose it later, and maybe I will in the end. But I'm not crazy yet. Not stupid either. I might be a coward. But I've come this far. All I have to do is hold on a bit longer, get what I came for, then run like hell back to Pottsburg. Where I can spend seven nights a week in therapy. Scream, cry, and climb the walls.

But not yet. Not yet.

She pulled herself from the bed, slowly, carefully, like an artist's mad construction pieced from hollow birds' bones, held together with wire and glue.

Maybe the first step was simply to go out again. Just a short walk. Without the crutch of a canine escort. The idea made her breathless.

Right. All the more reason to fucking *do it.*

The front desk was deserted when she slipped through the lobby. The tiny hotel dining room dark, french doors closed and locked. No matter. Her mission was to keep moving forward, like a shark. To move and breathe, onward. Not to crawl back into bed and cocoon in the sheets like a caterpillar waiting on a pair of stunted wings that would never unfurl.

Caterpillar. Cocoon. Moth. Ugh.

"Oh no, you don't." She shook her head. "None of that." She walked faster, eyes fixed on the sidewalk, timing her breaths, stepping over the cracks. The air felt cooler, less humid. Maybe that freak heat wave was breaking. She thought of going back to the Merry Cat. A few people there were the closest thing she had to friends here. But no, she wasn't up for a blast of Cora's energetic wrath right now. Instead she headed toward the south side of the island, away from Ibo City. Which seemed quiet, even by its own standards. Aside from the rare whoosh of a passing car, she heard only muffled conversation, and faint TV noise from the shops and houses she passed. Once, a snatch of a weather report, something about a tropical storm in the Florida Straits. Well, that was pretty far away. And anyhow, she thought, 'tis the season for those now. Hurricanes usually fizzled out before making landfall, anyhow.

When she passed anyone, she kept her gaze on the sidewalk. After a few blocks, her breathing slowed and she stopped counting. The pinched fright-lines that had tightened her face loosened. Another mile, and asphalt gave way to marl, the crushed white clamshell paving that still smelled of the sea. Buildings were fewer, farther apart. They looked a good deal older than in Ibo City. Mostly clapboard, some finished with stucco-like stuff called tabby—wood coated with a mixture of crushed seashells, lime, and water.

The town librarian had told her about that. But she'd remarked that very few of those structures were left on the island. Yet she counted a couple dozen on this stretch alone. Dreary, blocky little bungalows like the old, cramped coal-company housing back in Pottsburg. Strange. Hadn't Nick Yulee said most of the locals out here lived in trailers? Yet she hadn't seen a single mobile home, aside from the vintage, immaculate aluminum Airstream camper in one driveway.

She walked on. The lowering winter light gathered and

pooled on the edges of leaves, hung glowing, unearthly, ready to drip molten silver. Branches shook and clashed in the slight breeze like muffled chimes, as if summoning all in hearing to attend some ethereal gathering.

She crossed her arms and walked faster. Ought to go back soon. But it felt good just to be out, on her own. Not cowering in a small room. Not a quivering loser.

Strange, no cars sat before the houses out here. As if everyone on this side were away on vacation. She did see one parked in front of a yellow clapboard bungalow. In its backyard children ran and played, shouting, swinging on an old tire. Their happy cries floated away on the dusk like the calls of nesting birds. Somebody at this place was obviously a collector. The car was a shiny, perfectly preserved Oldsmobile Rocket 88. The squealing children ran past through the front yard, not even looking her way when she paused to admire it. She stood and watched for a moment, since they didn't seem to mind, or even notice.

Finally she walked on, the crushed shells cracking under her sandals. Another block, and the houses disappeared altogether. Brush and palmetto scrub lined the road, tangled with vines, full of shadows. It must be getting late, she thought. Better turn back. Guess I've been out longer than I meant to be. Still, the fact that she'd walked alone, for the most part without fear, made her reluctant to stop yet. As if turning back would break her concentration. Break the spell.

The road narrowed. Another house sat up ahead, larger than the rest. In front of it stood a mule hitched to a battered green wagon. Now that was weird. Like some kind of re-enactment, as if she'd stumbled into Colonial Williamsburg or something. As she drew nearer, a tall, dark-haired man came out, unhitched the reins, and swung up to the creaking buckboard seat.

Something was odd about him, too.

The screen door slammed. A young woman came down

the front steps and called out, "Don't forget my package, hear?" She stood with hands on hips, watching the mule plod sullenly off, hooves kicking up pale plumes of dust. The sunburnt man's heavily-muscled forearms flicked the reins as he passed Lucy without a glance in her direction. People here sure don't mind being rude, she thought.

The woman stooped to yank up a lone dandelion straggling beside the tidy brick walk. And as she studied that bent back, the sturdy laced shoes, Lucy realized what seemed so out of place: their clothes.

The man had been dressed in loose-fitting trousers and homely plaid button-down shirt. Suspenders. OK, not so odd. But he'd also worn a hat—a battered fedora. Just like the one her grandfather sported in the black and white photos from her parents' house, now stored in a shoe box in her apartment. In these he always stood stiffly facing the camera, head on. In later ones holding her own baby-small hand, engulfing it in his huge liver-spotted one, face shaded by the hat's felt brim.

She slowed and considered greeting the woman, who wore a gingham house dress like the faded ones Eugenie Lee favored. Except she wasn't old like Eugenie. Her chunky-heeled shoes were neatly laced, and she had a rolled fifties-style perm, like you saw on reruns of *I Love Lucy*. Those upswept cat-eye glasses mimicked the ones her own grandmother, a fashion resister, had worn till she died. She'd called the rhinestone-studded frames her "Cadillac eyes."

Both grandparents, so old by the time she came along, had clung stubbornly to these stodgy styles; a great source of embarrassment to Lucy as a child. They'd always worn those clothes, those shoes, those glasses, more or less. Yet . . . yet here it all looked new. Who would've thought she'd stumble onto vintage clothing freaks in the middle of nowhere. Maybe they'd lucked onto a chestful in their attic. Or ordered them off eBay.

But the young couple looked comfortable, not self-consciously trendy, not costumed from a funky online thrift shop.

It nagged at her. Jarred somehow the slowly-returning faith that she could still make sense of the world. A new, sharp elbow in her belief, so recently shaken, that time was linear and properly placed, not filled with lurking phantoms waiting to pop out and shove ugliness and terror in her face. Or reach out from the bland digital box of an iPhone. Or turn a sickly old woman into a one-way radio made of flesh and blood, then rearrange the very atoms of her being into something as wispy as wheat chaff blown across a field.

Lucy, struck dumb in the middle of the road, realized she was gawking like a tourist at an ordinary person in front of an ordinary house. If the woman noticed, she gave no sign. A final tug at the weed, and she chucked it out into the yard to wither and die. Then dusted her hands, straightened, smoothed her apron, and looked up. Directly at Lucy, who flinched—a voyeur caught in the act.

"Oh, uh, hello," she said to the woman. "Sorry, I didn't mean to—"

But the quaintly dressed housewife looked right through her. Sighed once, heavily, into the rosy, faintly shimmering air. Without a word, she turned away and went back inside.

God, some of the people on this island were beyond rude.

Disgusted, Lucy started walking again, slowly, as if moving underwater. The very air had substance now, and she was forced to push against it, willing her legs to move on. Uneasily aware she was alone, that Hercules was shut away in her room. Though why she felt threatened now was not clear.

Go back, she decided. Enough for one day. She turned around.

The road back to town was gone, enveloped in a low, hazy fog. Even the houses she'd just passed were no longer visible. To the east the glow intensified, as if the sun were setting behind all that haze. Impossible, she thought. It's got to be too early for sunset. And not only that: back toward town meant heading *east*.

So it would have to be a rising sun. But that was even more impossible.

She froze, paralyzed by confusion. The fog on the road gathered itself like a live thing and rolled forward to meet her, covering trees, bushes, the ground. The familiar, suffocating fear returned with a cattle prod jolt. The sudden dropping sensation, that hated carnival ride jerk. She looked around for reassurance, the sight of just one normal, unconcerned person. The road was empty but for her. The fog still backlit, its deep rose tint now shading to pink orange, as if she moved through an early morning instead of late afternoon.

The first fingers of mist reached her, clammy tentacles that made her skin crawl. The tourniquet around her chest tightened, released. Her heart, with each erratic beat thrummed *run . . . run. . . run*. She'd had enough such attacks in the last few weeks to know they passed after a few minutes. Stranded in this strange, lonely spot she felt no better for the reminder.

I need help, she thought. If I have to walk into that blind clammy fog to get to the hotel again, I'll just start screaming.

She glanced back at the yellow house with the prim yard. The front door stood ajar. Had it been open before? Who cared? It looked like an invitation. Compared to this shifting, roiling landscape, it looked . . . safe.

Without another thought she crossed the perfectly manicured lawn, climbed the stairs to its porch, and stepped inside.

The front room, with its angular blond furniture and gleaming china figurines of black impalas and reclining panthers looked tidy as a vintage *House Beautiful* cover. The pine floor had been scrubbed and bleached to bone whiteness, punctuated with handmade rag rugs. By the front window stood a cedar tree anchored in a bucket, hung with silver tinsel and red and green glass balls, lighted with waterfilled glass tubes that bubbled and winked.

Wow. Someone was having a real Norman Rockwell Christmas.

And the furniture . . . "Danish Modern," she murmured wonderingly. When she was two, she'd cut her lip falling against the sharp corner of a similar blond wood coffee table at her grandparents' house, and her parents had rushed her to the ER in a panic for stitches. A faint scar still marred one corner of her mouth. Yet the old folks had kept the coffee table, and she'd skirted it with fear from that day forward. She'd seen it again a couple years ago, battered, cigarette scarred, and dusty, when she'd cleaned out her father's attic.

These pieces didn't look old, though. The fair wood gleamed wax smooth, no dents or burns or waterglass rings.

"Hello?" she called, uncertain how she was going to explain her presence, but unwilling to go back out into that creeping fog. She crossed the living room and passed through an archway, running one hand over the cool, impersonal surface of a retro end table that was all right angles.

From behind louvered swinging doors came the splash of water, a clang of heavy pots, the careful clink of glass on glass, the wet slap of a dishcloth. She felt drawn toward this homely clatter, which blended perfectly with the furniture, the house, and her childhood memories. Taking a deep breath, she walked through.

Sunlight streamed through square windows topped by ruffled valences. On one sill stood a ceramic rooster, colorful, red-crested, stiffly poised to announce the dawn. Nothing like the scruffy black chickens at the Day house. The counters were blue and white tiled. Next to them a deep white-enameled sink shone like a hospital basin. A Hoosier cabinet held dishes, the same Apple Blossom pattern her mother had inherited. Plates and coffee cups were set to dry on striped cotton dishtowels.

And there was the woman she'd seen outside waving the man off on his plodding way toward town. She was folding laundry, humming a tune. A black leather satchel like an old-fashioned doctor's bag slumped on the pine table.

This woman looked strong and capable. Sure of herself. She would know what to do, with or without a college degree. Would know instantly what was real and what was not. She'd be full of practical advice for anyone smart enough to take it.

"Excuse me." Her voice quavered. "I, uh, don't mean to startle you but . . . well, I'm lost. OK, not exactly lost, but sick, or . . . I don't want to be a bother, but—"

The woman didn't look up. Didn't scowl or laugh or order her out. Just kept humming and folding, folding and humming.

"*Please*." She felt mortified at the pleading note creeping into her voice. "Could you just—" She reached out to stop the robotic lift, fold, and stack. Her hand passed through the woman's sleeve, arm, hand, even the dangling pair of pants half-folded. A vague tingling, as if she'd lowered her hand into a fish bowl teeming with tadpoles.

She lost her balance and stumbled, as if the floor had shifted beneath her feet. She recoiled, staring at her own hand in horror. *Impossible.* When she tried again her outstretched fingers disappeared *into* the print clad back as if it were a pool of floral patterned rainwater. The same sensation, as if the atoms of surrounding flesh and cloth were colliding with hers.

She stepped back, fingers pressed hard to her mouth to seal off a scream. The woman calmly smoothed the last shirt, then gathered the neat stacks and turned from the table.

Now she did cry out.

Before her stood Esther Day, though a much younger edition. Face unlined, eyes bright, but undeniably the same blunt, plain features, unmolested by time and gravity. And then the . . . ghost? . . . shifted her burden, smoothed her hair, and walked right through Lucy.

A knock on the door halted her. She turned toward the sound and Lucy saw anticipation or perhaps apprehension, cloud the slightly bulging blue eyes. The Esther ghost set the laundry back on the table and smoothed her already tidy hair again. Brushed invisible lint and wrinkles from skirt and apron, biting at her lips until they blushed a darker red. Walked to the kitchen door, waited a few deliberate seconds, then opened it. A handsome light-skinned black man, young, tall, and broad-shouldered, stood on the back stoop. Without a word he stepped inside.

The midwife smiled and embraced him. He gripped her upper arms as one would a child's, and gently but firmly pushed her an arm's length away.

"Can't come here any more, Esther," he said. "It's not right. We both know it."

She frowned. "What? No, we already talked about—"

"I know, I know. Not like I just now figured that out. Been weighing on me a long while. You got a husband. I'll be off to school in Tallahassee come next September, and . . . It's *dangerous*. Just got to stop."

"But Julian, you can't! You promised me the—I mean, didn't we have a wonderful time? I look forward to your visits. It's all I have to look forward to. And the Book—oh, never mind that. It's not important. Though it would mean a great deal to . . . to my work."

He looked even more troubled. "I know what you said 'bout that, about bringing the island up to date. Scientific. Progressive. Like me studying agriculture instead of just dropping beans in the dirt for some cracker farmer. Sounds like sense."

She smiled.

He shook his head and sighed. "Esther, the Book—it's

my Mama's. I never go against her wishes. Nor lie to her. I tried to sneak it out once, but she came inside just as I laid a hand on the cover. Like she *knew*. Never said a word, but—I won't try again."

"Oh, never mind. I don't care about that, darling!" Esther broke from his grip and clasped his waist. Her averted face looked cool, calculating. "Forget about the silly old thing. Just don't leave me now, not to him. Why can't you understand! It's not so much the Book now. I'm afraid. See, I—I'm going to have a baby. And I don't know—what'll he do when he finds out, if it's not his child, but yours?"

Julian's eyes widened. "What? But you said he never touches you, that he can't even—and you knowing all that real medicine, I thought what we did, that it was safe. That you wouldn't allow this to happen. Oh, Jesus God Almighty," he whispered. "I'm a dead man." He pushed her away roughly.

She plucked at his shirt. "He'll kill me when he finds out! I have to get rid of it. To do that safely—to do it myself . . . there must be a foolproof way. In the Book."

He flung her hands off and stumbled to the still-open door. When he clutched the crocheted lace that curtained its window, it tore away in his hand. She rushed after, stopping at the doorway, gazing out. He was already a distant figure, fleeing into a dark stand of trees, a white scrap of curtain trailing from one fist.

Esther laid a shaking hand on the knob, as if to pull the door shut. One hand stroked the torn curtain, the last thing Julian Koumari had touched. Suddenly she turned away, expression flickering from studied anguish, to rage, and then—with almost eerie speed—back to the same cool calculation as before.

She gripped the scalloped neckline of her house dress in both hands and wrenched until the material tore raggedly. Then took a deep breath, closed her eyes, and

raked her unpainted nails over the smooth white flesh of
face and breasts. Long deep scratches appeared, pink
furrows that began to ooze blood. Finally she hiked up her
long skirt, jerked white cotton underwear down, and
stepped out of them. She blotted her lacerated chest with
these, until the pristine cotton bloomed with red splotches.

She gripped the cloth for a moment in clenched hands,
with a distracted look. Then dropped the stained scrap and
turned to survey the kitchen. A hand shot out. She swept the
neat stacks of folded laundry off the table. Then, a pair of
ceramic salt and pepper shakers shaped like tomatoes, which
shattered against the gas stove. Next a knobby milkglass
vase holding a Christmas-red amaryllis. And finally a pair of
the Apple Blossom cups, which exploded on the checker-
board tile floor, spraying multi-colored shrapnel.

Panting, Esther surveyed the mess of water, clotted spices,
cloth, and gleaming shards. She nodded. Then, lips working as
if she were trying to decide which expression now fit these
circumstances, she turned back to the open doorway. Stopped
short, and raised a hand to cover her mouth.

Lucy followed her startled gaze.

Now on the stoop stood not Julian but a lanky teenage
girl in a simple white uniform, a red bandanna around her
hair. Her skin was an exquisite shade of cinnamon and
cream, her face a study in confusion and dread. She looked
in at the mess, then back at Day.

"Mrs. Esther, why you do that?" The girl's tone was
tentative, but hoarse, deeper than you'd expect. Add a few
hundred thousand cigarettes, and it could be the voice of . . .
Eugenie Lee. The midwife's teenaged assistant.

The two stared at each other, then Esther Day brushed
past the trembling girl. She staggered a few steps out into
the side yard, doubled over, clutching her stomach, and
screamed. A wordless keening wail that made both Eugenie
and Lucy flinch.

Two neighbors came running. The man, a napkin flapping from the neck of his stained T-shirt, looked annoyed. The woman wore an expression of mingled fear and hopeful curiosity. Soon a third man appeared in the yard, suspenders dangling, carrying a shotgun. A heavyset older woman trailed him.

"Hell, what's all this racket?" he grumbled. When he spotted Esther rending her hair into a rat's nest, he stopped abruptly. "Miz *Day*?" he breathed, gaping at the bloodstained dress, the clawed breasts spilling from it. "What ails you?"

She shook her head and screamed like a deranged bird. The man circled her, free hand making ineffectual shushing motions. During his third orbit the neighbor women held a whispered conference. The oldest, with a head full of pincurls and the face of a rouged pig, stepped forward and slapped the midwife's face.

"It was a man. A big nigger," Esther blubbered, a hand-shaped bruise already rising on her cheek beneath the smears of blood and tangled hair. She clutched at the shreds of her dress, as if just realizing how exposed she was. "He . . . he forced me! I thought he was gonna k-kill me." She slumped to the grass, moaning.

Eugenie Lee, who'd been hovering by the kitchen stoop, rushed out toward them. No one paid any attention; all eyes were still on Day. Lucy followed the girl into the yard.

Between breaths she said, "Beg pardon, mister, missus. I seen it all. But that were just Julian, Julian Koumari. From Revelation. He come like always, to, uh"—she cut her eyes briefly at the huddled midwife, then stammered on—"to chop the wood and haul water, like always on Thursdays. But Julian would never hurt no woman—white nor black. Especially Mrs. Esther! Why, you all *know* Julian."

Both men's eyes narrowed. The women whispered to each other again, shaking heads.

"She's right," Lucy said. "I saw what happened too."

No one even looked her way. They really can't see or hear me, she marveled.

But Eugenie had stuttered to a halt, her anguished expression one of sudden, perfect comprehension. Judging by Esther's furious glare from beneath sweat basted hair, her assistant had made a huge mistake. Jumped in at the wrong place, given the wrong information, and way too much of it.

This was all real. Lucy understood that now. *She* was the ghost, not they.

But how had she stepped back into a morning in 1950s Florida? And why, after dismissing these pictures in the air as harmless hallucinations, was she now trapped inside one herself? Yet she could forget her own predicament while caught up in this strange, twilight drama of past and present. Moving in what must be some sort of spirit realm, some alternate universe not explained even by string theory, she'd become a specter invisible even to its ghosts.

Her mind took off again, sorting impressions and ideas like pieces of a jigsaw puzzle. Esther Day had claimed she had no children. Yet she'd just told Julian Koumari she was expecting. Of course, any number of things could explain that. She'd miscarried or aborted. Or, lacking the resolve or skill to perform a procedure on herself, gone on to have the child, which then had died of some illness. Or perhaps— and this thought made Lucy shiver—she'd killed it after giving birth?

Now what would happen to Julian Koumari, once the town decided he'd fathered a black baby on a white woman, willing or otherwise? A white, *married* woman. Good references from Eugenie Lee wouldn't mean spit. In this time, all that *would* matter was that he was black, and had left proof of his encroachment on a white man's property.

Her attention was suddenly pulled back to the passion

play in the side yard. Eugenie was wringing her hands,
trying to recover her mistake. "Oh, please . . . look here
now. He didn't do Miss Esther that way. She so hurt and
scared, she just mistaken. It weren't Julian . . . maybe a . . .
a stranger. Y'all folks *know* him!"

It had to take tremendous courage for her to speak so
insistently to white adults who'd expect her to keep her eyes
lowered and answer "no'm" or "yessir."

But the skinny teenager stood her ground, trembling, as
a crowd of angry whites gathered. Men who'd been getting
ready for work, or were already passing by on their way
into town, in coveralls or white rubber watermen's boots,
bound for the sawmill or a fishing boat.

Soon more women left kitchens and vegetable gardens
and drifted up, chattering. A few took hold of Esther Day,
clucking, shaking heads over the shredded print dress, the
lacerated skin. They hoisted her and steered her into the
house. A few men ran back to houses or trucks or wagons,
and returned with guns and pipes and coiled rope. A farmer
in overalls led two sad-eyed dogs that bayed mournfully,
straining at their leashes. "I say we find him and string him
up," he shouted.

"Burn him, more like," said a waterman, spitting in the
well tended grass.

"Burn the whole fucking place down," growled a fat
man with shaving soap still flecked on his wobbling chins.

They gestured and argued. Then pointed south toward
Revelation.

Eugenie Lee stood apart from the mob as it surged and
ebbed, finally dividing like some deadly amoeba. Perhaps
she was too frightened to even think of hiding. Or perhaps
she understood, with the instinct of the small and hunted,
the erasing power of complete stillness. She stood alone
and tearful, mouth working soundlessly, listening to the
violent talk. Suddenly, she turned and bolted into the

woods across the shell-paved road, shoving through tangled grapevine and palmetto. Seeing her take flight, Lucy knew it was true. She was witnessing the beginning of the end for Revelation.

FOURTEEN

Scraps of mist floated past like magician's scarves as the mob reached the fishing pier outside town. A steady stream of men were converging there, too, in battered Ford pickups or hump-backed Chevys. Or on foot. Or, in a couple of cases, by wagon. They milled about slapping backs, punching shoulders, sorting lengths of rope, loading shotguns and rifles and pistols as if preparing for a turkey shoot. One kept snapping a bullwhip. It was a bizarre mix of carnival and mob.

Drawn against her will, Lucy had followed in their dusty wake. Seeing their growing menace made her glad to be invisible. She hovered, watching with increasing dread, wondering what to do. Or whether, in this existence and form she could do anything at all.

A sudden hush fell over the assembly, as if an official dignitary had just arrived. A mule-drawn wagon rolled to a stop at the edge of the crowd. The same one driven by the man she'd seen earlier in front of the Day house as he'd waved goodbye to Esther with one hand while the other slapped reins on the mule's rump.

He'd been smiling then, this thick, bear-like fellow with tightly muscled forearms and a beer gut, the handsome face marred by broken capillaries on cheeks and nose, and the crooked, bitter cast to the mouth. His narrowed eyes were cold and opaque as blue glass marbles. Though he gruffly greeted those who surged forward to offer sympathy and vengeance, she doubted he really saw them. But he looked fully capable of killing, without apology or guilt, anyone or anything unfortunate enough to get in his way.

Jars and jugs of clear spirits were passed around with ritual solemnity. A few stragglers joined the crowd. One was a slight, well-dressed fellow who didn't speak to anyone, but stood apart, faintly smiling, as if this were a play he'd already seen—one whose ending he knew, and had enjoyed.

He seemed familiar.

When he turned to look her way, she caught her breath. It was the madman from the Magnolia House visitors' room. He nodded and tipped his gray fedora. She understood then that he alone of all those present could actually see her.

The bottles passed hand to hand. A few skiffs were launched from the ramp of hard packed clay, while larger oyster and shrimp boats cast off from dockside moorings. One bird-dog reminded her of Nick Yulee's boat. She stepped closer to it, putting more distance between herself and the slight man in gray suit and vest.

Two sweating unshaven old boys in coveralls and rubber boots loaded the boat with rope and cans of gasoline, assisted by a teenager with acne and an adenoidal whine.

Was there any way to stop this tragedy? Maybe doing so would bring some other disaster to the future—or rather, her present-day world. Yet how could she just stand by, if . . . She stepped down into the boat, thinking, *Maybe when we arrive I can warn the people first.* Somehow. Yet she already knew that no one had been able to do that. It was sixty years too late to avert this massacre because in reality it had already happened.

Still she felt a faint hope. She had nothing else. No idea of how to get back to her present, the hotel room, her dog. Her life. But if she thought about all that right now, she might go insane.

The others in the boat paid no mind when she sat beside

the boy, who stank of sweat, dirty socks, and spoiled fish. They cast off, joining the ragged flotilla straggling over the water, rowing or running motors slow and quiet. The boats hugged the shore without running aground on shoals or oyster beds. She supposed the vigilantes intended to land at Revelation hidden by the trees and brush through which she'd first spotted the ruins from Nick Yulee's speeding bird-dog.

No wonder those crumbling foundations had made him uneasy. No doubt his grandfather, perhaps even his father, was one of these drunken avengers. Maybe the old man used to set little Nick on his knee and chortle, saying, "Let Grandaddy tell you about the time we gave the niggers a lesson to remember."

A bottle of whiskey was tossed back and forth between several boats. A man hissed curses as he fumbled and almost lost it in the murky water. She thought of her phone, on the desk back in her hotel room. Not that she could've called anyone now. But her cell held the final sounds of Revelation's life. What would become of that recording, what would the finders make of it, if she wasn't ever able to return?

Surely you'd need to be more than drunk, she decided. Mind-numbingly, brutally soaked in alcohol, to do what these men were muttering about. Having wives, children, brothers, parents of their own, how could they? Or was it exactly what those wives and sisters and mothers expected, even demanded of them?

She stood up cautiously, expecting she might rock the small craft. But perhaps she was weightless as well, for it didn't list at all.

Would a warning from the future impress the mob? It might look ridiculous to pose like Cassandra in a rowboat, but what the hell. Lucy raised her arms and shouted, "Stop! Go back! What you're planning is wrong, evil. You'll suffer for it later. Be damned by the whole world. By your own children. It's murder, not justice. *Because nothing happened the way she said!"*

Wind whipped hair into her face and mouth until she choked on it. The boat lurched and she grabbed the boy's shoulder to keep from falling overboard. He didn't look up, just twitched as if bothered by a mosquito.

They obviously didn't see or hear her. Her fingers clutched nothing but air. Yet she felt queasy. Did ghosts get seasick?

Was that what she was now—a ghost?

No one gave her an awed glance, or folded a hand and extended pointer and pinky in the age-old sign to ward off the evil eye. No one crossed themselves, or even paused with paddle raised in mid-stroke, mouth agape. No engines throttled back. The spotty teenager she'd leaned on frowned and scratched that shoulder with dirty nails.

I'm not here for them at all, she thought, sinking back onto the salt-damped floorboards. All I can do is bear witness, while taken on a tour of Hell.

But then, why are they so real to me?

A sudden jolt threw her into the slimy bilge, where the smells of rotting fish scales, old beer, and stale piss made her want to vomit. As the hull grated roughly on sand, her forehead struck the forward bench seat. Or rather, passed into the damp wood, leaving her with a faint, tingling impression of splinters and flaking paint. Yet she felt no pain. Scrambling up as the others leapt to their feet, she spotted a white strip of beach; white-washed buildings past the trees. The south side of Ibo Key.

Madness had come to Revelation.

A stout red-faced man barked orders at the arriving boats. "Sam, pull your skiff back out. Bo Franklin! Early Watson! Y'all belong to anchor out there. You other boys go pick 'em up. And don't get my damned guns wet, hear?"

Lucy scrambled out just before the skiff launched again. She stood on the beach as all around her men unloaded firearms and work-scarred hatchets and slithering coils of rope. Others were dragged up and down the shore in an awkward dance by panting hounds whose yelps and howls were muffled with makeshift rag muzzles. The slobbering, lunging dogs dug furrows in the sand, eager to begin the hunt. One slipped his muzzle and loosed a long, mournful howl.

The sound broke the spell that bound her. Sent her running toward the cluster of buildings glimpsed through the trees.

She emerged from the woods and stumbled around the side of a two-story white clapboard house, the building closest. She hung on one porch post gasping for breath. Over the front door a sign creaked and swayed in the salt-tangy breeze: FLOWERS' GROCERY DRY GOODS. The painted letters were all there now, sharp and clear. Two big display windows were outlined with strands of big red and green Christmas lights. A man swept the porch slowly, methodically, whistling "Rudolph the Red-Nosed Reindeer." Something about him seemed strange. After a moment she realized what: he was white.

Wait, she thought. Isn't this Revelation, the all-black community targeted by an approaching mob? Then she remembered Eugenie Lee had said a white man in town had helped some escape. That was why a few had lived to tell what happened and warn others not to come back.

"*Mr. Otis Flowers, who run the general store. He took in women and children. Hid us under the floorboards, in the basement, till the lumber train come through and they pulled us aboard. He counted on those crackers not to burn him out, 'cause he was white. They would've, in a minute, did they know who was hid in his cellar.*"

Perhaps Flowers, given warning, could stop the massacre before it began. Reason with the mob before the killing started and they got an unquenchable taste for blood. But how could she make him see and hear her? No one else had.

Except the gray suited man on the edge of the crowd. The one she'd first encountered in Magnolia House. Who was he? What did he want from her?

The storekeeper gave a final flick of the palmetto-fiber broom, leaned it against the railing, and stepped inside. She looked up and down the neat broad street, paved with crushed white shells, lined with other white-painted buildings, curtained windows decorated with flower boxes. Neat cottages. A barber shop. A hardware and feed store. The full blue skirt of a woman's dress was just disappearing into the small bakery. Past that rose two small churches.

The place seemed a ghost town already, probably because the men would already be off at work. In the sawmill, or logging the woods, or out on the Gulf, fishing.

A faint chorus of baying brought her up sharply. Move, damn it, she thought.

A black-suited man of forty or so, in clerical collar, was just stepping out of the nearest church, white clapboard with a small bell tower. *AFRICAN METHODIST EPISCOPAL CHURCH, Services 8 AM Wednesday and Sunday,* read the hand-painted sign anchored in a neat emerald square of winter rye. A minister was a man of God, more likely to believe in Good and Evil, even of things beyond normal understanding. Perhaps he would be more receptive to perceiving a woman who at the moment was apparently neither entirely flesh and blood, nor spirit?

She dashed out into the street. "Reverend? Sir! Listen, please!"

He was chatting with an elderly light-skinned woman in a white blouse and polka-dot skirt, her felt hat trimmed with pheasant feathers. Behind them stood a crèche. Its wooden lean-to sheltered plaster figures of a dark skinned Mary and Joseph. The stout woman was setting the baby

Jesus carefully in its wooden, straw filled manger. The baby's shiny plaster face was white with ruddy pink cheeks. Lucy caught the scent of orange blossom perfume even before she reached them.

". . . so Deacon Johnson told me, you best not miss that supper meeting." Her high girlish voice was at odds with the solid, corseted figure.

"Thank you for offering, Sister Kellam." The minister had smooth mahogany-hued skin, a kind but careworn face, and stooped shoulders. Laugh lines bracketed his mouth, but his eyes looked red-rimmed, sad. "I'd hoped to count on you. This not being Atlanta or Washington, news of young Dr. King's work sounds like a fairy tale from a far-off country."

"Amen, brother." The woman turned back to him, Baby Jesus safely tucked in.

"But the time is at hand. The word must be spread," he added. "Shout it from the rooftops if that's all we can do. Your presence will be a blessing, as always." He grinned. "And so will your sweet potato pie."

She laughed and wobbled off on black patent high heels that looked a bit too small.

The minister turned back to look at the crèche for a moment, then sighed. He patted his coat pocket as if he'd forgotten something. Lucy reached for his shoulder but couldn't grasp the material or the man wearing it. She punched his arm, clawed at his back, but he remained insubstantial as air. "They're coming," she shouted, inches from his ear. "A lot of angry white men want to burn this town! Listen, you've got to hear me! People will die!"

The minister frowned. He shivered as if chilled. Then shook his head, turned away, and walked in the opposite direction from that Sister Kellam had taken, pausing to greet two men in dusty coveralls and heavy work boots who were getting out of a Ford pickup. They nodded and went into the hardware store. The minister walked on a few more paces, then stopped abruptly, as if he'd come up against a wall.

A large mob was striding up the middle of the unpaved street.

"Oh God," she whispered. "It's too late."

She ran across the street, back to Flowers's store, pounded up the steps and through the door. The storekeeper, tall and thin, wore black-rimmed glasses and a starched butcher's apron now. He stood behind a glass display counter, like Jimmy Stewart playing small-town grocer. The case was heaped with glistening slices of pink smoked ham, thick red and white slabs of bacon, moist red beef roasts leaking bloody juice into white-enameled trays. Flowers was slicing pork chops and wrapping them in brown paper, still whistling. "Silent Night" this time.

"Mr. Flowers," she cried. "Please, please hear me!"

The storekeeper whistled another stanza, wrapped and taped another package.

"Damn it!" She shook a fist at the oblivious grocer. "What the hell do I have to do to make someone listen!"

She reached for the first thing on the nearest shelf, a can of peaches, ready to throw it at his head. No luck, she couldn't get a grip. Damn you, Flowers, she thought. You could help me if only . . . Flowers. Flower. *Flour.*

Next to the canned fruit sat sacks of bread flour. But her fingers passed through these too. She glared at the plump paper sack which seemed to symbolize all that was wrong with this insubstantial world. How she hated it. *Fall, damn you. Fall off the damned shelf then, and destroy yourself.*

The bag swayed. It skittered a few inches, bumped a silver can of early green peas, then toppled.

Flowers looked up in surprise. "What the heck," he said mildly, as a fine pale cloud rose from the bare pine floor. "Mary Louise! Come on out here a minute, sugar."

A plump woman in a shirtwaist dress, a pencil tucked in her tight perm, emerged from the back. "What, Otis. I'm trying to—I swan! Who made this mess?"

He shrugged. "Nobody. It just flew off there. Think our shelves are gettin' warped?" He smiled. "Or maybe five-pound bags of flour can fly now."

The woman tsked. "I'll clean it up. Just let me finish adding these figures before I forget what I was about."

"Okay, honey." He cocked his head. "Hm. Somebody's kicking up a ruckus. I'll just step outside a minute, see what the shouting's all about." He came from the counter, passed Lucy, and stepped onto the porch.

She barely gave him a glance, still staring at the powdery drifts on the pine planks. But she was hearing something Eugenie Lee had told her on the Day front porch, as if the old woman stood beside her again, whispering in her ear. "All the children in the swamp, we were cold and shivering, frightened all night long. But we were led safe out of the lion's den by a woman in white."

Lucy had nodded. "A woman in a white dress. Or you mean a nightgown?"

Eugenie had frowned and shook her head. "No ma'am. She was white all over. Hair, skin, everything."

Lucy had lowered the notepad, wondering if she'd heard right. "You mean, like . . . a ghost?"

"No, child. An angel of the Lord, with pure white wings and glory dust trailing behind her. Called to lead us to safety."

Eugenie's voice seemed right beside her. Or inside her. Then it was gone. But what exactly had she been saying? What did this remembered fragment mean? Lucy raked trembling fingers through her hair, pressing to ease a throbbing in her head.

A triumphant shout rose outside. She ran out to see what had happened.

At first, the street looked deserted again. A mutter of voices came from the far end of the street, past the church, from men clustered around something on the ground. Angry shouts rose. One of the mob drew back and kicked at a dark, dusty bundle once, twice, three times. As the others joined in, it jerked and flopped. Lucy's hand rose to cover her mouth. The sprawled figure was the AME minister.

Across the street, the pair who'd gone into the hardware store stepped out, then froze when they glimpsed the mob. The youngest wheeled and sprinted around the building, but the older man froze like a startled deer. Three angry whites were on him then, demanding, "Tell us where Julian Koumari lives!"

The man shook his head, shrinking back. "Please, boss. Don't rightly know where he's at this morning."

One of the whites slammed his head with a pistol butt, then jerked him upright again when he sagged.

"Maybe if this coon lost a few parts, it'd improve his memory," said a fat man in oil-stained blue coveralls.

Two attackers forced the old man to kneel, then pushed him face down in the dirt. They held his arms outstretched while the coverall-clad one raised a small hatchet.

"No!" Lucy screamed as the blade descended. Was this the same old man whose apparition had frightened her on the sidewalk outside Esther Day's?

A pickup was huffing up the street, riding low, its rusty bed full of men waving whiskey bottles, guns, and clubs. A barking hound perched like a live ornament, paws skittering and sliding on the metal hood. The men whooped and shouted, looking back and pointing at something out of view. As the truck passed, she saw one end of a rope lashed to its back bumper. The other was tied to a man's raw, bleeding wrists. He hung limp, clothes in shreds, coated with dust and blood.

"Whoo-ee! Caught us a little black rabbit! Sure run like

hell. Wouldn't talk, so we give him a ride to town," a man sitting the bed hollered to three gathered around the groaning, bleeding old man. "Gonna tow him back up the road a couple miles, see if that changes his mind."

The vehicle made a lurching U-turn, throwing two celebrants out onto the street. As it passed, the trussed man lifted a battered face, eyes wide with pain and fear. He was still alive. Lucy clenched her fists until blood grew sticky on her palms.

The driver ground the gears and the truck bucked, lurched forward, and jolted away. Beneath the cloud of exhaust it left, another smell weighted the air. Not the pleasant woody, resinous scent of a fall bonfire, or a woodstove. Not the warm, tallowy smell of a lighted candle. A chilling mixture of all three, with the acrid stink of melting wire thrown in.

The smell of a house afire.

A few cottages sat on the main street, but most were clustered behind the stores, one street back. All clapboard, painted white or pale yellow, with green or blue trim. Mums and marigolds grew in window boxes and along walkways, a bit leggy so late in the season, but stubbornly blooming thanks to the unusually warm December. Lucy ducked down an alley between storefronts, toward the heart of that little neighborhood, pursued by distant shouts and gunshots.

A red tricycle stood abandoned in front of a neat yellow bungalow. A Christmas cactus bursting with pink blooms was balanced on the porch railing. A cedar wreath on the screen door bounced as it banged shut behind a slender young black woman. She cupped hands to her mouth and called, "Dwayne! Dwayne, come on in right this minute! You hear me, child? *Dwayne!*"

No answer. His mother raised her hands again, then clamped them over her mouth, muffling the cry dying on her lips.

The white mob was rounding the bank, headed for her

yard. She stepped back, eyes darting left and right, terror eloquent in the stiff way she moved, like a person stopped one pace short of a coiled rattler. She edged back inside, too late. The leaders shouted and pointed; the crowd surged forward.

The front door of the yellow house slammed shut; a bolt clicked. Men were already climbing the steps, heavy bootsoles echoing like a marching army's. The first to arrive pounded and shook the latched screen door. One used an axe to break the flimsy hinges. They pulled it off, then put their shoulders to the solid inside door, battering in unison. It held. A skinny, pimply boy stepped up from the crowd in the yard, offering a crowbar. A triumphant shout went up as the frame splintered. Rioters pushed inside like a swarm of demons furloughed through Hell's front gate.

First there was no sound, only silence like the held breath of a mouse hunted by a hawk. Then shouts, running footsteps, and piercing shrieks echoed through the walls. Moments later the grinning men emerged, the last three bearing the struggling woman overhead. Torchbearers rushed forward to set the eaves and railings aflame.

"My baby, Lord God, get my baby out!" the woman shrieked.

A man jeered, "One less pick'ny, umpteen to go!"

Those carrying her laughed and threw her down in the grass a short distance from the fiery tinderbox that had once been a home. A lanky red-haired man turned to face the mob. "Look here, fellas. I ain't been educated as a preacher. But seeing as today's verse is simple—an eye for an eye—I take that to mean a woman for a woman, too. Am I right?"

A cheer went up.

"To get things warmed up, I'll go first!" he added.

Amid raucous laughter and shouted obscenities, men pressed forward. Only a few turned away, faces twisted in shame or disgust.

The last of them emerged from the burning house, leapt the porch railing, and began flinging handfuls of tinsel around. "Merry Christmas, boys!" he cried in a loud falsetto.

Lucy stood unable to move, feeling as if she were trapped in a terrible surrealist painting. Then she turned and fled up the street, away from the drunken shouts, the woman's hysterical pleas.

She ran heedlessly, noticing only at the last moment through drifting smoke that someone was heading her way as if to cut her off. She threw up an arm instinctively just before they collided. This time, the eerie frisson was stronger, like a brief electric jolt. She wasn't knocked down, but the tingling lingered.

She slowed to look back. A young black girl was racing across the lawn she'd just passed, breath rasping, thin arms and legs pumping.

Lucy put her hands wonderingly to face, chest, arms. *Eugenie Lee.* She passed right through me, crossing the road. But I felt it this time.

Had the girl noticed that strange contact? Could Lucy be gaining solidity, becoming a visible part of the nightmare landscape she'd been thrust into? She'd demanded to be seen and heard, but then if she was—what would happen when the crazed mob noticed *her*?

Eugenie was burrowing like a rabbit into the thick hedge of azaleas edging a white two story with green trim. Lucy ran to the still-swaying branches, but Eugenie was already out on the other side, squeezing through the porch railing, then sidling along the front wall to the door. She huddled there, glanced around, then pounded on the bottom panel with the heel of one hand.

The door opened a crack. "Child, what on earth?" said a voice. "Get inside. You look like the Devil and all his demons after you!"

A pair of strong brown arms drew the girl inside. And

Lucy heard the muffled sound of the mob coming. Behind them, a disheveled Otis Flowers darted from one man to another, pleading, shaking his head, gesturing frantically. She couldn't hear the grocer above the angry hum and roar of so many raised voices.

Two men broke away and turned back. One grabbed Flowers' collar, the other jabbed the business end of a shotgun into his chest. The storekeeper went white and silent. The shirt grabber shouted into his shocked face, spit flying like foam from a mad dog's lips, "Leave off, Otis, or we'll string you up next!"

A last vicious jab of the barrel, and they let go, shoving him down. Flowers crouched in the dust, a hand to his chest, watching the ugly human tide surge like hurricane-whipped surf through the quiet neighborhood, setting fire to houses and trees and the occasional car or truck. Battering doors down, breaking windows in silvery crescendos of splintering glass. The grocer flinched, and backed away, his face wide-eyed with fear, but also lined with impotent rage.

Forget about him helping, then. Might as well try to stop a tidal wave with his bare hands. The momentum of this mob would not be slowed by the entreaties of ten rational men, much less one skinny merchant.

Flowers rose and limped away, looking over his shoulder every few steps. No doubt concerned about his wife being alone at the store.

Turning back, Lucy saw someone climb the steps to the house that'd just taken in Eugenie Lee. Three more followed, and she recognized two of them. One was the fisherman she'd hitched a ride with; the other had fallen from the truck dragging the dying man like an old gunny sack. They hammered the door with fists and the butt of a revolver. "Ever'one inside come on out here right now!"

No one emerged. Instead, a volley of shots rang out, and

the Ford truck man fell backwards, a bloody hole where his face had been. The fisherman clutched his chest, grimacing. He back-pedaled and fell through a splintered railing.

A shocked silence fell over the crowd. The third man beat it hastily from the porch, falling back a safe distance in the yard.

A lone outraged voice lifted over the crowd. "Do you believe it—the goddamn niggers got guns!"

The words alone would have sent a shiver through Lucy, but the voice frightened her more. Because she knew it now. The high, jolly, good-natured lilt. The outraged speech had come from the smirking man in gray, who stood now within the crowd. Part of it. Egging them on.

She pressed her back against the fence, hoping to blend with its weathered pickets. If he noticed her this time, he gave no sign.

The dead were carried off and the others spread out, each with a flaming branch or club. They advanced again, circling the house. More shots came, but these missed any living target. That seemed to encourage the rioters. Two suddenly rushed up and hurled lighted torches onto the roof. The shingles smoldered but the flames died. Another shot came from a side window. The pimply teenager from the skiff clutched his left arm, screaming like a little girl.

The mob moved back behind the fence, muttering angrily.

"Hell, let's don't burn 'em up too quick. We oughta get our hands on the black bastards what shot Ray and Shorty," said the blue-coveralled guy.

"Yeah, they won't get off easy. We'll cut their black asses in little pieces, one at a time!"

A murmur of agreement rippled through the group. A few stayed to keep watch while the humming central mass moved on like locusts, devouring the neighborhood.

Lucy waited outside the house for a while. Eugenie Lee must still be inside. She'd obviously escaped at some point. But how—had she ever said? Lucy tried to replay the recording in her mind, to recall everything the old woman had said. She'd escaped the burning town and lived many more decades. That much was certain. But how would Lucy herself return? Had she changed the future by stumbling onto a foggy portal to the town's past? Perhaps she'd have to remain, trapped in a replaying nightmare. She didn't know if she was still also in the present, merely a spectator at a ghostly reenactment or had been flung back bodily into the past. Or perhaps she'd simply gone insane, her body sitting catatonic in a room somewhere while inside she lived out a horrible waking delusion.

Wearily, she slid to the ground and ran hands over her face. Horror had slapped her so many times in the last hour she felt numb. Did sanity or madness really matter if she was trapped here?

She pushed those despairing thoughts away. Eugenie Lee's words, the ones she'd heard again like a ghost whisper in the general store, swarmed like gnats in her brain. If only she could form the mass into some kind of sense, a plan, perhaps she'd understand how some had escaped, and even go with them.

All the children in the swamp . . . were led to safety by a woman all in white.

A woman wearing a white dress?

No . . . She was white . . . all over. Like an angel.

You mean . . . a ghost?

No. It was an angel of the Lord. Wings of glory dust trailin' behind her.

If that wasn't a delusion, or canny mythologizing by an old woman who'd survived a great horror, then what could it mean? A woman in white. No—white all over. Pure white. Covered in glory dust . . . so then, white dust? White . . . dust.

She felt like a fool. How could she not have thought of it back in the store? *If only the mess I made is still there,* she fretted, darting between storefronts toward the main street. Running for all she was worth, back to the general store.

Amazingly, the door was still neither closed nor bolted. Either Otis Flowers had decided he and his plump wife were in no danger, or else he'd given up, decided to meet his maker with open arms. Neither one was in sight.

Lucy ran up the aisle, panting, nearly skidding through the white powder that glowed almost phosphorescent in the dim light. She knelt there, scrubbing the stuff into her hair, her skin, her clothes. Most of it fell away through her insubstantial fingers. Instead of giving up, she recalled how the bag had flown from the shelf when she'd directed all her enraged energy at it. She concentrated now on the pile of fine white all-purpose flour, willing the dusty grains to rise, be picked up, to cling like talcum.

At first the flour dust simply lay there, inert, a puff occasionally drifting away as if a draft had swept the floorboards. As if she were in a giant snow globe. "Stick, damn it," she muttered. "Give me form and substance."

She wasted no more time with her clumsy fingers, no more substantial than air, but simply *willed* it to her. At last a few grains rose and adhered to her palms. She rubbed these into her arms, her shirt, her face. As long as no one could hear her, there was nothing she could do but watch or flee. But if the town's residents could at least *see* her, even for a few moments . . .

Then those good old boys would shoot you dead, nagged the voice of self preservation. *To them, you'd be nothing but a haunt. They'd piss in their pants, then shoot you to pieces.*

Her hands slowed. Maybe . . . but maybe not. Then came

another head-ripping question, one surely never posed on "Jeopardy": Could a person be killed by bullets fired before she'd even been born?

She shook her head and kept rubbing, finishing arms and feet. Her back was mostly out of reach, but that couldn't be helped. She threw a few handfuls over both shoulders, then rose like a dusty alabaster statue escaped from a museum.

Just then Mary Louise Flowers stepped out of the back office, pencil still tucked into her tight perm. Her look was strained, but her voice determined as she carried a push broom, dust pan, and galvanized bucket toward the spill in the aisle.

"Now Otis, I'm just gon' clean this stuff up. Like I said, nobody'll come in here and hurt us, long as we mind our own business. Stay back there. Those men surely wouldn't lay a hand on a white Christian woman. Work on the books, play solitaire if you want. But if I don't get up and do something, I'll jump right out of my skin!"

She rounded the meat counter, then stopped, gaping. The dented metal pail rang hollowly as it clattered to the floor. "What in the name of gracious heaven!"

Lucy glanced back just in time to see Mrs. Flowers— probably a life-long Baptist—cross herself. Then, like a wraith, Lucy slipped through the open doorway, a bright swirl of sun-lit white motes trailing behind like glorious angel wings.

Now that she was visible, Lucy took her cue from Eugenie Lee and kept close to walls and fences. She had no illusions about single-handedly stopping a rabid mob in its tracks. The very first sight of her might awe or frighten them. But, much as she hated to admit it, her inner warning was on target. They'd most likely treat the phenomenon of her pale self as they treated anything different from themselves: kill, and think about it later.

She wanted to work her way back to the big green-trimmed house. When and if Eugenie Lee and the others decided to make a run for it, probably well after dark, she had to be there.

In a grassy spot on the opposite side of the hedge bordering its yard, she huddled in shadow, beneath a riotous, fragrant clump of winter jasmine. A pair of attackers passed by so close she could've reached out and grabbed a pants leg. Should she try to frighten one off, just for practice? But if they shot her now, she'd never get a chance to help the children in the house. Then no Eugenie Lee, no future, no . . .

No. For now sit and wait to discover what part she was meant to play.

The sun packs up early in December, between four and five, and then gray twilight sets in. If this short day seemed very long to Lucy, it must've been a tormenting eternity to the besieged residents of Revelation. Long before the fiery orange ball had dropped into the quenching Gulf, the town had been lit with a sunset orange glow from dozens of crackling fires.

As far as she could tell, only a few people remained barricaded in houses, holding off the attackers. An occasional gun-shot echoed, but the two sides had mostly hunkered down to wait each other out. For how long, though? The mob could send back to Ibo City for supplies. The people of Revelation could not.

A few men who'd not participated in the burning and killing and raping had left early in revulsion and disgust. Still, most remained. At first, she'd wondered at such dogged patience. Until she realized they must be waiting for the rest who lived in Revelation—those who'd gone off early to work at the mill, in the woods, on the winter-grayed waters of the Gulf, or across it on the Florida mainland—to return home. Maybe word would reach some in time to head them off. Perhaps the smoke of the fires would be enough warning. But surely most of the men would still try to come, hoping to protect their homes, to save their families.

She gave in to fatigue and rested her forehead on her knees. The whitewash of flour sifted from her skin in mealy crumbs, speckling the ground. Her eyes smarted and watered, stung by drifting smoke that stank of burnt wood and singed cloth and a fainter, sweeter smell—like roasting pork—that made her stomach clench. She tried to focus on the notion that people were still alive next door. The hope she could somehow help them.

She was half-dozing when shouting snapped her head up again. Cries, the thunder of running feet. A voice boomed excitedly, so near her hiding place she shrank back: "They's some comin' back! Now we'll see some action!"

She stood to peer over the bushes. The remaining sentinels had left their posts in the yard, pelting off to join the rest. Something was happening down the street, if the shouting and barking dogs were any indication.

She crawled through and reached the house just as people came dashing out the back door, past woodshed and outhouse, disappearing into dark pines a hundred yards back. All women and children, no men. She hesitated, then followed.

The rag-tag group darted tree to tree, ducking, panting. Mothers with babies tied on their backs or in arms. Young children dragging whining toddlers. A few grandmothers hobbling arthritically, but keeping up. Their leader was a tall, middle-aged woman with light mahogany skin and thin strong arms, wearing a brightly patterned dress. She urged everyone on, taking a visual roll call as they bolted past.

Eugenie Lee had a fat baby balanced on one hip, struggling to push through hanging moss and branches. "How far, Auntie Solange?" she called. "This baby sick. And she so heavy. We need to stop soon."

So the leader was Solange Koumari. Lucy ran faster, to keep her in sight.

The tall woman paused to let Eugenie catch up. She took the baby, then slapped the young girl's face hard. "Don't tell me how tired you getting, 'less you're ready to lie down in the pine shatters and die right now."

"No, ma'am," Eugenie mumbled, fingering the welt already rising on one cheek. She took the baby again and hoisted it higher, then ran quickly on.

But where were they headed? The thick pines and mangrove swamp might offer hiding places. But the white men had dogs and apparently lots of time. Unless the refugees had enough boats to carry them away to safety with motors fast enough to outrun other boats.

They waded through a low swampy area, then splashed through a tidal pool. Lucy heard the muffled lapping of waves. Solange Koumari raised a hand and halted the group.

"Here we stay," she said. "Just before dawn the lumber train comes. Tracks behind town lie on the far side of those four big pines. We go out then, flag the train down."

A mother cradling an infant looked up. "What if they won't let us on?"

"Then we will be killed. But many who work on it are Negroes like us. I believe they will help." She turned suddenly to a young woman whose belly was huge with late pregnancy, and laid a more gentle hand on the girl's sweaty forehead. "How are you faring, dear one?"

The girl gave a shuddering sigh. "Worried about Charles, mostly. What if he leaves the mill, comes back and—" She closed her eyes. "I'm all right, Mama. Only, it feels tight. Here." She pressed trembling fingers low on her stomach. "Don't hurt, though."

"That's good, then." Solange smiled. "Your Charles will take care of himself." But when she turned away, she looked worried.

Lucy hung back, trying to decide what to do next. If they'd just circled the perimeter of town, and were near the railroad tracks . . . those tracks also ran right behind the general store. She'd stumbled across the rails when first approaching Revelation from the south shore. If only there were some safe, secluded place they could wait until dawn. Dogs would have no trouble finding them here in the woods if the mob thought to send them in.

All she could think of was the store. It certainly wasn't secluded . . . so who would suspect it? Apparently Flowers would be left alone, as long as he didn't try to interfere. Though if any of the mob entered the grocery, say, to get food . . . she shook her head. That wouldn't work.

Yet hadn't Eugenie Lee said there was a storage cellar? That women and children had hidden there until they could escape. Yet Solange Koumari said nothing about going there. What if the men discovered the Koumari house empty, and came looking for them with dogs?

Abruptly the healer rose and faced her frightened little band. "There is nothing else I can do now but petition the *loas,* the spirits of *voudon.* Expect no help from human hands here. Nor, it seems, from the white folks' God. Do you all agree?"

The women's gazes fixed on the tall, imposing Koumari. Though some seemed shocked or disapproving, they kept silent. A few nodded. Everyone still looked scared.

"Very well. Lower your heads and close your eyes. You will not speak, even if bitten by a snake! Do not interrupt, especially when the *loa* appears. It will be at your peril, if you do."

The women and older children nodded solemnly. Even the youngest kept still and quiet, watching with wide eyes.

Solange frowned, muttering, "More than one candle might be seen. No willow tree . . . at least I have a bit of flour in my bag. I must use this great old oak and pray

Maman Brigette will not take offense."

She drew a cloth pouch from her skirt and poured thin lines of white dust—it *is* flour, thought Lucy, what a coincidence—to make a simple design on the ground beneath the oak.

Then she replaced the bag and pulled a small, wickedly-curved knife from another pocket. She held her right wrist over the flour markings. The blade flashed silver, the movement so quick Lucy didn't understand at first what had been done. Then she saw dark drops falling like a shower of small red roses which spread and bloomed on the flour markings. The healer was dripping her own blood in a slow, deliberate pattern to overlay the white design.

Solange then pinched up some blood-soaked flour and dirt between thumb and finger, and ate it. Lucy had seen films of similar ceremonies in Haiti, though none of those had ever conveyed such a sense of both reverence and desperation.

The tall woman stood and addressed the huge oak as if it were a person.

"Mademoiselle Brigette! *Grande Maman*, most ancient of the dead. I cannot light your way with many candles, as custom demands for you or your honored husband, great *Baron Samedi*, lord of the cemetery. But I beg you, forgive your devotee this unavoidable insult, and hear my plea, in honor of my dead mother who was so long your faithful *mam'bo* . . . we have great need of you tonight!"

Solange stepped closer and grasped a low thin branch. "In the name of Maman Brigette." With the same sharp blade, she sliced it free, then held the severed limb out as if offering it back to the tree. "Mademoiselle Brigette, behold the lash which evil men have cut to strike you and your devoted servant. I bring it now that you may teach them the awful lesson they deserve." She knelt, then lowered herself and lay with outstretched arms, as if she embraced the earth itself.

Lucy was mesmerized but also feeling more and more anxious. A good show was all very well. She knew a mam'bo was a voodoo priestess. And that Baron Samedi was, in Haiti, the much-feared bogeyman of the night, haunter of dreams, similar to the Christian concept of Satan, though a bit less malevolent. But what if Brigette, this oldest of goddesses, didn't pick up the phone?

She looked down at her own arms, her clothing, still faintly glowing white in the rising dark. In this costume, I could pass for a spirit of some sort. Perhaps . . . perhaps even a priestess like Koumari would be fooled—if I kept my distance. Then it would be up to me to lead them out, maybe to the store. But if they can't hear me, I can't tell them what to do. My one advantage is, I know the future. If they'll only follow!

She stepped out of the trees and walked slowly, she hoped gracefully, into the middle of the huddled group.

"*Grande Maman*," Solange whispered, eyes widening. "You appear . . . differently. Yet it *is* you, the Oldest of the Old. Maman Brigette." She fumbled at her neck, and Lucy saw a dull shine, a chain of tarnished silver. "I offer this as my poor gift."

Lucy raised a hand to wave it away, shaking her head imperiously. If Solange touched her and brushed off bits of flour, the woman might realize the glowing white spirit before her was not the least bit divine. If she could just maintain the charade long enough to get them all to the back door of Flowers' store! She pointed at Koumari, then inclined her head at the group. All kept their faces carefully averted.

Good so far. Lucy made a broad, sweeping gesture with one arm: *Follow me.*

It was full dark now, a moonless night. For that, at least, Lucy was thankful. The glow from the burning town gave enough dreadful illumination. One by one her ragged followers emerged silently, fearfully, from the woods. One by one dashed across clearing and railroad tracks, then disappeared into trees on the other side. She held her breath, counting as a shepherd tallies sheep. Expecting any moment the raucous halloos of bloodthirsty men, the chilling bay of a hound.

Neither came. Apparently other luckless inhabitants were occupying the mob's full attention.

The group followed her a quarter mile or so. She held up a hand to halt at the edge of the pines, then crossed to the loading platform at the back of Flowers' store. Where the train would stop.

She climbed the steps. The storeroom door stood ajar; wooden cases of empty soda bottles were stacked outside waiting to be loaded. She peered past the half-open door into the interior. Flowers sat bent over a battered, paper-strewn roll-top, chewing on the eraser end of a pencil. He sighed and stuck the pencil behind one ear. A ledger sat illuminated in the golden circle cast by a brass gooseneck lamp.

She slipped back out to the tracks, beckoning the bedraggled band from the woods. Their footsteps on the creaking platform must've alerted the storekeeper, for he rose and stood, back pressed to the desk, eyes narrowing as they entered. He'd probably feared the hungry mob had arrived to ransack his store, because he looked amazed at the group of women and children, headed by the erect Solange Koumari. If he noticed Lucy he gave no sign.

"You are our last hope," Solange told the astonished man. He looked around at the old women, the pregnant ones, the wide-eyed children, all staring solemnly back. Glanced toward the front of the store, then down at a braided oval rug by his feet. Without a word, he bent, jerked it aside, and pulled open a trapdoor. A cloud of dust flew up.

"Down these steps," he whispered. "Not much light. Got to feel your way. And for God's sake, hurry!"

Some time later Lucy raised her head and rubbed stiffening neck muscles. She drifted again toward sleep, forehead on knees, but something nagged at her consciousness. A muffled shrilling that came intermittently. A dull vibration that faintly shook the hard, unforgiving floorboards.

She raised her head, for a moment bewildered by the surroundings. The room was dark, except for the dim orange glow of a low-wattage bulb at the top of the narrow stairs. All around the shapes of sleeping women and children huddled or lay curled among cardboard boxes of canned fruit and vegetables. Faint snores and soft, even breathing were the only sounds.

Now she remembered.

They were in Flowers's cellar. Not a true basement like the one beneath her apartment in Pennsylvania. This was only a bricked-in space beneath the raised first floor of the general store, damp and cobwebbed, which the storekeeper used for storage.

After he'd waved them down the steep, creaking steps, they'd settled on the floor. The women kept mostly silent, though a few prayed quietly. The children whined about being hungry. One woman produced a crumbled square of corn bread from a pocket, and divided it carefully. Another had a jar of water. One little boy, looking proud, pulled fuzzy, lint-flecked slices of dried apple from his pocket.

The children had drifted one by one to sleep. Gradually, so did the adults. All but Solange, who sat near the stairs, back straight, in an attitude of listening.

Lucy had stood watch in a shadowy corner until she'd

slid down the wall in exhaustion. Now she watched again, too. Would the mob suspect and come looking down here? She drew her sleeves over her wrists; it was chilly now. There had been rain clouds before sunset, thunder like distant drums. Surely her powdery goddess disguise had mostly flaked off. Perhaps she was no longer visible. Koumari had not glanced at her once since they'd left the woods.

At last she crept to the stairs, intending to go out and see where the mob was now.

"You leave us now, *Maman*, at our greatest time of need?"

The voice startled her. She paused, hand tightening on the rough banister.

The Koumari woman was staring at her. "I've observed your form growing faint. Perhaps you feel I have not been a faithful follower, but only call on you in times of need, like a spoiled, greedy child. It's true these people do not honor you as I was taught. You might be right to turn your back on us."

She held out her hands, palm up, imploring. "But hear me, please. If we die this dawn, it only means our time has come. But this persecution of our brothers and sisters, our children, our friends, will continue. If we must die, can you give some sign there will be an end to this suffering? That we will not be treated"— she took a deep breath—"like animals, at least in times to come?"

If only I could tell you, Lucy thought, how different things will be in even twenty years. But then she thought of Ibo City. Different, yes. And yet, at times, much the same. Was anything, for that matter, completely different anywhere—in Alabama, in New York, in Los Angeles, in Europe, in Africa, the Middle East—except on the surface? She might as well say to the pleading woman before her: *There will never be an end to hate, to suffering, to ignorance or fear. No matter the color of your skin, the texture of your hair, the name of your country, or your religion. Human life remains an endless cycle of hate, bloodshed, and death.*

She turned to face her. What would be an appropriate gesture? Finally she extended her arms toward Solange, then folded them gently against herself, as one would gather up a small child.

The tear-streaked face before her grew calmer. The desperate gaze slowly relaxed from worry to acceptance, even something like peace.

Feeling like a coward, and a liar, Lucy fled up the stairs.

She glided past Flowers, asleep in the desk chair, head resting on the green blotter, a hand splayed on the ledger, the pen fallen from his fingers. A splotch of India ink like a dark bloodstain marked the otherwise blank columns. He snored in muffled jerks, like an old engine in need of attention. His wife was nowhere in sight, but Lucy heard Bing Crosby's voice floating down from above, singing "White Christmas." Mrs. Flowers must have the radio on upstairs. That gentle voice, the irony of the holiday song, were too much to bear.

She fled through the back door and climbed from the loading dock. Standing on the tracks, she heard that shrill sound again, louder now. A glowing cyclops orb was moving slowly toward her through the morning fog. A whistle shrilled. The lumber train was approaching Revelation. She turned back to go alert the refugees in the cellar. They were already slipping silently from the open door behind her.

My part is over, she thought. Now all I can hope to do is get back. To my own life, my own time. Retrace my steps back down the road that led me from Ibo City.

Perhaps, by the time she'd walked it, things would be back to normal, as she'd left them, over sixty years in the future. But if not—what then?

A hellish glow lit her way back to the main street. She kept to back paths and alleys. The shouts and whoops of the mob grew fainter as she slipped away, through the fiery ruin of a place that had once been a lively town called Revelation.

FIFTEEN

Lucy slipped behind the smoking trunk of a fire-blackened magnolia, its glossy green leaves only a charred, skeletal memory. She heard an engine start, then another. Several carloads of rioters were leaving. The vehicles she'd seen earlier, parked before tidy homes that were now little more than charred fireplaces and smoldering ash.

After the last pickup in the drunken convoy disappeared, she ventured out. Revelation was silent except for the crackle of flames, the snap and pop of embers. Behind her, the grocery store stood alone, a soot-flecked white elephant mourning the burning carcasses of fallen companions.

She staggered down the road, feeling like the lone survivor of an air strike. Instead of shops and homes and churches, the blackened fossils of scorched, upright timbers clawed at the night sky. Glowing embers and thinly writhing flames beneath cast weird, distorted shadows. She shivered even as the heat seared her face. Her clothes clung, soaked with sweat, too much like the steaming bloody scraps sticking to the corpses lying here and there in the street.

She staggered on to the crossroads, where the shell of the AME church belched smoke. Its huge wooden cross had been ripped from above the door. The blackened

201

corpse lashed to it was surely the minister. She walked past, biting hard on the inside of one cheek, welcoming the pain, the shedding of her own blood. The hurt was real enough to assure her she was not dead, too, and in Hell. It also kept her from screaming. She looked away and walked faster.

Without warning, someone darted into her path. A girl, breathing hard, wrapped in tattered clothing like graveyard rags. Without glancing at Lucy she dashed past into the rubble of a house. She snatched up a few packages from an overturned icebox lying like an open coffin in the yard, then vanished into the shadowed woods beyond.

Lucy strained her eyes against the darkness after her, and spotted more figures huddled in the trees. A few steps further on ragged scavengers were clambering silently among fallen timbers and blackened bricks, searching for something. Survivors, food, clothing, cherished possessions? Two were small children, faces blank and shocked as the survivors of any great war.

A tall, broad-shouldered boy in torn, sooty overalls and a plaid shirt lifted a cloth-wrapped side of bacon from the ruins of a kitchen. He stopped suddenly, frozen in the tense, wide-eyed pose of a deer in the presence of a hunter. When he and Lucy stared at each other for a moment, she recognized him. The young man who'd fled Esther Day's house. Her secret lover, Julian. Solange Koumari's teenage son.

The smoky rubble shifted, and he staggered. A pendant swung from the neck of his shirt, swaying like a hypnotist's bauble on a thin black cord, glinting in the moonlight. Too quickly for her eye to follow, he was gone.

His necklace had looked familiar. Her hand crept up to reassure herself, to caress the silver medallion around her own neck. She groped at the fabric of her shirt to feel its familiar contours, the smooth ripples of soft silver, the heavy serpentine links. She found only cloth and bare sweating skin. Medallion and chain were gone.

"No," she whispered, turning to look again after Julian. When had she dropped it? He must've found it on the ground, picked it up. "No—wait!"

She wanted to go after him, but which way? A breeze off the water shoved at her. The rumble of thunder grew more distinct. She began walking again, more quickly, but the sky opened and drenched her in cold rain. The drops stung like sleet. She hugged herself miserably, but kept plodding.

Rain hissed and sizzled in the embers on either side. Steam rose all around, as if she'd stumbled into a sauna for the damned. She needed sleep; her knees trembled, her vision blurred. To lie down, just for a while. She looked around and choked out a laugh, a bitter echo ending in a sob. What mattress, what blanket, what pillow had not been turned to charcoal? She'd have to curl up in the ashes like Cinderella, but never to be rescued.

If Hercules were with her she could pillow her head on his side. His thick coat always smelled of fallen leaves and shampoo and warm dog. But now she might not ever . . . her eyes stung. She shook her head and stumbled on, to a dull humming that seemed to come from everywhere and nowhere. Perhaps the short-circuiting wires of her overtaxed mind.

One more step. The road wavered, tilted, and suddenly rose, just as in the old Irish proverb, to meet her. The main street of Revelation had become a broad stream of muck studded with sodden gift-wrapped packages, torn clothing, broken crockery, jagged glass, empty brass cartridges, smashed holiday ornaments that winked up at her like fairytale jewels. She collapsed slowly onto it, letting the damp earth take her weight, welcoming its embrace.

SIXTEEN

Her next awareness was of an aching that possessed her entire body. She groaned. Was shrapnel ripping through her nerves? No, just a jolt of pain from the cracked, unhealed rib. Something beneath her dug into her skin. Hard, cold, cracked . . . like a road . . . like a deserted road . . . in the woods.

She tensed, expecting a brutal kick that would snap more bones.

After lying there a little longer, not breathing, not moving, curled like a mollusk in its shell, she pushed herself up slowly, wincing. All around the night was bordered with a red glow. From above, whispering, like the rustle of cloth. Or perhaps wings. She threw herself down again, arms curled over her head, eyes clamped shut.

When something touched her, she shrieked and flinched away. It prodded her wrists, her hands. Caressed her back. Then came a curious tugging sensation, as if someone too weak for the task was doggedly trying to lift her. She slapped at the hands, willing herself to leap up, to run, but her outraged muscles would not obey.

So she'd die in this dark, mysterious place, hard and cold and damp, comfortless as an unmarked grave. She gave up then. Gave in to the despair she'd felt on waking. Well, she thought, why not face my killer? At least see my last place on Earth.

Her eyes opened again on darkness thick as blood, though the glow of distant fires was gone.

Maybe I'm already dead, she thought. Sightless in purgatory. But the touch of those hands . . . a dead, senseless corpse wouldn't have felt that.

Suddenly they returned, stroking her face, her back softly, gently, now comforting and familiar. Like the hands of angels. Gradually a faint glow lightened the dark. But if she opened her eyes, perhaps that was all she'd see: gray and more gray, blotting out the whole world.

The color of moth's wings.

She bolted up screaming, flailing, brushing at herself, as if cockroaches were crawling over her face, under her clothes, inside her skin. "Leave me alone!" she screamed.

Instead there came another tug, then a stomach-wrenching drop. A sense of impossible acceleration, into and then *through* the gray light, before darkness closed in again and blotted out all senses.

Who knew how many hours had passed since darkness blotted out the indifferent, unceasing gray? But some time later she felt herself surrounded by a warmer, soothing dark, like a child safe beneath the covers. The hands were back, pulling at buttons, gently undressing her, tucking the sheet tenderly around her shoulders. She gave in like a little girl too weary to fight bedtime. A low pitched lullaby drifted to her, slow, a bit sad, sung in a husky voice that carried a whiff of tobacco.

She sighed and settled into the comforting softness, wincing once at a faint jab from her cracked ribs. The lulling voice faded, and she slept.

Dawn made red shades of her eyelids. The comforting dreamsong had been replaced by an even, sawing buzz. Hercules's asthmatic snores.

The light coalesced into the glow of the unshaded bulb in the hotel room's ceiling fixture. She was in bed. Back in her hotel room. But that was impossible. The last thing she recalled was falling amidst glowing ruins like a giant's jumble of pick-up sticks, the smoking timbers pointing accusingly at the stars. Heaps of smoldering furniture. Ash-blackened bricks. Litter scattered like after-hours at a carnival, trampled into muck tinted with blood. The oily stink of kerosene. Bodies like blackened logs wrapped in charred tatters of cloth. Women and children bolting for the woods while men with guns took casual aim. Everything tilting at a crazy angle as she fell.

She clutched at the mattress as if she were at sea on a small, unsteady boat. Oh, how she'd like to think it had all been a dream. But she recalled too clearly the crackle of flames eating wood, the dreadful sweet stink of cooking human flesh.

Beneath the glow of the overhead light she lay tangled in the sheets, naked except—to her relief—for the silver medallion and chain. Where had she dropped the chambray shirt and khaki shorts she'd ventured out in earlier? Her bare skin felt damp. A watery drumming on the roof; slow, steady winter rain. An echoing drip from the tiled bath. Perhaps she'd just taken a shower? She shoved hair out of her eyes, wincing when a ragged fingernail tore her scalp.

A streak of blood smeared her fingertips. Two nails had broken off, one down to raw pink quick. She felt her hairline, found the warm stickiness. Her other hand was uninjured, but caked with grayish-white granules of . . . flour?

Not a dream, then. The terrors she'd seen and felt and heard were not hallucinations or a belated traumatic reaction. Yet, how could she believe or explain it?

Several years ago she'd read a book called *The Serpent and the Rainbow*. Wade Davis, anthropologist and ethnobotanist from Harvard, had gone to Haiti to discover the ingredients in legendary "zombie powder," a concoction of Datura plant and poisonous sea-toad that paralyzed the victim into a living-death state. Made them the walking dead, disposable, perfectly suited for slave labor. Davis's unorthodox method had been to ingest the botanical drugs in question himself, then record the results. This time he'd nearly lost his sanity. She remembered shaking her head at the harrowing ordeal he'd *voluntarily* undergone. What a fool, she'd concluded. What a fucking show-off.

Whereas she'd taken no drugs, natural or otherwise, yet seemed almost in the same state.

She looked down at Hercules, who snored on, oblivious to her emotional storm. So much for the psychic abilities of animals. She wrapped herself in the sheet and slipped out of bed, stepping carefully over the dog's tail. She crossed to the window overlooking Water Street and hammered at the lock, then forced the sash up its warped tracks. Leaned out to bathe her face in misty rain. Nausea swelled in her throat. She gritted her teeth, willing it away. After a few deep breaths the rain-washed winter air made her feel better. She was starving, though. When was the last time she'd actually eaten?

But the stark memory of all she'd seen, or thought she'd seen . . . even though it had happened long ago. It turned her stomach.

Up the street, the faint happy sound of bluegrass music leaked from unshuttered doors and windows, drifting on mist. So lively and innocent she was tempted to get dressed and go out. Not that she could tell anyone, but . . . just to sit in the comforting presence of other human beings. To let the whine of a well-played fiddle convince her life was straightforward. That problems could be solved—if not in the morning, then later, with a little work.

A fiddle. Probably Yulee's band then, Scratch. His father and grandfather had no doubt been part of the lynching that had taken an innocent town apart. The shouting, murderous mob spilling down the unpaved streets. Also it explained the horrified look Nick had given her when, that evening out on his boat, she'd joked about the curl in her hair having African origins.

She turned abruptly and crossed to the dresser, intending to throw on some clothes and make herself go get some food. She didn't know what time it was—where was her phone? Obviously some places were still open. She closed the window, and the music became a distant soundtrack.

On her way to the dresser she stumbled over a sodden pile of cloth.

Dirty clothes. She snatched up the bundle in irritation, then caught her breath and let it tumble slowly, piece by piece, from her hands. Damp grains of sand, greasy patches of soot, larger crumbs of a white sticky substance stuck to her fingers. She rubbed her palms together slowly, staring down at the shirt, the shorts. If she'd needed more proof, there it was. Wood smoke, damp earth, the tangy reek of fishy salt marsh, the copper of dried blood.

She looked around and spotted her hiking boots turned toes-in beside the bed. She bent and ran a finger over one worn sole. Dried reddish muck crumbled and sifted to the floor, along with some flat, shiny, multicolored flakes. She frowned and tweezed one up, mystified. A fragment of thin colored glass. A shard from a broken Christmas ornament.

She dropped both shoes in the wicker trash basket by the door, stuffed shirt and pants in on top. Enough. She'd leave the island at first light.

She yanked her suitcase off the closet shelf and started tossing in journals, books, clothing.

Her cell rang. Hercules groaned and opened his eyes. Came over and nosed her palm. As the iPhone continued to play her ringtone, he looked from it to her. She stood twisting a T-shirt over the open suitcase. Finally she dropped the tortured bit of cloth and snatched it up.

A barrage of voices, a blast of music, the clink of glasses hit her ear like a slap. A man's voice shouted, "That you, professor?"

"Who's this?"

"Sorry. Pretty loud here." Sound was suddenly muted, by a shielding hand, she supposed. There came a muffled shout, "Hey! Keep it down a minute, damn it!" Then he was back. "Sorry—it's Nick. Nick Yulee? I just . . . oh, hell. Thought maybe you'd want to come down and sit a while. We—the band, that is—we're at the Cat till one."

"Oh." She thought of his appealing grin, the way he played the fiddle, the possibility of food. Her stomach growled. "Don't know. I, um, don't think—"

"Right! Don't think," he said quickly, cutting her off. "I'd like to see you. For a few minutes, even."

She stared at her phone, its blank face no help. Just when she was getting out of this creepy hellhole. "I'm about to leave. Packing. I don't have time."

Silence. More muffled background noise. A sigh. "Uh-huh. Well, guess I don't blame you. Better get a move on. That tropical storm out in the Straits? It's headed our way now. Leading edge s'posed to hit by dawn."

Shit. She clutched the cell and nodded as if he could see her. "Oh. Right. Heard something in the car, but wasn't really paying attention. It's a bad one?"

"Category Two right so far. But you know how that goes." He chuckled. "Or maybe you don't. You're not from Florida."

She frowned. What did that mean? "But if it's going to make a direct hit here . . . I mean, aren't you supposed to evacuate or something? Go to the mainland?"

He laughed. "Well, yeah, supposed to. But locals always wait it out. I never left for one yet. Some of the fishermen even stay out on their boats."

He paused, and she heard him swallowing something, a beer maybe. Suddenly her throat felt parched.

"We just duck when the wind takes the roof off," he said.

"Hmm." He sounded half-drunk. Well, that wasn't her problem. Thank God.

"So, won't change your mind?"

She hesitated. "Well, um . . " No! What the hell was she thinking? "Sorry. But thanks for asking. And the weather report. I appreciate it, but I've got to go."

As he began to protest again, she quickly pressed END, feeling rude. But she really did need to leave.

Back to the closet. The last two shirts hanging. A folded pair of jeans. A half-empty bag of Purina chow. She stepped into the tiny bathroom, swept shampoo, soap, brush, comb, sunblock from the tiled counter.

At a tap on wood, Hercules barked softly. She stuck her head out of the bathroom. Yes, someone was knocking. She rolled her eyes. If it was that drunk fiddler . . . but no way he could've gotten here so quickly. She crossed and rested fingertips on the cool brass knob. Reluctantly turned it, and opened the door the length of the chain.

Eugenie Lee stood on the landing, looking real and very grumpy. Her knees almost buckled. She took a step back. The tiny woman smiled, worn face creasing into gentle seams. Impossible—but who was Lucy Fowler to ever use that word again? Somehow she couldn't feel afraid of gentle, gruff-voiced Eugenie Lee—woman, apparition, whatever the hell she was. After last night perhaps few things would ever frighten her again.

The chain rattled off, swung like a pendulum. "Look," she said quickly. "I don't know what's going on. If you're real or some kind of . . . magician or illusion, or—Christ! I can't believe I'm even talking to you. But I'm packing and leaving. Now."

"You can't." The old woman slipped in past her. "Too

late and a dollar short, as my mama used to say."

Lucy held her ground, but Hercules backed up before Eugenie, hackles ruffled, a faint rumble deep in his throat. "Hush, you young pup," she scolded. The dog whined, then lay beside the bed, eyebrows working, gaze shifting anxiously back and forth between Lucy and the old woman.

"Well, my mama used to say it's never too late to try to fix a mistake," Lucy shot back. "All I have to do is pay the bill, throw these things into the car, and go flying back up the road to Pottsburg."

"Pssht. No place ever made that's far enough away from fate. Leave now, and you put your own two feet on the road to Hell, dragging every soul on this island along. Still believe you come here by chance?"

"What? No, I think—

"Then you a fool. Who you expect sent all those clippings about the country midwife? Not Miz Esther Day. Were *me*. You had to come back, even if I got to reel you in like a pan fish."

Lucy stared. "Come *back*? That's the craziest thing you've said so far. I've never been to Ibo Key in my whole life."

Eugenie shook her head slowly. "Poor ignorant creature." Then she said, slowly and patiently, as if explaining the ways of the world to a small child, "'Bout time you know, I guess."

"What? I've got to—"

"Esther tried three times to abort that baby. Use every trick she knew: drink pennyroyal tea till she near heave her guts out. Sit over a wash pan of carbolic acid and boiling water till her shaking thighs can't hold her up no more. Third time, she use a coathanger. She try to make me help, but I wouldn't for love or money. So she grab that bent piece of wire thinkin' to do it herself."

"Oh my God," said Lucy, horrified, thinking of the pain, the blood. To do that to yourself . . .

"Crazy. But-a course she was out of her mind by then.

Hanger should've killed the baby and her too. Esther nearly die, but then she live on. Keep gettin' bigger, and bigger. Sick to her stomach right up to the end."

"The end?"

Eugenie Lee nodded. "Seven months, two weeks, and one day after the lynching at Revelation, she give birth. To your mama."

Lucy sank onto the bed, eyes locked on the frail but terrible figure. "My *mother?*" she whispered.

Eugenie nodded. "Told that murderin' snake of a husband the little girl was born dead. Not that he'd a kept any high-yellow child. A pretty light-skinned baby with a full head of curly black hair. Borned dead—so *she* said. Only I guess you know different. She give her away in secret, the shameful fruit of her so-called ordeal."

Lucy nodded unwillingly.

"Well, look at yourself," said Lee. "Go on."

She turned reluctantly to the clouded pier glass by the hotel door. A tall olive-skinned woman with dark eyes, a wide mouth, a rounded nose (which her adoptive mother had always insisted was Irish), and abundant curly black hair. Some reddish highlights. Broad shoulders. As broad even as Solange's, as Julian Koumari's?

No. It couldn't be. Because . . . then it was *all* true.

"No." She clenched her fists. "If you're trying to make me believe that . . . that Esther Day is my . . . *my grandmother* . . . and that boy I saw?" She bit her lip. "I mean, the one I *thought* I saw . . ." She shook her head. "Of course my mother was adopted, I always knew that. OK, it's true I was never told much about my biological grandparents. But they, I mean my *real* grandmother and grandfather, the ones who adopted her, they didn't even *know* who—oh, damn it!"

She pressed her fingers to her forehead as if that would still the pounding in her brain. No one had ever spoken of origins in her family. Whenever she'd asked, her mother said, "I really don't know, honey." Or, "Who cares? Your Grammy and Poppa were just happy to get a healthy, beautiful baby. And then we had you!"

They never seemed to understand. *She* cared. No clues, no legacy of where she'd begun, except . . . her fingers crept up, touched the medallion, caressed it. Esther Day, her grandmother? Julian Koumari, her . . . grandfather? And Solange Koumari, her *great-grandmother*?

But that would mean . . . God. Had there been more to her grandparents' reticence than solicitude for some young woman's reputation? Reluctance, even shame hidden behind the tall sash windows and cool front porches of her childhood—in Richmond and Vermont—because their perfect, beautiful, miracle baby, the lovely but secretive mother of Lucy—also happened to be part black?

Not that it mattered. No, wait. Of course it mattered, sixty years ago, and now. Hadn't her stay in this cursed place just shown her how much?

Not that it matters to me. She didn't quicken her pace or look over one shoulder when a black man passed on the sidewalk, did she? Or automatically lock her car doors when the faces in a passing neighborhood suddenly were no longer white. She had black friends, too.

Then why did she feel so incredulous? So . . . angry? Did it matter that now she ought to check off different boxes under "ethnic origin"?

It must. Because she felt as if she'd been wronged, somehow. Singled out.

The old woman stood with hands clasped, waiting. But Lucy's head was throbbing, she couldn't string two thoughts together.

At last she stuttered, "Then, if . . . I mean . . . you'd just better explain some things! Like why you arranged this scheme to get me here, so many years later. And why Mrs. Day is in that place with those crazy geriatric murderers.

And what I saw in the house when you vanished right before my fucking eyes! Was that some kind of trick, or a hallucination . . . or . . . *what are you, anyway?*"

"Fair enough." Eugenie Lee nodded, lips pursed. "Old Esther, she keep track of your mama and then you, all this time. In secret, she think. But I seen the letters. The folks she give that baby girl to? She lied, saying she was one-eighth colored, like those fancy girls in New Orleans. Octoroons? And when those folks see her—such a *pretty* baby, so light-skinned—they don't care. Maybe don't believe it.

"And Esther keep track of it all, like an accountant. But never want to meet either of you face to face."

Lucy frowned. "Then why the continued interest?"

"I think, deep down, she know she open the door to real evil. Her hands stained with all that blood. What happened to Julian, to all of Revelation. She and God both know it was her begun it. Later, when all her other babies come— well, it was too bad." Eugenie's eyes avoided Lucy's for a moment. "But how could she face either one of you when she'd as good as killed her daddy, your granddaddy? All to save herself. Not only that. She killed a witch."

Not with her own hands, but with lies. Then something else occurred to Lucy. "But after that night there *were* no black people left living on Ibo Key. They all ran away, the ones still alive. None ever came back, even to vacation. You said so yourself. Why did *you* stay?"

The old woman's look turned bitter. "Oh, I board that train with the rest. But didn't ride it on up North. How could I, being partly to blame? I had to stay. Yes, it become a whites only place—not that you'd find that rule writ down anywhere. Except for me. Esther Day told them I was a credit to my race. One of the good ones. A colored girl who know her place. Who told on the wicked! What else could she say, me as good as her accomplice, and she needing to keep my mouth shut? Mr.

Turner, he tolerate me. Call me 'Esther's pet nigger.'"

Lucy winced. "Nice."

"And me, I smile and nod and work my tail off. Because I helped kill Revelation as sure as if I'd pointed out the way, when I say Julian Koumari's name."

"But it was an accident! You were trying to help."

The old woman's sigh was the sound wind makes across a scorched, empty place. "The heart don't reason like that, child."

"How could you stay here, with her!"

"Where else? Go live in a strange city up North, afraid, ashamed, wondering when my people would find out what I'd done? Discover who the fool named Julian to the white men? I had plenty of time to think about it all, later. Did I speak up, unasked, for spite? Maybe. Maybe wanting him myself, being outdone seeing him with Esther. *That's* the wickedness I have to answer for. Here I lived in shame, but was needed."

Lucy frowned. "Needed?"

"To help Esther work . . . and to make sure she never, ever forget."

Lucy's mind reeled imagining that awful partnership, endured for many decades like prison shackles. Resenting, mistrusting each other. Surely hating.

"Why bring me here now?" she whispered.

"Because now *you* the one needed."

"Me! For what?"

"Esther try to tell you, but her mind ain't up to it no more. Sixty year gone by, and Revelation still a graveyard. But honey, the dead don't forget. Sometimes they live on. Their curses surely do. And so now something—maybe the Devil, maybe something else—come to collect his due. And you the only one can stop it."

She barked out a laugh, nearly choking on her own sour spit. "Me! But I don't even believe in the, in a—any kind of devil."

Eugenie ignored this. "As for why Esther in that place . . ."

She stopped laughing. "Yes, tell me."

"A week before you get here, I tell her I sent for you. That I was gone tell the truth because it was our only hope. She was so outdone, she pick up a chair, and she—" Eugenie broke off in a fit of coughing.

"She what?" Lucy folded her arms and rubbed them, though it was warm in the room. "What did she do?"

"The thing she dream of day and night for nigh on six decades. Not that I hadn't wished the same on her."

"For God's sake, just tell me!"

"Why, she killed me, child," said Eugenie Lee gently, smiling a little. "Raised up her hand against me. Smote, and killed me dead."

SEVENTEEN

Lucy stared at Eugenie Lee, unable to look away from the thin dark wraith before her. She swallowed, throat clicking dryly. "She, um, *killed* you?"

Eugenie nodded. "Lifted one of them nice antique Windsors in the dining room. Brought it down on my head hard enough to knock me into Glory." She grimaced wryly. "Though this ain't exactly what I expected Glory to be like."

Lucy could think of no response to that.

"Pssht. Don' look so puny. I been reconciled to it. Maybe I even goad her on to do it. Pain in my lungs been getting worse. So when I say you'll be here soon, well, she fit to be tied. Keep asking why I trying to send her to the grave. And I say, 'All those years ago, when you tear and wound yourself, and lie fit to beat the band, you pound the first nail in the coffin for Revelation.'"

"Before you named Julian Koumari and sealed the casket," Lucy said, then wondered, Why am I defending Esther Day? Maybe blood was thicker than all the water and land and time between here and her previous so-called life.

The grief-etched lines in the old woman's face deepened. "A fool girl without the sense to keep quiet. But after the words was out, what else could I say to all those angry crackers? Would they listen? All I could do to run back to Revelation fast as my feet would fly, and warn the town."

"Not fast enough," Lucy whispered. Her eyes no longer

219

saw the hotel room, but fire and rage and bloody murder.

"No. Not fast enough to do most folks any good. But I got to Auntie Solange before the lynch mob. And we run into the woods, made our way to the general store and hid."

"I know." Lucy leaned forward. "So they did escape?"

"Some did, when the train come. But you know that."

"I didn't for sure. But you said, some. Not all?"

The old woman bowed her head. "When the lumber train come around midnight, we was ready. Only a handful of the mob stayed. But a few guns and hatchets can do a lot of butchering. We hoped they hadn't taken a notion to wreck the tracks. And praise God, they didn't. Those men had no regard for life—not ours, anyway. But plenty for some white company property.

"When the train pulled in to Flowers's loading dock, the lumber company men already knew something bad wrong. Conduc-tors and brake men hanging out all along the sides, looking around. The engineer was white, but a righteous man, praise Jesus. He slow almost to a stop. One of the brakemen, he reach out and jerk me up by one arm onto the platform—oh, it hurt, but I didn't care! Then push me inside, out of sight. All the children was lifted up by men like angels in blue uniforms, snatching them right off the side of the tracks and up into a moving heaven. Most of the women, too. But not all.

"Solange's daughter Marina so big in the belly, she lose her balance, slip on the tracks. They couldn't stop the train fast enough. She fall under the wheels and they cut her in two. I heard screams, hers and her mother's. All the little children cover their ears and cry. When they drag the poor girl away, wasn't a prayer of saving her. Blood soak the ground like rainwater. Her mama bent over, trying, though. But she die in seconds.

"When Auntie Solange straighten with her daughter's blood up to her elbows, on her dress, even in her shoes, she don't scream or tear her hair or cry. Her back stay straight.

But she curse Ibo City and Ibo Key and all the people who
live there. Then pull a knife from her bag. Everyone step
back. What this crazy grieving woman going to do with that
wicked blade?

"But I knew, because I work with Esther. If she can't
save her daughter, she would try to cut the baby from her
belly. A Koumari woman never afraid to use a blade."

Eugenie paused, a look in her eyes Lucy had not seen
before, even when she'd spoken of the lynching before.
Pure hatred. But—for Koumari?

Before she could ask, Lee continued in a rush. "Yet just
as that knife touch Marina's bloody dress, another sound
come. One I dream about for over sixty years.

"The mob had flushed Julian from his hiding place in a
burned out house, and came dragging him along, a sorry
sight. Beat, bloody . . . they'd sliced his ears from his head
like you prune leaves from a tree. Blood ran from his
mouth, they already took his tongue, too. Like nasty boys
who torture animals, they get bored and go looking for new
ways of killing. From the coils of rope they carry, they plan
to tie him to the tracks. Let the train have what was left."

This was what had happened to her . . . grandfather?
Lucy covered her face with her hands. "Enough."

Eugenie went on as if she hadn't spoken. "Turner Day
in the lead, carrying a noose. By then everyone on the train
but Solange and her dead girl. When the trainmen who got
off to help see the mob they hop back on right quick. Who
could blame them? Solange Koumari turned from her dead
child, her unborn dying grandchild, her own salvation on
wheels. She stand straight as a fence post, and face those
men down. She look at her mutilated son, then down at her
dead girl, and holler out words. They wasn't in English.

"The sounds stop those men cold.

"She say, 'It may be that all the gods, yours and mine,
have deserted our people. You slaughter children like

animals, so you are welcome to this tough old flesh.' The men all look at each other but make no move toward her.

"She raise her arms and cry, '*Maman Brigitte*! No time to observe the rituals now. But hear me. If the blood of my blood does not return in two generations to punish our enemies, give this place over to your husband, Lord of the Cemetery, Baron Samedi! Curse it once for my son, once for my daughter and her child, and once for me, your unworthy follower. Destroy it! Let their own puny Devil take the souls to burn for eternity. Accept this, my offering!' Then she run forward and plunge the knife into Julian's chest.

"Before anyone could grab hold she turn that same blade and drive it into her own heart. Blood splash the men still holding Julian's arms. They drop him quick . . . that's all I saw. The train was rumbling and clanking, moving away. We left Revelation. Because it was already dead by then."

Tears were streaming down the old woman's cheeks. How could a ghost cry?

"But still, you came back."

Eugenie laughed. "Girl, don't you listen? I never left this cursed island. When the train slow to pass through Ibo City, I jump from the platform of the last car. See here." She drew up her skirt to reveal a long, puckered white scar that ran from above the knee to just above that ankle. "My punishment. Not enough blood to wash away the guilt, but I drag myself to the Day house in the dark, and hide in a tool shed. I fell out from fear or tiredness. At first light I make Esther open the door and let me in."

"And she did?"

"Oh, yes ma'am. Wasn't I the only other one who knew the truth? She was bound to keep me on, keep me quiet—or kill me. I didn't care which."

"But what . . . I mean, *why*? Why not leave and never look back?"

"All alone, shame shadowing me like crows' wings?

God had a part for me to play here. To be Esther Day's helper, her reminder. To be a vengeance unto her."

Lucy simply could not accept this. "That can't be the only reason."

Eugenie once more evaded her gaze. "No. Not the only one. Even though I hated those white men for all they done . . . I hated *her* more."

Lucy nodded. "Esther? Well, sure. Who wouldn't?"

Eugenie sighed. "No, not *her*. Solange Koumari. Because of what she already done to me—and to others. And had meant to do to us all. All the girls."

"But you said . . . I don't understand. Why hate Solange? She died!"

"A town of white people full of hate, happy to have any reason to kill is bad enough. The law say they can't own us no more. But imagine this: still they hold you captive every day of your life. Watch what you do, what you say. What you touch, eat, get to buy in stores. The ones we allowed to walk into.

"But Solange imprisoned us, too. The town's doctor. A witchdoctor, she might be called, back in Africa. Under the old laws, they have more power in the village than the head man, the chief. At church meetings, at business meetings, Solange say, 'Forget the whites. We keep to our own stores, our own churches. Our own customs. Bring them back, live them, spit on white ways.'

"She was brought up on tradition. Bound and determined to enforce them, the old ways. But how? Through the women, forced on the little girls."

Lucy shook her head, lost. "You mean she told them how to dress or talk? Who they could marry?"

"More than that. She could take away more than you can dream, and change a life."

"How?"

"When I was little, I was fascinated with my body. You

know what I mean. Liked to touch myself, because it felt good."

Lucy stared. "Well, uh, that's not unusual. I mean, it's normal. Children don't feel shame, until someone humiliates them."

Eugenie laughed bitterly. "Oh, really? Well, back then my mama worry and she bring me to Solange. My parents decide it's shameful—a little girl so pleased with herself. Solange agree. Praise them for coming in time. 'How else will you keep her pure for a decent husband?' she ask. 'I have a cure, written down in the Book.' Well, that was enough.

"One night they carry me, still sleeping, from my bed to the Koumari house. For a special treatment, my mother said. I didn't understand. Thought she meant medicine, like the cherry tonic we got dosed with every spring. Instead they held me down on the floor of her back room, where roots and herbs hung from the rafters to dry, and spiders spin their webs . . . do you see it now? *My own mother held me down.* And then, with her sharp dirty knife, Solange Koumari cut me. Cut away those parts that give pleasure, then sewed me up so I never touch myself again. Could do nothing, not even pass water but in pain and shame."

"Oh," Lucy moaned, closing her eyes in horror.

In classes she'd read about female circumcision, still practiced in some countries, on thousands of little girls. At age six or so, a girl-child was held down while her outer genitalia were cut away, labia and clitoris. Without anesthesia. The woman 'operating' might use a knife, or a broken piece of glass, then sew the wounds up, leaving a small opening for urination. If the little girl didn't bleed to death or die of infection, she was bound to be a virgin until she married. Then be cut open and stitched up again repeatedly for sex, for childbirth.

God, how ignorant, Lucy'd thought back then as she'd sat reading her new soc-anth textbook at Barnes & Noble, drinking a latte and wincing. Later she'd looked 'infibulation' up online and seen human rights groups were protesting diplomatically to the governments of those countries. "Terrible," she'd muttered. "Bastards." And then she'd forgotten. A far-off horror that didn't touch her.

She felt sick, hollow. "Oh, Eugenie, how could they, your own parents?"

"I wasn't the only one stitched together like a dress seam. The slightest touch made me scream. 'You will heal,' said the old witch, 'and grow up to marry a decent man. All good men want virgins.' Why, she'd done it to her own daughter. Everyone pointed out Marina Koumari to their children, what a good young woman should be! That was enough for my folks.

"Auntie Solange's words carried all the weight of Africa, of our ancestors, the stolen heritage we could only hold onto scraps of—with our nails, our teeth. And we did, we hung on so proud!

"They took me home crying and bleeding. Put me to bed, kept saying I'd had my appendix out. My appendix! As if I hadn't been there, didn't know what they really cut away." She laughed without humor. "The next day they give me a rubber baby to play with. Fed me ice cream. A week later, when I could hobble around, I slip out and bury that ugly blue-eyed doll in the woods."

Lucy nodded. "OK, so you stayed for revenge. And your parents—I guess they were killed? But they'd all been horrible to you, and you wanted to escape."

Eugenie shrugged one shoulder. "So I thought then. Why not work for Esther Day, help her, to spite Auntie Solange. But also hurt her for murdering Revelation, at the same time. Hurt them all. Course I ain't God. But I knew no matter what else happened—whether Esther kept me or killed me— her time would come.

"So to answer your question—no, they aren't no black folks left in Ibo Key, not to this day. Except one." She smiled faintly. "And now, not even me! But I was always invisible after that day; a shadow, a haunt. My hands might move, my mouth talk—but not too much. I attended with Esther at hundreds of birthings. Especially her own. Always thinking, Her time coming—yes, Lord, bring it on! Just as Solange Koumari's had. But not before she cursed this Key, all the men and women and children, three times over. Once for Marina, once for Julian, once for herself. And all for the dead of Revelation."

"Curses always work by threes," Lucy murmured.

"Huh," said the old woman. "So you know *something*. Yes, missy, by threes, and sometimes can be changed. But this one can't be lifted. When those beasts come to kill us, they also curse *themselves*. Which doom mean the most? All I know is, the last blood kin of Solange Koumari—meaning you, child—is here. And so is the Devil. Someplace. Solange and her Book might call him Baron Samedi. I expect it just different names for pure evil."

"Oh, come on." Lucy shook her head. "I never even believed in the traditional Christian Devil, and religion was shoved down my throat enough Sundays. As for the African or Dahomean or Santerian or . . . whatever . . . version, well, OK—I learned about those. But I don't believe—"

"You think the whole world turn on what *you* believe?" Eugenie laughed. "Sister, whether you *believe* or not, evil is here. *I* wouldn't give a damn if it took every last man and woman off to fry in hell. But you part of it, too. So if you want to live . . . well, this devil may not look like some movie boogyman. You got to find him out, and stop him."

"Oh, like I'll just spot him on the street, and—" Lucy stopped, because for a moment she'd glimpsed, in the mirror over the dresser, a figure, a man in gray. The skeevy one from Gulf Rest. The same one who'd slunk around the edges of the murdering mob. Who'd also seen *her*. But now from behind him something else seemed to rise, a huge winged figure. Like a bird or a gigantic moth. "And—and what if I don't? What if I just leave now?"

"Won't matter none. He find you anywhere you go. And then this town is doomed."

"Why should I give a damn about that?"

"Because then so are you. And that child you carry, too."

Wind shrieked, rattling loose panes in the hotel window. Lucy didn't know if she felt more like laughing or screaming. "Don't be stupid. There's *no child!*" She realized one hand was cradling her stomach, and dropped it abruptly. "Anyway, I . . . you can't know that, and I don't believe it." Remembering sweating, crazed Tim Carling standing over her. Punching, kicking as she cowered on cracked asphalt. But the blood test had been negative. She'd taken the morning-after pill to make sure. And the home test kit . . . she'd even had a period since . . . hadn't she? "There's nothing there," she insisted. "But even if there was, I wouldn't have it."

Eugenie Lee spoke again, the words slowly flaying Lucy. "That part up to you. But the other . . . you are included, missy, and no one gon' ask if you like it or not. If you *want* to or not. Solange cursed *all* the descendants, maybe not having enough time to think on what that meant. Not knowing a white woman already carry her new grandchild. Made no exceptions, even for the children of Julian. And because you are the child of Esther Day also. All this island is cursed. You both will die with the rest, here or elsewhere. So you'd best get your damned lazy ass off that bed, and get ready."

Lucy shook her head. "What the hell for?"

"To beat the devil, you got to find him first."

"The man in gray?" she whispered.

Eugenie Lee shrugged. "Gray, white, black, green. Who care what color he turn out, this time round! *Get up.*"

Lucy squeezed her eyes shut. God! Why couldn't

everything—this nagging old bitch, the spinning room, the whole damn island—just go away? She didn't want to hear reasons why she had to stay and save some rude, racist people who—for some unknown reason—liked living on this stupid pile of sand.

Nor did she want to save a supposed child which no test or drug or exam had apparently detected or prevented. Because otherwise . . . otherwise, what? Some hokey curse, handed down by a fearsome, conniving dead woman—who, by the way, was also her long-lost great-grandmother—would befall her? Right.

She was choking on a laugh, but held it back for fear she'd never stop. Until they took her, ranting and raving, to live at Gulf Rest with the rest of the wackos. Then she could bicker and play cards until demons came and dragged them all to fucking Hell and back. Maybe.

Damn. Now she was starting to think like them: crazy as shit. As if everything that had happened in the last few days wasn't just plain crazy.

As if it were all for real.

Could she believe in the power of the dead to watch, and hate, and finally reach out from the grave to clutch at the living? And what about those dead? What about Eugenie Lee, was she already in hell—or some other, middle place, a kind of purgatory that allowed visits back to the living?

According to her studies with Dr. Grove, in some places this would be routine thinking. A fact of the culture. But did *she* believe in an afterlife, in Hell? Could she believe, in other words, in any of the things she'd studied, as anything other than fanciful tales relayed over the years by imaginative people, worthy human beings ignorant merely due to isolation?

And then there was the Book, the one she'd wanted so much to find. That seemed unlikely now.

"One last thing," the old woman's cracked whisper went on relentlessly. "Solange give me this for safekeeping. She break it in two, just before we leave her house and run for the woods. She give the working half to me, t'other to her son. Tol' me, 'Keep it safe, you'll know what to do with it later.' And when like a bad dream I creep back to Revelation, afterward, past where the men leave Julian to rot by the tracks, I take the other half off what the crows left of him. Hid it in them baby things Esther send with your mama to the folks who took her for their own. Kept my half, though *later* been a long time coming. But at last I know."

What was the old fool droning on about now? Her mother was dead, she had been for years. Lucy rubbed her face, wanting to blot the words out. Angry ghosts, dead people, voodoo curses, mad relatives, dead relatives, a freaking devil, for God's sake—all merged into one sickening stew. The words battered at her head like fists on a door.

A shining object spun across the space between the open doorway and the bed. It struck her in the chest and tumbled down onto the mattress.

She groped in the sheets, picked the thing up, and held it to the light. What winked back looked like the working end of a large skeleton key.

She stood so quickly the room spun, but that didn't matter. Her other hand was already reaching for the medallion around her neck, a thumb tracing the rough edge of the intricate design.

As if she'd practiced the motion all her life, she brought the two halves together.

They fit perfectly. The soft metal warmed beneath her hands, a hot welding-together, so painful she had to let go. Tiny blisters rose on her fingers. The broken serrated shaft didn't fall back onto the bed.

The Ibo Key was whole again.

"Unlocks the Book." Eugenie's voice came to her now

as if from far away. "Unlocks the *loas*, too—the spirits of
what you call voo-doo. Solange, she say it *voudon*. All in
there, the power to make and unmake. To quicken or kill. Or
so it say . . . in the Book."

"Then why didn't it work for Solange?"

Eugenie shook her head. "Ain't I worried that myself
like a hound with a knucklebone. Not enough time? Not the
right words? Maybe she lost her belief, or broke her vows
to those gods she always claim to call on. Don't know the
answer to that, child."

Lucy looked up from the now-complete medallion. The
old woman had come closer; she was standing right beside
her. "But where is this Book? Will you help me find it?"
When she reached out instinctively to touch one thin,
withered arm, her outstretched hand only passed through a
fading image.

"Do what I can," came the ghost of a whisper. "But no . . .
soul . . . no mortal help . . ."

The old woman was gone. Where she'd stood a small
black bird hopped, its wings tipped in red, breast mottled as
if with fresh blood. The blood of Revelation. Its sleek black
head was cocked, a bright black eye gazed right at Lucy.
She heard the rustle of dry, feathered wings, and tensed.
But it was only the little bird taking flight. The flapping of
its small wings seemed magnified a hundred times, though,
as if a whole migrating flock were crossing the room. It
swooped and flitted through the open window, and was
gone. But the sibilant sound remained, becoming the
whisper of many dead voices within her head.

We all go with you.

EIGHTEEN

Visiting hours at Gulf Rest had just begun. Cars crept into the lot, disgorging family groups who drifted across the lush green, bearing offerings before them like Magi: flowers, fruitcakes, potted poinsettias, boxes papered with reindeer and holly.

They scattered at the intersection of neat cement walks, heading for various cottages. One woman balancing a potted Christmas tree left a glittering wake of tinsel, as if marking her way back through a dark forest to the parking lot. A chubby toddler stumbled along, gaze fixed on the box of candy canes clutched by an older sister. Men lagged behind wives, hands pocketed, whistling.

On a stone bench under a drooping willow, Lucy sat with her laptop, observing each person who passed over its raised screen. Assessing and dismissing one after another, even the children. Nowhere did she see a thin, malicious face smirking above some sort of gray outfit.

To beat the Devil, one must first encounter him. Who had said that? But neither Satan nor Baron Samedi was listed on 411.com, or in the Yellow Pages under *ARCHANGELS—Cast Out.* Really, was the guy she'd glimpsed truly ancient evil incarnate? More likely merely a man; a very sick one, but no more a demon than she. And yet . . . what about his presence at the massacre? If he was local he might've been a grandfather, a great uncle of some

231

current resident. But she'd first met him here, so here she'd stay, for a while at least. In case he ambled by among the dutiful crowd.

Sorting and rejecting, she tried to appear just another visitor, taking a Facebook break on one of the home's teak benches. Like a car on an icy road, her mental wheels were spinning, trying to gain traction.

After the specter of Eugenie Lee had metamorphosed, then vanished, her hunger had faded, too. She'd fallen asleep and dreamed.

She was sitting naked on a straight-backed chair in front of the full-length mirror hung on the closet door. She felt a strange sensation, a strong pressure between her legs. She'd spread her knees and saw, in the mirror, a baby emerging head first. Yet she'd felt no pain, no fear. She held her hands out and the baby slid into them. It was a boy who had no umbilical cord. There was a birth mark like a strange scrolled cross on the child's stomach. And then the baby slowly turned its head, and the eyelids fluttered open. He had the same blue eyes, the exact facial features as Nick Yulee.

She'd sat up in bed sweating, mouth filling with saliva. Gray light was just filtering through the windows. Staggering to the thirties-era toilet bowl, she hit the cold tiles hard enough to crack her kneecaps, but already retching too violently to care. Between spasms, thinking, *So this is what morning sickness in Hell feels like.*

She remembered what Eugenie Lee had claimed. But why Nick Yulee? He certainly wasn't . . . he couldn't have had anything to do with . . .

She'd moaned, "Oh Christ." Grabbed the edge of the sink and hauled herself up. Then, one hand braced against the rim, she splashed cold water on her perspiring face.

After that she had dressed very slowly and carefully, to avoid turning her head or looking up or down. The slightest motion made her want to heave her guts all over again. She crept down the stairs to let Hercules out into the alley, whispering "good morning" to the clerk. Then stood well upwind while the dog performed his morning ritual of sniffing and peeing, peeing and sniffing, then finally dumping a load of . . . ugh, she couldn't even think about it. The desk clerk had frowned at them through the open side door, but she didn't care.

By then though she'd felt marginally better, and ordered plain toast in the dining room. But when it arrived the yeasty smell of whole wheat brought sour bile to the back of her throat. She'd pushed the plate away. Straining a few sips of black coffee and some watered-down orange juice past gritted teeth, she left some bills on the table and retrieved Hercules from the room. Pregnant? Impossible. But just in case . . .

She found a pregnancy test kit in the island's general store and smuggled it past the inn's front desk in a brown paper sack, feeling weirdly guilty and transgressive. But why? Her problems, her actions, were nobody's business. Not here.

She was so anxious by then she could barely force herself to pee, but when she was finally successful and had waited exactly the prescribed time, the stick reassured her—no pink line. Ha! She was fine. Silly to freak like that. Still, she decided to get another kit later and do it over again, later.

They went back down the stairs. Just as the dog was jumping into the back seat, a truck passed. The face that did a double-take above the wheel was Nick Yulee's. She'd averted her eyes and slid quickly into the Toyota. The sight of him forced her to wonder: why *was* she still lingering in Ibo Key? He'd probably been wondering the same.

Well, for one thing, by now it was impossible to dismiss the past few days as wild imagination or post-traumatic hysteria. There on the hotel room floor had lain a pile of wet clothing reeking of saltmarsh, dead fish, and charcoaled wood, all sprinkled with beads of damp white flour. If the burning town hadn't been real, then what was it—an elaborate practical joke involving all of Ibo Key, their lines rehearsed, dressed up in vintage costumes?

Secondly, most solidly, hanging from the chain around her neck was the transformed medallion, now in the shape of a finely wrought silver key of ornate scrolled design. Two separate parts which had warmed as if hotly attracted, and then welded together suddenly, magically, with no seam apparent.

Third, she'd had the promise—made by an apparition, a ghost—that she could flee to the ends of the earth and still be pursued and felled by some unspecified but lethal fate awaiting all on this island. She, and the supposed fetus. Which of course wasn't there. The test had proved that—again.

And finally, there was the putative Book. According to Eugenie Lee, and also poor deluded Esther Day, it held the answer to saving everything. In her mind, it represented the chance of a lifetime. She'd gone through quite an ordeal already. If at all possible, why shouldn't she have it?

She put the car in gear and pulled out onto Water Street.

But where was this arcane tome? Buried, burnt to ash, tucked whole and blackly-mildewed in a sooty chimney at the ruins of the Koumari house? She wasn't even sure which foundation that one had been. And had seen nothing like a bound set of pages in Solange's possession as they'd fled. But that event had been so chaotic, the night so dark. A *small* book might be easily concealed. But if it was large and thick, with a fancy leather binding, one of the mob could have spotted and made off with it as booty. Though she couldn't imagine any of the men she'd seen recognizing an old book as a thing of great value. Or wanting to hang on to one for so many years.

But if someone had, how the hell would she find out what they'd done with it?

She sighed and looked down at the screen again. The Facebook photos and postings—old now, she hadn't updated since before the attack—blurring under her distracted gaze.

A voice near her left ear whispered, "Clever girl. Don't give up too easily."

She tensed and nearly screamed, but instead forced herself to calmly turn her head and look at the man who'd just sat down next to her.

He wore a gray tracksuit today, its strange weave wavering in the late-morning sun with an electronic rainbow shimmer, like a distorted television image. He offered a thin-lipped smile.

She cleared her throat and recovered her voice. "So I've, um, found you again."

"Have you?" He looked around, eyebrows raised. "Well, I suppose. Not as hot here as at the last place, eh? And certainly not as exciting. By the way, could you slide over a bit?"

Lucy did so gladly. He merely edged closer. She scooted farther, until the wrought-iron arm of the bench dug into her hip. Not looking directly at him, she ventured, "The last place was a long time ago, even though it was only last night."

He smacked his forehead. "Of course! Give the lady the prize behind door number three. But wasn't that a hoot?"

She closed her eyes. "Give me a break. You're just a man, some creep playing Evil Psycho. Obviously all this has nothing to do with a poseur like you."

He swiveled to face her. "My, my. Sticks and stones, sticks and stones. Still, I can hardly let that go by. Not good for the image." He shook his head. "Speaking of provocation, how long have you been tempting fellow students with rides home late at night?"

"What!"

"The boy really did like you. That weak little scholar."
He tsked. "It wasn't easy to make him draw blood. Had to
push harder than is usually required. Naturally, he suffered
agonies of remorse and horror and all that garbage. After
he, I mean *we*, had our fun with you. A minor annoyance.
He expressed himself only a little there at the end. I let his
acting out go on a fraction too long, I'm afraid." He shook
his head. "So messy, at the end."

Struggling not to jump up and bolt, taking slow, deep
breaths to calm the rising nausea, she said, "You, um, you
mean Tim. Then . . . that was you. Not him?"

"Not me, *not me*," he whimpered, mimicking Carling's
quiet voice so well she did want to scream.

Of course, that detail had been in the newspaper. But
how did he know what Tim sounded like?

Tears leaked from his merrily squinched eyes. "Oh, oh.
That was a good one. NOT ME! Of course it wasn't him,
the stupid twit. He didn't have the balls—or as they
quaintly say down here, the chitlins—to do anything so
deliciously wicked. Not on his own. I must say, no one
wants to take responsibility for his actions these days.
Haven't you noticed?"

She was trembling so hard her teeth clicked. "Th-then if
that was you, and y-you . . . what name should I call you by?"

"Of course it was me all the time. And a delightful time
it was, my dear."

When he winked, she noticed his pupil was not round,
but a narrow black slit. Just like—

"For old times' sake, you may call me . . ." he paused,
fingering one shimmering cuff, "Mr. Gray."

She caught a faint sulfurous reek, like summer wind
blowing over a rotting landfill.

"So you're on a crusade. Or no—a quest! That's all the
rage for girls these days in fiction and movies. Going to beat
the Devil, like Daniel Webster in drag? Or perhaps you'd

prefer to deal with one of those gentlemen I introduced you to inside?" He inclined his head at Magnolia House. "Think back. Weren't those old geezers leading the pack at the massacre? Whereas *I* was merely an innocent bystander."

Lucy stared at him. The old men, the card game, the quarrel . . .

"Tsk, tsk." He shook his head. "What good is an expensive education if you don't notice details?"

Some children ran past, laughing. "Watch me, Gramma," a small girl shouted, and did a clumsy cartwheel in the grass. A frail white-haired woman applauded from her seat under a shady oak. That was when, with fresh horror, Lucy understood. *They* had not been here sixty years ago. These happy, laughing kids. Any of them related to the murderers, no matter how distantly. If she were to believe, well then . . . they were doomed, too.

Her companion shrugged. "Their own fault if they get in the way."

She turned on him. "Doesn't hanging out with mentally ill nobodies ever make you feel like—oh, I don't know—the underworld's biggest loser? Or is it more exciting here? The cut-throat bridge games, the daytime soaps, the meals on trays with plastic cutlery, the wheelchair races, Wednesday Bingo?"

His pale cheeks grew rosy. Another whiff of sulfur, and a singed under-scent. "We are not here 'all the time,'" he growled. "We come and go as we please. Unlike some people who think they can walk on water—risky showboating, that, *we* don't even like to cross—well, never mind. Anyway . . . the four gentlemen stay here, bound by our little secret. Some of their spawn did leave and go on to greater fame. Nor will they escape my attention. In good time. You may have read about it?"

He kept saying "we." What did he mean by that? She shook her head.

"The supermarket firebomber? The sniper in California?

The charming lady in Alabama who drowned her children in the bathtub because God told her to? No? Pity. Don't you ever go online?"

"I try to avoid tabloid crap and cute cat videos."

"Ironic, considering your origins. Well, I can give only so many hints. From here on out, no more free rides. Dig up your own information. And by the way." He glanced at his watch, a Mickey Mouse Timex. "If you find any interesting reference works lying about, consider turning them over. If you were to *offer*, well, I'm a bit of a collector." He raised an eyebrow. "I could offer a trade. An undiscovered fairy tale manuscript, a Gnostic scroll. If you like that sort of thing."

She wondered how he would use the Book. Or maybe he just didn't want her to have it. "Thanks, but . . . no thanks."

He stood abruptly and brushed off his pants. "Once finished with this quaint little fishing burg . . . well, I've always wanted to see the Haunted Mansion, and ride the Teacups! Spin, spin, spin. . . ."

Just then a toddler ran shrieking past, young mother in hot pursuit, startling Lucy. When she looked back, the man in gray was gone.

She drove slowly back to town, so lost in a whirl of insane thoughts she crossed the center line twice, the second time nearly colliding with a pickup. The long, outraged wail of its horn jolted her back to sweating awareness and a death-grip on the wheel.

She felt trapped in a crazy folk tale. Who was the devil, demon, lunatic she'd just encountered? Above all, where was this Book everyone spoke of? If she could find it, some of her problems might be possible to solve. Wasn't that what Eugenie Lee had said? She hadn't yet been to see the woman Yulee had mentioned, the amateur, unofficial historian who kept old documents and books about Ibo Key. A regular lending library in her home, he'd claimed, and that she might let Lucy peer into the boxes she'd stored against the day the fabulous Ibo Key Historical Society and Museum would be built.

But what was her *name*?

"Damn," she muttered, cursing her inability to remember names, unless they were mythological figures. Those she had no trouble with. She usually tried to connect people to mnemonic devices . . . nope. Nothing came. Did this mean she had to see Nick Yulee again? She supposed, with a mixture of wariness and anticipation, that it did.

Inside Anhinga Tours, a couple stood at the counter, arms linked, signing off on a rental return. Nick was swiping a credit card and didn't look up when Lucy entered. She waited by the door, back to the counter, perusing a rack of sun-faded postcards with curling edges: *Southern Exposure*. A brunette standing on a dune, turned from the camera, smiling over one shoulder, minus the bottom half of her bikini. "Oh, clever," she muttered, and jammed it back in the rack.

Yulee called, "Back in a minute," and escorted the couple out. He returned, wiping his hands on a rag. "Sorry, but there's a marine advisory out. The hurricane. So I'm not renting any more—"

She turned and faced him.

He looked startled, then wary. "I won't say another word. Every time I open my mouth it runs you off." He slid back onto a stool and crossed his arms, snowy T-shirt a stark contrast to his deeply tanned skin. His face was wind-burned, and the raised white curve of scar stood out on his cheek. "So . . . is 'hi' safe?"

She had to smile. "Yeah."

"Didn't expect to see you here. This mornin' it appeared you were getting a late start for the mainland."

She shrugged. "That was the plan. But . . . I was

wondering . . . the other night you mentioned a woman who keeps historical stuff. I forget her name. Do you know her number, or where she lives? I wanted to stop there. On my way out of town."

"Oh." He looked disappointed. "Um, yeah, Mrs. Waters. Velma Waters, over on Saltmarsh Road. Can't call her up, she doesn't keep a phone. Hates the sound of a ringing machine, she says. I could take you—"

"No thanks," she said quickly, then regretted it when he looked hurt. "It's just, I'm in a big freaking hurry, and don't want to take up your, uh, working hours."

"Jesus, I mean *Hay*-suess, is coming in about fifteen minutes. He can watch the store. But if you're in such a big hurry . . ."

She avoided his gaze. "So short on time, well—you just wouldn't believe it. Could you write the address down?" She spotted a block of Post-its on the counter and slid it toward him.

When he took it, their fingertips brushed. He frowned slightly, then sighed and scrawled a few hasty lines.

"Thanks," she said, backing toward the door. "I really appreciate it, Nick."

"Hey, no problem. And listen, professor?"

She didn't correct him this time, just hovered in the doorway, eyebrows raised.

"I don't know a good way to say this, exactly. But since you're leaving, what does it matter." He placed his hands flat on the counter, looked down at them, then flexed the one that'd brushed hers a moment ago. "Anyhow, I hope whoever it was did whatever he did to you, that the bastard is dead now. Or good as."

She caught her breath, then turned away and ran for the car.

The yellow one-story cottage had a deep porch and a neatly edged square of yard delineated by a weathered picket fence.

The roof had twin peaks, as if two smaller houses had been joined side by side. She walked up a curving brick path, climbed the steps and knocked. A hand-painted sign hung above a split-oak market basket:

Natural history proves it true—
Women and elephants never forget. —Dorothy Parker
RETURN BOOKS HERE, PLEASE.

A quick tapping of footsteps, and a thin, gray-haired woman stood on the threshold, a cashmere cardigan draped across her shoulders. She blinked out at Lucy like an owl from a tidy cage. "Don't believe we've met. You a winter visitor? Looking for a good book, I expect."

"Um . . . yeah." She tilted her head, trying to look both competent and friendly. "Nick Yulee told me—"

"Nick! That sweet boy." Her voice warmed. "Well, *man* I should say now. Even if he is grown, hard to think of him as anything but thirteen. Hopeless at diagramming sentences, but what an imagination. Oh, but I'm yammering about the past. Here, step inside."

She drew Lucy into the dark and shut the door firmly behind them.

As her eyes adjusted, she saw why Nick had called Velma Waters the town librarian. The front room was furnished in Victorian mahogany and floral brocade. But floor to ceiling, the walls were lined with shelves. Even over the windows and doorways. An oak card catalog served as a coffee table. Atop it sat index cards, a jar of pens, and a stack of books.

"Wow. How many volumes are in here?"

Waters smiled. "After twenty thousand I stopped counting. A hobby that got the best of me. Now, what're you interested in—mysteries, science fiction, romance? Hmm."

She narrowed her eyes. "No, no. You've got a serious look. Foreign authors. Mahfouz or Cheng Nien. Maybe Borges. Am I close?"

"Uh, well." How best for a stranger to ask to root through boxes of the woman's precious Ibo Key history? "I'm not really here for a novel."

"No?" A frown passed fleetingly, but the expectant smile remained.

"I had a question about, um . . ." She thought hastily. "About birds. One kind in particular." She described the strange black and red ones that seemed to follow her around the island. "Are they native to the key?"

"Hmm. Wait one minute." Mrs. Waters pulled a dog-eared Audubon guide off a shelf. "One of these, I guess you mean. The red-winged blackbird. No? Hmm. Well, there's the spotted-breasted oriole . . . but they don't normally come this far south."

Lucy looked closely at the second color photo, then shook her head. "That's definitely not it."

The woman sighed and slid the book back in its place. "Afraid that's the best I can offer. I'm familiar with the local ones. Another hobby. But I've never seen anything exactly like what you describe. Must be a migrating species. The winds sometimes throw the poor little things off track. Anything else I can help with?"

She nodded, trying not to look too eager. "Well . . . I'm studying folklore at Pottsburg University, up north. Writing my dissertation on folk medicine and, uh, legends in your area."

"How exciting! And don't we just need a book—a good one, I mean. I wrote a pamphlet myself, once. Out of print now . . . not that it would compare with a real academic study, heavens no." She shook a teacherly finger. "I knew you didn't look like a snowbird." At Lucy's puzzled frown, she added, "A tourist, honey."

"Oh. Right. Well, I'm looking for information on the

area called Revelation."

Silence. The woman stared at her intently, searching her face as if it were a map of her intentions. What she expected to see, Lucy had no idea. She braced herself, prepared to be promptly thrown out. "I'd understand if you don't want to let me start digging into boxes of old papers. You could call and get a reference from my university," Lucy added in a rush, then remembered the woman kept no phone. "Oh, wait." She dug out her iPhone. "Here."

"Gracious! No thank you." Mrs. Waters eyed the cell as if it were a giant squirming cockroach. Then the frown smoothed away. "I'm not a native of the Key. Not even a native Floridian. My people hail from south Georgia, though, so I know small towns. If you've been asking around here about such as that, you probably haven't gotten much cooperation. Most folks like old skeletons to stay in the closet, not come out and rattle their bones in the street."

"I guess not," said Lucy, glancing at a stack of leather-bound books. How old, she wondered. If I could just—

"And you hope to publish whatever you find, one day."

"Uh—yeah." She mentally crossed her fingers. "I mean, well, there's a possibility."

Waters sighed. "Understand now, I wasn't living here yet, back then. But I can guess what it must've been like. I'm a Southerner of a certain age, so you may be assuming certain things."

Lucy shook her head. "Oh, no! I'd never—"

Waters smiled. "Well, you'd be wrong. My mama and daddy brought me up to hate violence, and detest bigotry. Those things really don't have such neat geographical boundaries, no matter what the media likes to show."

"You're right, Mrs. Waters. It's easy to assume things."

"Yes, well . . . I fell in love with this place many years ago, back when fishing was still the main industry. Watched the boats chase each other to the docks every afternoon, smelled the spiced shrimp cooking, saw the slow, easy way things were done. That was before I knew of its . . . history. This island used to be called 'Queen of Gulf Coast Fishing Towns.' I loved it then because it had *refused* to change, to tart itself up like Key West, to troll for tourist money. But over the years—a comment here, one there. Well, I put two and two together. It made me angry. Still, I wanted to stay. Can you understand that?"

She felt her shoulders sag. Obviously the woman was about to say no, very politely, in detail, and at great length. "Sure. I suppose so."

"All these years, I felt guilty not doing or saying something about that poor murdered community. Didn't have the faintest idea *what*, but . . . I suppose I kept hoping someone else would do it for me, so I could go on loving the Key with a clear conscience. A reporter came to town once. I might've talked to *him*, but then . . ."

Lucy blinked. The suicide guy in the car, thirty years ago, with a bullet in his brain?

Mrs. Waters paused and shook her head. "People in Germany or South Africa or Bosnia might feel the same way. Can't change history, so why not let the memory fade away? But you only have to read the news to see that's the wrong answer. Some young black men were killed in New Jersey recently, run down like dogs just for visiting a girl in an Italian neighborhood. The other day, on CNN, there was that segregated high school prom in Texas—or Alabama? Anyway, it's time someone told the world about Revelation. A wound needs air and light to heal."

Lucy straightened. "You mean you'll let me—thank you, Mrs. Waters!"

"Please, honey. Call me Velma. You weren't in my English class." She sighed. "Once your visit gets out maybe folks will stop talking to me, too. Won't be popular, that's a fact! But I'm not running for mayor. Nick must've sent you for a reason. Come this way, honey. All I have is in the back."

Down a short hallway, past old black and white photos of people in strange bathing suits, of men with cocked fedoras and devilish grins, of fishermen posed next to big catches. At the end, Velma opened the door to a cramped room. Dust motes floated like plankton in the light filtering through 1950s metal Venetian blinds. Cardboard boxes were stacked against the walls, double and triple parked, so only a small square of floor remained open, in the center.

She dragged one box from a corner and dusted her hands smartly. "Now, you may be disappointed. This is all I've got. Most of the records were destroyed decades ago."

"By the fire, of course," Lucy agreed, eyeing it, disappointed already. One small cardboard cube, with the label of some old Tampa tobacco company pasted on its sides: SAILOR'S FRIEND. A girl in an old-fashioned middy blouse was waving goodbye to a departing schooner.

"I'll leave you to it. But remember"—the retired teacher frowned sternly, as if Lucy were a student in detention—"I know just what's here, and expect to find it all back in good order before you leave. I'll be right down the hall, cataloguing. Stick my head in to check on you soon." She turned away authoritatively on one blocky heel and left Lucy alone.

She sank to her knees before the sealed cardboard box. With the serrated shaft of the medallion key, she slit the brown paper tape on its flaps, then slowly folded them back. A smell of musty old paper, mildew, and a faint hint of charcoal enveloped her, as did a cloud of powdery black mold. She rubbed her nose, sneezed. "Shit," she said. No tissues. After a moment's hesitation wiped her nose on one sleeve. No time to waste hunting for Kleenex. What if the Book itself, or at least a clue to its whereabouts, were contained in this plain brown box?

She carefully lifted out the top rustling layer.

A few newspaper clippings. Yellowed legal documents. Creased black and white photographs. A huge, mummified roach. "Ugh," she said, and flicked it across the room.

There, under the papers, lay a small black book with dry leather binding that threatened to crumble in her hands. She nearly stopped breathing. Until she read, stamped on the cover in gold script: JOURNAL. Looking closer she saw it was mass produced, probably less than thirty years old.

Her stomach clenched. She feared for a moment she'd be sick again. But it was just disappointment. She laid the journal aside and picked up one desiccated, yellowed clipping.

NEGRO ASSAULTS WOMAN IN IBO KEY
Suspect Flees Scene; Many Join Search.

Ibo Key, Dec. 18—A group of deputized citizens attempted to apprehend a Negro wanted in an alleged attack on a white woman yesterday. The citizens were met in the nearby town of Revelation by armed accomplices determined to prevent the arrest of the suspect. Shots were exchanged, and the resisting gang barri-caded themselves in a house. Intermittent fighting continued until two white men were brutally killed. The Negro casualties have not yet been determined. The Governor had no official report of the race riot at this time. Lacking official information, he did not wish to comment on whether any steps would be taken by the state to restore order. Hope was expressed by white residents that the Crane County sheriff would assemble a body of men to protect white citizens should racial disturb-ances spread to the mainland.

Her fingers tightened on the yellowed scrap. But that's

not what happened, she thought, setting it aside to look through the remaining clips. They too were dated that long-ago day, or the next, or three days later. Small articles headlined

RACE RIOT ENDS IN SEVERAL DEATHS

REVELATION RAPIST DIES
WHILE RESISTING ARREST

ORDER RESTORED IN IBO KEY DISTURBANCE

She shook her head, disbelieving. The tone was of genteel relief that such a "potentially violent situation" was now under control. But respected citizens of Ibo City, The weekly *Abaton Pilot-Courier* stated, had even more fears: "Negroes are likely stockpiling kerosene and gasoline to firebomb the island and nearby mainland towns." White casualties were still listed as two. The "colored" body count remained "undetermined." Most of the so-called outside agitators, another article claimed, had fled. But local law enforcement and the Klan were both looking for them.

She crumpled the fragile newsprint in clenched fists. Then, realizing what she'd done, hastily smoothed the paper out.

She set these aside.

Next she unearthed faded black and white photographs, brittle squares with serrated edges. Their backgrounds had grayed in spots. The kind of old photos she'd been allowed to look at sometimes as a child, gingerly balancing a heavy embossed leather album with thick black pages on skinned knees.

In the first, three little dark-skinned girls in fluffy white organdy dresses stood before a church, flanked by a distinguished-looking man in clerical collar. She frowned. Her fingers tightened on the small square. It was the AME minister she'd tried to warn. In the background sat the church whose cross she'd seen a blackened corpse nailed to. She studied the girls, but couldn't decide if they were familiar. It'd been so dark in the woods, then the basement.

The next two photos stunned her. A car parked before the Flowers' general store. Two whites, a man and a woman, just visible inside it. A black woman clad in a dark dress and apron, doctor's bag at her feet, was holding up a white infant so the camera could capture its tiny disgruntled face, wrinkled as last winter's apples. The woman was Solange Koumari, smiling confidently. In the background, blurred figures walked past, carrying bags or parcels.

In the third, larger photo, gangly children sat on the steps of a frame building, posing for a group shot. Those in the back rows peered over or around their companions. One held up two fingers behind a classmate's head, crowning him with horns. All wore white shirts or dresses, and clunky lace-up oxfords with white socks. Carefully printed across the bottom was

REVELATION ELEMENTARY SCHOOL, NOVEMBER 1960.

Where were those children now? Retired, with children and grandchildren of their own, scattered around the country. Or small, shattered skeletons lying in an unmarked mass grave? When she traced a finger over the writing the letters blurred.

She laid the photos face-down, gently, on top of the clippings.

All that remained was the journal. She picked it up and carefully opened the front cover. The pages were warped, water-rippled, foxed with brown spots. The title page so faded she could barely make out the writing. Beneath *This Journal Belongs To* was scrawled a name almost oblit-erated by a water stain. She got up and walked over to a floor lamp, turned it on the brightest setting, and held the page directly underneath. Here she could make out some letters:

N CK YU E

"Oh!" Shocked she nearly dropped the book. *His* diary? But why was it in here?

Opening it at random she read.

Today he (Grandaddy I mean) had some folks over to play cards. He took the jar out like he always does + set it on the table. Let's deal old Julian Koumari in, boys, he said. An they laughed, like they always do. It not funny so why [unreadable]. Nobody else's grandpa keeps a pickled hand in a jar in the garage.

A few pages farther, she deciphered:

Went to fish today by my self but HE said hed come too so we can have a man to man talk. Oh hell I thought, thinking sex but no. He told me about all the land Id inherit when he dies and how I got to make something of it. And take care of my mom always. He took out a bottle and drunk all before we got out to his fishing spot. I don't want it, I said to myself—I guess too loud. He hit my face. Not that land, I tol him. You no grandson of mine he said but a true son of bitch. My head hurt all right and I wish again hed just die. Except then the land he murdered for and hid [a water spot] in the Daniel field will be mine. If thers such a thing as ghosts

*theyll come after me but HE stole it I
DON'T want it. Never.*

The sound of footsteps made her jump. "I see you
found his old journal. I just recalled that's where I'd filed
it. It's not really Revelation material of that period, of
course, but . . . I'm not sure he'd want it to be read."

"Oh, I haven't really looked at it yet." The lie came to
her without thinking. "This really is Nick's old diary?"

She nodded. "It was. You see, I had my seventh grade
English class keep journals for the whole year. Nick turned
his in like everyone else."

"So you kept it here all these years?"

"Goodness no. That's not the journal I asked him to
write for class! That one was neat and rather boring and got
a solid B minus. This is his own. He kept up the writing
after the assignment was over. For a year, anyway. I was
surprised, as you can imagine when he brought it to me
after school one day. Though I guess it made sense. Even
then I was accumulating papers, loaning out books
sometimes.

"He told me he couldn't keep it in the house, for fear
his grandfather might find it. Herbert Yulee was a violent
man. His son, Nick's father, had already died in a drunken
accident. His mother was a tiny, silent woman. Pale as a
ghost. Herbert drank a lot, and often. It made him even
more violent."

"Oh." Lucy felt a flash of sympathy, could imagine a
young, frightened boy at the mercy of a staggering,
shouting ogre.

"You won't know any of this, but Nicky learned the
fiddle from old Mr. Oatey—the restaurant man?—and got
very good on it. Still is! But when his grandfather found
out, back then, that he'd been sneaking over to the old
man's to learn to play, he beat him so badly the boy missed
school for a week.

"Back then, taking a belt or even a board to a child wasn't considered abuse. Not the state's business and certainly not some nosy schoolteacher's. I'd seen some terrible bruises on Nick before. Once I asked where they came from and he said, 'I fell off the fence out back.' But he looked over my shoulder, not at my eyes, when he said it.

"Still, I tried to talk to his father after the fiddle incident. You've seen that scar on his cheek?"

Lucy nodded, biting her lower lip. She'd assumed it was from a fishing hook, or maybe a bar fight.

"The day he returned to school, that side of his face had been laid open. It was still bleeding, a gaping wound. I took him to Mrs. Day's little clinic. Her assistant, that nice Miss Lee, sewed it up. He finally admitted his grandfather had done it. Hit him in the face with a boat hook because he'd lost a crab pot. Well." She sighed. "That night I went to their house. The mother—that thin sliver of a woman—she hid in the back."

Lucy frowned, recalling the night in Oatey's when she'd asked why Nick called his band "Scratch." He'd just fingered the pale, raised crescent on his cheek, but said nothing.

"Herbert threatened to kill me some dark night if I didn't mind my own damned business. Called me a nosy old bitch, and worse." She laughed bleakly. "Nick had been keeping this diary in a hole in a big old oak, but it was getting wet. He knew it wouldn't hold together much longer."

Lucy frowned. "So you put it in the Revelation box because you knew his father, or grandfather, had been at the massacre?"

"No. I didn't know that, though it wouldn't surprise me. I moved here long after that. But I'd vacationed here, loved the wildlife and all. I'm a bird-watcher, as I said. But that's not important. Nick asked me not to read the journal, just to keep it safe. So I have."

She was surprised. "You never read any of it?"

The other woman blushed. "Well, just a few pages," she admitted. "There's no excuse. I'm ashamed to admit I did break his trust on that."

Lucy willed her own face to remain neutral. "Why'd you put it in here, then?"

Velma said slowly, as if thinking back, "He told me his father started cutting firewood near the tree he'd hidden it in. That scared him, so he took it out. I asked where he wanted me to keep it. He said, 'Just put it someplace safe, where no one'll be looking through things.' So I thought of this box. I never add to it, and no one ever brings me new items, or asks about it. Seemed a good bet. When I told him, he said that was a fine choice. And that it . . ." She paused and cocked her head, bird-like again. "Yes—that it belonged there."

Lucy looked down at the journal again. "So he knew it was here. And that I'd probably . . . Mrs. Waters, may I stay for a while and read? I know you don't want the things taken out of the house, and I think I've found some . . . material."

Velma frowned. "I don't know. You think he might've written about Revelation? But he wasn't even born. I don't see how. But I declare, that one . . . he's an old soul. I knew it the first time I set eyes on him. And he sent you, didn't he, knowing what you're looking for."

She nodded. "He said . . . whatever I needed, well . . . it was OK with him."

The older woman looked relieved. "So he knows you. He trusts you. It must be all right."

Was the hot blush creeping up her neck visible in the light of the single floor lamp? Lucy was beginning to feel very small indeed. But she had to find out, any way she could. "Hey, would you, um, like to call him?" she asked, surprised at the calm sureness in her own voice.

Velma hesitated, the conflict between politeness and old promises clear on her face. "Oh, no," she said at last. "I'll take your word. Why, how else would you know to come and look, if he hadn't told you? Anything else you need?"

"One thing, yes. There's supposed to be a book . . . an old, rare one. It was very important to Revelation, to some of the people there."

Mrs. Waters frowned. "You mean like a genealogy, a record of births and deaths? Or a history of the town?"

"No. Kind of like an old herbal, or a book of cures . . . a collection of lore. A *grimoire*, they used to call such works. It'd be of huge interest to a historian or folklorist."

The other woman looked mystified. "Never seen or heard of anything like that. I'm sorry."

She left. Lucy slumped against the jamb, seesawing between disappointment, relief, and guilt. The journal felt warm in her hand, almost alive. A thing that didn't belong to her and she'd simply appropriated it. Till now she'd had no idea what lengths—or depths—she'd go to get what she wanted. Now she was pretty sure, even beyond this mild misleading of the innocent: Lie, cheat, steal. Whatever it took.

She took a break to let Hercules out of the car for a quick walk. Then hurried back inside. The warped journal was sitting where she'd left it, and she stared at the leather rectangle, trying to imagine a very young Nick Yulee's implicit trust in his teacher. Decades later, she'd broken that trust between them. Her fingertips brushed the cover tentatively. But shame wasn't enough to make her put it back in the box.

With a sigh, she slowly opened it to the marked place, feeling as if someone were watching. But even shame was not enough—not nearly—to prevent her from reading more.

After twenty or so pages she stopped, closed the book, and shook her head. Herbert Yulee had indeed been at Revelation. A young man then. His hobby late in life, aside from getting drunk and beating his family, had been boasting about what happened there. Showing off souvenirs, like the withered hand in a jar of 'shine he kept on the fireplace mantle. And a big silver railroad pocket watch, which he used to dangle before little Nick when he taught him to tell time, "by old Reverend Nigger." Lucy recalled the watch the AME minister had consulted. The same.

No mention of Solange Koumari or her book, so far.

She read the few remaining pages. The last entry made her dizzy.

> He kept me out of school today. We
> went to the land he rents to Mister
> Daniel. They was all working. Rafe
> Daniel had a new John Deare harrow.
> Some men had come out to see it work.
> When it they ran over the south field,
> it churned up some white things. Made
> a awful racket. Every one walked out
> to look. Mr. Daniel was cursing to
> beat the band.
> Then I saw what got hung up in the
> blades. BONES. Lots of broken leg
> bones, and skulls. Some small as a
> cat's head. Not cow bones I don't
> think. Baby skulls and bones of arms
> and legs all busted up. Like Mr.
> Daniel had meant to grow people
> instead of green beans.

She lowered the Book, sickened, reminded of her dream of a burning town. A giant plow furrowing a mass grave for bodies still alive.

She took a deep breath, and read on.

> But the men just laughed. One kicked
> a skull like a football. Guess you

dint plant those niggers deep enough,
Hurl, he said. Else we'd have a whole
new crop by now. Grandaddy laughed too
and passed a bottle around. Like it
was a party. All I could think was
what he said before. That this would
be mine. One day, when he was dead.
Well, I hope I die first then. I hate
my grandfather. He is THE DEVIL. I
wish him back to Hell.

It was dusk when Lucy got back to town. She parked in front of Nick's shop, but didn't get out. She'd been unfriendly, even rude. Then had misjudged him, and now was still using him, all the same.

She sat with hands clenched on the wheel, gazing at the building, the water beyond. When had she become so good at deceiving and lying. So . . . greedy?

No, she told herself angrily. It wasn't greed. She needed the Book to avert a terrible disaster. To save this island. She'd been *summoned* here, for God's sake.

All right, it was partly for her own benefit, too.

Hercules poked a wet nose over the seat back and nudged her shoulder. *Are we getting out or not?*

"Okay, *okay*," she told him. "Let's go in."

But when she entered the office, it was not Yulee behind the counter, but a young Hispanic man. An inch of ash clung to the end of his cigarette. "Help you, lady?" he asked, grinding the butt into an empty bait tin.

"I was looking for Nick. Are you—"

"Jesus," he said, smiling. "I help out Thursdays, Fridays, Saturdays. You must be a new friend. I never seen you before." He looked her up and down.

"No, not exactly." She stepped aside so Hercules was visible. "Will he be back tonight?"

His gaze flicked to the dog. "*Un perro grande*, that is.

Yeah, but he didn't say when. But, hey, mama, just go on down to the Cat. You know where it is, right? He's there talking to Cora."

She hesitated. "Maybe I should wait. I don't want to interrupt anything."

The boy gave her a shadow of his previous grin. "He won't mind."

She finally decided to walk the few blocks to the café. The last time she'd been there, Cora Cisneros had told her off. Well, who cared about the bad opinion of a small-town short-order cook? The café owner was nothing to her. Besides, it seemed now Cora hadn't been far off the mark.

Hercules sank to the pavement at the entrance without being told. Lucy closed the gate and reached for the front door handle. The hanging jungle of pothos and philodendron draping the front window framed Cora and Nick sitting at a corner table. Cora jerked a thumb at the back doorway. Nick vanished through it, and she sat again, smoking furiously, scowling like a Notre Dame gargoyle.

Lucy was reluctant to intrude. As she recalled, nothing was in that back passage but two closet-sized restrooms, one hand-labeled *Gulls*, the other *Buoys*. And an ancient, wall-mounted payphone . . . but who didn't have a cell these days?

A freshening breeze tossed dry leaves and paper scraps against her legs, spinning them into ankle bracelets, making her shiver. Was she afraid of a cook? She pushed the door open and walked straight to Cora's table.

She tried for pleasant and casual. "Hi, Cora. I'm looking for Nick." Then braced herself for a storm.

The older woman raised one eyebrow, unsmiling. "Yeah? You and ever'one else. Sit down, take a number. He's on the phone." She rose. "Take my seat. Some people got work to do." She pushed through the swinging doors and disappeared into the kitchen.

Well, that hadn't been so bad. Lucy sat, pushing a heavy

white mug with coffee dregs and Cora's shade of lipstick to one side. A full cup sat at Nick's place. It smelled fresh. She'd like some coffee too, but damned if she was going to stick her head in the kitchen to ask for it. She gazed at the fragrant steam rising from the mug, imagining putting her lips to the rim and taking a sip. Just one.

What a thought! She rose and walked to the passageway, intending to let him know she was there. Near the doorway she heard his voice rising in anger or excitement.

"Already told you what I want done with the land," he was saying. "What'd they offer? No, no. That's not—what d'you mean, more than it's worth? You don't know what it's worth! You got no idea. . . . Look, when I'm ready to close, you'll be the first to know. After the firm. Hobdy, Kirby and Arguelles. In Tallahassee, right."

When he leaned against the paint peeling wall, Lucy saw his broad back, tousled black hair, one arm braced against the door to the men's restroom. *Land, offer, law firm.* Was he going to sell his share of Revelation?

Oh yes, his dreaded birthright. He really did want rid of that nasty little inheritance. Developers could build fancy waterfront condos for the rich. Old bones don't work their way up through concrete foundations. Or did they? She thought of the one in her backpack, so weirdly carved, that Herc had dug out of the bushes a few days earlier.

When she looked again, Nick's free hand was gesturing. She couldn't see his face. But his tone was pleasant. He chuckled like a man who'd gotten what he wanted and could afford to make jokes.

He's going to sell it, she thought. Even knowing how it got to be his. That there must be survivors somewhere afraid to come back to claim their property. What about the words he'd scrawled years ago, in a cheap black journal that rested again in a dusty cardboard crypt: *I hope I die first.* The boy who'd written that wouldn't try to profit from a field of splintered bones. From mass murder.

But that child was buried, like old bones, in a man's body. Who knew how much of that abused, unhappy boy remained? Maybe so little that the adult Nick could take money from strangers happily if it meant he'd be rid of an unwanted legacy. With enough cash he could put a thousand miles between himself and a ghost town.

Soon he'd hang up, come back out into the dining room. Fine. Then she could ask him. She backed away and snatched her bag up from the floor by the chair. She glanced at his coffee, cold now, remembering how she'd wanted to put her lips to the same china rim his had pressed.

Not now. She turned and walked out. On the crude brick patio she paused long enough to whisper, "Herc, come. Hurry up."

But the patio was empty. Herc wasn't where she'd left him. "Hercules!"

Now was not a good time to talk to Nick Yulee. But where was her dog? She looked up and down the sidewalk, behind the coquina wall of the patio. He was gone. Herc never wandered off.

Forget Nick Yulee. Once given the command, Hercules stayed. Maybe he'd gone back to the car. But why? He never—

She hurried down the narrow sidewalk, back to the boat rental office.

No dog waiting at the Toyota. The shop was closed, and it was getting dark. She had to find him. He could get hit by a car, stolen, lost. There were snakes here, poisonous ones. She'd go all the way down Water Street, check the side streets too. Get in the car and drive around. Or wait— maybe he'd gone back to the hotel! She ran across the street and pounded up the front steps.

The dolorous guy in black was behind the desk. She rushed up, out of breath. "My dog," . . . "did he . . . come in? . . . Did you see him?"

The clerk looked at her dumbly. "N-no. Should I check your box for messages?"

"From a dog?" She slapped the counter. "I'm looking for my German shepherd. He can't leave messages."

"Yes ma'am." He leaned away and she realized she'd been shouting "But if he does," the clerk added, "I mean, come in and not leave a message, I'll, um . . . what would you like me to do?"

"Just keep him here till I get back." She caught sight of herself in the long mirror behind the desk: wild eyes, leaves and twigs snarled in springy dark curls that resembled a wind-combed Halloween wig. No wonder the clerk had been startled.

Well, no time to waste on reassuring him right now. She rushed out the front door.

The wind was stronger now, breathing life into street litter—crumpled coffee cups, Styrofoam takeout boxes, crumpled paper napkins—flinging them into her path. She leaned down to peel a sticky ice-cream-bar wrapper from one ankle. No sign of Hercules. After checking all the side streets, she turned back for the car.

A block from the car she heard a metallic clink. A jingle. Dog tags? She turned eagerly, but it was only a white-smocked aide from Gulf Rest striding up the sidewalk, a hand in one pocket, jangling change. She stared with such disappointment his steps slowed. He looked over one shoulder, then cautiously back at her. Before he could say anything she veered off toward the car—and collided with Nick Yulee.

"Whoa, Miz Fowler. Cora said you were lookin' for me." He caught her shoulders and held her at arm's length. The aide sidled past, giving them a wide berth. "Hey. What's wrong?"

She realized she was clutching at his jacket as if she was drowning, and it was a life preserver. She released the cloth abruptly. "Nothing. It's just—I can't find Hercules."

"Seemed too smart to just run off. But maybe I'm not the best judge of—"

"You can let go," she said. "I'm OK."

"Oh sure. Sorry. Want help looking? I'm playing a set at nine, but that's three hours off."

"I'm sure you're too busy to form a search party for a lost dog."

He stared until she looked away. "OK," he said quietly. "You hate my guts. Is it my personality, my clothes, the scar on my face, or something beyond the help of plastic surgery? Could you pause in flight just one second and tell me that? Maybe I can go buy some self-help book and fix it."

Her first instinct, which shocked her, was to hit him. Then to turn, walk to the car, and drive away. Instead, incredibly, humiliatingly, she began to cry. Which made her even more angry.

"Come inside," he said gently, "or I'm probably going to get jailed for something. Not that there's any lawmen in town. It'd have to be a citizen's arrest."

She choked on a laugh, then sobbed.

"Oh, man. Let's go." He steered her into the marina office. She didn't feel like resisting any more.

"I don't hate you," she said, after he'd shooed a gawking Jesus out the back, and returned with a Styrofoam cup. She took a gulp of lukewarm black liquid and gagged. "Oh my God! What is this stuff?"

He shrugged. "It was coffee, yesterday morning."

"Eww." She almost laughed. "It's not you, Nick. It's just—oh, shit. I don't know how to explain myself very well."

He cocked his head. "Who does?"

"I have a confession to make. Remember how you told me the other night about your old junior high teacher?"

He looked even more mystified. "It's Mrs. Waters you

hate?"

"No! Just listen." She told him about her visit. "And then I read your journal." She waited for him to get outraged. He just nodded.

"Uh . . . well, so," she continued in a rush, "I, um, decided I'd misjudged you. Not that I was entitled to judge in the first place. But, I mean, I had this impression of you as . . . as a—"

He looked at her solemnly. "Small town asshole? Gulf coast redneck? "

Her face flamed. "Well, uh, anyway, after I read the journal, I decided I was wrong."

"Hey, good news for me. But now? . . ."

"A little while ago I came in the café and overheard you talking on the phone to, I don't know, a developer, I guess. About your—the land. And . . . and you sounded so . . . so *pleased* . . . like you were going to—"

"Make a deal."

"Will you stop finishing my sentences? I hate that!"

"Not a developer. It was a woman from the Nature Trust. She called the office and Jesus told her she could reach me at the Cat. I lost my cell overboard yesterday, trying to help a tourist reel in a big grouper."

She hung her head. "Oh, God. Talk about jumping to conclusions. I think—no, I *know* I'm just as bad as Cora."

He frowned. "As bad at what?"

"Never mind. Go on, please."

"Anyway, it wasn't a developer. Scumbags? Well, who knows? At least they'd be nonprofit scumbags. Anyhow, I didn't send you to Mrs. Waters to find my diary. Maybe I shoulda thought of that. Doesn't take a rocket scientist to figure out what a history professor—"

"Grad student. Folklore. Not a—"

He threw up his hands. "Whatever. Fact remains, only one interesting, historical thing ever did happen around here. But not something the Chamber of Commerce, if we had one, would put in a brochure. And maybe—I dunno—maybe somehow I did want you to find it." He shoved hair back off his forehead. "About my conversation on Cora's phone: I didn't make a deal with anyone yet. That was just a discussion, and we folks down here are big on polite."

"Oh." She immediately thought of Cora in one of her spitting rages, but kept quiet.

Nick shook his head. "Condos or wildlife preserve, doesn't matter."

She drew back. "It doesn't?"

"No. Told 'em I'm not selling nothing to nobody. Now I'm telling you the same."

"But I thought you wanted . . . not selling?"

"No! How can I?" Then, in a rush, "Shit yeah, I'd like to get rid of the damned property. I never wanted it! The only thing my grandfather left me, besides a scar and a couple old fishing boats. Well, I took his fucking leaky boats, and made a shitty little business out of them, and then a slightly bigger shitty business. But I don't want that land, or to make any money off it, no matter how bad the tour business gets. My mother died last year, cirrhosis—"

"I'm sorry– "

He shook his head. "I'm not. God knows, nothing here on earth ever made her smile. Maybe she's happier now. But the land—what I'd *like* to do is give it back to the original owners. Whoever and wherever the hell they are. But it takes bucks to do that. Track people down, get lawyers, do record searches . . . all that crap."

He dragged a hand over his face, as if he'd thought for so long about this it all just made him weary. "Other people hereabouts 'inherited' parts of that land, too. Most of them, they'd love to sell. But my plot's the biggest waterfront piece. The one the buyers want most. If I don't sell it'll ruin all their swell plans, I guess. Well, tough shit. I'd like to be able to sleep . . . better than I do now. "

She touched his arm. "I'd like to apologize, and help you figure out what to do. But right now, all I can think about is, where's my damn dog." She forced a laugh. "I don't know what I'll do if anything's happened to him." He narrowed his eyes. "Not just a pet, is he? I notice he goes everywhere you do, and you're not blind. He's along even when it'd be a damned sight more convenient not to have a big hairy dog around. Maybe sometime you'll tell me why."

She stood abruptly, spilling the horrible tepid coffee on her jeans. "Shit! I can't sit here talking any more. I have to find him. There's a storm coming. He might be hurt. Maybe someone's taken him."

Nick rose and took the empty cup. "Awful big, toothy handful to kidnap. But wait up. I'll help you look."

Two hours of searching bumpy back roads and fish-stinking alleys in Nick's pickup, and of perusing the winter-sere yards of Ibo Key, turned up two stray terrier mutts, one bad-tempered, one-eared black and white tomcat, and a pit bull who deeply resented their invasion of his front yard. Luckily Nick knew their owners and was able to persuade them that their intentions were honorable.

At eight-thirty he dropped Lucy back at the hotel. "I'd keep on looking with you, but I promised to play for the Christmas Eve hurricane party. Fill in for a Tallahassee band that canceled out. You don't know what Cora's like if she's crossed."

"I can guess."

Christmas Eve. She'd nearly forgotten. In Vermont last year, when she'd gone back to celebrate with her father at the Hermitage, he'd been quarrelsome and refused to open his gift. Then kept mistaking her for her mother. He seemed altogether to have forgotten what the holiday was. But the doctors had warned her what Picks disease was like. "Thanks for trying. I mean, for helping."

"You really shouldn't be roaming around on your own. A bad storm's coming."

She frowned at him "What?"

He looked down, tapping the steering wheel. "Sorry. I mean, naturally you should do what you want, but be careful. You don't know the area—or these people—very well."

About as well as I want to, she thought. "I don't think I'll be going out again tonight. I'm hoping he'll come back to the hotel."

Nick smiled. "Well, he is a smart dog."

"Yes. Well . . . thanks."

She headed for the Island House. She'd meant what she said to Yulee. The previous evening's foray out on her own had landed her in the middle of a nightmare. One that obviously wasn't over yet.

Nick Yulee watched until Lucy disappeared inside the hotel, then made a U turn and drove slowly toward home to change clothes and pick up equipment for the show.

A block away from his street, a large oak branch thudded like a leafy club onto the hood of the truck, bounced and fell into the street. He sat straighter, peering up at the sky. The wind had picked up since he'd let Lucy off. The palms lining Water Street were swaying, fronds lashing the night sky like cheerleaders urging the storm on. He parked in his shell-paved drive and opened the door. A gust rattled the pines in the side yard. Cones dropped like grenades, one grazing his head. Suddenly the air felt much colder.

"Shit," he hissed, sprinting for the porch. "Must be one hell of a toad strangler on the way."

NINETEEN

"**O**h, Dr. Fowler, you're back. Your dog hasn't, um, checked in," said the same clerk. One eye was twitching. "A good night to stay put, according to the weather channel."

"Thanks." She pushed wet hair off her face and turned away for the stairs.

"Oh, wait a minute," he called. "You do have a message."

She snatched the sheet of paper from his hand. Her name was scrawled in round, childish script. Maybe someone had found Hercules.

The note had a pastel border of kittens batting at balls of yarn. The imprint said *From Esther's Desk*. She frowned. Had Day been released from Magnolia House? Why now, in the midst of a storm? The message at first glance seemed like a bad poem, penciled in the laborious script of a first-grader.

> Oh where, oh where
> has your little dog gone,
> oh where, oh where can he be?
> Until you find me a good book to read
> He'll stay down here next to me.
>
> See you after break of Day!
> – Best Regards,

An Admirer

Her fingers tightened on the paper until it crackled. "Who brought this in?"

The clerk wrung his hands. "I couldn't say. It was on the counter when I came back from the restroom. About an hour ago. Bad news?"

She was about to stuff it into her pocket, then hesitated. She smoothed the paper out again. The naive, rounded handwriting was very different from the looped, slanted scrawl on the earlier note from Eugenie Lee. She peered closely at the fat, curved "A" in "Admirer." Two tiny marks projected from the top of the letter, like . . . oh shit. Like horns.

"Oh my God," she whispered.

The clerk's eyebrows lifted. "You all right, miss?"

She ran out, taking the steps two at a time. Crossed Water Street without looking for oncoming cars. The faint, discordant twanging of a band warming up drifted down the street.

He has Hercules. The horrible man—devil—whatever he is. He's got my dog, and what will he do to him? What's he already done?

So he wanted the Book badly, too. But why?

Right now, who cared. She had to find him, in order to find her dog. Maybe once she did have it, she could bargain with him somehow. He'd even offered to trade for something else—she couldn't recall what, exactly, and didn't care. She just wanted Herc back.

Though she had no intention of giving such a rare find away, either.

But where to look? As she stood transfixed on the walk, a salty gust pushed her back a step. In this storm, it wouldn't be safe to drive out to the exposed southern tip of the Key. Anyhow, if looters had carried the volume off sixty years ago, it could be in the attic of any house in town. Or already burnt to ash decades ago, in the fire.

But Eugenie Lee and Esther both said it *did* exist. And *he* still wanted it. So there you have it, she thought. The scientific, unimpeachable testimony of a crazy old woman, a chain-smoking ghost, and—maybe—the Devil.

Well, that would have to be enough for now. She dug for her keys.

A moment later, the Camry revved and she backed away from the marina office. She couldn't search every home in Ibo City, but she could look in one. Because after all, who in town was most likely to have kept such a thing, all these years?

She made a U-turn, in the direction of the empty Day house.

It was time for dinner at Magnolia House. All five tables were occupied, with only one empty chair. The diners were all mesmerized by the dessert that'd just been served: pumpkin pie with a dollop of Cool Whip. None looked up as a slight, gray-haired man slipped into that last available seat.

When Esther Day, sitting across from him, glanced up, her plastic fork fell soundlessly to the carpeted floor. "Lord God," she breathed, eyes widening.

He gave a thin smile and bowed slightly.

She looked right and left for help. But since dessert always occupied the residents for a good ten minutes, the aides on duty took the opportunity for a break. The nursing supervisor, a stocky fifty-year-old, was visible through the glass window of the office. She'd slipped back there to catch a couple rounds of *Jeopardy* on the twelve inch flat-screen on the counter.

Two aides were in the linen closet. They'd shut the door but hadn't bothered to engage the lock. It swung open halfway and Esther saw them. Both were married, but had been eating dinner together for the last three weeks, comparing the flaws of their respective spouses.

Last week she'd seen the man pinch the woman's butt cheek in the doorway of the nursing office. Three days ago the woman had let her hand brush the crotch of his scrubs as they'd passed in the hall, when she was escorting Esther to physical therapy. Just the night before, as Esther—sleepless despite a nightly dose of Xanax—had looked out her window and seen them making out in a car, in the staff lot. A guard patrolling had swung a flashlight their way, which sent the male aid shooting out the passenger side and scrambling into his truck.

Now they were humping like shameless dogs. So enthusiastically the woman's head kept slamming into a shelf stacked with towels. Esther couldn't believe it. She'd delivered that brazen harlot herself, forty years ago. Her name was Justine. How on earth would the hussy explain those facial bruises at home?

As if they were right next to her, Esther heard Justine say, "Hold on one little minute," her words muffled by terrycloth.

"Whore of Babylon," she whispered.

The thin man across the table raised an eyebrow. "Takes one to know one."

Esther pushed back unsteadily from the table and stood. Her chair toppled with a clatter. She pointed at him, the loose flesh under her arm quivering like a jellyfish. "I know who you are. You're—"

He nodded. "Back to collect on a debt."

She opened her mouth to shriek, "Oh my Sweet Jesus, don't you see him, he's come!" But fear so tightened her vocal cords the words hissed out in a harsh whisper. Two patients looked up from their pie, at Esther standing rigid at her place, pointing at an empty chair. But residents here often made cryptic, unfathomable comments. They lowered their heads and resumed eating.

The gray man reached across and took hold of Esther's extended index finger, shaking his head as if deploring a terrible breach of manners. With a quick jerk, he snapped the finger bone just below the second joint.

Esther shrieked and dropped like a loose boulder onto the table, flattening her untouched pie, squashing it into the green and red holiday tablecloth.

He slid his grip to her wrist, as if checking for a pulse. "Hmm. Coronary thrombosis, I'd say," he murmured. When he let go the arm thudded limply next to her blood-engorged face, eyes bulging unseeingly at her neighbor's dessert plate.

The other residents looked at Esther with more interest now, while scraping their plates clean. The thin man stepped around the table and laid one pale, long-fingered hand against a mottled cheek. "Didn't think I'd forget, did you, dear?" He bent and kissed the tip of one ear, which poked up through thinning white hair.

He vaulted to the tabletop and clapped sharply, standing above them all. "Attention, please. I've come for four of my special friends. One final task before we all move on to the next . . . thing. Come now, gentlemen. You know who you are. Stand, please."

One by one four elderly men stood. Two looked puzzled. One, eyeing his half-finished pie, seemed annoyed. The fourth, a thin, bent cotton swab of a fellow, looked sly and eager.

"Ah, my old poker buddies. Franklin, I see you're getting the idea, at least. In even a dim constellation, there must be a brightest star. So, onward. There's a storm on the way."

The remaining residents glanced from Day's lifeless body to the door, forks halted in midair, as the four men trailed out, heads bowed, as if following an invisible drum major.

"Here now, what's the ruckus?" said the nursing supervisor, returning from the office. She looked around at the four empty chairs, then at Esther, lying still across the table, face in the pumpkin pie.

"Lord have mercy!" She crossed herself. "Bailey, Justine! Get the hell out here and clean this mess."

The porch light was on when Lucy pulled to the curb outside the shuttered Day house. Who'd left it on, and why? She let the engine run, listening to the end of a weather bulletin. The hurricane was shearing off west; apparently it would only brush them now. She killed the ignition and again looked reluctantly at the otherwise-dark house.

Wind bowed large branches overhead, its moaning occasionally rising to a sharp whistle. Winter leaves fell in a crisp, dry rain, then were torn away on the next howling gust. The only other sound was the faint *tick-tick* of the Toyota's cooling engine. No Hercules panting in the back, no cold nose nudging her shoulder.

"Well, don't suppose anyone's coming out to greet me." She fingered the crumpled note in her pocket. *A good Book to read.* Could it simply be sitting on a shelf somewhere?

A wet fistful of leaves slapped the windshield. She looked up through them at the peaked roof. First floor, second, attic? At least, no basement; not on a subtropical island. But she'd have to find the attic stairs. Sighing, she opened the glove box. At least she had a flashlight. "Here goes," she muttered.

The unlocked front door swung open on a black silence still as a held breath. Lucy inhaled deeply, slowly breathed out, then groped for a wall switch. She clicked the two she felt, off and on, with no result. One must be for the porch light. But that was disconcerting, since no matter which way she pushed the switches that outside fixture stayed on, while inside all remained dark. She swung the flashlight up so that its long pale beam probed like a glowing scalpel at the murky guts of the house. Which seemed different. It felt . . . hollow.

She swung the light around again. "What in the world?"

The place had been cluttered with dark Victorian heirlooms and angular fifties modern, before. That had been the day she'd found Eugenie Lee in the . . . the . . . .

No. Don't think about that.

Now it was empty. Not a stick of furniture in the front room. Remembering those staring eyes set like peeled boiled eggs into the seamed, grimacing face, Lucy suppressed a shiver. She arced the light away, to illuminate the empty hall stretching right and left from the foyer. The dim walls, papered with faded roses, corners peeling, were set with rows of closed doors like the shuttered eyelids of a many-headed beast.

"God, get a grip," she muttered. Or she might run out screaming, right off this island, without her dog or anything else she'd come for.

And your life still under a curse you wish you didn't believe in.

Second floor, then. Taking another deep breath, she set a foot on the first creaking riser.

The landing was piled with broken furniture, ruptured cardboard boxes, old television sets, plastic bins full of vintage soda bottles and empty coffee cans, a foot-pedal sewing machine. Other unidentifiable junk stretched into the dimness like the cluttered mind of a lunatic. Apparently the Days had never in their lives thrown anything away.

There came a whispering, the dry rustle of brittle paper. She jerked the flashlight over and up shakily, illuminating another, narrower staircase up.

To the attic. Why not start at the top? A smaller area to search, from what she'd seen outside. The second floor was giving her the heebie-jeebies anyhow.

She started up. The pine railing had a moleskin coating of soft dust. The air was choking with mildew. Dancing motes swam like airborne plankton in the flashlight's underwater glow. When she sneezed, the echo was cut short, swallowed by a hungry silence.

At the top landing stood what looked like a small closet door. She tried the knob: locked. Rattled it, and the whole thing shook, door and frame. Powdery dust and crumbled bits of wood showered her head.

"Dry rot," she muttered, dismayed at the sepulchral echo. She leaned one shoulder and shoved hard. The crumbling molding splintered, cracked, gave way.

The sudden momentum carried her inside. She swung the beam around, lighting corners and alcoves. The attic walls were paneled with sloppily-painted beadboard; the ceiling sloped sharply away from the roof's peak. A wind-whipped branch scratched at the panes of the room's only window, a small circular one like a ship's porthole she hadn't noticed from the street. In the already-dimming beam, she saw that other than a blanket of dust and the musty-sweet smell of long-dead mice, the room contained only one thing: a carved chest banded in tarnished metal. The wood was dark; ebony or black walnut. The design was stylized, strong and irregular as some Haitian folk-art carvings she'd seen at the university art gallery, brought from Port-au-Prince.

"It's African," said a woman's voice, behind her.

Her dropped flashlight rolled across the warped floor, strobing sections of wall and ceiling crazily before coming to rest in a corner. Lucy scrambled for it. Fear pierced her chest like an electric drill. Panting, she snatched it up and spotlighted a figure standing just inside the door.

Eugenie Lee grinned. "Look like you expecting old Scratch himself."

"I don't know who or what to expect anymore." Lucy gritted her teeth to stop their chattering. "For all I know, that's who you are."

The woman—or ghost, or whatever—smiled. "Evil dwells in every soul. Yours. Mine too. Else doing good be no real challenge, would it? Only question, which weighs heavier inside: the bad or the good?"

Lucy fidgeted impatiently. Philosophy was all very well in the classroom, but she had more practical concerns. "I got a note—"

"Good. Afraid that pale skinny clerk wan't never coming back from the toilet. When he did, he almost overlook it there on the counter. Like a snake close enough to bite him. And so you come."

"The note, you mean. But who sent it? Where's my dog? And is that damned book here?"

"Still full of questions. No wonder. Wasn't me who left *that*, it were *him*. You know that already. He got your pup, but that's the least of your worries."

She huffed, "Oh really? What do you think's the biggest?"

"This sea chest here belonged to Solange. Brought all the way from N'awlins. Her mama's, hand-carved by an *Ibo* in Africa, to start . . . who been a, well, most folks would say, witch doctor." She laughed. "Or maybe something more polite nowadays—alternative medicine practitioner? This island was a way station for slaves, smuggled direct from Africa, to get sold. Shipped on to Louisiana, Alabama, Mississippi. They call it that still, not knowing why. A sort of living-on, though not much consolation to all those black folks dead on the voyage, or whipped to market like hogs."

This was all she could stand. "Please, please no history lesson. If this is Koumari's trunk, and the famous so-called voodoo book's inside, that's all I care about right now."

The old lady nodded. "Be my guest, child."

She dropped to her knees before the heavy casket. Locked, and solid as a boulder. No dry rot here. She hammered at the padlock with the flashlight, but only cracked its plastic grip. Then she tried to lift the box, but the weight was amazing. She shoved, straining and grunting, but could only inch it across the floor.

She wiped sweating, trembling fingers on her shirt. "I can't open it. Sure as hell can't haul it down the stairs. How'd it ever get up here?"

"After Solange and Julian die, the mob went to burn their house. First they loot it, of course. Found not much— kitchen things, furniture, dried herbs, oils, some batik cloth.

"Like most conquerors, Turner Day bound to take some trophy back. And not settle for an ear or a hand to keep in a jar of 'shine, like Herbert Yulee. Day want payback for the insult to his property—his woman. There, in Solange's bedroom, 'gainst a back wall, he discover the finest thing she owned: this box. He make six men help him carry it back. Then give it to his wife."

Lucy looked up in disbelief. "Esther had it all along?"

Eugenie nodded. "Who else long to own it? When she open this, she find her precious Book."

"That must've made her happy," said Lucy bitterly.

"Why not lift the lid. See for yourself what-all she reap."

The chest gleamed like a giant onyx, exotic, out of place in its setting, the rough dusty boards of this attic. She stroked the lid, then fingered the cold metal of the catch. "It's not even rusty."

"Pure African silver. Soft enough for a strong bare hand to mash. But too thick to break. Like us, it only give and bend. Anyhow, no need."

Lucy moved the light closer and peered at the design. Then recognized what it reminded her of. What it . . . matched. She clawed at the neck of her shirt. A button pinged and rolled away across the floor. She fished out the silver chain, medallion swinging from it.

"I have the key," she whispered. "I had half of it all along." The metal no longer felt cool, but warm in her hands; almost alive. The tarnished silver glowed dully, seemed to waver and twitch.

Eugenie Lee nodded. "Blackbirders headed to the Gulf ports, they liked to steal folks from the Ibo tribe. Strong, stoic, work till they drop. Good for working the rice and sugar plantations. The ones survived the sea journey they kept shackled in pens where the farmers' market sit now.

At auction time buyers come from the mainland. Leftovers got taken on to Mobile, New Orleans, other ports. That the *real* Ibo Key, in your hand."

It slid smoothly into the lock, turned easily. When she lifted the heavy lid, cold musty air like a breath from the grave filled her lungs. Inside, on top, wrapped in yellowed newsprint, lay five small bundles. She poked one tentatively, then flinched as the desiccated folds cracked, revealing tiny . . . bones?

"Oh my god," she whispered, recognizing the tiny, fragile skull of an infant. She closed her eyes. Beneath the top layer she'd glimpsed more paper-shrouded bundles.

"All Esther's babies here now," Eugenie murmured.

She means me too. But Lucy didn't want to be included in this pitiful, doomed family. "How . . . how many?"

"Nine. Never lost a single baby *she* midwifed. Just like that newspaper article say. But after your mama, all her own died. Miscarried late. One come out with no eyes, no nose, no mouth."

"But everyone said she never had any more children. People would've noticed. Would have known!"

"Esther, she big-boned. Later on real heavy, too. Got good at hiding a belly, especially after the second one died. Some babies gush out too early on a hot wave of blood. Others born perfect but stone cold, cord wrapped like a lynch noose around the neck. Or sometimes with a hole in the chest, where a heart ought to be."

"God."

"Turner grow bitter after the first three, so she don't want him to even expect a child no more. Things go worse for her when he disappointed. She go out into the woods when her time come, with me along. Bite down on clean rags to muffle the screams and moans. Together we deliver those poor, lost souls. Then she bring each one back here, wrap it up to put away with the others."

"Why not bury them there, in the woods?"

"Eugenie curled her lip. "Wouldn't be *Christian*, would it? Here she get to come and kneel and grieve and hate all she want."

"Her personal punishment from Solange Koumari's curse."

Eugenie shrugged. "Part of it. The other part was the Book."

"So it *is* here, underneath . . . these?" Lucy took a deep breath, and reached back inside. She lifted the first mummified bundle gently. It felt hollow as a dried seed pod. She sobbed and set it aside, wiping her fingers on her jeans. These desiccated cocoons, wrapped like meat from the butcher, were her aunts and uncles. Yet now, with their secret grave finally discovered, she couldn't wait to pull them like worthless packing foam from their coffin, digging for the bigger prize.

Will I stop at nothing; have I no shame? At that moment, she hated Solange Koumari, Esther Day, and Eugenie Lee. But she hated herself more. *Only question, which weighs heavier.* Her stomach lurched. She swallowed back bile, then reached for the next bundle.

At the bottom, beneath folded, faded quilts and stacks of wrinkled, yellow linens, lay one last object. A small leather book, plain black. It looked like the Bible Lucy's mother had given her after she took Confirmation. Its cover was spotted with mildew and felt smooth as worn velvet in her slick, sweating hands. No words were stamped on its cover, though. The spine was hinged with leather straps attached with silver studs. It smelled of dust and age and tanned, long-dead skin.

She bit her lip when she remembered: The Haitian slave revolt. Human skin.

She opened it slowly, carefully, to a bright, hand-painted frontispiece. *La Livre des Loas*, it read. The page was bordered with fanciful green and red snakes twined around skulls, with crowing roosters, black-feathered chickens, and exotic tropical birds at each corner.

The Book of the Spirits, she said softly, grateful for having slogged through four years of undergraduate French. And knowing from Dr. Grove's graduate anthropology class about *voudon*, and that *loa* meant ghost or spirit or god. Otherwise, how would she ever be able to—

Suddenly she understood the other half of Solange's curse. "Esther wanted this thing, like, forever. But when she got it, she couldn't even use it. Could she?"

"No." Eugenie shook her head. "Couldn't read a word of French. And who she gone ask to translate? If she take it to the college over in Gainesville, well. . ."

"Yes. To a professor," said Lucy. "He'd sure know what it was, what it was worth. Would ask where she'd gotten it. Maybe even want it for himself."

Eugenie laughed dryly, without humor, then coughed. "She try a special dictionary once, make me write away special to order it. But all these words not even in it. They not even all French. She couldn't make sense of it still."

Lucy sighed, shaking her head. "So here it stayed. After all the trouble and blood and lies and murder. All she could do was bury her dead children with the big prize."

A blast of wind shook the walls. The attic rattled as if a lumber train were passing through the rooms below.

"Or maybe she put them babies in there thinking it bring just one back. Who can say. Now you found it, what you do next?"

"I, uh, I don't know yet. Take it back to the hotel and look through. Try to read some of it."

"Better hurry. Don't have much time left."

"The storm—"

Eugenie nodded. "An old song say, 'Storm, lightning, wind, rain. The devil coming to the island with lightning for wheels.' Well, he not coming alone."

Lucy frowned. "I thought it was supposed to pass us by."

"Them weathermen, what they know?" Eugenie shook her head. "He gone wait for you at the dead town. 'Round midnight." She nodded. "To gather up souls. Here, anywhere they hide. Hunt 'em down like rabbits for the pot. Same way the women and children of Revelation were hunted. You too. And your child. Unless you can change his mind."

"Who is he, exactly?"

Eugenie Lee shrugged. "Do it matter? He change shape to suit him. To suit whatever evil call him up."

Lucy's hands tightened on the Book. "Let's say you're right. How could I do that? Change his mind, I mean."

"Sacrifice," said the old woman, hidden in shadow now. "Always, always they want a sacrifice." The light dimmed until the splintered doorway and landing beyond were visible through her wavering form.

So—a fatted bull calf before an Old Testament altar? A glossy black rooster decapitated by a chanting Santerian priest? A white-robed virgin on a stone slab, breast bared to a gleaming blade? Damn it, this was no horror movie, this was her *life*. "What kind of sacrifice?" she shouted. "Wait a minute!"

The vanishing ghost only whispered, "Time to drop this weary burden. Take it up and do what you can, now."

"No!" Lucy ran after the fading wisps that had once been the old woman. "No, you're not leaving me now!"

"Can't hold on another minute." The words dropped

from empty air. On the attic floor lay a small bundle of black and red feathers. Was that what—or whom—the birds had been all along? She touched the feathered body, hoping for some sign of life. It felt stiff, too still.

"But I needed your help," she whispered. "I need *you*."

Except for the howl of the storm, and an occasional creak of timbers, there was silence. At last, not knowing what else to do, she slipped the small, dead bird gently into her pocket.

TWENTY

Rain fell in cataracts from the green-glowing hurricane sky. Her Toyota rocked in the gusts, pelted by water and leafy debris. The potholed road to Revelation had been covered with tall tufts of winter-burnt grass, but they were sodden and flattened now. The way grew more and more narrow, more deeply flooded, until she panicked at the approach of a single car, the only one for miles.

The rusty black Jeep passed in low gear, crammed with laughing, shouting teenage boys. It threw up a sheet of muddy water like liquid wings, slewing on the unpaved road. Just before the backwash flooded the windshield, one guy lobbed something shiny. The crushed beer can bounced with a hollow ping off the hood.

She gritted her teeth and gripped the wheel harder. Otherwise she'd be hydroplaning off into the ditch.

Who else but drunken partiers would be out tonight? Joyriders too blitzed on Schlitz to care about being drowned, crushed by falling trees, or mangled in a wreck. Or perhaps a woman foolish enough to risk her neck on a wild goose chase. Wild ghost chase.

"Whatever," she muttered, wiping sweat from her eyes, leaning forward to peer through a smeared waterfall of windshield. *Concentrate, or you're gonna lose it.* She switched the wipers to high and turned the de-fogger on full blast.

In a movie, now would be the time the hero called on

help from some higher power. A gunslinger, a ghost-buster, a flying super-hero. Or how about God? She had not been to church since she was a teenager. She'd never gotten down on her knees anywhere else, since, and prayed to Him for anything. She wasn't an atheist, had even been confirmed at twelve. But that'd been expected, her parents' idea. Well, maybe it was time to get off the fence.

A hard wrench of the wheel, as the gale suddenly shoved the little sedan far to the right. She tried to avoid fallen branches; finally gave up and ran over them with a scrape of metal undercarriage, hoping nothing important had been torn off. Every few minutes a burst of water hit the windshield, as if a giant sprinkler were rotating above the tops of the swaying, creaking oaks and pines. She might as well be driving blindfolded.

So why press on? For a dog she loved, whose presence let her imitate normal life, and act as if her will hadn't been shattered. It wasn't for the fabled Book, a supposed *grimoire* she hoped would make her career. That object of desire— small, mildewed, actually pretty unimpressive-looking—lay on the passenger seat beside her.

So was she risking her life for an island full of people she barely knew and, in some cases, didn't even like?

The pro-birth crowd, who often seemed to care nothing about children once they were born, would probably insist her concern must be for what she was told now nestled within her. As for how it had come to take up residence, to invade her body, linger to sprout . . .

She inhaled deeply, several times, forcing away that memory. Yet she'd taken deliberate steps to ensure no conception, no souvenir of that night would exist. She'd used tests since that assured her they had worked.

How could she ever look at such a child, had there been one, and not think of a deserted road so much like this one? Not see that contorted, evil face, its desperate eyes, the bared teeth. A face familiar yet totally alien, intent only on maiming, humiliating, and finally killing her.

OK, she could give a baby up, as her grandmother had done after her mother's birth. But how could she bear to have such a thing even growing inside her for the endless months it would take to be free again?

Of course there was another option. Her opinion had always been that abortion was regrettable but acceptable. How could she judge a stranger's choices, her problems, her needs? She'd never imagined she might have to make such a decision. She'd been careful—oh so very focused—when it came to birth control. Because no matter when life truly began, to end its possibility without even knowing what, if anything, was being lost—that had always sounded like more of a burden than she wanted on her shoulders.

Ha. Look at her now—speaking of burdens!

That some unplanned speck could one day be a person who moved and breathed and loved seemed as unreal as Eugenie Lee's dire warning that she'd soon be facing Evil Personified. Mr. Splitfoot. Beelzebub. Satan, the great horned demon of fables, medieval woodcuts, plastic Halloween masks at Walmart. A myth, an adjective, a dated metaphor. A church-inspired hoax. The villain of the longest-running story ever told, made simple and bad, all red and pointy, to keep misbehaving children and credulous adults on the straight and narrow.

Why not admit it, the voice in her brain piped up.

She was becoming resigned to this internal critic. Resigned, but not fond.

It's not for Ibo Key. Not really for poor old Hercules. Certainly not for some ridiculous bean-child. Or to stop a hokey curse. And not even remotely connected with Good or Right or morality. Because you've never really cared what those things are, or if you even have them in you.

It was true. She wasn't unselfish. Or good, or moral. That much by now she knew. So she must be undertaking this little adventure for herself. She'd chosen to study folklore because she was fascinated by tales and customs and art forms. Half her family tree had always been a mystery. She'd longed all her life to feel part of something. To belong, regardless of mistakes and failures. To fill the void, she'd read. Becoming, as she played alone, Little Red Riding Hood, or Clever Manka, or Persephone kidnapped on horseback to the Underworld. These tales had been her best, most uncritical friends. Later she'd dressed them in the more sedate robes of academia and made them the center of her life.

So, given a chance to confront the most infamous folk character of all time, in the ruddy, smoking flesh . . . how could she refuse? Because even as her rational mind still scoffed at the idea of a cloven-hoofed, goat-horned Master of All Demons. Fallen Archangel Lucifer, there was no denying she felt a real, palpable fear. Because, if real, then he'd defied God face to face at the beginning of Time, and doomed all humankind to sin disguised as knowledge.

Her hands clenched the wheel as one might a safety railing that blocked off a bottomless abyss. She flinched at every blowing leaf and tumbling branch on the road. Her face was damp with sickly sweat that now and then ran into her eyes and burned like sulfur.

An even rarer sensation had been growing along with the fear. At first it only nosed at the edge of her consciousness, like a needy dog seeking attention. But now, just minutes from the blasted, bone-seeded field that had once been a lively, living community, it swelled, crowding the anorectic specter of fright for elbow room.

Excitement. Sharp and intoxicating as the moment before the prick of a hypodermic of heroin. What a soldier might feel going into battle, a parachutist before a jump. Was it really so bad? To want that. Already she knew she'd crave more.

It's as if, she thought wonderingly, *I* was the one who was dead before. Cold and lifeless as the ashes of Revelation.

Nick Yulee squeezed into the payphone nook, like a hermit crab nostalgic for an outgrown shell. The phone, between restrooms, past the swinging kitchen door, was as far from the rowdy holiday-hurricane crowd as he could get. What a crappy time to have lost his cell.

A few minutes remained till the next set, so he punched in the number of the front desk at the Island House. As it rang, a blast of beer-scented laughter stabbed his ears. Christ, he thought. Seems like I spend half my life just trying to get a fucking word in. I ought to blow off this damned island and never come back.

He plugged his free ear with a finger. "C'mon, *c'mon.*"

That pasty clerk must be in the back again. Wasn't answering the phone part of his fricking job? He slammed a fist into the pockmarked wall and split the skin over one knuckle. "Shit," he hissed, sucking blood away.

"Nope. It's the Island House," said a voice archly from the receiver. "May *I* help you anyhow?"

"Uh, yeah. Gimme Lucy Fowler's room."

"I'll ring if you want, but she's not there. Went out an hour ago in a big hurry. Hasn't returned."

But she'd *said* she was going to stay in. Wait to see if the dog showed up. "Fuck. Did she say where?"

"Nope." The clerk lowered his voice to an intimate whisper. "Just between us, she was acting strange. If you ask me."

Nick curled his aching hand into a fist. Suppose I have no choice, you scrawny little peeper. "Why's that?"

"There was this message for her? When she comes in, I hand it over. But what was weird . . . when I picked up the paper her name was scrawled on one side. Now, I didn't mean to read it, of course"—Nick rolled his eyes. *Yeah. I'll bet*—"but I couldn't have anyway."

Nick held up a hand at Jimbo Ellis, Scratch's bass player, who was signaling the next set. Damn it to hell. "OK, OK, cut to the chase. Why not?"

"Other side was blank. But *she* got real ticked off when she looked at it. Even pretended like she was reading something there. *Twice.* Asked who'd sent it. How did I know—maybe the phantom of the opera. Then she rushed out like a bat at sundown. Uh . . . hello?"

Nick was hanging up, already turning away to run out the back door of the café. Scratch would just have to get along without him for the rest of this night. But Jimbo came over and grabbed his arm.

"Come on, man. Cora's having a fucking fit. I need this gig. Got a kid on the way, remember?"

Nick sighed. "OK, OK. One more set. Then I'm out of here."

Revelation looked much as the first time Lucy had seen it, only wetter. Tangled weeds and scrub, the huge skeletal tree, kudzu choked brick foundations, pines corkscrewed into grotesque shapes by decades of salt and storm winds. Amazingly, the dry-rotted hulk of Flowers' general store, which had already seemed held together only by a crazy-quilt stitchery of wild grapevine, was still standing. A shingle flew off the roof like a hell-bound bat as she watched, followed by another. Wild jasmine and trumpet vines whipped like carnival streamers. She hoped the store would hang together a little longer. If it fell, where would all those homeless snakes go?

She parked at the end of the main street. Wind rocked her car like a cradle, howling a monotonous threnody. The boat-at-sea motion made her queasy. She focused on the nearest steady object, a huge live oak several yards away. But as she stared the tree slowly took on an unnatural slant, shifting until it hung crosswise as if suspended only by moss and vines. Then, with a low tearing groan, it toppled in front of her bumper, spraying a shrapnel of dead leaves, bark fragments, and broken twigs.

Black mud ran like clotted blood down the windshield glass. This would be an ill omen in any fairy tale. But she was already here; too late to be heeding signs. She switched on the map light, picked up the dusty, black-bound book and propped it on the steering wheel.

The text was rough, archaic, printed on an ancient hand-operated letterpress. Some of the words were hard to figure out. Her first impression of the language had been premature. Now it seemed more a pastiche of medieval French, Latin, and what might be a transliterated African dialect. Or a creole, or island patois. Well, thanks to her studies under Dr. Grove, she knew two lodges of the French Illuminati had relocated to Port-au-Prince in the late 18th Century, bringing their European ceremonial magic along. She could read some words, guess at others, but . . .

She sighed and closed it again. Such a slim volume, yet it still might take days, weeks, to fully translate. The only reasonable thing to do was skim.

At first, what she read seemed ordinary, almost boring. She didn't need a cure for warts or a love potion. Or a charm to attract wealth. Well, OK, she could always look at that again, later. What exactly *did* she need—demon repellent? An exorcism chant, like in the movies? Something more powerful than home remedies for a nagging cough, or charms for the naive and lovesick. She snorted, thinking of how once, in a *botanica* on South Street in downtown Philly, among candles for saints and paper packets of dried St. John the Conqueror root, she'd seen bottles of Spirit-Away Floor Wax.

If only something in a bottle could clean up this place.

Then again, perhaps she'd just huddle in the car till dawn, experiencing nothing more frightening than a terrible storm. She could live with that.

She read on, translating slowly. Halfway through the

volume she found a more chilling passage.

Papa Legba, open the gate. Sing the hymn, and he will enter. Open!

There followed some hand-inscribed drawings of ve-ve, the symbols drawn on the floor or on the participants at ceremonies to call the loas. One, an ornate cross for Papa Legba, looked familiar. No doubt Grove had drawn it on the white board in one of his classes, or she'd glimpsed it in a research book.

An invocation was inscribed by hand, underneath this, in brownish-red ink the disturbing shade of a faded bloodstain.

Par pouvoir St. Antoine, Legba Antibon, Maitre Carrefour, Maitre Grand Bois, Maitre Grand Chemin, Legba Barriere, Legba Bois, Legba Caille . . .

The call to the spirit went on for two more lines. Lucy shuddered. Some of the chant was familiar from Haitian voudon. But the last thing in the world she wanted was to be invaded and possessed by a spirit—*any* spirit. "Forget that," she muttered, sighed, and turned the page.

After another half-hour of eye-burning concentration, she found something that looked more promising.

"Lanterne Noir de Desastre," she murmured. The Black Disaster Lamp. A ceremony used only in the most dire emergencies, it produced a new catastrophe in order to avert another. What was this if not a dire emergency for the inhabitants of Ibo Key?

She read further, translating aloud: "The ceremony falls . . . under the . . . protection of the, uh . . . cemetery gods." She frowned. "OK . . . Maman Brigette and . . . uh oh . . . Baron Samedi," she whispered. The same entities Solange Koumari had called on, deep in the pines, as Revelation had died.

Wasn't Baron Samedi really the Devil? How could she call on the Devil to help her outwit the Devil? Or were they different, separate powers? Good God. Why not try to count pin-dancing angels while she was at it. What a fool to think she might pick up an ancient book, study it like *Cliff Notes*, and expect to use it! Years of devoted study were required to become a Cuban *santera*, a New Mexican *bruja*, a Haitian *houngan*. Ha! Might as well try to build a nuclear bomb after a few minutes of speed-reading Einstein.

She tossed the Book onto the passenger seat and rested her forehead against the steering wheel. "*Shit*," she moaned. "Damn it to—"

"Don't give up before you started, child," a voice whispered near her ear.

She shrieked and looked around. No one but her inside. No one standing outside next to the window, out in the rain. But something odd *was* happening. Though the ignition was off, the FM dial glowed. The digital channel selector was scanning, racing rapidly past station after station. Her hand shot out to punch the power knob. It was already off.

Static burst from the door speakers. Then came a whole Greek chorus, distorted by interference. "Call on what you know. You have strength. But believe." Within the babble of voices, she distinctly heard the smoky, chastising tones of Eugenie Lee.

"But I don't know what, or—or who I believe in! Or what to do."

Wait. Was she really talking to her car radio?

A fresh burst of static. The scanner raced again. "Believe first in yourself. What good to *tell* you there's something beyond the world you sit in now? No name. No face. Call it what you will. And use what tools you have."

The green glow faded. The radio fell silent. She was left with the dull thump of her heart. In the Japanese Shinto religion, it occurred to her now, you didn't have to believe—but rather just *do*.

To use what tools you have.

Such as? She was alone in the path of a hurricane, expecting to meet the devil, or at least some lunatic who *thought* he was Satan. She had: a car, a flashlight, a book she couldn't quite read, a pretty silver key, and—

Oh yeah, she thought, let's not forget: a dead bird in my pocket. But OK—let's say it's true. That after the things I've seen lately, I do *believe*. Or else why am I sitting here at all? I spoke, over and over, to a ghost I thought was a living woman. I met a man who *seemed* to be then the personification of Evil. At the very least a mind-reader, a psychic psychopath. And now I *believe* I'm descended from people white and black, living and dead, from this island. Because of that, I may be in danger.

She took a deep breath. All right. I *believe* . . . inside me there's . . . a possible though unwanted baby . . . who's in danger, too.

Wow. That last one was the hardest. A ghost had been the angel of this annunciation. But how could it even be true, when she'd had not one but two negative pregnancy tests, and swallowed a drug designed to make sure she didn't conceive? True, she'd been horribly sick to her stomach—

She froze just then, astonished, at a strange flutter in her belly, like the tickle of a minnow slipping between the fingers of your cupped hands.

"Oh my god," she whispered. Was that it, inside her? How she felt about it, what she'd do—worry about that later. Right now she would assume they were all in danger on this damned, doomed island. *And it seems the only one who can stop the coming destruction . . . is me.*

"All right," she whispered into the cool dark interior of the car. "I may be just plain nuts. But yes. Yes, I believe."

She picked up the Book, and slowly began to translate; to read it yet again.

To make a black disaster lamp you needed a dried coconut shell or the shell of a sea-crab. Into this should go sweet castor-oil, *chevaux-negro de chien*—which Lucy took as Creole for black dog hair—sea water, soot, the powder of a corpse. Then half-bury it at the foot of a tree consecrated either to Maman Brigette or to her cadaverous husband, Baron Samedi. The lamp could make an enemy lose his livelihood, or take away his life. It could break up a family. Force a foe to leave the community. Or simply draw the anger of the spirits away from the living, and redirect their ill will to the uncaring dead.

"Talk about shotgun cures," she muttered, feeling like a doctor about to treat a mystery ailment with wide-spectrum antibiotics, hoping one might work. What she wanted was the third possible outcome—to send this demon in gray back to Hell.

Another hour passed. It was twenty minutes to midnight. The page with the black lamp recipe was the only section that seemed useful. She took a deep breath, braced her shoulder against the car door, and flung it open. Into a howling wind that fired rain at her like stinging buckshot, and tried to lift her like Dorothy, to deposit far off elsewhere, as she pulled herself along from tree branch to vine to splintered stump.

No coconuts would grow this far north, but she did spot the empty brown bowl of a horseshoe crab lying overturned in a marshy puddle. She tucked it under one arm and went on.

Next, sea water. No problem, right? A few hundred yards away lay the Gulf of Mexico. But, seaward, the monstrous waves clubbing the sand, the weird greenish-yellow glow of the horizon, took her breath away. Earlier, from Yulee's boat, the Gulf had seemed tame. Now it was imitating a disaster movie.

Yulee. Right now she wished for his company even more than his help. Though if she'd confided her new beliefs no doubt he would've driven her straight to the Gulf Rest admitting office.

Now, some soot. Easy—scraped from the nearest broken chimney with a shard of oyster shell.

Powder of a corpse? Hmm. The mummified bodies of her infant aunts and uncles were back in the Day attic. It would be fitting to make them a part of this. But she had no time to go back, assuming the road was still passable.

Well then, how about a generous pinch of the blood-soaked soil of Revelation? Into the shell it went, along with the rest of the ingredients she'd gathered so far.

Next, castor oil. That one really stumped her until she remembered the tiny flask of sandalwood oil in her glove compartment, a gift on her last birthday from Hal Prince. She rarely wore perfume, so it'd languished there, unused, ever since. A lifetime ago. Had it been pressed from castor beans? Who knew, but it was oil and would have to do.

Chevaux negro de chien . . . resting a moment back in the car, clothes sodden with rainwater and muck, she idly rubbed a palm over the seat next to her. It came away coated with . . . dog hair. From the cloth where Hercules normally sat. Poor guy, when would she see him again? Was he alive and well, or suffering torture she didn't want to envision? She forced herself back to the task at hand. Most of the fur there was black undercoat. She scraped up a small pile with her fingernails.

Cradling the cracked shell to her chest, so as not to spill the disgusting soup within, she half-walked, half-crawled, like a waitress in a war-zone, to the largest tree she could find. A huge water oak like the giant that'd nearly crushed her car. She dug between its roots, clawing at the sodden black mud, breaking nails, lacerating fingertips.

At last she set the shell lamp in the shallow hole she'd managed to excavate beneath the consecrated tree.

"Oh," she said. "Shit." Consecrated . . . what a bungling priestess she was, forgetting that detail. Should she go back to the car, try to find and decipher the appropriate ceremony, then no doubt have to search for even more ingredients? Her cell already read five minutes to midnight. As she looked at the screen, it flickered and read: NO SERVICE.

The time for research had passed.

Think, she admonished herself. When Solange Koumari had called on the goddess or spirit, Maman Brigette, what had she said, what had she done?

Of course, the goddess had not actually shown up. The answer to the distraught midwife's prayers had been Lucy Fowler in a liberal coating of Gold Medal, not some ancient island goddess. Or maybe . . . was Lucy's appearing on the island, out of time and place, actually the loa's response to the cry of a disciple? A dizzying thought. Perhaps Solange had figured that one out, which might explain her willingness to take Lucy as the real thing.

It seemed ludicrous. But then so did most everything else she'd said and done lately. The gods wanted a consecration ceremony? Coming right up.

She got out again and tried to stand, but in the rising wind and blasting rain had to finally settle for an awkward crouch. "Um, let's see. Now . . . I call upon you, Maman Brigette. OK, I know this is not your usual offering, but the circumstances are—"

Oh, hell, she thought. I sound like a bureaucrat at the DMV. Well, I'll do the best I can. Belief will have to count for the rest.

"Maman Brigette, accept my humble plea for help. Bless the black disaster lamp, your great tool, most powerful spirit. Please use it at the right moment . . . to drive our enemies, the ones who would destroy us, far from this place."

Hadn't there been something about turning harmful attention away from the living, toward the dead? Yes, a phrase . . . though what it had to do with sending the Devil out of town, she couldn't imagine.

"*Ce pas faute moi; ce pas moi minm qu'ap fait ca mal; ce mort-a!*" She shouted, the words torn from her lips to tumble away like pebbles in a raging river. *It's not my fault; I'm not the one doing this evil; it's the dead spirit!*

There. It was done. Now all she wished for was . . . company. Hercules or Yulee. Even the otherworldly Eugenie Lee. Hell, Cora Cisneros would do, at this point. If only I could call up Hal Prince, she thought. What would he make of my academic research now? She felt in her pocket for the iPhone again. NO SERVICE.

What spell would let you call a friend without a phone? She snorted, then straightened abruptly. Wait a minute. Call a friend . . . without a phone . . .

Dr. Grove had told the class last semester that when he'd been in Haiti on a brief research trip, he'd gone to a *voudoun* ceremony. "An unremarkable, garden-variety tourist show," he'd droned. "Except for one interesting development."

A chant was begun by the priestess, the *Mam'bo*. As a joke, Grove said, to summon a friend who'd failed to show up. She hadn't pulled out a cell phone, but simply taken an article the person had once touched and chanted some lines several times over.

At first nothing happened. The skeptics in the audience sniggered.

But a few minutes later a man had staggered into the circle. He'd been beaten bloody. Attacked by a gang who'd marked him for death. Suddenly, he told the priestess, inexplicably, the five muscular, armed assailants let go of him. They ran from the alley where they'd been beating and kicking him.

"This was no con, no Punk'd game," said Grove, smiling at the popular reference, a thing he normally left out of lectures. "From my seat I saw the blood, the bruises. The dangling, shattered arm."

The man had fallen to his knees and kissed the feet of the startled, swaying priestess.

But what had the woman chanted? Grove told the class she'd called the man's name several times. Then something about the family being assembled in one place . . .

Lucy closed her eyes and imitated the swaying of a Mam'bo she'd seen in a video on YouTube. She whispered, *"Ce' ou? Ce' ou que la'?"* Is it you? Are you there? And then, *"Toute famille a yo semble."* The whole family is assembled. And finally, in a hoarse shout: *"M'crie': mauvais ce' pou sorti; bon ami ce' pour entre'!"* I cry: evil depart; good friend, enter!

Close enough, she hoped.

But she had nothing belonging to any friend along with her. Except . . . she dove into the car again and rummaged in the back seat, for a long strip of leather.

Hercules's leash. What harm could it do? And if it somehow called him back . . . she began the chant again, swaying, first calling as if he'd simply wandered off into the trees. At the end she cried, *"Bon ami ce' pour entre'!"* and opened her eyes, peering hopefully down the flooded, overgrown street.

Still empty.

But perhaps he had to come from a long way off. The Haitian man hadn't appeared instantly, either. Maybe Herc was tied up, or injured.

Or maybe, her mind nagged, *you're just no good at this.*
She turned away from the street, shaking her head to
fling the negating words from her brain.

Or maybe this is just all a bunch of—

Suddenly, as if choked off, the voice fell silent.
This abrupt cessation of doubt unnerved her. She
turned, almost expecting to see the invisible, mind-fucking
critic there in the flooded street.

Instead, four figures stood outlined by the green and
yellow neon of the hurricane sky. Each carried an aura like
swamp fire. The street, which was a swamp now, reflected
wavering, oily yellow and orange patches, as if Revelation
still burned below its surface. Spirals of vapor rose in
arabesques like smoke from a leaking furnace . . . or fumes
from a barely-submerged underworld.

She took a step back. Had her amateur spell casting
accidentally called up fiends from Hell?

A voice spoke by her left ear. "Enjoyed your little dance.
But that first chant, under the tree? 'Not my fault, oh great
spirit,'" he quavered, in perfect imitation of Tim Carling's
hesitant squeak. "Tsk, tsk. As I said earlier, no one wants to
take responsibility these days. So disheartening."

Her heart lurched. She turned to see the . . . being . . . from
Gulf Rest standing behind her. The shimmery weave of his
shirt and pants was eerily unruffled by the wind that gusted and
howled around them. He looked dapper. He even—and
somehow this was most frightening of all—looked dry.

"Close your mouth, dear. It's rude to gape. I didn't
expect you to show. Woman of reason, academic
intellectual, and all that. Don't you find this scene a little
embarrassing, just a bit . . . *de trop?*"

When she tried to speak, only a squeak emerged. She
cleared her throat and tried again. "On—on the contrary,
it's . . . interesting. If you understood my field of study,
you'd know that."

He curled his lip. "Still time to leave. If you've seen enough to finish your little term paper."

She shook her head, but backed closer to the car. Fear numbed her arms and legs. "No, I—I was expecting something more traditional. You know, those manifestations of evil you read about. Some horror made larger than life before my eyes. Special effects, like fireworks at Disney World."

"*Disney World?*" A trickle of smoke threaded from his right nostril.

"Besides," she said quickly, fascinated by the smoky stream slowly dissipating in the rain. "Leaving won't do me any good, right? Just put off the inevitable."

He smiled. "Correct."

"So what now? I'm new to this sort of thing. Except on paper."

"And paper burns so quickly." A smile creased his face into sharp, hard lines. His teeth were small, yellow, pointed. "Special effects, eh. Such as doom and destruction? *Raiders of the Lost Ark* mayhem? Ashes, ashes, they all fall down. Or wait, wasn't that salt?" He rubbed his hands. The nails looked longer; pointed, too. "Afterward, there's the harvest. My favorite part. Who could ever tire of picking up nice fresh souls? So satisfying to hear the pitiful cries. To feel them squirming like naked, newborn mice in my collection bag." He reached down, lifted a sleek leather messenger pouch and slung it over his shoulder.

After one glimpse of the bulging, undulating bag, Lucy didn't look again. "What are the rules of this so-called game? Or has the winner already been decided?"

When he snorted, a puff of smoke shot from the other nostril. "Predestination, *phfft*. You can't believe in that. Dear one, this isn't the WWF. Outcomes are always subject to change . . . though I can't remember the last time things didn't go our way. Back in town, for instance."

He stretched both arms out, hands side by side like the

leaves of an open book. She took another step back—then realized that there, in the fleshy cup of his hands, a very small, high-definition screen was glowing.

First it showed a 1950s television test pattern. Then the tiny figures of a man and a woman in the green scrubs of Gulf Rest staff. As she watched they wrestled their way down a long corridor; banging into walls, tearing each other's clothing away. They fell into a room where a dozen people sat mesmerized around dining tables.

"But—that's Magnolia House," she said. "At Gulf Rest."

The couple stumbled into the tables, rolling naked in the remains of dinner trays, while the patients looked on. They jolted a body stretched across one table. The camera, or whatever was transmitting this bizarre tableau, zoomed in on sightless, staring eyes; a protruding tongue. The distorted, lifeless features of Esther Day.

The panting couple grew more frenzied, until everything—tables, half-eaten food, the rutting man and woman, the lifeless body—toppled to the floor. The patients stood and applauded.

Gray closed his hands as if praying—though that seemed unlikely. He opened them again to a new scene in his dreadful illuminated Book.

The interior of the Merry Cat, where a noisy crowd thronged. On an elevated stage, a band played beneath a crudely painted banner: *Merry Christmas! Happy New Hurricane!* It was "Scratch," and Nick Yulee was sawing at the fiddle like a man possessed, eyes closed, hair dripping, expression turned inward with intense concentration.

Jerkily, as if filmed by a clumsy hand-held camera, the scene swung past the stamping, yelling audience to the back of the café. Cora Cisneros burst from the swinging kitchen doors like a cuckoo from a clock, a butcher knife in hand. She pushed through the crowd to the makeshift dance floor ringed by pushed-back tables. Up front, two men sat clapping and stamping, singing along. One wore a dress shirt, and his red and green Christmas holly tie hung askew. A lawyer on vacation, a banker on holiday . . . or, maybe a developer?

In one smooth motion Cora stepped up and plunged the knife into the man's chest, then yanked the blade free. She turned to glare at his companion, who jumped up, overturning his chair, and ran out, shouldering past oblivious partiers. A highball glass flew out of the stamping, cheering crowd and shattered like a crystal grenade.

She wiped the blade on her chef's apron, then shouldered her way back to the kitchen. The swinging doors flapped shut behind her.

"Holy shit," whispered Lucy.

The screen went black. Beyond her the four naked figures danced and capered in the rising waters, slack greenish-white bellies jiggling and flapping. One had found a pair of stilts and was lurching around the tumbled bricks and broken foundations, howling at the cloud-draped moon. No, wait—not stilts. His legs had elongated like a heron's. Flying creatures, small, dark, and airborne, bats or maybe swallows, swooped and croaked around the prancing figures, escapees from a Hieronymus Bosch painting

"Losing interest already?" the demon asked. "A shame. There's more quality programming ahead. Look!"

Unwillingly, she turned back and saw an overhead shot of Water Street. Power lines were down, writhing and sparking like electrical snakes. Yet the town was still lit by a hellish glow from the seaward horizon, like sunset on a film running in reverse. Water gushed from the eaves of the Day house, which was sinking slowly into the mud and rushing water. Cedar shingles took flight from the roof of the Merry Cat like frightened pigeons, whirling in splintering tornados. The mullioned windows of the old Ibo City Savings Bank cracked like eggshells and exploded, spewing stained glass shrapnel.

On the marina pier Boy Jackson, the Bird Man,

crouched low, stringy hair plastered to his narrow skull. He held out a fish to a crippled pelican. As the bird hopped over to gulp it down he grabbed the bird's neck and wrung it, then slowly tore it to pieces with nails and teeth, scattering feathers and bloody organs as an offering to the howling hurricane.

She closed her eyes. The swirl of insane, gory images made her sick. She sank to her knees in the muck. But the screen was already shifting again. The Island House Inn sign rocked, swung, then ripped free and sailed down the street like a flying carpet. It took the roof off a careening pickup and decapitated the driver. The headless corpse steered onto the sidewalk, leaving broken bodies in its wake. The truck embedded itself in the display window of Key Artists Gallery and Gifts, wheels still spinning amidst glittering glass shards, broken shells, smashed mermaid paintings.

From side streets and alleys hunched figures loped. They climbed over the hood of the accordioned truck and scrambled into the shop, then reappeared laden with silver jewelry, seascapes, driftwood sculptures, weavings. They rushed off into the dark, cackling like nineteenth-century ship wreckers. The injured lying on the street and sidewalk writhed and moaned, their blood diluted to translucent pink stains in the rising flood.

Lucy dragged a sodden sleeve across her face. In the last few minutes, an idea had taken shape. "Well, um . . . "

Gray cocked an eyebrow. "Yes?"

"Nothing." She shrugged. "Except . . . wow. After such an impressive display, I was thinking to just give up. You've got better effects. More power. Even assistants." She pointed at the cavorting figures.

He looked sullen. "We didn't take you for a quitter. It's a bore to win by default. Very well; you may choose the contest, and even call on help. What will it be?"

She held up a hand. "One second. I'm thinking."

"Oh, please. What uninspired little game can your provincial mind concoct—Monopoly? Strip poker? Apples to Apples? I warn you, I'm universal champion at them all." He buffed his nails on a lapel, and flapped a weary hand. "Go on, pick your poison."

She shoved tangled hair out of her eyes, wrung the hem of her dripping shirt like a washrag. "I challenge you to a story-telling contest."

He rolled his eyes. "That's your ace up the sleeve?"

"And as my assistant, I'd like . . . Scheherazade."

His eyes bulged. His skin went livid. A wisp of ocher smoke curled from one ear. "But she's not *living*! Not even a real person!"

"They can only be real, live people?" Lucy tried to look shocked. "But you didn't say that. I mean, *you* aren't real, or alive, or human. . . are you?"

"Clever bitch," he fumed. "Well, if you think I'm going to stand asshole-deep in ooze on some miserable armpit of an island for a thousand and one nights, trading whoppers with a storybook character"—his angry flush faded to a peculiar pale green—"All right," he snarled, "I give you the first round. It won't help a whit in the end. Now it's my turn."

She folded her arms to hide her trembling hands. "Sure, whatever. I'm ready."

"A little contest of wit. Riddles. You may know that I have long stockpiled verbal puzzles. But before we begin—"

Oh god, she was not looking forward to this. "Hey. You know what else you lack here? Though I'm sure it was an oversight."

He huffed a sigh. "What now?"

"Background music. There's no sound track. Your backup dancers look stupid out there without any accompaniment."

"*Stupid?*" He glanced over one shoulder. "Hmm. Perhaps you have a point . . . in an age of music videos, mystic strains may inspire their gyrations, and fill in the tedious pauses." He raised one leathery gray arm. "Maestro . . . the music!"

TWENTY-ONE

After a long debate with himself—a mental chewing-out for being a fool and a busybody—Detective Bob Reshenko gave up and dialed the number penciled on his kitchen wall, next to the phone. One of six scratched there in the paint, the topmost being his son's home number in Los Angeles. Right below it was the Mountainside Subway's take-out number. His wife had chosen this pale yellow two years before she died. He would never have taken a pencil to it while she lived. He'd always respected her taste, though he wasn't much for home decoration, himself.

He'd done a lot of things in the years since then he wouldn't have dreamed of while she was living. Little things, really. But the one he'd never contemplated, surprising even himself, was getting interested in another woman.

Until the night he'd taken that Lucy Fowler's statement.

Well, that was Freudian. Or was it Jungian? One of those guys, anyhow. His wife had been a victim; he'd tried and failed to save her from madness and death. Unlike Marcia, Fowler hadn't retreated into her room, then into her own frightened mind, and finally, into an overdose of sleeping pills and the grave. The girl *seemed* to be doing OK. Still, he knew the signs. A tenseness around the eyes. The defensive way of talking. The occasional tremor in the hands.

She was still afraid. But also stubborn; too much so to

303

give in and retreat, to take time to repair the damage. People like her needed a guardian angel. But hell, *he* was no celestial being—just a nosy cop who hated to let go of a case. Yet he did want to help; that was why he kept calling.

One reason, anyway. All right, he should admit it. He liked her. She was way too young for him. Way better educated, too. He didn't expect reciprocal feelings. Keep it on a professional level. He'd decided to think of her as the daughter Marcia had always wanted, the one they'd never had.

He looked down at the phone in his hand.

That was why, no doubt, he was calling her long distance from Pottsburg on Christmas Eve. To see if she needed any reassurance from a paunchy fifty-year-old dick three hundred miles away.

Her cell was still playing a ringtone. Something folk he didn't recognize. What did they call it now . . . oh yeah, Americana. He leaned against the wall so he could see the television, sound off as usual. It showed the cheerful computer-generated hurricane map, that weird icon that looked like a runaway boat propeller still moving up the Gulf of Mexico. Last night the storm had been a Category Two with gusts in the high nineties, losing steam. Suddenly, today, it'd turned Cat Three with sustained gusts over 115 mph. Hurricane-force winds extended thirty miles out from its center.

Wind could be bad. But what the forecaster was agonizing about was a surge, that wall of water that builds up before a storm like a crazed surfer's wet dream. Only a surge doesn't stop at the beach. It continues inland like a giant wet fist, smashing and drowning everything in its path. The way Katrina had, in New Orleans. This storm, Roscoe, was gathering strength as it moved up the Gulf, sucking energy from the warm sea like a salty steroid cocktail. On its jaunt it would not make a direct hit on Ibo, but it would drop a heavy calling card on the tiny key.

His attention was jerked back by a voice-mail recording droning in his ear. "The person you called is not available. Please try your call again later."

"Shit," he muttered, and fished his wallet out, looking for the scrap with the hotel number she'd given him. Someone answered on the fifth ring.

"Uh, yeah—hello," said Reshenko, sheepish already, though he hadn't even asked for Fowler's room yet. She probably knew all about it, and what to do. Had probably evacuated to the mainland already.

No answer, only breathing.

"Hey, this the Island House? Trying to reach Lucy Fowler."

Silence. More breathing. Then, just as he was about to give it up as a wrong number, a man spoke.

He couldn't make out the words. "What's that, buddy? Sorry, can't hear you. Probably the weather, we sure got a bad connec—"

The voice rasped, louder, "No connection. It's the end of . . . the world. All . . . dead here." A crash of shattering glass, then nothing. Not even a dial tone.

"Je-*sus*," breathed Reshenko, staring at the receiver. "It's already hit?" What about Lucy? He slammed it back onto the base and stood chewing a thumbnail. Who did he know in law enforcement down that way—anybody? *Think.*

OK, there was Buddy Watson, sheriff in the county next to Crane. He should give old Bud a call, assuming *his* phone still worked. See if he knew anything about the situation. Like, if the three mile bridge to Ibo Key was washed out, or flooded, or . . . well, he wouldn't think about all the bad options right now.

He fumbled in the junk drawer for his address book. Where had he written that son of a bitch's number? Wells . . . Watters . . . Worth . . . Watson. Someday, he'd alphabetize the damn thing. Marcia used to take care of all that stuff, because he hated sitting still long enough to do it. Someday, when he had nothing else to do. Maybe on his deathbed. He squinted at the page, then started punching in numbers.

"I think the *kind* of music is very important," said Lucy.

The demon's lips twitched like coked-out worms. "Well of course. Bluegrass. The Devil's own music played on the Devil's own instrument. 'The Devil's Dream' is my favorite. Stimulating. Don't you agree?"

She tried to look surprised. "You mean—you really do play?"

He narrowed his eyes, the irises no longer round but mere slits, like a goat's. "You must be well aware, through your measly academic travails, that I *invented* the fiddle. And now—"

"You're going to play for me?"

"Not at all!" he fumed. "I said, *background* music. Though I might join in, if I could find a worthy accompanist. Hmm." He tapped his pointed chin thoughtfully. "Oh, I know. Your fisherman friend. This is all his, after all. He's the landlord around these parts."

"What? Not someone from town." She rolled her eyes. "It'll take them too long to get out here. The roads are a real mess. And besides—"

His eyes flashed red and green sparks. "Don't be a bore. Transport takes no time at all."

He raised his hands and clapped once. Then again. The air all around them wavered and jumped, like an old silent film jammed in a projector. And then, just like that, a man stood in the road, between the two of them and the four cavorting old madmen. One now wore either a Viking helmet or had grown a set of horns.

Nick Yulee still held the violin under his chin. He opened his eyes, lowered the instrument slowly, and looked around, blinking smoke-reddened eyes. He rubbed his face hard with his free hand. "What the hell," he mumbled. Then he spotted Lucy.

She was responsible for bringing him here, having suggested music in the hope it would be Nick the demon summoned. Maybe he'd forgive her this, since they were all doomed. Though perhaps he'd rather have had a small chance at salvation, rather than die by flood or falling tree or even at crazy Cora's hand.

"Nick," she said. "I'm sorry. I asked him to bring you here."

He wasn't looking at her, though, but at the demon. Nick's tanned face drained to a pale mask beneath the shock of black hair. "Jesus. What's *he* doing . . . he's not. He can't be!" Nick dropped the fiddle in the mud. It landed with the neck upright, as if also paralyzed into alert stillness by what its owner saw.

She turned on the demon. "What'd you do to him?"

He took a step back, a hand on his chest. "What did I—? Explanations are so tiresome. Here's the simple version: you see your own tiresome idea of Evil Incarnate. To you I look like—Hitler? John Wayne Gacy? But he, of course, sees his. Hey, I'm adaptable."

And Nick Yulee's idea of pure evil would be—

"Grandaddy?" he cried. "But you're dead! Dead and gone. What the hell *are you doing here?*"

She splashed through mud and water to grab his arm. The muscles quivered like over-tightened strings. "Nick, that's not your grandfather."

"But I see—"

"I'm sorry. It's someone . . . something . . . even worse." She pulled him a few feet away and told him quickly of the Revelation curse, then. And about the rapidly approaching end of Ibo Key.

* * *

". . . That's the best I can explain, fast. Sorry to drag you out here. But if he wins, you'll die along with everyone else, even if you stay home and lock the doors."

He shook his head. "Jesus. This's pretty hard to swallow. But then, a couple minutes ago I was playing a gig at the Cat. And now, way out here."

She blinked. "You mean you believe me?" She suppressed an urge to bury her face in his damp T-shirt, to cry with relief. She wasn't crazy. Or at least not the only one. He smelled of cigarettes and some sort of lime cologne, and beneath it, a faint whiff of the marina: salt, sunblock, diesel fuel.

"Well, I mean, if I hadn't seen *that*." He gestured at the demon, who was tapping one foot a few yards away, ears smoking in the rain, face now longer, more angular. "Or what's been going on the last few hours in town. People are goin' crazy. Knifin', shooting each other. Looting. We—the other guys and I—had just decided to pack up and get the hell out after that last song. Except we couldn't really go anywhere."

"Why not?"

"Bridge is out. Waves smashed it all to shit. A couple cars were washed into the Gulf. Nobody can leave now. A couple fishing boats capsized trying to cross to the Crane County pier. All we can do is head for high ground, grab onto something, and hold on like hell."

"But you accept the rest. The curse, the Book, and . . . that he's—I guess—the Devil?"

"Hell, yeah. Makes as much sense as me playing the last bars of "The Devil Came Down to Georgia," and then suddenly I'm knee-deep in marsh mud six miles away. If you'd told me this last week, even yesterday, I would've laughed. So . . . what now?"

As she leaned closer to whisper, a bony finger tapped her shoulder.

"Let's get on with it. First, a little change of costume for the players. Approach!" the demon called in a booming voice.

The old revelers ceased leaping and shouting, and stepped forward.

He pointed a long-nailed finger and a fiery tongue of flame hovered over each man's head, then bent itself into a glowing crescent moon These horned haloes flared, subsided, vanished. And the four stood changed.

One was seated on a white metal-flake three wheeler. Naked, except for a pleased expression and a silver breastplate with ENFORCER glowing in neon across the chest. He clutched a large crossbow.

The second straddled a winged bull which gleamed red, eyes and all. He held a huge machete. His stringy gray hair had turned thick and black, swept back in a pompadour. His jacket was scarlet leather, and stitched across the front was PEACETAKER.

The third man's green jet ski wallowed and rolled on a rising flood. He clutched a spear gun shaped like Neptune's trident. His skin was green as phosphorescent algae. Beneath a huge tattoo of a gray shark on his bare chest was inked HAMMERHEAD.

The last was mounted on a gaunt yellow horse which pawed the ground, snorting gouts of maggots from inflamed nostrils. Its rider, who had once sported a sizeable beer gut, was now emaciated, skeletal. His eyes were dark pits unlit by iris or pupil. He alone had no tattoo, no label, no name.

"Death," whispered Lucy.

"Ah. You're not entirely ignorant of the so-called Holy Book, like so many these days." The demon coughed. "But don't confuse community theater with the Big Event. I sometimes stage a rehearsal for the final performance.

Rwanda? Bosnia? Always a dress rehearsal, of course." He clapped again, a bolt of sound that eclipsed the storm's thunder. "Run along, you four. There are souls to hunt."

They scattered. The jet skier skimming the roiling Gulf waters, the bull rider flying above the trees. The pair on horseback and motorcycle roared off overland, throwing up sheets of muddy water like wings. But even they hovered a few inches above the ground.

The gray man beamed. "My own dear boys. Now, while they're busy, you may audition," he told Nick. "But I warn you, I'm not an easy audience."

At a snap of those bony, sharp-nailed fingers, a leather recliner with waterproof canopy appeared. The demon sank back and crossed his legs on the footrest. His shoes were gone, apparently lost in the muck. His hairy ankles ended in silver cloven hooves. A frosted mug of beer appeared on one armrest, a huge remote control on the other. He tapped the black plastic rectangle and mouthed, *Only if I get bored.*

"Shit," muttered Yulee, sluicing rain and sweat from his face. "All right." He raised the fiddle, tucked it under his chin, holding the bow down in a shaking hand. He glanced at Lucy. "What . . . the hell . . . should I play?"

"A song that's a riddle. If you know anything like that." She glanced over her shoulder at the oak tree. No god or goddess had appeared in response to her summons. Not even Herc. So her Black Disaster Lamp must be a dud. Well, if she couldn't even conjure up her own dog—

Gray's nails drummed the armrest. "*Waiting.*"

She stepped forward, feeling like the emcee of a deadly reality show. "Now, uh, Nick Yulee will give a new rendition of . . . an old favorite." In folk tales the Devil was always fond of word puzzles. "It's also a riddle, of course."

Yulee raised the bow. He played several bars, uncertainly at first, then more surely. He lowered the fiddle and sang in a clear tenor:

Someone done stole my old black hound
how I wish they'd give him back.
He run the devil right over the fence
and the little devils through the cracks.

After the last line, he put two fingers in his mouth and gave an earsplitting whistle. Then he turned the violin over and poured rainwater out of the f-holes.

Gray clapped listlessly. "Your fingering slipped toward the end. I suppose that could be the inclement weather. But we must be professional under any conditions. Oh, and the answer to your song-riddle—Appalachian, no?—is simple: A vicious old sow and her piglets."

Nick looked at Lucy, nodded and sighed. "Yeah."

"My turn now," said the demon eagerly. "This one needs no musical accompaniment.

I walked down my Grandmother's hall,
and outside heard an old man call;
his beard was flesh, his mouth was horn.
Yet this old creature was never born.

Lucy and Nick conferred. "An old rooster. Flesh wattles, horny beak. Hatched, not born."

A glower. Thunder rumbled out on the water. The devil grew a few inches taller. "Then I suppose there must be a tie-breaker," he snarled. "Proceed."

She clasped her hands, reciting like a child called on in class:

Patch on top of patch,
leaves a hole down the middle;
answer truly this riddle,
and you'll win a gold fiddle.

"Not difficult at all. It is, of course, ah, a . . . brick chimney."

"Absolutely right! And here you are." She pried the fiddle from Nick's grip.

"Hey!" he protested.

"Shh." She held it out. "Truly golden in tone," she assured the demon.

The Devil took up the fiddle gingerly, as if it were a baby in need of changing.

"Play for us?" she begged. "Please. We've never had the chance to hear the best in the world. Not to mention outside or, um, under it. Right?"

When Nick looked doubtful she nudged him, and glanced back at the devil.

He nodded. "Uh, right. Absolutely."

"Think of it as a last request."

"Well, if you put it that way." The demon tucked the fiddle beneath his pointed chin. Plucked at the strings with two long fingers, using the pointed nails as picks, producing a cascading sound of silver bells, the waterfall tinkle of a wind chime. Then raised the bow, closed his eyes, and began to play.

"What's with the stupid kid games?" Nick muttered. "Isn't this life or death? Like, ours?"

"I'm stalling. Just try to be an appreciative audience."

As the demon closed his eyes, playing faster, she backed away slowly, toward the car. Slipped inside and grabbed the Book from the passenger seat, opening to the place she'd marked with an old gasoline receipt: the recipe for the Black Disaster Lamp. She ran a finger down to the final paragraph, titled *Rituel Ceremonie*. There were a few lines left she hadn't had time to say before the Gray Man had suddenly appeared. Perhaps if she finished, the spell would be activated, summoning Koumari's gods of the cemetery. But could she actually command them, assuming they'd agree to send the Devil to hell?

She glanced back. Nick had closed his eyes, swaying as if entranced by the odd, eerily beautiful music. She raised the Book, about to quietly recite the last lines, when she noticed the final words. *La famille vin prayer sang*! The family comes to pay for the blood.

What could it mean? She shook her head impatiently. What difference, what choice did they have? She took a deep breath, visualized the archaic words as flaming arrows to fire against an enemy. The back of her neck prickled. She glanced over at the fiddling demon.

His arms were folded now, yet the violin played on, still producing ethereal, exquisite notes. It floated before him, bow raking the bridge like a crosscut saw. Wild, discordant music poured forth. Despite all the rain the varnished wood was smoking. There was an expectant glitter in the demon's yellow irises, avid as a cat's with its paw on the mouse's tail.

She realized then what she'd almost done, and froze like a midnight traveler without a light who's walked to the edge of a vast, steep cliff.

"Go on," said the Devil, flapping a hand at her. "Have fun with your little Book. Take your best shot, my dear."

Of course he'd known what she was up to. Now she understood. He'd come for all of Ibo Key, yes—but for Lucy Fowler in particular. Somehow *she* was his only real challenge, though not because of great skill or intellect or persistence. It was something else, something that had originated outside herself. Part of her had descended from the cursed. The other part, from the woman who'd decreed their doom. She was of both worlds and so, really, of neither. In academic terms, a liminal person, betwixt and between. Only a deity could forgive; only a mortal could atone.

Or did it mean he could only half-destroy her? Maybe he needed her cooperation to add her soul to the hideous specimen bag. Was that why he didn't just take the Book? Surely he could. Maybe . . . maybe she had to offer it freely.

To sort of invite him in.

The family comes to pay for the blood. What remained of that family now but her ailing father—not marked by this particular curse—and she herself. And the life sparked within her? She wondered whether, if you fought evil with its own tools, you became one with it. Tumbled off that steep cliff into a bottomless pit blacker than a demon's vertiginous onyx gaze. A fall that would go on for eternity.

She snapped the Book shut and slipped it into her pocket. No. She wouldn't fall—not yet. But then what defense did they have?

Perhaps nothing but nerve.

She went to stand beside Nick, just as Satan was winding up his song. "The Devil is the Father of Lies," she scoffed. "The 'Inventor of the fiddle'? Right. I've heard better playing in a campus bar. The truth is, a guy named Amati invented the violin only about five hundred years ago. Maybe you hung out with Nero and his lyre, while Rome bur—"

The demon's face went a mottled purple and black, as if he were strangling on his own ire. Raindrops struck his skin, sizzled and vanished. With a snarl, he shot up a yard taller.

Yulee grabbed her arm. "Shit, what're you doing? We lost that crazy riddle match. Now you really pissed him off. He's mad as—as hell."

The demon hissed, "Enough games. There's room in here for you and you and all the greedy, pinched souls on this desolate sandbar." The leather bag slung over his shoulder bulged and squirmed.

"Just a minute," she said. "I understood that if . . . if I made a sacrifice . . . a certain kind of sacrifice, I could stop this whole curse."

He looked interested. "What is it you offer?"

What was left to give? No great fortune or beauty or talent.

She'd lost her oldest, most faithful friend, Hercules. But surely he was valuable only to her. The other, more traditional sacrifices? Innocence, virginity—both gone. No great love to renounce, no far-reaching fame, no first-born son.

Though she did have in her care, potentially, not one but two souls.

The gray demon smiled, as if he'd heard her thoughts.

Would she deliberately sacrifice anyone, even a merely *possible* soul, to save this place?

Nick stepped in front of her suddenly. "What about me? I'm a part of all this, too. Associated by blood. Take me instead."

"So chivalrous, Mr. Yulee. But frankly, meaningless. I'll get to you in good time anyway."

So there was only one thing left to give. But she couldn't figure out how. Like a most stubborn riddle, the answer eluded her.

The demon said, "Back in the good old days of the Inquisition, the courts gave the dear girls a small reprieve in order to first deliver their little bundles of joy. Then, poof!—off to the stake. Could I do less?"

Yulee pulled her around to face him. "What the hell does that mean?"

"I think—I mean, I'm pregnant. He knows. Apparently there's some question about whether he's, um, truly entitled to my . . . soul. So he'd let me live long enough to give birth, then—"

The demon chuckled. "Because I'm the most generous of angels, out of sheer good will I'd even spare a couple of the fleas crawling over this miserable water-bound burg. Your friend, here—and your unborn heir." He sniggered, then added softly, as if to himself, "And what a future tidbit *that* will be!" Then, louder, "Quite right, my dear. You're the perfect trade: half and half. Ashamed I didn't think of it first. Oh, wait—maybe I did!"

Gray laughed and the trees shook. Leaves and twigs rained down, then whipped away on the wind. "As a bonus, I'll send a dear old friend to pick you up. Oh, it will be priceless."

He stamped one silver hoof. A murky curtain of marsh water arced and fell back to earth slowly. Inside it a gray mass took shape, a mist slowly defining itself.

Lucy felt her knees buckle. Felt Yulee holding her up, heard him say her name. But she couldn't stop the screams wrenched like torn silk from her throat.

Great tattered wings fanned a hot wind over them, carrying the stench of sulfur and decayed flesh. The Moth turned a blank, insect gaze on Lucy. Tim Carling had metamorphosed now beyond even her worst nightmares, into the epithet he'd been tormented with in life.

The demon raised his arms and spread them wide. "'*And a great portent appeared in the heaven: a woman clothed with the sun, with the moon under her feet, and on her head a crown of twelve stars. She was pregnant and was crying out in birth pangs in the agony of giving birth. Then another portent appeared in heaven: a great red dragon, with seven heads and ten horns . . .*'"

He eyed Lucy's torn, sodden clothes. "Tsk. OK, so it's the B movie version."

She was sitting quietly in the mud by then, but mind and body still advised: *Let's bolt. Put many miles and at least one ocean between us and that.*

"There," said Gray, dusting palms off briskly. "I'll deal with the fiddler first. Then we can take our time, enjoy the *dénouement.*" He snapped at the hovering Carling. "Carry the man off. Dispose of him in any way you please."

She stared in disbelief. "But you said—if I—you promised to spare him!"

The Moth swooped, the flapping of his leathery wings like a thousand bats streaming from a cave at dusk. He shoved her aside, breaking her grip on Yulee.

Gray shrugged. "That's the Father of Lies for you. Now, up and away with him."

Before Carling took flight, a dark blur hurtled into Gray like a snarling torpedo. A chaos of noise, a blur of limbs was all Lucy could see and hear. Blood-chilling shrieks, hoarse growls, as a snarling creature bore the demon to the ground.

"Herc," she whispered.

The bristling shepherd pinned Gray with jaws and teeth and muscle, amid a dreadful snapping and tearing and rending of flesh. Mud and water flew as Hercules shook and worried his enemy. But slowly the pale bony hands tightened on the big dog's neck. The sharp nails blackened and grew to ragged claws. The skin of the clutching hands turned green as spoiled meat. A smell of singed fur and corruption filled the air.

A hot wind, the flap of wings, wrenched her gaze from that struggle to the one above. Carling's segmented arms wrapped Nick, dangling him like an owl's prey a dozen feet above the ground. He struggled to break free, but the Moth had insect strength and a hard carapace.

For a moment a blinding explosion in the chartreuse sky drew her gaze away. It looked as if a wing of B-52s were bombing Ibo City. The mutter and buzz of a motorcycle engine came on a lunatic gust of wind that uprooted a pine tree and sent it spiraling skyward out of sight. The apocalyptic emissaries were wreaking terror in town.

She turned desperately from one struggle to the other.

Do something. Anything.

Her cold fingers brushed the leather cover of the Book in her pocket. It brought Hercules back, she thought. Maybe the *loas* will still come and save us. If they arrive soon.

As he squeezed the life from Nick Yulee, Carling

looked detached as a mantis processing its next meal. His sliced throat gaped like bloodless lips. The night he'd attacked Lucy, his irises had appeared like clear aquamarines set in a twisted, demonic mask. Wide with terror, confusion, and revulsion at brutality the rest of his body seemed to revel in. Eyes that had reflected a trace of the gentle man trapped inside.

Was that man still in there, somewhere?

"Tim, it's Lucy. Remember? You . . . used to like me. I always liked you. I understand now that what happened wasn't your fault. That it wasn't you."

Gray wings beat the air as he hovered in place. The blank face tilted to stare down. His hands loosened a fraction. Nick coughed, sucking air desperately. He clawed at Tim's hands but couldn't break that armored grip. His face looked bruised and dark from oxygen-hunger. But at least he was still alive.

"Tim, you were a good man. A kind person. Then a horrible thing happened. I can't bring your life back. But maybe together we could set you free. You don't want to be a part of this, really."

A sudden high-pitched howl tore from Hercules. Lucy felt it as a blow to the chest. Crying, she forced herself to keep talking. "Tim—this whole thing is evil. But you were—you *are* human. You were always quiet, but so very smart. You have enough strength to free yourself. Otherwise how will you ever find peace?"

The thing tilted its head, as if considering. Then began to rise again, still holding Nick.

"Don't! You didn't want to attack me, I saw it in your eyes, only I didn't understand then. Listen—there's something else you need to know. A baby—it has to be your baby—is alive inside me. Would you destroy the only child you'll ever have?"

Silence. But he hovered in place, no longer rising.

"Tim, you were always first one with the answer in our classes."

The dead gaze bent to peer at the struggling Yulee, as if noticing him for the first time. Something like a faint light—a spark—seemed to be growing in those creepy, insect eyes. The Moth shook his head, then dropped like a senseless gray stone from the sky.

Another shrill howl spun Lucy around, just as the demon flung Hercules away. The dog hit the huge twisted oak and tumbled down to land among its gnarled roots, right over the disaster lamp. He lay limp, motionless. He'd come to save her, and he'd paid with blood.

Carling hit the ground, and let go of Nick, who lay as still as the dog.

Before Lucy could run to help him, the enraged demon grew even taller. He'd shed his gray suit altogether. He towered over them looking like a medieval woodcut. Dark congested face, cruel thin-lipped mouth, yellow goat's eyes, sharp knife-blade of a nose, long spade-like chin. Two thick, twisted horns jutted from matted curling hair. He was the symphonic devil from "A Night on Bald Mountain." His torso gaunt and muscled, his color not red, but a diseased gray-green.

So the Devil had appeared, looking just as she'd expect.

That thought seemed important, but both Nick and Hercules were injured, perhaps dying. And the only other being left to appeal to was no longer entirely human, no longer alive.

The demon roared, "My legions will feast on your souls. You will rise and put on flesh, only to be eaten again, for all eternity."

She flinched at that, thinking, *I have nothing left now to save us.* But then she felt a faint rustling in the pocket of her mud-splattered shorts. Her fingers slipped inside, closing on a hollow-boned bundle of feathers.

All that remained of Eugenie Lee. Lucy drew out the body of the red bird. It rested on her palm; shriveled, unbearably small. So pitifully dead. Yet there was *one* thing left. All she had. The feathered corpse felt lighter even than the dense, humid air. She kissed its paper thin skull. But what words to use? She thought of the church she'd gone to as a child. Of all she'd read. Of what she'd learned on this island.

"Please, God. Hear me now! Oh, blessed Mother and Holy Trinity. Please, Mother Brigette, hear me now. Anyone with the power of good, I beg you: help us in our hour of need."

With all the strength in that arm she flung the mummified bird as hard and as high as she could, a tiny messenger sent into the loud, reverberating night. It rose so high that for a moment she thought the bird *had* returned to life. Then it plummeted, landing beneath the oak tree near where Hercules lay torn and bleeding.

Her shoulders sagged. That was it. Everything she could think of, every bit of strength and knowledge she could muster. Every trick, every plea, and it had not been enough. She had no weapon great enough to win against an evil this strong. They'd lost.

She knelt in the mud beside Nick, and touched his still shoulder. As she did a glow spread from the bodies of dog and bird, as if a light had been switched on underneath them. It took a moment to realize the rays must be emanating from her makeshift Disaster Lamp. Could the mongrel thing actually be working? If there was any hope at all, she'd call on the deities one more time. "Maman Brigette, Baron Samedi! We, the believers, await your vengeance against our enemies!"

"Melodrama," snarled the Devil, scraping blood and muck from his dog-bitten face. "Peasant superstition. Look how far that got anybody."

The dead bird was rising again, as if drawn on a magician's invisible wire into the air. Like a stone from a sling, it hurtled and struck Carling in the chest. The bird vanished as if absorbed into the insect carapace. He staggered, then raised his face to the stinging rain and screamed.

The tortured shriek pierced Lucy's ears. She stared in wonder as the Moth began to change. His body writhed and twisted. Three round growths rose beneath the skin. From his right shoulder, one burst free with a tearing sound, throwing a shower of dark blood. Lucy's whole body jerked when she recognized what had just been birthed from Tim's dead flesh: a head, the face the dark, severe countenance of Solange Koumari.

Another tearing and rending as from Tim's narrow chest erupted the face of a black Botticelli angel, crowned with a multi-hued halo of tropical flowers. "Maman Brigette," whispered Lucy.

The flesh of his left shoulder bulged, gave way, and there emerged a cadaverous, ebony visage painted with a skull mask, whose eyes glowed like red embers. Baron Samedi flashed pointed black teeth in a charnel-house grin. The musty smell of graveyard mold filled the air.

So Papa Legba had indeed been the gateway for the spirits. And were they on her side? Her lamp had shone, at least, and worked.

Carling cried out again, from all four mouths, but now he sounded triumphant. His sick gray hue faded as if draining away into the sodden ground. His leathery wings grew and spread. The gray membranes lightened. From small buds on their surface sprouted the feathered pinions of a Sistine angel, ivory in hue. Except, here and there, for a small tuft of black feathers.

All four faces lifted as if to appraise the storm-tossed skies. Tim's arms rose in supplication or summoning. A fine blue net of lightning enveloped him.

Lucy was certain he would be consumed by it. But Tim was not a smoking corpse. Instead he gripped a shining curved sword that drew sparks when he lowered its point to the ravaged earth of Revelation.

She knelt and lifted Yulee's head. His eyes fluttered open. "End of the fucking world," he whispered hoarsely. She turned his face in Carling's direction. "Holy. . . holy shit." He winced.

"I don't think he—or they—will hurt us."

The demon known as Gray stood at least thirty feet tall now, dwarfing even the trees. Glowing cinders spewed from his open palms and fell sizzling into the mud. "I'll turn all of you to swine! Pig meat, barbecued ribs for the Hounds of Hell. Weaklings, I will roast your diseased, yellow livers. I'll—"

"Oh shut the hell up," Lucy said. "You're a boogeyman in a gargoyle costume. Not Satan, if there even is such a thing. A bookkeeper of lost souls, dressed up to scare children."

The would-be Devil roared, "Maggotty puppet, be silent!" He spit flames, but they fell short. "I take what I please." He howled and lunged, but Nick was faster. He threw himself at the demon, shoulder first. Trailing clouds of sulphurous vapor, it staggered and fell backward, cursing. Nick fell back, and this time, lay still. When she tried to go to him, the ground heaved up and split, forming a deep ditch between them.

From all four throats a rhythmic chanting rose, increas-ing in pitch until the empty overgrown field behind them exploded. Dirt clods, clumps of grass, broken branches, dented cans, pieces of rusty farm machinery spewed upward as if a charge had detonated. Among the flying dirt and leaves and trash glinted, here and there, gleaming white shards. These paler fragments separated from the rest and arced higher. They fell in a white hail, pelting the howling demon. Large and small, some rounded, some stick-like, some white, some yellowed, some smooth, some splintered . One fell at Lucy's feet. It was a human femur, crudely carved like the one Herc had unearthed from beneath the bush on Water Street.

A broken tibia slashed Gray's forehead. The gaping wound did not bleed, but he still shrieked in agony. Three skulls struck his shoulder and glanced off, splashing down into the mud and water below. The bone-shower grew heavier, until the demon was obscured in a whirling tempest of bone fragments.

Slowly the four-headed angel lowered his arms. Gradually the skeleton rain subsided. Gray stood buried to the waist in tibias, skulls, and femurs, coated with filth and leaves and powdery white dust, skin torn and pierced. He blustered and shrieked. And shrank, slowly but steadily growing smaller.

"*You* might escape this time," he snarled at Lucy. "But I will collect one soul before I go."

He reached again for Nick.

"No!" She turned to Tim Carling. "Go get him. Please, save the man."

Carling flew to Nick. Instead of lifting him, Tim dwindled, shrank, and slid like a wisp of vapor between his slack, parted lips.

Just then an ominous rumble came from deep underground, as if the earth were quaking at it deepest core. "No!" cried the demon. "Not yet—I'm not finished!"

He shrank to the size of an ordinary man, the guise he'd taken on at Gulf Rest. The horns and hooves were gone. He gave a high whistling shriek, like a teakettle boiling over, which shattered brick chimneys and ripped boughs from trees, whipping ropes of kudzu and grapevine through the air like flying serpents. He stamped a bare foot. Water and shells and muck around him bubbled, glowed, became a molten pool. Then Gray vaporized in a column of yellow steam, leaving behind only a rank, sulfurous stench.

The deep gap in the earth that separated Nick from Lucy slowly closed, healing itself. She ran to him. "You did it, you drove him away."

Nick's head sagged; he closed his eyes. Battered, torn, covered in blood, as if he'd run his truck into a brick wall; as if he'd gone through the windshield.

"Oh my God. Let me help you." She slid an arm beneath his shoulders.

He didn't speak or look at her again. As she pressed his body to hers, bracing to support his weight, it felt as if something pierced her belly. Not a pain, but more a jolt, or an electric shock. At that moment Nick went limp. His eyes rolled up and he slid to the ground.

The glowing wisp of vapor that had been Tim Carling's last incarnation escaped his open mouth in a visible last exhalation. It rose and formed again briefly into the many-headed angel that was Timothy and Solange and Baron Samedi and Maman Brigette, departing, rising slowly like sea fog burning off under a morning sun.

"Nick, get up. Please." Lucy grasped his arms, shook his shoulder. No response. She felt clumsily for a pulse but felt none in the wrists, or on the side of his neck. His skin was cool, clammy. She summoned her limited knowledge of CPR, and tried to breathe into him, for him. His lips were cold, slack. When she pressed an ear to his chest, to listen for a heartbeat, she heard only the hollow sigh of wind gusting off the water. "Nick," she said again, crying. "Wait. Stay here with me."

The electric flutter came again. She thought of the dead infants in the chest at the Day house, surely lost in the hurricane flood. And of the dream she'd had, giving birth as she watched in the mirror in her room, to a child with Nick Yulee's eyes. A baby with no umbilical cord, marked by a strange ornate cross. No, not a cross precisely, but the *ve-ve*, the mark of Papa Legba, gateway of spirits, summoner of the dead. Whose spell she'd invoked to call the spirits to enter.

Call the spirits. To enter. To enter me.

She closed her eyes and summoned the details of that mark again. Maybe she couldn't save Nick's body. But his spirit . . .

She groped in the receding waters and found an old roofing nail. Rusty, but so what? She'd had a tetanus shot, and time was running out. She took a deep breath, pulled up the hem of her shirt, and dragged the nail over the tender skin of her belly, hissing at the pain. She made a cross bar, then began to incise the ornate, scrolled details she recalled, the ones she'd seen on the body of the child in the dream. The blood that rose was washed away by the slackening rain.

She raised an arm to wipe water from her eyes, then looked at the symbol she'd carved in her own flesh.

Not as finely-drawn as in the dream, but it would have to do. When she pulled the Book from her pocket and set it in her lap, it fell open to the page she sought. She almost smiled. "Thanks," she whispered.

With a hand on Nick's chest, the other on her own belly, she bent beneath the endless drizzle of rain and read in a loud, clear voice, "*Par pouvoir St. Antoine, Legba Antibon, Maître Carrefour, Maître Grand Bois, Maître Grand Chemin, Legba Barriere, Legba Bois, Legba Caille . . .*"

But at the end of the chant, she took a deep breath and

kept going. "Nick Yulee, whose soul hangs in the balance, I invite you in. Nick, do not depart! Come into me. Come into—"

Unlike in the painless labor and birth of her now not-so-strange dream, she was slammed with a stabbing pain, as if Cora had slammed the same knife she'd killed the doomed customer with into Lucy's abdomen. She screamed and doubled over, rocked by the waves of burning, undulating pain. She writhed and panted, but did not let go of Nick, twisting her fingers into the cloth of his shirt, gripping hard to make sure she didn't break the connection.

Finally, as abruptly, as it had come, the agony subsided. She hung her head, panting, waiting to see if there'd be more.

The faint rev of a motorcycle engine carried across the water. The four horsemen had been loose on the island all the while they'd battled Gray. But now the buzzing echoes died away, and it was quiet. Except for a sound she hadn't heard since before the hurricane had begun. A trill, a warble, one long fluting note. Bird song. Tentative at first. Then clear and strong, as a hundred more joined in.

Looking down at Nick Yulee's still, battered face, what did she feel—sadness, loss, joy at still existing, herself? No. Only numb, and barely alive. She stood at last, and waded through the receding water, only ankle-deep now. To the hollow of twisted roots that cradled the broken body of her faithful, her best old friend. "Herc," she whispered. "I'm so sorry."

She knelt and stroked the matted fur on his side. Faint smells clung to his pelt, disturbing hints of how far he must've journeyed to reach her: singed hair, sulfur, acrid smoke. He, already cool to the touch, coat crusted with mud and blood and something like gray ash.

"Through fire and brimstone," she murmured. "My good boy."

His brown eyes were open, looking serenely on

something in the vast distance she could not see. If there was an afterlife for animals, could any creature deserve it more? She buried her face in his damp fur.

She tried to lift him, but his dead weight was too much. She'd have to go back, get help, lead people out here to get them. To bring their bodies home.

As she stood, there came a strong fluttering, a faint scrape and pull in her belly. She put a hand there. It felt almost as if . . . there were two beings inside her now. Could it be true? No way to know, yet.

She stood and turned to look out at the horizon. "See that pink glow?" she said aloud. As if Nick and Hercules could both hear. "Sun's coming out. The storm must be gone."

Then, she started walking.

* * *

When Buddy Watson could finally commandeer a boat in Washington County that hadn't been shattered or sunk by the hurricane, he called up his Crane County counterpart, as a favor to his old fishing buddy, Bob Reshenko, who was waiting by the phone up in some burg in Pennsylvania for a call back. Sheriff Burgess had told Watson the Coast Guard was on the way to evacuate the island, that things sounded pretty dire.

So Buddy would call up Bob Reshenko, just as soon as he could scoot the borrowed sixteen-foot sport fisher across the shallow channel and leftover chop between the mainland and the Key. He was really pushing the cranky old Evinrude, because Reshenko swore this was life or death. No shit, he thought. That was one sumbitch of a hurricane.

When Watson neared the Ibo bridge he cut the motor, just to stare.

There *was* no bridge. Nothing, where one had stood for almost six decades, since he himself had been nothing but a rug rat.

He gaped at the empty three-mile stretch from the Big Bend coastline to the marshy Ibo Key shore. No connecting road now, just snapped pilings like the open mouth of an old bull gator with rotten teeth. Creepy, how nature could do so much demolition work in just a few hours, with nothing but wind and water, could knock a place back into the last century.

Hugging the shoreline, north to west, he saw toppled trees, floating debris, a dead bull, the carcass of a gaunt yellow horse, a wrecked motorcycle, and lots of washed-up crap on the beaches. But not much real damage, inland.

He rounded the point across from Snake Key and turned for the Ibo Channel. As usual he looked left, toward downtown and Water Street. Then pushed his ball cap farther back, and looked again. No, his eyes had not deceived him.

Ibo City was gone.

He throttled back, because all the channel markers were missing, and used a long branch scooped out of the water to feel his way in to the concrete seawall and pier behind where Anhinga Rentals used to be. That was the only place left to tie up. The other piers, built of wood and farther out in the channel, were gone. Oil drums, tires, dead animals, broken trees, various parts of houses—including a bathtub with a wet raccoon peering anxiously over the side— floated past. He steered gingerly around some snarled line and tied up next to two Coast Guard launches. They were the only other boats in the basin, unless you counted all the ones capsized or sunk. Or the drifting scraps that used to be skiffs, dinghies, and bird-dog boats.

"Jesus H. on a pony," breathed Watson. "Where . . . I mean, what in the hell?"

A woman in dungarees and Coast Guard cap reached to take his line. He tossed it up, still gaping, then followed when she offered him a hand.

"Holy shit," he whispered, turning slowly round and round.

Broken palm fronds, shattered oaks, splintered pines were snarled and woven among fallen power lines that covered Water Street like a giant game of cat's cradle. Roofing shingles lay everywhere, like chips from an abandoned poker game. A few concrete foundations.

"Jesus, Mary, and Joseph, look at Cora's place," he whispered. The painted sign for the Merry Cat swung from a single standing beam. The rest was gone, except for a huge Vulcan stove which hulked in a forest of broken siding and snapped beams like a stainless-steel rhinoceros.

The sign tilted in a sudden breeze, creaking.

"Seen Mrs. Cisneros, the woman who runs the restaurant?" He asked one of the men standing on the deck of the cutter.

He frowned, shook his head. "Nah. Seen her daughter, that Starr girl. She told us her mama left near the end of the blow, got on a weird lookin' cycle with some creepy old biker dude. Said Cora was laughing. But the poor kid was in bad shape, all beat up—looked like a drowned rat. Who knows?"

Nothing remained of the Island House except the first flight of lobby stairs, truncated abruptly at the missing second floor landing. The oranges, apples, broccoli and bananas strewn everywhere like edible confetti he assumed had blown in from the farmers' market, though he couldn't pick out its foundation in the general debris.

As he stood staring, a small group emerged from beneath a dripping canopy of half-fallen trees. Another Coast Guardsman was helping them along, carrying a crying, muddy toddler. An older woman led a dazed younger one by the hand. Two teenage boys followed, looking around in awe, even admiration.

When the older woman turned her face toward the pier, he recognized her. "Hey, Miz Waters!" He waved. "It's

Buddy. Buddy Watson, from over to Rawlings? I was in your seventh-grade English class, the year you taught high school there. You, uh . . . you all right?"

"Chester!" A grin creased the smudges of dirt. "So it's Buddy, now, is it? I don't really approve of nicknames. Well, I'm good as a body can be in a mess like this. My house is probably on the highest ground around. Still standing, only it's got no roof. These here are my neighbors. I went out and got 'em when their trailer blew in." She looked kind of proud of this. "I hear a big wall of water came right down the middle of Water Street, and—" She stopped and looked around as if noticing for the first time where she was. "God help us. It's true."

He sprinted across the street and caught her arm. "I'm sure He will eventually, ma'am." Gently he took the elbow of the younger blonde woman with her, who looked as if she might be in shock. "But right now let me give you all a hand."

"This is Lissa Ellis. Her husband Jimbo was at the Merry Cat, playing bass in Nick Yulee's band. She was home minding the little one. He, uh . . ." Mrs. Waters lowered her voice. "He hasn't turned up yet."

They both looked at the rubble beneath the still-creaking sign, then back at young Mrs. Ellis. She seemed oblivious to their scrutiny, and everything else.

"Don't suppose you know anything about an out-of-town woman, a grad student name of Fowler? Been staying at the Island House." He tried to keep his eyes averted, but they were drawn with awful fascination to the jutting staircase that led to nowhere.

"Oh, yes! I did meet her. Just yesterday, wasn't it? But honestly, I don't know what's become of her. Seemed to be friendly with Nick Yulee. You remember Nick, Chester. Or wait, probably not. He was five or six grades behind you." She glanced at the bare foundation of the boat rental office.

"Don't know what's become of her," she repeated, in a whisper. "Or him either. Oh Lord, I hope—" Her eyes filled.

Watson patted her shoulder. "Sooner we get this young lady on the cutter and over to county hospital, the better." He lifted Lissa Ellis like a child and called over his shoulder, "Come on, Miz Waters. I'll help you on board. Bring that baby over here, folks! We're getting you all outta here right now."

He wondered if his cell would pick up a signal out here. He really wasn't looking forward to calling Bob Reshenko.

Lucy didn't have to walk after all. Her Toyota started on the third try. It did stall several times on the road, in low spots where the water was so deep it drowned the engine. Nick's truck would've forded these points like a wading shorebird. But she didn't want to think about Nick right now. Each time she did, she put a hand to her belly and cradled it. What if—

But no. She couldn't think about that any more.

She was so exhausted she saw things on the road that shouldn't be there: dark figures that scurried and splashed away from the oncoming car. Twisted creatures that didn't look human—exactly—but were too large to be any of the local wildlife. She locked the doors and decided she wasn't getting out of the car for any reason. Not even if the engine died altogether.

In fact, she was so tired that when she pulled into what used to be the south side of Ibo City, at first she didn't notice the tangle of trees and power poles and wires that blocked Water Street. Didn't recognize the area as downtown at all, and barely hit the brakes in time.

She stopped inches from a live wire sparking and dancing in front of the bumper. Keeping an eye on this deadly, manmade snake she got out and looked ahead. Instead of the familiar waterfront, she saw a hopeless snarl of broken poles, downed pines, broken windows, siding, smashed appliances and, here and there, bright rags of sodden clothing. A Christmas tree lay on its side in the road, ornaments still attached.

On the west side of Water Street, where Yulee's business had stood, was now—nothing. Except for a knot of people, and two large white official looking boats riding mild swells near the curiously barren pier.

Oh, God. Nick's building. All his boats. He'd never see . . . of course, he'd never see this. But—

A man was waving at her from the now-vacant lot. She looked down at her torn, stained clothing, felt the caked mud and powdery salt and crusted scratches on her face. Wasn't that a Coast Guard boat? They must be evacuating the island.

She stumbled toward the disheveled, stunned-looking crowd milling at the dock. At this moment she felt completely like one of them, and also completely apart. In all the world, they might be the only ones who could begin to understand what had happened. The only ones who'd ever believe her story.

A story she didn't plan to tell, though, for a long, long time. Much later, when she knew how it was actually going to end.

"Hi," she said to a young woman in a Coast Guard uniform, who offered her a hand. "Maybe you can help me out."

Acknowledgments

All of the following souls played some part in the creation of this novel, and are due many thanks, if not large quantities of chocolate. The late James Allen was my first agent, and even now I miss his wicked sense of humor. Rob Crane, Tom Dye, Doris Galen, Diane Galen, Pete Gallagher, Mary Ann Johnston, Lin Poyer and Dr. Frances Williams all read various drafts of the manuscript and offered illuminating comments or exciting new historical material. Frank Green, mentor and teacher of the first order, made these pages fit to be seen by applying his keen editorial eye. Andrew Zack, then at Putnam/Berkley, was the first editor to have faith in my stories when he acquired *Black River* and then ordered, "Start another novel immediately." Editor Tomas Algard, at Egmont Boker in Oslo, liked that first novel so much he also published a Norwegian edition of this second work back in 1999. Most of all, though, I'm grateful for and awed by my talented daughter, an artist among artists, and my husband, one of the hardest working writers in the business.

About the Author

ELISABETH GRAVES, descendent of an old Florida family, grew up in a small citrus-industry town not far from Disney World, her first employer. A former wardrobe assistant, theme-park waitress, seafood-joint cashier, graphic artist, advertising copywriter, and forensic librarian, she grew up in a somewhat haunted house on a Central Florida lake that's home to many an alligator and poisonous snake. She likes to read the headstone inscriptions in old cemeteries in her spare time. *Black River*, her first novel, was originally published in English by Berkley Books, New York, and in Norwegian by Fredhois Forlag, Oslo, as *Sort Elv*. *Devil's Key* was originally published by Egmont Boker, Oslo, in 1999 as *Svart Frikt*.

Northampton House Press

Northampton House LLC publishes carefully selected fiction, lifestyle nonfiction, memoir, and poetry. Our logo represents the muse Polyhymnia. Watch the Northampton House list at www.northampton-house.com, and Like us on Facebook—"Northampton House Press"—to discover more innovative works from brilliant new writers.

CPSIA information can be obtained at www.ICGtesting.com
Printed in the USA
BVOW08s1116220516

449075BV00001B/1/P